PRAISE FOR

"This was one of those feel-good romances that leaves you smiling! I loved the banter and teasing Aspen Hadley works into all her dialogue and found myself equally laughing and swooning throughout the book. A fun, lighthearted romance that I highly recommend."

—Summer Dowell, author of *It's Just Business*

"*Just Enough Luck* was a fantastically cute romp through the ranch of my dreams and the cowboy to end all cowboys. I laughed, I sighed, I laughed some more, and I fell hard for this adorable couple. The perfect book to remind us what we love about love!"

—Rebecca Connolly
Author of the *Lost Creek Rodeo* series

Other books by Aspen Hadley

Simply Starstruck

Blind Dates, Bridesmaids & Other Disasters

Suits and Spark Plugs

Halstead House

Just Enough Luck

ASPEN HADLEY

SWEETWATER
BOOKS

An imprint of Cedar Fort, Inc.
Springville, Utah

ISBN 13: 978-1-4621-4094-7

Published by Sweetwater Books, an imprint of Cedar Fort, Inc.
2373 W. 700 S., Springville, UT, 84663
Distributed by Cedar Fort, Inc., www.cedarfort.com

Library of Congress Control Number: 2021947110

Cover design by Courtney Proby
Cover design © 2021 Cedar Fort, Inc.
Edited by Rachel Hathcock

Printed in the United States of America

10 9 8 7 6 5 4 3 2 1

Printed on acid-free paper

For my two real-life cowboys

My grandpa Roy Campbell
The first cowboy who threw me onto the back of a horse as a tiny girl and taught me to love those big, wonderful animals.

My brother Ben Ridges
The boy who made me into a real cowgirl, who always laughed while we galloped through the hills and dusted me off when the landing was hard.

Both of you are in heaven now, and I imagine you riding horseback together through the clouds. I hope when it's my turn to join you, you'll be waiting with a "good pony" and a mountain to explore.

Chapter One

It turns out there might be such a thing as too much good luck. I know, I know. Who says that? Well, if I hadn't had such a run of good luck lately—and I'm talking extremely unbelievable, my-mom-thinks-I'm-lying-to-her-type-stuff—then I wouldn't be driving up a sketchily paved road in northern Montana headed to the Drake family ranch. You read that correctly—ranch. Who has those? Sure, I've got friends with second homes or mountain cabin getaways, but owning a family ranch is on a level that I'm totally unfamiliar with.

Maybe you haven't heard of the Drake family, so let me enlighten you. Drake Enterprises is a financial planning company started by the father, Robert, and handed down to his oldest son, Alexander, about five years ago. They have loads of cash—enough cash to make your eyes cross and give you goose bumps just thinking about all the times you could say 'yes' to something rather than 'I'm broke.' Alexander is on the cover of finance magazines all the time, and the fact that he could be a model isn't hurting anything. So, yeah, if you're good with nothing more than looking at covers and dreaming about the men on them, then Alexander is your kind of guy. If, however, you're like me and you actually read the articles inside, then Alexander is like the handsome prince of the financial world with his looks and his brains. I'm telling you, he's big stuff in my corner of the world.

I'd only applied for this job on a dare from my best friend, Kayla. We'd both graduated from college two years ago and had been working at entry-level corporate positions ever since. I was working as a personal financial advisor for a national bank chain, and Kayla was working as an interior design assistant. While we were grateful for the income and finally having enough money to eat fresh fruits and veggies, it didn't mean we'd left our dreams behind. We still laid in our one-bedroom apartment, facing each other from our respective twin beds, and weaving fairy tales about our future.

After a particularly frustrating dinner with my family where my older sister's success had once again been waved in my face like a matador's red cape, I'd returned to our apartment, determined to find something better in terms of employment. Kayla, loyal friend and hater of anyone who made me feel bad, had immediately joined in the search. Together we'd hunkered down in our tiny bedroom, laptops and phones out, and she'd stumbled across a listing for Drake Enterprises. Her head had popped up and she'd immediately tossed her phone on my lap.

"Luce, isn't this the company that the hot guy on your finance magazines owns?" I'd glanced down and nodded. She'd continued cheerily. "He looked amazing on last month's issue. I've spent a lot of time dreaming about having his perfect lips pressed against mine." She'd disappeared momentarily into her head, and then shaken it and given me a dreamy smile. "Anyhow, this is your dream job. You should apply."

It had taken me a minute to pull my gaze away from the tiny digital image of the perfect man, and then I'd had to blink a few times when I'd seen the job listing for a senior financial planner. My toes had curled under me, but I'd kept my face calm. See, the thing is that attractive guys aside, I'm really into numbers. They're my jam. It was the reason I'd majored in finance with a minor in business management. Added to that was my psychic-like ability to make stock market predictions. Seriously, if I'd been born in another century, I'd have carried around a crystal ball and spoken in a spooky voice, and everyone would have come to see me because I'd have been freaky accurate.

"This is a high level position," I'd replied as I'd scanned through the listing.

"Yes, the senior part of the title suggested that."

I'd stuck my tongue out at her without taking my eyes off the screen. "I only have two years of real world experience, with much smaller clients than Drake Enterprises has. There's no way my skimpy resume would even make it through the initial HR process." I'd tossed her phone back to her bed across the room even though I'd really wanted that job. "They'd laugh their heads off at me for even applying." I'd sighed. "Maybe someday."

She'd snagged her phone and waved it at me. "I'll pay you twenty bucks if you at least work up a resume and send it in." At this I'd lifted my eyes to meet hers. She'd smirked at me from her little twin bed pushed up against the wall of our small room and reached up to smooth her dark brown bangs out of her eyes.

"You don't have twenty bucks," I'd replied, amused.

"This is how much I think you should apply."

I'd sighed again, twisting my lips back and forth, and leaned back against the wall, straightening my legs to let my feet dangle off the side of my bed. "You'd miss meals for this?"

"I'll eat at work. The pot just went up to thirty dollars."

I'd laughed and tossed a pillow her way. "We won't make rent if you keep upping the ante."

"I dare you to do it."

Ugh. Why with the dares? I always caved to her dares, and it usually backfired on me. One time she'd dared me to put Jell-O powder in the showerhead because our sophomore year roommate was just the worst and had some bad karma coming her way. Unfortunately I'd gotten busy and distracted and showered before the roomie had, so the joke had been on me. Still, a dare was a dare and I was no marshmallow. I'd held up my hand and wiggled my fingers in the universal 'toss it this way' sign, and she had done so with a grin.

"When you land this job," she'd said, "you owe me a big dinner, because you'll be super rich."

"Super rich to us would be buying chicken to go in our Rice-A-Roni."

While I'd never expected it to go anywhere, I'd actually put some effort into a resume and applied for the job. Guess who nearly died of surprise when I'd been called for an interview a week later? Me. Kayla was less surprised, having that cool best friend ability to see all my good qualities. When I'd told her the news she'd grabbed my hands and danced us around the apartment.

One week after that I had a job offer I couldn't refuse, and another week later I was driving a rental car into unknown territory, trying to pretend I had this.

After I accepted the job and Kayla had once again danced around our apartment, she'd pulled up a picture of Alexander Drake on the internet and swooned onto her bed with glassy eyes before predicting I'd be engaged by Christmas. I had no illusions that my relationship with Mr. Drake would ever be anything but strictly professional. However, a terrible best friend had planted that little nugget in my overly analytic brain, so I could thank her for all the obsessing I was going to do over the next little while. What if I started accidentally flirting? Sure, the fact I'd had zero serious boyfriends should keep me from worrying over whether I was a flirt or not, but it didn't. Maybe I had an inner siren that had been silent all these years just waiting for a fellow numbers nerd to awaken her.

The biggest question you probably have is how I had landed a job so obviously over my head. First, as stated earlier, luck, luck, luck. I'd never lost complete faith in my fairy godmother, and now I had proof she was alive and well. Why else would my resume have been plucked from the pile? In thanks, I'd whistled the "Bibbidi Bobbidi Boo" song from Cinderella once a day.

Second, I had borrowed a pantsuit from my older sister, Daphne, and wowed Mr. Drake with my math skills and scary predictive abilities.

Okay, in fairness I should probably mention that I'd nearly choked and failed the entire thing. Let's get real here. You can't be cool as a cucumber when you walk into a conference room and sitting at the head of the table is the guy whose face you've been staring at on a glossy magazine cover. Ladies, he looks better in person.

Thankfully, I'd reeled my own daydreams back in and gotten down to business. Mr. Drake had tested me by asking about a certain stock, and after crunching some numbers in my head and thinking on it, I'd predicted it would rise. He'd been dubious, and the rest of the interview had been pretty standard with questions about my schooling and work experience.

However, when my prediction came true only two days later, he'd personally called to invite me back. I'd borrowed a second pantsuit from Daphne and gone in for a chat with the board. The actual board. Around a huge table in their top floor, glass-walled conference room. I'd managed not to stutter, and somehow they'd managed not to laugh at my inexperience and youth. Their job offer had knocked my socks off.

My sister said they hired me because they can get my skill set for super cheap as a recent graduate with only moderate experience. She's not wrong; she's just mean sometimes.

Somewhere in the glow of accepting this ridiculous job opportunity and thanking the board members, a small bomb had been dropped when Mr. Drake had asked me to stop at his personal assistant's desk for some instructions. I was thinking HR stuff, you know—name, social security number, bank info for paychecks, and so on. Nope. Pamela Lin, chic and stoic assistant, had handed me an airline ticket to Great Falls, Montana, and explained that I'd start in one week, living on-site at the family ranch during their annual sabbatical. I'd had no less than a million questions about sabbaticals and where I'd live, and how awkward it would all be. But I'd pasted on a devil-may-care grin, nodded like this was totally normal and expected, and driven home with the ticket clenched in my hand.

Kayla's expression had frozen too at first, but she'd bounced back quickly and become a champion researcher on Winterford—the tiny town that the ranch was nearest. We'd learned something I'd already feared—October in Montana is a far cry from October in Las Vegas. Kayla had kept me from falling into a pit of fear, and together we'd scoured the local department stores for cold-weather clothing. This hadn't been an easy feat in the desert, but as always, online ordering came through for the things I couldn't find locally. In the end I felt I was as stocked up as possible, and before I could fully grasp my new situation, my best friend had dropped me off at the airport to fly into the unknown.

Her parting words had been, "Don't mess this up."

Yeah, thanks for nothing, Kayla.

The flight into Great Falls had been pleasant enough. Landing in Great Falls had been a little less pleasant when fifty-five degree temperatures went from something I'd read about on a screen to something prickling against my skin. The people of Montana did not share my same feelings, as those weirdos were traipsing about in jeans, t-shirts, and sandals, acting like it was the middle of summer. I'd heard of these people. They were the same variety that came to Vegas and walked around with bright red faces and sweat rings on their shirts.

While I watched my luggage come around the carousel I couldn't stop thinking about how I'd be spending the next month at my super hot, mega rich boss's private family property trying not to accidentally put out a 'come to mama' vibe. Let's make it clear that I'm not trying to harass the man and I want this job, but there's this evolutionary pull to combine genes with the best possible partner. To make matters worse, he's young enough to be in the running, you know? Like, he could be a viable option for romance. So, even though this is supposed to be his vacation time—even if he apparently can't be bothered to actually stop working—this is no vacation for me.

Circling back to the theory on too much good luck: too much of a good thing can flip over pretty darn quickly into a bad thing. Too many donuts? Thighs for days. Too much soda? Heartburn and regret. Which was exactly why I was expecting things to be all downhill from here. According to Kayla, during the texting frenzy while I'd sat in a frigid airport waiting for my rental car, I'd crossed over into being dramatic and pessimistic and I should at least wait for something bad to happen before totally freaking out. Oh, and then this little bomb had dropped:

Kayla: Don't worry about meeting the entire Drake family. They'll love you.

WHAT? How could I not have thought of that before? Of course they'd all be there. This was the annual *family* retreat, and that didn't mean just me and Alexander chilling on the porch.

The fact that I'd missed this glaringly obvious truth was a slap in the face. How high was my head in the clouds? Sure, I'd been busy panic packing, online ordering, researching the location, and finishing out the last week of my old job, so I'd been highly distracted. Add in Kayla's daily texts with pictures of wedding dresses and her leaving Post-it notes with 'Mrs. Lucy Drake' written around the apartment, it was a small miracle I'd made it this far at all.

Once Kayla had planted that seed, I was forced to initiate an immediate web search on the entire Drake family while sitting with my head between my knees on a cold airport chair. According to a variety of websites, the family would include father, Robert; mother, Priscilla; and Alexander's younger brother, Daniel. Pictures proved they were all beautiful people, well-dressed and smiling happily, and well . . . this was happening. This family was about to open their doors to me, and while I'm confident in myself, I'm also nowhere near their sphere of existence. So, yeah, intimidating.

Here's what you should know about me. My name is Lucy Moore. Never Lulu. That nickname gives me hives. I'm Luce to those I'm closest to. I'm twenty-four years old. I have that kind of brown hair that's a little lighter on the top and darker underneath so everyone thinks you're highlighting your hair, but the reality is that my hair just doesn't know what color it wants to be. I love fashion but rarely pull it off. I have dark eyebrows, blue eyes, and I wear glasses with leopard print frames. I'm known for my bright red lipstick, which Kayla says is my signature look, but I feel silly saying that myself so I let her do it for me. I have an older sister, two loving (though a little absent) parents, and you already know about my best friend. I'm from Las Vegas, but I don't gamble or hang in the casinos. And I don't appreciate everyone thinking Vegas is all party. Real people live there too. I always tell the truth, I'm endlessly curious. I have a tendency to get in over my head, and too often lack a filter between thoughts and speech.

This—this is the person going to the Drake family's ranch in the Montana wilderness for at least a month.

Eventually my rental car showed up and I climbed in with sweaty hands and a mind spinning out of control, along with a strong desire to hurl. The first thirty minutes of the drive from the Great Falls airport to the small blip of a town called Winterford was white knuckles and deep breathing. The last hour was wondering if I'd gotten lost and accepting just how much my sister would like being an only child. Truly there was nothing in sight. This was big country, with all the space you could imagine. From now on when people talked about overpopulation of the world I was going to show them a picture of northern Montana and let them know I thought we'd be okay.

My worries about being lost eased as I saw a mountain range rise up in the distance, followed by the outline of buildings, and at last a sign welcoming me to town. Population: 1,204. I hadn't spent a lot of time in small towns, but I didn't see a population of that size supporting much by way of shops and entertainment. Should be interesting. I slowed the car as I entered the town limits, watching the buildings of Main Street pass by in a sort of stupor. This place was straight out of a postcard or an old black and white show. I wondered if I'd have time off each week and could come here and window shop. It seemed that window shopping in a town like this should be on my bucket list. If Kayla were here she'd be friends with every one of those 1,204 people before leaving town. In fact she'd probably have been running for mayor and forcing me to act as treasurer, which was kind of my unofficial position in all aspects of her life.

Before long I was out the other side of town and headed toward the mountain range in the distance. According to Pamela, assistant of few helpful words, the Drake ranch was about five miles out of town. I was supposed to look for a big iron archway on my right-hand side with the name The Lucky Wolf welded along the top. I wondered how they chose that name. Maybe the older Mr. Drake thought of himself as a wolf or something. Who was I to judge? If I had to name a ranch I'd probably have gone with the terribly boring Whispering Pines or something even worse like My Place.

The gigantic iron archway rose out of the scenery just as the road began to climb toward the foothills. I put on my blinker and slowed the car as I passed from the pavement onto dirt. I hoped the road didn't get too much worse because this little two-door hatchback wasn't built for terrain. On a whim I stopped the car under the arch and decided to get out and video chat with Kayla. She'd never believe the size of that arch, and I thought the little car would give good perspective. I cut the engine, grabbed my phone, and hopped out. Evening was approaching and I took a moment to breathe in the fresh, cool air. Then I coughed and decided two deep breaths were enough. No need to pipe frigid air into my lungs. Let them acclimate awhile first.

I unlocked my phone and hustled to the other side of the road where I could get a full shot of the arch and my tiny rental under it. I couldn't help smiling and imagining Kayla's reaction. The archway was unapologetically showy, with intricate iron work across the top and the two sides anchored in humongous white stone columns. A howling wolf was positioned at the high point of the arch, and I kind of loved it. I snapped a picture and then turned to get a selfie of myself with the arch too. My glasses were a little foggy from the temperature change, but I pushed them higher onto my face and grinned. The fog would just add an element of reality to the shot.

Then I called Kayla. She answered on the third ring, her big smile filling up the screen.

"Hey, you're alive." She grinned. "And not even hyperventilating at all."

I returned the grin. "Not even a little bit. In fact, I'm looking forward to the challenge. The Drakes are going to love me."

"Goes without saying." She nodded as her eyes drifted to the background, and I turned the phone to give her a slow panorama of where I stood, ending with the arch.

"Check that thing out," I said from outside the picture.

She was silent for a moment, taking it in, before saying, "I've always said subtlety is overrated."

I chuckled. "I just hope I have the right place. If only there was a landmark of some sort . . . "

"A sign would be helpful, for sure," she agreed. "People can get lost on these country roads."

"I do think the wolf is kind of cool."

"Agreed. It's a power move and I like it. The mighty wolf guarding the equally mighty Drake family. Nice."

I turned the screen back toward me. "When I first got out of the car my glasses fogged up." I blinked a few times, glad the fog had gone as the lenses adjusted to the air temperature. "It can't be a good omen. I may freeze to death out here."

"Good thing we found all those beanies in the bin at Goodwill."

"Fact."

"You might want to wash them first, though."

We chatted lightly for a few more minutes, her reminding me that I was the best human she knew, and me reminding her that she needed to stop leaving dirty dishes in the sink because they'd stink after a month of me being away. The light-hearted back and forth settled my nerves in a way nothing else would have.

I scampered back to the car after saying goodbye, beginning to feel the cold seep in and anxious to get the heat running again. Except, rather than open the door, I chipped a nail on the handle as it slipped from my grasp. I looked at my nail, confused. That was strange. I tried again and the handle didn't budge. However, this time the car alarm went off. Nice. What was a car of this caliber doing with an alarm anyhow? Trust me, no one was trying to steal it. Street value on this baby was probably zero. I tugged once more on the handle and grunted when it remained locked. I walked around the entire car, trying both handles and the hatchback several times, always hoping for a different result. Nothing changed, but it was possible that the squawking of the alarm grew louder. I kicked the tire on principle.

With a big sigh I decided to look up Pamela's number and see if there was any way I could get some help out here, but when I dialed it went straight to voice mail. The only other number I had for her was her office phone, and with it being a weekend there was no way anyone at the Drake Enterprises headquarters would be there to answer. *Obviously* I was unprepared for this emergency. Time for another tire kick.

Darkness was falling, because I was in the northern-most part of the United States and the sun sets really early here in the fall months. I was wearing skinny jeans, tennis shoes, and a flannel shirt that Kayla swore did not make me look like a lumberjack. Sadly, I had no jacket, no beanie, no delightful little scarf Kayla had given me as a 'you got this' gift when she'd dropped me off at the airport. They were all inside that beeping little monster. Maybe I should start walking. At least walking would keep me warm, and I really doubted this road led anywhere other than the Drake property.

I turned to face the dirt road heading off into the tree line and took a step. But wait . . . was this place called The Lucky Wolf because it was in wolf territory? Now, I wouldn't say I'm chunky, but I'm definitely more than a little morsel of meat. I'm a healthy woman with curves and, yeah, some cellulite, so I'm for sure looking like a pretty big score for a wolf family. Which means instead of walking, I decided to climb onto the roof of the car and lift my phone straight ahead, flipping on the flashlight

Maybe from this high point I could see the wolves coming with some warning. Warning I would not get if I followed that road into the forest.

I've never climbed anything faster than I climbed that car. There was a moment where I think the front hood caved a bit, but I wasn't worried about that as I scrambled higher. I stood on the roof and lifted my hands in the air, holding my phone up and turning in slow circles.

Nothing was coming, but that didn't mean nothing was there.

Chapter Two

Still standing on my car five minutes later, I began another rotation, now talking out loud to my phone. "Come on, little buddy, I know you can find any wolves hiding in the dark forest. " I aimed the phone straight out in front of me, parallel to the ground, still spinning in slow circles. This time I raised my voice and called out, "Okay, fairy godmother, you got me into this so I need your help getting out of this." I finished the circle and scowled when there was no change. "I can't believe you'd ditch me like this. What kind of magical creature does that?" I yelled at, you know, my fairy godmother.

A rustling sound nearby made my head shoot up. Wolves? No, it wasn't wolves. It was a man on horseback. I couldn't see the upper part of his face clearly, but I could see his mouth and it was smiling—not just a friendly 'hey partner how you doing' smile, but an 'I heard your crazy talk and am amused' smile.

"Seems like a tough way to learn you can't depend on your fairy godmother," he said. His voice was nice, I'd give him that. It was sort of relaxed and deep, as though he wasn't worried about much in life. I'd probably have liked it more, though, if I'd heard it the first time in a less embarrassing setting.

I nodded because it was a good line, and if the roles were reversed I'd have been laughing too. "I feel very let down."

He chuckled and pushed the brim of his hat back as his horse came to a stop near my car. He tilted his head back to look up at me standing on the roof, and my smile dissolved as I recognized someone whose face I'd just recently seen for the first time on my phone screen during a lunatic internet stalking session. This here was

12

Daniel Drake, younger brother to Alexander. The man was pretty easy on the eyes like his brother, plus that whole attractive cowboy vibe was really working for him. His smile was definitely not disappointing, but all of this was proof that my luck had, indeed, run out, because if it was still holding we'd have met tomorrow morning with me in my business clothes acting like a professional, not standing on the roof yelling at a fairy tale woman.

"Your car seems angry," he said, pulling me from my thoughts.

I turned off my phone flashlight, sat down, and used the front windshield as a slide back down to the ground, shooting off the hood and landing in a way that made me stumble a few steps (once again proving I shouldn't be worried about my ability to accidentally attract a man). Thankfully, I felt a little more in control now that my feet were touching the earth again.

I hooked a thumb over my shoulder to point at the car. "First, this is not my car. It's a disappointment to cars everywhere, but it was the only thing available at the airport. Second, I've locked the keys in it and kicked its tires repeatedly, so, yeah, it's angry."

Daniel slid out of the saddle, his feet hitting the ground in a way that spoke of ease and comfort, an action he'd done thousands of times. He certainly did not stumble. He held out a hand to me. "I'm Daniel Drake," he said.

I barely caught myself before announcing that I knew who he was. Instead I took his hand and shook it just as my car let out an earsplitting sound and went quiet. I jumped and spun around to glare at it. I would have probably kicked the tires again, but really, it was time to be professional now that a member of the family was watching me. I tried all the doors again while Daniel silently stood nearby. No dice.

"Well, I guess that's it. I'm locked out, and I think the car just died. I was hoping to avoid calling Triple AAA, but I guess there's nothing left to do," I said when I'd returned to where he was waiting.

"No Triple AAA out here, but we have some tools in the barn. Let's head there."

I looked warily into the darkening forest and hugged my arms around myself. "How many wolves are in there?"

His gaze followed mine. "I'd usually say zero, but I guess you can't be totally sure."

I nodded and stood up straighter. "Okay. Let's do this." Maybe with a horse by my side the wolves would stay away. "I'd like to note that I'm not a dummy who wanders into dark forests with strangers. If I didn't know who you were, I would have waited with the car. That's all."

I started walking, assuming he'd walk with me. When he didn't, I turned to look back. His expression was unreadable, because I didn't actually know him, but it seemed like he had a tick or something in his right cheek that kept making it tug up.

He nodded. "Good to know. Seems smart for a woman on her own." Oh, yeah, my little speech. I was making one heck of a first impression here. He walked his horse forward to me, climbed on top, and said, "Give me your hand," while leaning toward me.

It was clear he meant for me to join him on that gigantic animal, which was just the worst idea ever. I learned a lot of things in college, but one course I never took was how to ride double on a horse with a total stranger. The delicate art of climbing aboard, balancing, and hanging on for dear life while leaving some space between our bodies was lost on me. I won't go into detail of how I got onto said horse, but it involved some very embarrassing grunting and me possibly yelling at this guy. He didn't deserve it, exactly, but he sort of did because he started chuckling halfway through and wouldn't stop.

"How far to the mansion?" I asked once I'd gotten my balance. I found a handhold on the back of the saddle and leaned away to make some space between our bodies.

Daniel chuckled again. "Mansion? Allow me to reset your expectations. There's a regular size house about two miles from here."

My cheeks pinked with embarrassment, and I was glad he couldn't see it. "All I was told was that this place is the Drake family ranch and retreat. That's what I get for letting my roommate's mind run away with the idea."

"Roommates can be dangerous that way."

We rode in silence for a few minutes, me not having a clue what to talk about, and him seeming totally at ease. I listened for the sound of snapping branches and watched for glowing eyes in the trees, but so far things seemed pretty safe even as the light was fading into full dusk. It was both eerie and peaceful as we made our way through the forest. A city girl like me was used to constant noise, and I was in awe of the silence.

The temperature had fallen and the only warm part of my body was where my legs and backside were in contact with the horse. I'd seen enough romance movies to know that I could scoot closer to Daniel and borrow some of the heat coming off of him, but I held myself stiffly upright and shivered a few times even though his blue and gray flannel shirt looked like the answer to my heart's desires.

"You can lean closer if it'll help you stay warmer," he said, reading my mind.

Nope. Not happening. I stayed silent and tense, willing my body not to shiver again.

He tried a different approach. "I made a huge assumption back there that you're Alex's new employee, but I didn't catch your name."

Oh, right, we hadn't bothered to introduce ourselves past his 'Hey, I'm Daniel Drake,' and my car shrieking.

"Lucy Moore. Mr. Drake hired me last week."

He glanced at me over his shoulder. "You'll probably want to drop the Mr. Drake stuff around here, seeing as there are three of us in residence. My dad, Alex, and me." He turned to face forward again. "Go ahead and save Mr. Drake for our father. Alex and I just go by our first names."

"Uh-huh." Last thing a new employee was going to do was waltz in calling the man Alex. Even thinking of him as Alexander in my own head was pushing it. Did this Daniel person not understand how awe-inspiring his brother was? "I'll ask your brother what he'd prefer I call him."

"Don't trust me?"

I shook my head and startled when my chin grazed one of his shoulders. I'd leaned closer to that warmth without even realizing it. My hands had strayed too and were inching toward his waist and away from the saddle. Yikes. I quickly moved back to a proper polite distance.

"I don't know you," I replied.

Internet stalking had told me only that Daniel was not interested in being in the spotlight. Not exactly character reference stuff.

"Fair enough. Can I be there when you ask Alex what he wants to be called?"

I wanted to roll my eyes, but it would be wasted on his back. "Nope."

He shrugged. "Plan B always involves eavesdropping, and I'm good with that."

At this I felt my first tug of amusement. Who was this guy? "How old are you?" I joked, the words out before I could catch them.

"Twenty-eight. Age doesn't matter, though, when it comes to brothers and being annoying. I will always be the little brother."

I grinned. "I'm the little sister."

"Can I call you Lulu?"

My grin became a scowl. "No." Of all the nicknames to try, that one? Yuck.

"Wow, I found a sensitive spot there. Just so you know, I don't think you should call me Dan."

I huffed a breath out. "I wasn't going to."

"Good." I saw a grin tug his cheek. "You can call me Mr. Drake."

At this I wanted to drop my head forward in defeat, but his back was in my way, so I just groaned loudly. "Do most people call you Dan?"

"No. Only my brother, which is how I like it."

"So you prefer Daniel, and I prefer Lucy. Are we good?"

He nodded. "We'll be good if you'll scoot closer. Your shivering is starting to scare my horse."

Now, I don't know horses, but this one seemed as calm as a beast that size could be. I wasn't buying it. "Nice try."

"Come on, you're cold and I'm warm."

"True, but it sounds creepy when you say that."

Daniel laughed and I found myself grinning. "First law of Montana? Stay alive. You're the only one who finds it strange to cuddle up to a near stranger for heat. I promise."

His words made sense, and another big shudder coursed down

my back as I debated. Cold won. I scooted closer to the saddle and leaned forward so that my front was pressing along his back. Rather than wrap my hands around his stomach—because seriously—I balled my hands up against his sides, taking fistfuls of his shirt. Heat seeped from his flannel shirt into mine, and I almost sighed with relief. Sure, my back was still chilled, but this was helping.

"When we get to the homestead I'll send my guys to get your car unlocked and drive it back."

I wasn't sure how they'd accomplish that, but he'd said it so confidently that I didn't bother asking. "That would be nice. Thank you." I turned my face and pressed my cheek against one of his shoulders. He smelled clean.

"Sure thing."

We rode the rest of the way in silence, with me occasionally switching which side of my face I leaned against him. I kept my eyes open, taking in the scenery as my mind struggled to make sense of this curve ball. I was riding on a horse, behind Alexander Drake's younger mystery brother, in the forest of Montana. I couldn't wait to call Kayla tonight.

We'd entered some trees as we climbed into the foothills, but then the road had turned back downhill and the trees had cleared into a very large meadow. Nestled in the side of the hill, looking over the meadow, was a large log home. Daniel was right, it wasn't a mansion. It was, however, larger than most homes I'd been around. From our viewpoint slightly above, it appeared to be shaped like an H, spreading low and flat. It was made of log, but not the rounded ones. They were square and modern, and fit comfortably into the hillside. There was a barn off to one side where the land flattened out, and on the other side were four small cabins. All of the dwellings had smoke coming from chimneys and light coming from the windows. The scene was welcoming and a half.

"That's the place. Sorry to disappoint you, but nothing is covered in gold and jewels."

I pulled a face. "Yes, yes, eating my words back here."

He aimed his horse toward the main house. As we approached the massive double front door, which was in the center of the horizontal section of the H shape, the door opened, splashing soft, warm light onto the covered porch. I recognized Pamela as she came down the stairs to meet us. She was wearing jeans and a sweater, her chin-length black hair perfectly in place. She had no expression on her face, as though me riding up behind Daniel on a horse was an everyday occurrence. Her fingers tapped a staccato beat on a notebook she carried in one hand.

"Welcome, Miss Moore," she said when we came to a stop.

"I think she's a robot," Daniel whispered to me as he turned to dismount, bringing our faces very close for a second.

A little jolt went through me as our eyes met, but I managed a small smile at his joke. His eyes—brown apparently—crinkled in response before he agilely landed on the ground. He reached up to me, and I swung my right leg over the saddle, put my hands on his shoulders, and appreciated him lifting me down. I mumbled my thanks and took a step back to a more proper distance.

"Where's your car?" Pamela asked, thankfully pulling my thoughts away from broad shoulders and warmth.

"Oh, it's . . ."

Alexander Drake came out of the light-filled front door before I could answer. He looked more relaxed than he had in his office building, wearing a sweater and slacks. I couldn't help but stare as he came down the steps to stand next to his assistant. He looked like he'd just finished a photo shoot for another magazine cover, this one called *Hunks at Home* featuring his very delicious person. I could imagine him quoting me financial statistics by firelight, me lounging on a rug and watching the way the flames teased his blue, blue eyes. He'd ask my opinion and I'd lean closer . . .

He spoke, which was good because I'd almost dipped into the crazy pool there. "Looks like you've had an adventure," he said, taking in the horse and his brother with one quick look. His face was passive and his tone polite, almost like he was commenting on the weather or traffic. "I'm assuming you had a car at one point."

"Yes." I clasped my hands in front of me. "A rental that uh . . ."

Daniel jumped in at my hesitation. "Yeah, there was a slight problem, but luckily I was out riding and came across her. I'll send Jarrod and Steven down to take a look and bring it on in. Nothing the guys can't handle."

While Daniel spoke he pulled his cowboy hat off his head and casually ran a hand through dark brown hair, the ends curling around his fingers. I found it amusing that I'd ridden for two miles behind him and couldn't have said what color his hair was. It was a lovely color, dark and soft looking, the same color as Alexander's, although longer. There had only been a handful of pictures of Daniel online, so this was my first chance to really see the brothers side-by-side, and the differences were noticeable.

Daniel's face was relaxed, warm, amused. His actions were open, the way he stood with his arms relaxed by his side and one knee bent, his hip jutting out.

Alexander, on the other hand, was formal and gave off a slightly disinterested vibe. His hands were clasped together in front of him, his posture straight as an arrow.

Night and day, warm and cool—yet both so handsome my eyes wanted to pop out of my head. While I had no idea what Daniel was like, I did know that I was ridiculously intrigued by Alexander's mind as well as his good looks. He seemed to be the whole package, and I couldn't wait to unwrap it and find out more.

Daniel, seemingly unaware of my scrutiny, plopped his hat back on his head when he'd finished his explanation and turned to lead his horse into the barn.

"Welcome to The Lucky Wolf, Lulu," he said as he passed by me with a nod.

"Lucy." I nodded back, grateful beyond belief that he hadn't told them that *I* was the problem the car was having. "Thanks."

Pamela's voice pulled me back from watching Daniel walk away. "Follow me, Miss Moore, and I'll show you were you'll be staying."

Alexander turned from where he'd also been watching his brother and gave me a courteous smile. "As my brother said, welcome. Miss Lin will get you settled, and I'll see you at dinner."

"Sounds good," I replied, anxious to put this awkward arrival behind us and make a good impression.

I turned to follow Pamela's small form as she headed toward the cabins I'd seen off to one side. We rounded the end of the main log homestead, as Daniel had called it, and the four small buildings came into view. Unlike the main home, these were made of logs in the traditional cabin style but were definitely new additions that looked modern and cozy. A well-tended gravel walkway picked up from the parking space and continued along to the very last cabin, with small shoots for each individual building. It felt like something you'd see in a travel ad. I liked it immediately.

"There are four cabins," Pamela said as she marched along purposefully, the sound of gravel crunching under our feet. "You and I will share the first cabin, which is reserved for guests. The others are used by employees. One for the cook, one for the land maintenance crew, and one for the ranch hands. It should go without saying that we are not welcome in any of the other cabins and we are not to disturb their work or their rest."

We reached the first cabin, and Pamela took the two steps up to a small sitting deck off the front door. She turned to look down at me, and I assumed she was looking for agreement from me that I'd be leaving the workers alone.

"I promise I won't bother them," I said with a totally innocent look on my face, which made her roll her eyes as she reached for the door.

"I've spent my life watching attractive women like you."

I was caught off guard by the comment, but she didn't elaborate. Instead she turned to enter ahead of me—so, yeah, pecking order. My title of Senior Financial Planner meant nothing to her.

I entered and was pleased at the coziness of the space. It was in the style of a studio apartment, with everything being open in one room. Along the back wall were two beds, each pushed up against an outer wall with enough space for two dressers between them. To the right was a kitchenette and a small sitting area. To the left was a doorway into a bathroom. It was all done in browns and greens, and with a fire going in a pot belly stove next to the kitchenette it felt very charming.

Until the ice queen opened her mouth.

"Your bed is the one on the left. I've already ordered a screen for us to set up between the dressers for privacy. We share the bathroom and the kitchen, but I've labeled my things and expect you'll have your own to use." Oh boy did I want to salute, but I'm not a martyr and I fully understood that this woman had the power to make my life miserable. So, I nodded with a smile. She continued, "The family employs a cook and we can take our meals in the house three times a day. At seven thirty, one o' clock, and seven o' clock. If you'd prefer to eat out here you are welcome to go to town and purchase your own groceries."

That would be a hard pass from me. I'd never been so excited about something in my life. Three meals a day, provided, cooked, and most likely cleaned up for me? Total dream come true! Kayla would flip when I told her, which reminded me . . .

"Question?" I dared to speak. Pamela lifted an eyebrow, perfectly plucked and shaped I might add, which appeared to be her invitation to proceed. "Is there WiFi service here?" I had a feeling my phone data would drain very quickly if I had to rely on it out here in the sticks.

She nodded. "Yes."

I waited for more but wasn't going to get it. I guess braiding each other's hair and swapping licorice ropes could be taken off the list.

"Okay, thanks. I'll just go into the bathroom and wash my hands and face and stuff."

"My things are labeled," she replied.

I smacked my lips together. "Yep. Understood."

She gave me a quick once over, and her shoulders lost some of their tension. "Dinner is in an hour, so I suppose this one time you can use some of my soap to wash up. I'm . . . not the same size as you, so I don't have any clothes you can borrow. Hopefully your things will arrive soon."

I looked down at myself. I hadn't noticed that my pants were dusty, but I'd been riding on the backside of a horse for half an hour so it made sense. While I didn't need her to actually point out our size difference, she wasn't wrong about my clothing. I wouldn't be making it to dinner unless Daniel and his employees showed up with my things. I couldn't meet the Drake family and uphold my goal for a good first impression if I showed up like this.

"Would it be terribly rude of me to skip dinner if my things haven't arrived?" I asked her.

She shook her head. "In this case, no. I can make excuses for you."

"Okay." Then a thought occurred. "They still dress up even though we're out in the country?"

"Well, the permanent staff doesn't. But you aren't staff, so you're held to a higher standard."

If I wasn't staff, what was I, exactly? I'd find out soon enough, I supposed. I nodded. "Okay."

"I'll expect an update by 6:45 in order to let the cook know if she should set a place for you or not."

I gave her a thumbs up, and she went directly back out the door. I was surprised I couldn't hear the clip-clove of her little cloven hooves as she walked away. I slapped all the dust off my jeans that I could and flopped down on my assigned bed. Staring at the ceiling, I went over everything that had happened that day, until I had myself laughing hysterically. I should be crying, yes, but it was just too much. I'd met my boss's cute brother while standing on top of a car and yelling at my fairy godmother. I'd then had to snuggle up to said brother for warmth while on my first ever horseback ride. I'd just been given strict no-sharing orders by my boss's elfin assistant, and I'd most likely be missing out on the first meal I hadn't had to cook myself in months.

"Welcome to Winterford, Lucy," I said out loud. "It's all uphill from here."

Chapter Three

The first thing I noticed when my alarm went off was that it was cold with a capital C. I'm talking penguins would need a sweater. The room was still mostly dark, with hints of sunrise coming through the blinds in the cool blue shades of morning. I tugged the big green comforter up to my chin and pulled into a fetal position on my side. Last night I'd thought the potbellied stove was the cutest. This morning I realized it also served a purpose and I'd need to remember to add wood before bed. The second thing I noticed was a huffing and puffing sound, followed by repetitive thumping. In confusion I listened harder. It was coming from inside the cabin. I leaned up on my elbows and looked around until my eyes landed on Pamela in the seating area where she was doing some sort of exercise.

I must have made a noise, because she turned my way while I was still working on getting my brain to understand what I was seeing. When I realized she was looking at me, both eyes popped wide open like a deer in headlights. Should I fake sleep? Should I speak? What did she want from me in this moment . . . well, other than for me to disappear so she could have the space to herself?

She spoke first. "I have a calisthenics routine I do each morning." She dropped down and began doing push-ups. "I trust it won't bother you."

"Nope," I replied, well aware that she wasn't really asking a question. I watched her bust out two sets of twenty push-ups as easily as though she were lifting a spoon to her mouth. "Probably a good way to start the day," I mumbled, my voice coming out frog-like.

She stood and began lunges. "It's more for my mind than my body. I have to stay sharp to work with Alexander Drake."

Her words made nerves flutter in the pit of my stomach, and I relaxed back onto my side, squeezing my body into a tight ball. In the end, I hadn't made it to dinner with the family last night. Daniel had sent two of the men who worked here to get my car unlocked and delivered, but it had proven to be trickier than expected. While I owed both of them a big favor for their efforts on my part, my clothes and toiletries hadn't shown up in time. Thankfully, Pamela had returned with a plate of food for me before I'd totally passed out from hunger. I'd eventually gotten to shower and gone to bed with a full stomach and clean body.

"How long have you worked for him?" I asked her.

She didn't pause in her lunging. "Five years. When he took over the company from his father he hired me. I've been with him ever since."

I could see why he'd chosen her as his personal assistant. Pamela Lin appeared to be tough as nails. She gave off a no-nonsense vibe that most likely kept everyone in their place. It would be interesting to see how she was with the Drake family and if she could turn off the bossiness in a family setting. I was less interested in seeing how our month of cohabitation was going to play out.

Pamela did a few stretches and then sank down to the carpet, ending in a sitting position with her legs crossed and her hands resting on her knees. "I have ten minutes of meditation. Please stay as silent as possible."

That was going to be a small problem since my bladder had begun squawking at me. "I need to use the bathroom. I can be quick," I said hesitantly.

She opened one eye and gave me one of her famous nods. I threw off the covers and skedaddled into the small bathroom feeling like a kid who'd been given a hall pass.

* * *

The bright blue sky that greeted me when I stepped out of our cabin a little while later made the cold weather seem a little less bothersome. I tugged my adorable gray suede jacket closer and paused at the bottom of the steps, letting my eyes follow the progress of a cloud across the otherwise empty sky. There were sounds of life around me, but they were very different from the city sounds I was used to. I could hear animals from somewhere nearby, and a slight breeze made the leaves above my head quiver as a few of them fell. There were also voices in the distance calling out to each other, and I watched as a few men crisscrossed the big open space in front of the main house. The entire scene was so homey that I headed toward the house feeling a little more confident. I'd given myself a big pep talk while I'd dressed in my power red sweater and black slacks before straightening my long hair and putting on my makeup. Mr. Drake had hired me for a reason, and I was going to remind him of that today. Even more, I was going to remind *myself* of that. I wasn't a fresh-faced schoolgirl with her head in the clouds. I'd gone to college and worked for two years in a related field. I had a mind for numbers. I deserved this chance, and I wasn't going to mess it up.

I walked the short path to the main house, my black boots crunching on the gravel, and entered using a side door into the kitchen that Pamela had pointed out the day before. The smells of cooking immediately hit me square in the face, and I couldn't help a smile at the sight of the big long wooden table before me, piled with food. People were coming in from other parts of the house, and a man behind me cleared his throat to politely alert me to his presence. I quickly scooted out of the way, and he gave me a nod as he walked in and took a seat. The men who were employed by the family all seemed to be on the younger side, and I somewhat self-consciously reached up to smooth my hair as I felt their curious eyes on me.

I understood enough about ranch life, thanks to Hallmark movies and historical fiction books, to know that women were most likely scarce and I could be seen as an interesting distraction. I hesitated, taking in the scene.

The table was long and made from the same wood that covered the exterior of the house. It looked long enough to seat at least a dozen people, and the chairs were filling fast as cheerful conversation and morning greetings filled the room. Alexander was seated at the far end of the table next to Pamela and across from an older gentleman whom I recognized as his father, Robert. Mr. Drake had the same dark coloring as his sons—even if his hair was now streaked with gray—but it was clear that Alexander favored him more. Both were lean and tall, with close cropped hair, and I doubted they even realized they were dressed the same in slacks and wool sweaters. An older woman whose picture I'd also seen, Mrs. Priscilla Drake, pulled out the seat at the head of the table, a smile on her face as she chatted easily with those close to her. Mrs. Drake had lighter hair, down to her shoulders and styled perfectly in soft waves. Her eyes were bright, her face only lightly made up, and she gave off an easy feeling that reminded me of the way Daniel carried himself . . . well, at least as far as I knew him.

I took a moment to look at everyone else. There were four men, all dressed in work clothes, with their hats sitting politely on their knees under the table, sneaking glances my way and chatting lightly with each other. They looked clean but by no means dressed up. The three family members who were already seated, along with Pamela, however, were dressed nicely, and I knew it would be best to take my cues from them. In addition to the four workers, I knew that the family employed a cook, and I'd been told her name was Willow. I glanced toward the kitchen to see a thin woman bustling around. She didn't fit whatever mold I had in my head about a country cook. Her light blonde hair was pulled up high in a messy bun on top of her head and a bright paisley patterned headband wrapped around her forehead. She was wearing jeans and a plain white t-shirt, tennis shoes, and at least a dozen bracelets that clinked around on her wrists as she worked.

"Pick a seat, any seat," a familiar voice said from my side, interrupting my thoughts.

I turned to find Daniel standing next to me. I'm not too proud to say I was somewhat relieved to see him. He seemed easier to strike up conversation with than the rest of his family, or Pamela, and I wasn't sure if the ranch employees would be cliquey or not.

"There's not assigned seating or something, right?" I asked.

He shook his head. "We only have reserved seating on the yacht. Here we're more relaxed." I wasn't sure if he was joking or not, which he appeared to find hilarious. "I'm kidding." He laughed. "Even on the yacht you can sit wherever you want."

I rolled my eyes, not about to ask if they actually had a yacht, and picked an empty seat at the opposite end of the table as Alexander, though not on purpose but because it was all that was left. Daniel sat down across from me, a grin still on his face. I noticed his hair was wet as though he'd come straight from showering. He too was wearing a plain t-shirt and jeans, and I wondered how he'd come into the room without me noticing.

"For the record, we don't own a yacht," he leaned across the table to whisper. "We sold it when we bought our own private island."

At this I made a face, but before I could respond a booming voice rose above the idle chit chat.

"Good morning, everyone," the older Mr. Drake called. Everyone stopped talking and turned to give him our attention. "We're excited to kick off our annual family retreat and look forward to catching up with all of you. Also, you may have noticed that we have a new face in our ranks. Welcome, Miss Moore." He gestured a large hand in my direction, and now all those faces were looking my way.

I swallowed my nerves and forced a pleasant smile while pushing my glasses up higher on my nose. "Thank you. I'm happy to be here."

Mrs. Drake laughed. "It's kind of you to lie, but I doubt you were very excited when you found out your first day of work would be on vacation with the boss's family, as if starting a new job isn't hard enough."

I relaxed and managed a more natural smile. "I enjoy a challenge."

Mr. Drake tipped his head toward me with a polite smile. "Well, you've certainly landed yourself a big one here. We'll try to do our best to keep you from running away screaming."

Everyone laughed and shot me smiles or words of welcome as plates began passing up and down the table. The man seated on my left was named Steven. He had a winning smile, and his green eyes gave me a quick perusal as he handed me platter after platter of food. I asked a few polite questions and found out that he was one of the ranch hands who helped out with the animals and equipment. I wasn't trying to be rude, but I dropped my end of the conversation once my plate was filled with pancakes, eggs, bacon, and fruit. I felt almost greedy in my excitement. I must have had a smile on my face because Daniel commented.

"You look like a person who's been starving all her life and just arrived in heaven."

I looked up and wrinkled my nose. "My usual breakfast is a protein shake from Costco. I feel like I've stumbled into a wonderland. Are all the meals like this?"

He nodded. "Willow is really great at what she does. She's even better at getting overly involved in your life, so be warned."

I took a big bite and closed my eyes as the fluffy pancake and sweet syrup glided across my tongue. "She can give me all the life advice she wants to if she keeps feeding me."

"I'm going to remember you said that," Daniel replied lightly.

"Famous last words," Steven added.

I raised my eyebrows and pointed my fork at each of them. "You forget, I'm only here for a month."

Daniel smiled as he dug into his own heaping plate of food. "A lot can happen in a month."

* * *

The office at the Drake ranch was more in keeping with my assumptions about what I'd find here. Decorated in dark woods and warm reds, with bookshelves, a settee, and three desks, it was nothing short of elegant. A set of windows on one side of the room overlooked the wooded area at the back of the house and let in some much needed sunlight. Alexander was sitting at the biggest of the three desks and gestured for me to take a seat across from him when I entered after finishing my breakfast.

I did my best not to stare at him as I crossed the room. I mean, really, I'd been around men all my life, but there was just something about him that made me feel awkward as I sat in front of him. He leaned back in his office chair crossing one leg over the other. I watched the movement and wondered, briefly, if he practiced the move. It was very graceful.

"I've been looking at the stock you recommended when you interviewed the first time," my new boss said when we were both settled. "It continues to do well, and I'm pleased with that. I've recommended a few clients add it to their portfolios, and I'm satisfied that it will be a good solid investment," he said.

"I'm happy to hear that," I replied calmly, even as my heart gave a leap at the compliment.

"I'm planning to dive right into work, and I wanted you to be clear on the expectations. Our work hours will be less than when we're in the office because, regardless of how busy I am, this month is supposed to be dedicated family time. You, Miss Lin, and I will work from eight to one daily. You'll have your afternoons and evenings off." I was okay with that and offered a nod. "Because I've required you to be on-site with me, you'll still be paid your full salary even with the shorter hours." At this I nodded sedately again, even though inside I was wiggling with happiness. Food, full pay, a beautiful setting. What wasn't to like? "Do you have any questions for me?" he asked.

I pretended to think about it, because the one question I really had was a dumb one and I wasn't sure if I should actually ask it. Finally, I licked my bright red lips and pushed it out. "I'd normally call you Mr. Drake, but as your brother pointed out to me yesterday, there are three of you living here right now. Do you have a preference for how I address you?"

Based on the flicker of surprise in his expression, my question had not been one he'd anticipated. Awesome. Even Pamela turned away from her work to glance my way. I avoided her eyes entirely.

"You can call me Alexander. When we're back in Vegas, Mr. Drake will do."

"Sounds good."

"Miss Lin will get you set up with a computer and internet connections. Your desk will be that empty one facing hers." He gestured and I took the hint to go ahead and migrate over to that area.

He uncrossed his legs and went back to focusing on his computer while I headed to my new workspace. I could hear the click-clack of keys being typed on as I sat down at my desk and looked around the top, noting it had all the basics. I wondered what my desk would be like at the Drake Enterprises home base in Las Vegas. I wondered if I'd have an office. Oooh, maybe I'd even a name plate.

"I didn't think to bring a picture of my family," I teased, looking up to see Pamela watching me.

"You could have told me you weren't sure what to call Mr. Drake, and I would have given you direction," she said in a low, annoyed tone.

"Do you have a picture of anyone on your desk?" I redirected.

"No." She looked away from me and slid open a drawer from which she drew out a piece of lined paper. "Here is the information you need to get your computer set up and connected to the WiFi. Once you're all set up, check the messages in your new work email address, which is also listed on that paper. Mr. Drake has already sent you some stocks he'd like you to investigate, along with some current investments that he wants your feedback on." She opened another drawer and pulled out two thick blue folders, which she passed to me. "The email will explain these too."

I took the paper and file folders, not at all surprised to see her handwriting was impeccable and the instructions detailed enough for a kindergartner to understand. Again, I resisted the urge to salute her and instead offered a small smile before turning to my computer and pushing the ON button. While I waited for the computer to boot up I took a moment to look around a little more at the room we were in. Especially the bookshelves. No self-respecting book nerd like myself could contain their excitement about all the shelves. I wondered what they contained and how the Drakes would feel about me borrowing something to read.

A tone sounded, letting me know my PC was ready for action. I followed the instructions, and before too long I was reading through the promised email from Mr. Drake. I sank into the numbers and information like an elephant in a mud puddle, rolling around in it and getting gooey all over. I loved this stuff. I especially loved that he hadn't started me out easy but rather had thrown me into the deep end.

Ready or not, I was on the job, and I was going to blow the socks off this thing.

Chapter Four

I discovered a little something my second day on the job. Daniel was not an active part of the family corporation. His job was to live at the ranch and take care of a herd of sheep. Being that I'm plagued by curiosity, the second I found out there were sheep on the ranch, I was suddenly thinking more about sheep than I ever had in my entire life. Sheep look peaceful, but I started to wonder how loud a whole herd of them would be and why I couldn't hear them from where I was. The whole idea was ridiculously intriguing, as I'd never been around barnyard animals. I'd especially never thought I might be able to hear one from my desk. Horns honking, sure. Sirens, doors slamming, engines revving, yes. I can push all that to the background and ignore it. But when a person is forced to sit at a desk and listen for potential bleeting, or baa-ing, or whatever you'd call it, while also trying to make your new boss happy, it makes for a long morning. The minute the clock struck one p.m. I got antsy. Not only was lunch at one o' clock, but it meant I was off for the day and could explore a little. First order of business was going to be learning about sheep.

Unfortunately, it's never good form for the new girl to bust out of the office first. I was obligated to wait until Alexander and Pamela turned off their own computers and began preparations to head out. The day before, this hadn't been an issue. I'd worked until dinner, wanting to get started on Alexander's requests and get myself settled in and familiar with everything. Today, however, I was jumping out of my shoes with anticipation. For sheep. I was all rared up over woolly animals. If only my mother could see me now.

Finally Alexander and Pamela left the room, and I snuck a text off to Kayla before leaving myself.

Me: I just found out the brother raises sheep. Sheep! Investigation begins after lunch.

I didn't expect to hear back quickly, as she was at work and her terrible boss watched her cell phone usage like a hawk, so I followed my work colleagues down the hallway into the open living space where people were already entering from outside. After the three meals together yesterday and breakfast this morning, I was more comfortable with the informal setup and happy to sit wherever a seat was free. I'd also had a chance to meet the other employees on-site and visit a little more with Steven. I confirmed my initial thought that two of the men were gardeners/landscape crew, and two of them helped Daniel with the sheep ranching stuff. Did you call it ranching when it wasn't cattle? Anyhow, I'd been happy to text Kayla last night to let her know that I was surrounded by young, muscular, outdoorsy men and I was not taking that for granted. Sure, I wouldn't be acting on it in any way, but that didn't mean I couldn't appreciate the view for the next few weeks.

She'd begged me to take candid pictures and send them to her. I was still considering it.

A delicious waft of cooking smells met me once I entered the big living space—it would never get old—and I nearly closed my eyes in rapture. Willow had done it again. I was going to need to schedule in some exercise every day, because this body was not used to eating so well and wouldn't know what do with all these glorious calories. I glanced into the kitchen to offer her a smile in gratitude, and she grinned back in acknowledgment. I reached for my chair and started to pull it out, but before I'd even budged it, it was given a tug and I lost my balance a little. A warm hand wrapped around my upper arm, helping restore my balance, and I looked quickly to the side to see Daniel's smiling face above me.

"Allow me," he said.

"I don't think the purpose of gentlemanly behavior is to make a girl land on her backside," I replied with a shake of my head, my lips tugging up.

He let go of my arm and wiggled the back of the chair until I sat in it. "I guess I should have paid more attention to all that stuff my mom kept saying." He sat next to me and took off his cowboy hat, draping it over his knee and then running his hands through his hair. It really was a remarkable color of brown, dark and rich, like coffee or dark chocolate.

"You know, my favorite candy bar is the same color as your hair," I said, because why just think something when you can say it out loud? Ugh.

His eyes, really the most brown I'd ever seen, swung my way and he grinned. "I think that's the nicest thing anyone's ever said to me."

I pulled a face as a small pulse of embarrassment made my chest tingle. "I doubt that very much."

Thankfully my shoulder was tapped on the opposite side as a basket of rolls was passed to me by Jarrod—the other rancher sheep guy. His fingers brushed mine as he handed over the piping hot and pillowy creations. I held back my inner impulse to jump at the contact and pretended it hadn't happened. I stared into the basket, thinking I could be happy eating nothing more than a plate of rolls and jam for lunch. I was proud of my restraint, taking just two before passing the plate along to Daniel.

"These rolls look amazing," I said to him.

"Once again, you say that like you've never seen food before. What do you usually eat for lunch?" he asked.

I shrugged and reached for the pot of corn chowder making its way around, this time avoiding Jarrod's hands. It had probably been an accident before, but still. His blue eyes lit up when I thanked him for passing the soup, and I turned toward Daniel quickly. The pot was large and warm, and required both my hands to lift it, which left no way to serve myself. Daniel, seeing my dilemma, dipped out a portion and filled my soup bowl for me. Then he filled his own bowl and took the large pot out of my hands to keep it moving down the line. I thanked him and took a spoonful of the soup, blowing a little to cool it off.

"That bad, huh?" he asked.

Without taking my eyes off my food I replied, "What's that bad?"

"What you usually eat for lunch. So bad you can't even talk about it?"

I took a bite and closed my eyes as the delicious, creamy, warm liquid slid around inside my mouth. "Oh my heavenly days," I mumbled. "Let's just say what I usually eat for lunch isn't even in the same stratosphere as this soup."

He joined me in eating, and I enjoyed listening to the conversations flowing around me, uninterested in joining in myself. I wondered how many times I could ask for the chowder to be passed back to me before I'd get a double take from my new boss and his family. I figured seconds were probably complimentary to the host and chef, but thirds would cross the line. Still, it would be silly of me to pass up the opportunity to eat food like this when I had the chance.

"What are your plans for this afternoon?" Daniel asked as he put his napkin next to his bowl and leaned back in his seat. With the way his hands were splayed across his stomach I was guessing he'd eaten more than he'd needed, which oddly made me happy for him. A satisfying meal is one of life's joys.

I swallowed my last bite and pushed my bowl away, removing the temptation to ask for more. I was stuffed. I turned to Daniel and said, "Sheep."

"Come again?"

"Sheep. I'm on an information-seeking mission." I too leaned back in my chair and stretched my legs out in front of me. Yep, full to the rafters.

"Is there anything in particular you're hoping to learn?"

I scrunched up my nose as I thought. "Are they smelly? Does the wool feel as soft as sweaters? Are they nice or grumpy? Can you pet them, or will they mess you up if you try? You know, just the usual stuff."

I could see the corners of his mouth pulling, but he held a straight face. "'Will they mess you up if you pet them' isn't usually one of the top questions I get asked."

I cocked my head to the side. "Why not? It seems pretty basic to me."

He nodded slowly, his eyes crinkling, but he still kept a smile at bay. "Do you have a plan for answering these questions? Were you hoping to sniff them?"

I made a face. "I can't imagine a sheep letting a total stranger walk up and sniff it." He cracked and I was rewarded with a smile. "Besides, I'm sure my answer to that question will be pretty clear when I get to the sheep pen."

"How do you plan to find out if they're nice or grumpy?" he asked. He sat up straighter and leaned forward, elbows resting on the table, his head turned in my direction.

"Not sure. Sometimes you just have to see what happens."

"And sheep are an area where you're willing to just go with the flow?"

"I wouldn't be sitting at this table with you right now if I wasn't okay with taking risks," I replied. Score one for me.

His face grew serious, and he leaned closer to me until I could see tiny golden flecks that I hadn't noticed before inside those brown, brown eyes. "Want to know what I think?" he asked in a low tone that did funny things to my breathing. "I think you're probably a girl who could take on just about anything." He casually sat up straight and pushed his chair back from the table while I sat there with my head whirling and my fingers pressed tightly together against my stomach. "If you really want to learn about sheep, go change your clothes and meet me in the barn. I'll give you the whole tour."

He didn't wait for an answer but scooted his chair back in, put his hat on, and took his dishes to the sink before heading out the side door. There was nothing for me to do but rise to the bait. I'd once again gotten myself into a situation, but I was actually curious about sheep and didn't see many other offers coming my way. This was my shot to answer the burning questions that had filled my mind this morning, so I was going to change my clothes and meet some sheep.

As I changed into jeans and a pink flannel shirt I felt a little guilty about roping Daniel into giving me a tour. If she knew, Pamela would definitely lecture me on leaving the family alone to enjoy their time together and finding a better use of my time. The thing was, I was looking forward to exploring, and it wasn't entirely my fault that Daniel had been roped into it. In fact, I hadn't asked Daniel to show me the sheep, so yeah, I was probably only 30 percent at fault, and I knew enough about numbers to not lose sleep over that figure.

I threw on a pair of old sneakers and then put on a jacket. Lastly, I pulled my hair into a ponytail, refreshed my red lipstick, cleaned my glasses, and tucked my phone into my back pocket. I'd definitely be taking pictures of the sheep. I wondered what their names were, or if they named them. I supposed it would depend on if the sheep were for profit or hobby. Heaven knows the Drake family didn't need the profit, so they were probably hobby sheep. The phrase "hobby sheep" made me chuckle to myself as I walked down the slope to where the barn rested on a flat stretch of meadowland.

I arrived at the barn and walked through the big, double wide doors that were open. From a distance the barn didn't look quite as big as it felt now that I was inside of it. The outside was painted the traditional red with white trim, and I thought it was picture perfect sitting there in the valley.

Steven and Jarrod, the two guys who did animal ranching stuff, were moving about, but in the wide expanse of the barn they hadn't seen me yet. I opened my mouth to call out a greeting, but I heard my name and paused, curious.

"Daniel said that Lucy girl is going with him to see the sheep today," Jarrod was saying. "I'll take her to see anything she wants to see around here."

I wasn't expecting that, and I felt heat climb into my face as Steven joined in.

"She's real pretty. Seems nice too."

"Nice enough to get cozy with, am I right?" Jarrod chuckled and I took this as my cue to call out.

"Hi, guys," I said loudly, trying to act as though I hadn't heard their words. Words that made me feel awkward and flattered at the same time. Kayla would say I should milk the attention for all it's worth, but that had never been my style.

"That pink suits you," Steven said kindly, his head turning casually in my direction while he held a crate of tools in his hands.

I blushed yet again. "Thanks."

"There are flowers that bloom here in the spring that are just that color," Jarrod added with a smile. "They're real pretty."

"I've been meaning to thank you both for rescuing my rental car," I said.

Steven waved it off, but something in the flash of Jarrod's eyes made me expect a flirtatious comment. In the end he just shrugged and said it wasn't a big deal.

I smiled, making a mental note to get them a thank you of some sort for rescuing my car, because it was a big deal and I appreciated it. Maybe tomorrow I'd go into town and see if there was something I could purchase. Like toe warmers for this weather. I tucked my hands into my pockets. Good grief. If this was October, what was going to happen in the actual winter months?

"Hey Hungry, you look cold," Daniel greeted as he came out of a stall on the other end, thankfully out of hearing range, leading the same horse we'd ridden before.

Oh, hooray, another new nickname attempt. "It's Lucy, and why are you getting out a horse when I wanted to see sheep?"

He walked toward me, leading the huge beast. "Because the sheep aren't that close today, and I figured you'd rather ride than walk."

I made a clicking noise. "Sadly, you were wrong. Walking will be good for me after how many bowls of chowder I just ate."

He nodded. "I personally don't enjoy walking on a full chowder stomach. The way it sloshes around in there begging for release really creeps me out."

I tried not to smile. "And riding on a horse keeps things from sloshing?"

"Not really. But at least this way if you need to make good time to a bathroom, a horse can get you there fast."

I put my hands over my face and shook my head. "Oh my gosh, Daniel."

"Climb on board. You can snuggle me for warmth."

I looked up. He was standing close, the breath from the horse's nostrils puffing the air near my face. I took a step back, uncomfortable with something so large and unknown being right in my space bubble. For the record, I'm talking about the horse.

"Do you realize that the more you talk, the worse things start to sound?" I asked.

"Another thing my mom keeps trying to tell me."

At this I did laugh, and his face lit up at seeing my smile. "You might want to go into town more often to talk to women. You're out of practice."

He reached forward and zipped my jacket closed before I could understand what was happening. Then he turned toward his horse and nudged him so the animal was standing with its side to us. "It's because the two women in town are my grandma's age. They think I'm adorable no matter what I say." He tipped his head toward the horse. "Let's mount up."

"Do I get the back seat again?" I asked.

"Do you know how to ride a horse?"

I shook my head. "Yesterday was my first time."

"Do you want to learn now?"

I shook my head again. "Today is about sheep."

He grinned. "Then, yes, Lulu, you get the back seat."

I groaned. "I hate being called Lulu. Don't you have a truck we could take?"

He put his foot in the stirrup and swung easily into place, landing square in the saddle. "Ironically, this horse's name is Ford. So, turns out we're taking a truck after all."

He reached his hand down toward me and I placed mine in his, totally unsure how this would work. Warm fingers wrapped around my smaller ones, making me realize how chilled I was. He slid his foot out of the stirrup and directed me to put my left foot in. Once my foot was in—practically doing the standing splits, thank you—he gave my hand a tug and told me to jump. As I felt his tug and tried to leap into the air, another set of hands wrapped around my waist and lifted. I squeaked in surprise at being launched off the ground by an unexpected force but couldn't look behind me because I was being propelled forward and had to focus on not missing the target all together. Once I was seated on top of the horse, I looked down to see Jarrod grinning up at me.

"Uh, thanks?" I said. He touched the brim of his hat and sauntered off. "Was that weird, or do you ranch guys always manhandle the new girl?" I muttered to Daniel.

He put his foot back in the stirrup and looked at me over his shoulder. "I think he was attempting to be a gentleman. When you live out in the sticks you get pretty excited about a lady showing up."

"Right. Like you with trying to pull out my chair at lunch."

"And here I thought I'd done such a good job of it," he joked. "I know it's bad timing to say this after you just finished complaining about our overly friendly behavior here, but you're going to slip right off Ford's round rump if you sit that far back." He chuckled.

I focused in on where I was sitting and obliged, grateful for the excuse to get closer to the heat coming off of him. It would be so nice to have a stove inside of my body like it appeared he did. He gave Ford a gentle nudge with his heels and we rode out of the barn, turning away from the house to cross the large meadow area. I didn't see any sheep in sight. Which meant I had some time to ask a few pressing questions.

"So . . . you live here full time?" I asked.

"I do. I care for the sheep, keep the house maintenance up to date, look after the land, and anything else that needs doing."

"Did you grow up in Vegas?"

"Nope. We lived in a small town in Southern Utah, actually, before my dad's company took off. I was about fourteen when we moved to Vegas. A few years after I graduated, my parents bought this place. After visiting a few times I asked to take over here. Everyone was happy about that. Alex because it left him as the clear company man, and my parents because it kept me engaged in the family." He gestured to the scenery around us. "I get all of this."

I playfully let out a big sigh. "But no women to practice your gentlemanly behavior on. You must be so happy that Pamela Lin arrived this week. I think the two of you will do very well together."

He nodded, his hat nearly scraping my forehead. "Looks like my fairy godmother didn't bail on me like yours did."

I laughed out loud and relaxed until my hands were resting comfortably on his sides.

The ride to the sheep took about thirty minutes, and we chatted only a little, but I didn't mind. I was soaking in the landscape and wondering what it would be like to live this far removed from everything. The tree line surrounded the homestead portion of the property, creating a natural barrier that made it feel like the real world was kept at bay. I could see living here being both freeing and restrictive. I'd miss the convenience of grocery stores and movies, gas station soda fountains, and burger joints. But I wouldn't miss traffic, crowds, pollution, or small living spaces. Here you could stretch out and relax. Still, it wouldn't be easy to do that with snow drifts up against the windows for three months of the year. Then again, he did have that room full of books.

As we crossed over a small rise and into the foothills, I began to notice white spots spread out in the distance. The sheep. They looked so tiny and picturesque grazing and lounging in the mid-day sun with their fluffy wool coats wrapped around them. Daniel led us down into the middle of the group . . . flock . . . herd? Whatever they were called, they sure didn't seem to mind Ford walking right in with two humans on his back.

"What are the chances I'm allergic to sheep?" I asked as I scooted back to allow Daniel to dismount first.

He waited to reply until he was standing firmly on the ground looking up at me, those brown eyes filled with amusement. "Have you ever owned a wool coat or wool sweater?"

I shook my head and slid up into the saddle, this time determined to dismount the same way I'd watched him do it. "I'm a desert girl. We don't really do much wool." I slid my left foot into the stirrup, or at least tried. His legs were quite a bit longer than mine, so it required me grabbing onto the saddle horn and leaning way to the side in order to reach it.

"Here, let me . . ." He reached for me, putting one of his hands on my thigh and one on my lower back, trying to keep me from toppling off.

"No, no, I've got it."

I pointed my toe and finally got purchase. I started to swing my right leg around, but things were off balance and Ford was tall and I was kind of a total newbie, so, I toppled. Do I need to actually admit that I landed on Daniel, or did that go without saying?

There was nothing soft about that man. No cushy tummy or soft legs. Nope. Nothing but hard muscles and pointy hats. We laid there for a startled second on the ground, him on the bottom and me with my back pressed to his chest staring at the sky. Somehow his arms were around my stomach, but trust me there was nothing indecent or exciting about it. Ford turned his head to look down at us, and I swear he rolled his eyes at me.

"Honestly, I think you're probably a bigger danger to the sheep than they are to you," Daniel said, and I felt the words press against the back of my head. Poor fella probably had a mouthful of hair. His arms fell away from my middle, and I rolled over onto my hands and knees before pushing up to a kneeling position.

"This wouldn't have happened if we'd taken a truck," I retorted, trying really hard to not react how I normally do when I'm embarrassed, which is with chattiness and laughter. I could have broken the man. "Are you okay? Did I snap your spine?"

He turned his head to look at me and his hat fell off, flopping to the ground. First he dimpled, and then his mouth opened wide with laughter. "Snap my spine? I work on a ranch. I've had worse things happen to me already today."

"Huh. Well, for me this is in the top five worst things. I can't say I've ever had a man cushion my fall from a horse before."

I stood and offered him a hand, which he surprised me by taking. It was clearly symbolic, because there was no way I could actually lift him to standing. Still, I did some tugging and we got him situated in an upright position. I hurried to grab his hat off the ground and dusted some vegetation off before handing it back to him. He pushed his dark hair back with one hand and settled the hat onto his head with the other.

I let out a long, loud, slow breath and licked my lips. "So . . . about them sheep." I let the 'p' in sheep pop.

41

"Yeah, time to learn some stuff." He started walking and I followed him.

Things I learned that afternoon:

Sheep don't really smell bad. Just a little animal-like, but not stinky.

I'm not allergic to them.

They don't want me to pet them.

They're more aloof than grumpy.

Their wool does not actually shrink in the rain, and they do not require gentle hand-washing or dry cleaning.

Chapter Five

I t's really unprofessional of me to even think this, but there's just no denying that Alexander Drake is seriously swoony. I kept glancing at him behind his computer the next morning while we worked quietly, soft classical piano music playing from hidden speakers. His dark hair looked like he babied it, his blue eyes were bright and intelligent, his lean jaw was the stuff of romance novel fame. Don't even get me started on his beautiful, perfectly manicured hands. Nothing at all like his brother's hands, which were work-roughened. Alexander didn't tease or goad me, and he didn't send me traipsing through a pasture to see if a sheep would let me sniff it. Alexander was a gentleman. He always called me Miss Moore. Our conversations were serious and thoughtful, despite being only two sentences long. He respected my boundaries, never attempting to assign me some silly nickname. His clothes were pressed and clean, not covered in hay and mystery dirt smears. What I knew of him was perfect. Of course, it would really put Alexander over the top if he could give me the time of day. Daniel at least talked to me.

Pamela cleared her throat, and I blinked a few times, hoping she'd think I'd been woolgathering and unaware of exactly where my eyes had been. I slowly moved my gaze down to my computer screen and typed wildly for a few moments as though inspiration had struck. Actually, I was busy typing Lucy Drake over and over, which was one heck of a sweet-sounding name, if you ask me. A little flirty, a little high-class. It was nice.

What I was not doing, at all, was thinking about how Daniel's hair had been wet again at breakfast this morning. It was almost black when it was wet, and the ends curled around his ears and neckline. Did that mean he showered twice a day? Because I could not see a person working in that dirty setting and then going to bed without washing it off, and for all of his playful ways, he wasn't a slob.

Pamela cleared her throat again, this time a little louder. Sadly, I actually had been woolgathering, and even more disappointing was the fact that this time my eyes had been focused on her pixie-like face.

"Sorry," I mumbled.

"Is the work that boring?" she asked.

I shook my head and smiled. "Not at all. I just get lost in numbers." Her look said she didn't believe that. "Sort of how you get lost in your morning mediation?" I tried. At this she dropped it and looked away.

One more quick peek at the handsome and never rumpled Alexander Drake, and I was back to the task at hand. I really did like numbers, and I really did have something to prove. This was only my third day on the job. I might be silly sometimes—hey, I'm twenty-four, and it's not like anyone is fully formed at that age—but I did take myself seriously and knew this was a job I couldn't mess around with. So, after a pep talk about work being a daydream-free zone, I focused back in.

Alexander had sent me some more investments and stocks to look over, along with a few client portfolios. I decided to start with the client portfolios, figuring a great way to learn about Drake Enterprises would be to see who their clientele was. Since my brain likes order, I started at the top of the alphabet, clicking on a file named Harry Agaard. The good news is that it didn't take long until I was completely sucked into Mr. Agaard's world. The man was diverse in his investments, willing to take risks, yet he was almost eighty years old, and somewhere he was losing money. This was not the time of life when money should be hemorrhaging. I dove deep into every inch of that portfolio, consumed by the numbers flashing before my eyes as I took notes on a note pad. Then I found it. My eyes grew larger and I sat back heavily in my chair.

"Well, would you look at that," I mumbled to myself.

Pamela's head shot up. "What?"

I ignored her, typed furiously on my computer, hit the PRINT button, and walked the few steps to where the printer was now making a buzzing noise as it prepared my paper. A little adrenaline was pumping as I celebrated finding that needle in the haystack. Alexander was going to be pleased, and I'd help dear old Harry Agaard hold on to some of his money. Poor Harry, to be eighty and worried about where the money was going and where more would come from. I imagined him worrying at home, wearing a cardigan and sipping cold tea, not knowing that miles away was a young wonder woman who was about to bring him good news.

The paper came out of the printer, and I hustled the few steps to Alexander's desk. "I have something of interest on the Agaard portfolio," I said when he looked up at me.

He held out his hand for the paper, not offering me a seat, but I didn't hold it against him. Surely he was too caught up in amazement over my financial prowess to be bothered with his normally perfect manners. He read the paper, his brow crinkled in thought, and then he turned to his computer, where he typed for a few seconds, most likely pulling up the file for himself. Still no offer for me to sit, and now my adrenaline was slipping away. Was this not what I thought it was?

Finally, he looked back at me, and there was almost a smile on his face. "Well, Harry told me he was unbeatable, but you did it. Good work."

He'd said most of the right words, but some were missing and some were just confusing. "Thank you?"

He shook his head slowly, his smile growing until he was practically showing teeth. I couldn't believe it. "I can't wait to call him," he said. "He owes me a steak dinner for this one."

Yeah, for sure I was missing something important about this conversation. Like, all of the important parts. "I'm not sure . . ."

Alexander leaned back in his chair and clasped his fingers over his mid-section, which I was coming to understand was his favored pose when he wasn't typing something. "Harry Agaard is an old family friend. He's invested with us for years. When I told him I was hiring a young person with limited experience as my senior planner, he couldn't understand why I'd take such a risk. I told him he needed a more open mind, but he felt there would be others more suited for the job. So, he proposed to prove it to me by changing up his portfolio and putting something small, nearly undetectable in that would cause him to lose money. He didn't believe you could find it, but you did. The rules were that I wasn't allowed to direct you specifically to his file and that you had to notice and find it yourself. Here you are, day three, and the game is already won."

Then, Alexander Drake did something that was so beautiful it almost made me forget that I'd been at the center of a patronizing bet. He chuckled. White teeth flashed, and that same dimple his brother had was buried in his left cheek. His blue eyes sparkled, his hair shone, and yet I could barely enjoy the show for the sinking sensation in my stomach.

"So, I gather he's not an older gentleman living on a small income who will be devastated by financial losses at this age?" I managed.

His smile remained as she shook his head. "Not at all. Harry is very wealthy, which is why I expect to truly enjoy my winner's dinner."

I nodded. "Well, then I suppose congratulations are in order." I tried, I really did, to keep a smile on my face and my tone light. I knew it came out half-hearted.

"No, you deserve the credit, not me. Well done."

I swallowed hard and returned to my desk, head held high even though I felt a flood of feelings I wasn't sure what to do with. Was he being a jerk, or had he been standing up for me by agreeing to the game? Did it show that he truly believed in my skills? If so, that was flattering and I could work with it. But, still, he'd engaged in a bet with me at the center, and it wasn't sitting right. I guess I'd have to think on it a little more before I knew how to feel.

By the time one o'clock rolled around I had a headache and just wanted to talk to Kayla. Sadly, her boss didn't allow her to take personal calls during work hours, so I sent a text telling her to call me the second she could. I wanted to skip lunch, but my stomach had other plans, so I made my way to the kitchen. I was hoping I could just grab something and go eat alone in the cabin while wearing stretchy pants and listening to some depressing music. I needed to sort out what had just happened.

Luck, that fickle thing, was on my side. Today's lunch was sand-wiches, chips, apples, and individual bottles of lemonade. Every-thing was already in a box, with a label letting you know what kind of sandwich was inside. I saw one labeled 'Ham and Swiss' and snagged it with a quick thanks to Willow before I shot straight out the side door.

The air was cool and my tights were thick, but not thick enough to keep goose bumps from breaking out on my legs as I made the trek to the little building I was planning to wallow in. My thoughts were caught up in my crumbling vision of Harry Agaard and Alex-ander Drake. Harry wasn't old and needy, and Alexander's shine had chipped off a little too. It was probably a good thing about Alex-ander, though. He wasn't a god, and I should try to stop seeing him that way. However, that was going to be easier said than done. He might be just a man, imperfect and too handsome for his own good, but he was still a level up from what I was used to, and I seemed to have zero control over my body's response to him. I was finding it impossible to separate the flesh and blood man in that study from the magazine cover model fantasy I'd built up in my mind. Ugh, my head felt like it was on a carousel going around and around again.

I made it to the steps of my cabin and was pulling open the door when Daniel's voice called to me from farther down the pathway where the other cabins were.

"Are you skipping lunch?" he asked with a wave. "It's not like you to miss food and social time," he said, and I was struck by that statement.

He came to a stop at the bottom of the steps and looked up to meet my gaze. For some inexplicable reason, it was like all the sounds quieted and all I could hear was his soft breathing and mine as I analyzed why he'd say that so confidently, like he actually knew me well enough after two days to get away with it. He wasn't wrong. I loved food and I loved people, but still, a woman wanted to main-tain some sense of mystery.

I pushed my glasses up onto my nose and blurted out, "Your brother used me to make a bet." So much for womanly mystery.

His mouth opened and closed while he decided what to say. While I waited for him to speak I noticed that his eyes were the same shape as Alexander's perfect ones. Two brothers with perfectly shaped eyes. The world wasn't fair.

His eyebrows dropped down. "What?" was the word he landed on, and I regretted saying anything. I really had no idea how close he and Alexander were. Maybe they shared secrets in a bunk bedroom and took a morning horseback ride together.

"You know what, he's your brother. I'm . . . forget I said anything."

His lips twisted while he seemed to think. "Tried, can't forget it. What happened?"

I rubbed my lips together and tilted my head. "Didn't mean to say it. Keeping it to myself."

He looked down and noticed my box lunch. "Are you planning to eat solo then?"

"I was planning to put on stretchy pants and overanalyze my morning before crawling into bed and binge watching bad TV dramas."

"I think that's a solid plan A you've got there. Can I offer a plan B?" He took off his hat and slapped it against his leg, releasing dust that sparkled in the sunlight before falling down to his feet.

"There's a ham and Swiss sandwich in this box, so your plan B will have to be pretty amazing."

He grinned. "I know it's cold out here for a southerner like yourself, but how about a picnic in the hayloft of the barn?"

I thought about it. It sounded fishy to me but also really cool because I'd read a lot of historical romance and haylofts were kind of a thing. And, really, when was I ever going to get another chance to go on a hayloft picnic? I pretended to ponder. Then I opened the box and sniffed the sandwich. I pretended to ponder some more until he finally slid his hat back on his head and turned to walk away. I cracked up, appreciating in that second how he'd lightened the mood considerably.

"Fine. Let me get changed."

He turned back around, and his dimple signaled that he'd known all along which way I'd crumble. "I'll grab a box of my own and meet you at the barn."

I changed quickly into jeans and a UNLV hoodie that Kayla had apparently sneaked into my luggage. It was fuzzy and gray with the red logo splashed across the front. I owed her a thank you because a hoodie was exactly what I needed today. It felt like a little hug from her at a time I really needed the support. I brushed my hair back and pulled up the hood before I wandered outside again. It was the middle of the day, and the high was a whopping fifty-four degrees. That was middle-of-the-night temps at home, and I was chilled. Plus, I felt a little emo, which meant hoodie up.

"Way to represent," Daniel said when I approached the barn carrying my lunch. I gave him a questioning look. "The hoodie. University of Nevada, Las Vegas. That's where I got my degree."

"You have a degree? I thought you said you came here after high school."

He pulled a face and turned toward the barn. "I said after I graduated. Plus, I'm a Drake. Do you really see me getting away with not going to college? I have a degree."

"What in?" I asked.

We walked toward the side of the barn where there was a smaller side door. "Do you doubt me?" he asked as he pulled open the man-door and allowed me to step into the big barn ahead of him.

I waited until he'd come through and closed it before carrying on. "No. I'm just curious."

"I have an English degree."

"So the books in the study are yours?"

"Most of the books are mine."

"Is it safe to say you have a grasp of historical novels, then, and knew exactly what you were saying when you invited me to a picnic in the hayloft?" I asked as we came to stop in front of a huge ladder that went straight, straight up. His eyes filled with humor, and he offered me a short nod. "Oh my gosh, is my virtue safe with you?" I almost, *almost* made it to the end of that sentence before laughter caught up to me.

His expression was amused, his stance relaxed when he said, "You told me you're a girl who likes to take risks."

As usual, my words came back to haunt me. My mouth flopped open. "Be serious."

He sighed. "Obviously you have nothing to fear from me." He paused. "Is it a problem that I invited Jarrod to join us? I've seen the way he follows you around with his lovesick gaze."

I pulled a face and ignored the statement because it was eerily accurate. "Just two teensy questions," I said. He raised his eyebrows in the universal invitation to ask away. "Do you read classic literature to the animals, and what are the chances that I'm allergic to hay?"

His head fell back, his hat almost coming off, as he said to the sky, "What did I do to deserve this one?"

I grinned cheekily and tucked my lunch box against my body with one arm as I started to climb. I almost giggled three different times on the ascent, like a fourteen-year-old who'd snuck away on business her mother wouldn't approve of. I held it together, even though the feeling of light happiness continued to fill me, and stepped into the huge hayloft with a smile. While Daniel climbed up behind me I took the chance to look around. Huh. It really was filled with hay. Bales and bales of it. Cool.

"Impressed?" he asked. I could hear the joking tone in his voice.

I responded in kind. "Truthfully, it's pretty average as far as haylofts go, but at least it's warmer up here than outside."

He shrugged. "I'll take what I can get."

He motioned toward a stack of square bales that would make a good seat and I followed along, wondering if hay was soft or stabby to sit on. Yes, I'd done a hay ride before, but these days that really means a wagon with a little bit of hay strewn where your feet rest. I reached out a hand and tested one while Daniel took his seat on another. Satisfied that I wasn't going to have a puncture wound, I sat. Verdict: hard and stabby. Not someplace I'd be hanging out much unless I brought a blanket to sit on. We both opened our boxes and placed items on our respective bales, not bothering to talk while we got set up our food before digging in.

I was happy to find no offending mustard on my sandwich and mentioned it to Daniel. "Don't you think it's kind of presumptive of someone to put mustard on a sandwich without asking first?" I said around a bite of ham and swiss. "I mean, everyone loves mayo. It's non-threatening, creamy, gives some moisture to the whole situation. Not mustard, though. It's an invader. Gets in there and makes itself known above all the other tastes."

"I'll have to compliment Willow on standing up to invaders."

I used a napkin to wipe my face and took another bite. "She deserves gratitude for so many things."

He seemed to enjoy watching me enjoy eating, which was strange, so I redirected by asking him more about the ranch and his job here. He was happy to entertain me with stories about how the family had initially tried running cattle first before quickly realizing they weren't interested in a serious ranching operation. Sheep were less work, cheaper to buy and raise, easier to feed, and perhaps best of all, they gave Daniel a sense of purpose. He didn't think he'd get that same sense of purpose if he was living there with nothing to do but make sure the water heater kept working.

"Did you ever think when you were getting your English degree that you'd live your life as a sheepherder?" I asked.

He shook his head. "Nope. I never thought my father's business would take off like it did and our lives would change so drastically, either."

I popped open my bottle of lemonade and took a swig. "If you were working the job you'd wanted as a kid, what would you be doing?"

"Well . . ." He smacked his lips together. "I'd be the worlds' best ice cream cone maker."

"Nice." I saluted him with my lemonade. "I'd be driving a school bus. Just think of the power. You, and only you, can open and close the door and use the microphone. With one flick of a switch you swing out a stop sign and make traffic bow down to your commands."

"Why didn't you follow your dreams?" he asked with a really admirable straight face.

"Honestly? I guess I realized that no one who *wants* that kind of power should have it. I have a natural tendency toward dictatorship that isn't attractive."

His lips twitched and he glanced away for a moment. The sight of his eyes crinkling up around the edges, and his dimple peeking out, made something happy dance in my stomach.

At last he looked back, apparently under control, and said, "Lucy Moore, I applaud your humanity."

I dipped my head in a very regal manner. "Thank you, kind sir."

"Now, tell me what you meant about my brother making a bet over you."

And, cue the cold water dousing my happy stomach dance. I put the lid on my bottle of lemonade and began packing my trash back into the little box, fidgeting about as I tried to find a way to avoid answering his question. The thing that was so hard was that I was starting to feel really comfortable with Daniel, like I had an ally and friend here, and I didn't want to let him down by saying something possibly negative about his big brother. Sibling code says, "I can pick on you, but no one else can."

"Lu?"

At this my head popped up and I pushed my glasses back into place. "I will only tell you if you stop calling me that."

"Lu? It's cute. I don't know why you hate it."

"I don't have to give you a reason, other than it makes my back feel itchy every time I hear it," I huffed out.

He must have seen something in the mulish set of my face that caused him to retreat. "Sorry. I meant to tease, not to annoy."

"It's a fine line."

"Someone recently mentioned that I may need some more practice with women." His face was repentant, and I immediately got over it.

"Okay, we're good."

I told him what had happened that morning with Alexander and Harry Agaard. Daniel was an avid listener, cocking his head to the side and focusing on me in a way that almost made me blush. I wasn't used to that. People rarely held other people's gazes for the whole story but flicked their eyes around and fidgeted while listening, or jumped right in the second they could. When I was done with the story I still didn't know if I should feel complimented or patronized, and I said as much to Daniel, explaining that I wasn't trying to be easily offended or to overreact.

"Hmm. Let me think for a second," he said.

We sat without talking, his gaze on the hay at his feet for a minute or two. Below us were the shifting sounds of animals in their stalls, and I found it comforting to hear them snort and chew while outside I could hear a few birds. I knew that the lunch hour was almost up and I'd need to let Daniel get back to work, but for now I was content to sit in the stillness and see what he thought about the situation.

"Okay," he said at last. "I know Alex better than you, so here's what I think. He's always been sort of reserved and didn't really do all the typical kid things. He was always more content to be studying or working two part-time jobs as a teen. In college he didn't go to parties or dancing on the weekends like I did. He always chose single rooms or studio apartments, while I was living with eight guys in total chaos.

"Because of those things, I think that sometimes he's not the best at seeing how his actions might affect others. Don't get me wrong, Alex has a good heart, so I really don't think he did it to bring you down in any way. It was his way of proving that you were the best and he'd scored big by hiring you. Bonus points for making Harry lose. Overall, I'd take it as a compliment that Alex was willing to put your skills up against Harry's experience. Plus, you won. He's loving that, and he'll value you even more as an employee now."

"So it wasn't a sexist, patronizing thing?" I chewed my lip.

He shook his head. "No. Alex may be oblivious, but if he were actually sexist and patronizing he'd never have hired you in the first place, much less bet your abilities against Harry. Your gender and age had nothing to do with anything, and that's the exact point he was trying to make to Harry."

"So you're telling me it was a compliment, in a weird way?"

"Pretty much."

I thought about it for a few heartbeats and agreed to give Alexander the benefit of the doubt. I didn't know him so was unsure of his motivations. He didn't know me, so he couldn't predict how my feelings might have been hurt. We were still within the first week of working together. I could forgive this little fumble, especially if it was helping me to secure myself in his good graces. If it happened again, though, we'd have a sit down meeting about it.

I hopped up, a smile blooming on my face. "This has been an excellent lunch. I don't even feel like binge watching horrible TV dramas."

He stood slower, gathering his things. "I'm glad."

I walked toward the ladder and he followed. "I think I'll head into town to check it out and buy a little thank you gift for Steven and Jarrod for rescuing my rental car. Do they have any favorite candies or something you know of?" I asked as I swung a leg over the top rung and started down.

"They get thank you candies and I get used as a landing mat?" he said from above me, referring to yesterday's dismount disaster.

I paused in my descent and looked up at him. "You got the glowing pleasure of my company in a hayloft."

"Oh, is that what that was? Thanks for telling me."

I made a face. "You've spent too much time up here alone on this ranch."

I took the last step off the bottom rung and looked up to watch him coming down. I was struck by how confident and graceful he was. He was much more comfortable on that ladder than I was, and when he reached the bottom we stood facing each other.

"Any ideas for Steven and Jarrod? Seriously?" I asked.

"Steven likes baked goods, and Jarrod likes hard candies," he said, although he didn't sound really excited about offering the information.

"You sound a little mopey," I stated, wondering if he was playing or if he really felt left out for some reason.

"They won't share."

I laughed. "What do you like, then?" In all fairness, he'd rescued me as much as they had.

"Jelly beans," he replied with childlike enthusiasm.

"Jelly beans? I used to be so disappointed when the Easter bunny left them in my basket."

He folded his arms across his chest. "I stand by it."

I held up my palms. "We had a perfectly nice lunch. Let's try not to ruin it over barfy pieces of flavored gelatin." He opened his mouth to retort, but I hurried and grabbed his boxed lunch remains from his hand. "I'll take your garbage in. Have a good afternoon." I scampered out to the sounds of his amusement.

Chapter Six

Here are some of the things I looked up on the internet during my first week of living in the middle of nowhere, northern Montana. In no particular order:

Do snakes live under cabins?
Can snakes sneak into cabins?
Do horses bite?
Can you die from a horse bite?
How to survive when lost in the wilderness
What to do when wolves attack
Techniques for living with difficult roommates
How to properly dismount from a horse
Pitfalls of office romances
What to do about a difficult coworker
Do sheep gang up on people?
How to tell if your boss is into you

Actually, the "how to tell if your boss is into you" searches were done by Kayla, who insisted on sending me list after list of behaviors to watch for. They were pretty amusing, which led to me sending her all the searches I'd come across saying it isn't worth it and you're better off finding a new job before dating a coworker. People thought crushing on your boss was an even worse offense. Kayla remained unconvinced.

For my part, while I was trying my hardest to see Alexander as a regular guy, it was going to take me a while to stop staring every time I caught sight of him. The man was attractive—I don't care who you are. Having Kayla pep-talking me to death wasn't helping either. Every time I'd get my head on straight, she'd remind me of how pretty and smart our babies would be.

To make matters worse, my love life had been Death Valley on steroids. I was parched and he was a tall glass of water. Ha ha, yes, I actually thought that. Yes, I'm humiliated by it.

Overall, in spite of my see-saw fascination with Alexander, I'd have to say my first week had been a success. I'd slipped into a pleasant routine of working until lunchtime and then exploring, or lounging in the afternoon and evening hours. I'd run into town for the thank you gifts and had the pleasure of watching Steven and Jarrod blush so hard their faces turned purple while they gripped the brims of their hats in front of their stomachs. It had been oddly satisfying to be the cause of such a reaction. After that they'd jockeyed for position by me at breakfast every day, and I'm not too proud to admit that having two young cowboy types flirt your shoes off isn't a bad way to start your day.

I'd also purchased a book of Sudoku puzzles and loved to sit on the tiny porch of my cabin working on them before the air cooled too much, or in the cozy sitting area near the stove before going to bed.

Then there was Daniel. We had ended up having lunch together every day outside the house somewhere, which I'd enjoyed even more than the staff members' flirtations. I hadn't had a guy friend like this before, and I liked it a lot. I was starting to understand more why Kayla dated so much. Guys were more comfortable to be around in some ways.

Today was Saturday, which meant no work and that the family was off on a "togetherness experience," whatever that meant. I'd swallowed down a laugh when Mrs. Drake had announced it at breakfast. Her eyes had held that mom sparkle that meant she was thrilled and the men were in for it. Trust me, if your mom is that excited about an activity, then you can bet it's something she's always wanted to do and you've always said no to doing it. Daniel had avoided my eyes, apparently knowing I'd be full of questions. Joke was on him, because those questions could wait until they returned from their experience. My mind was a steel trap.

Willow had invited me to join her in the kitchen mid-morning for some baking. I'm not sure how she looked at me in my knit sweaters, leopard print glasses, and bright red lipstick and thought, *Here's a girl who wants to bake*, but I'd happily accepted the invitation. Now that I think about it, maybe it was my drooling at mealtimes that made her think I'd want to be around food on a Saturday. I'd have said yes just for the food, but I was also motivated by the fact that she was my only option for female companionship. Pamela was a viper waiting to strike at the slightest hint of weakness on my part, and Priscilla was kind but on vacation with her boys. Okay, and I thought maybe Willow would let me lick the spatula.

I entered the kitchen area through the same door as always and found Willow pulling ingredients out of the large pantry and lining them up on the work island. As always, she was in a t-shirt and jeans with her hair pulled up and tied off with some sort of scarf. This scarf was long, with pink and green strings that ran down her back.

"Morning, Lucy." She grinned, and her bracelets jingled as she offered a wave. "Come on in. I thought we'd start with some cinnamon rolls for tomorrow's breakfast and then move on to cookies for an afternoon treat."

I watched her bustle around, whistling a zippy tune, moving as fast as a hummingbird. She seemed to have endless energy and was unfailingly cheerful every time I saw her. I couldn't understand that. Spending all my time in a kitchen would have made my eyes cross and my attitude stink. Cooking felt like a lot of work for only fifteen minutes of eating time, followed by a lot of clean up. But to be fair, she probably felt the same way about doing Sudoku puzzles and planning out investments.

"Your outfit is too cute to mess up. Go snag an apron, and by the time you've got it on I'll have everything ready to go," Willow called me back to earth.

I did as asked and came to lean against the island, looking over everything she'd placed there. The good news was that I recognized everything. My mother was a wonderful cook, and I'd helped her a time or two in the kitchen as a child. Those had been happy times spent with my normally busy mother, but cooking had never truly interested me beyond making sure my body was fueled. I believe that's why my mom gave up on having me join her. I regretted it a little bit, because we hadn't found anything else in common.

Willow and I chatted easily as she gave me directions when she wanted help and told me to step back when it was something she'd do herself. I learned that she had recently celebrated her forty-third birthday, was married once to a member of the armed forces, and had moved to Winterford when things had gone south in the relationship. She had no children, which was fine by her, and she didn't even own her own car, instead making use of work trucks when she went to town for supplies.

"Why Winterford?" I asked, wondering how a vibrant woman would have heard of this place. "Did you have family in the area?"

"Nope. I was looking for a job as a cook, and the Drake family had an opening here."

Well, sure. Jobs are a big factor in where you live. "Is it hard living here year round with just men for company and all that snow?" I asked. "Or are there, like, quilting bees you get invited to?"

She shook her head, a smile of amusement lifting her lips. "You do realize that not all country women tie quilts, right?"

I blushed and nodded. "Yeah. Sorry."

"Don't worry about it." She passed me a large bowl to grease. "Daniel and his crew are easygoing and kind to me. It's not hard to make three meals a day for only six people." I supposed that was true if it was your only job and not something you had to squeeze into your day. "Plus, we don't eat nearly as fancy when no one else is around. I don't mind snow that much. I have inside hobbies for winter and outside hobbies for summer. It's a good life."

"If I was the cook they'd get cold cereal, PBJs, and frozen pizza every day," I admitted.

She laughed. "I think they're all half in love with your pretty face and would happily eat whatever you gave them."

My mouth dropped open. I had never been a girl who wrapped people around her finger, so the fact Willow thought of me that way was startling. "I doubt that." I frowned.

She patted my arm. "I have eyes. Take the compliment. Besides, you've made things interesting for them, which isn't a bad thing."

I was desperate to redirect, so I asked, "How often are the other members of the family here?"

She handed me the mixer full of bread dough before answering. "Probably about three times a year. In October they stay a full month. The other times it's more like two weeks, although Robert and Priscilla have been coming more often lately. Retirement is a beautiful thing."

"Do you like having everyone around, or do you prefer it to be just the regulars?" I dared to ask.

"It doesn't matter, really, what I think. I was hired to cook and manage the house, so I do that regardless of who's in residence." She had a point. A job was a job.

I plopped the bread dough into the greased bowl, and she covered it with clear plastic cling wrap, then moved it to a counter in the sunlight to rise.

"Time for cookies," she chirped.

She grabbed another large mixing bowl and passed me the recipe for chocolate chip cookies. "These are Daniel's favorite. I sneak in some shredded coconut and ground walnuts, and no one can figure it out, but they love them." She smiled. "You start gathering the dry ingredients in this bowl."

I followed the recipe and gathered ingredients while she asked me questions about my own family and life in Vegas. "Not much to tell," I responded as I scooped cups of flour. "I have one sister, Daphne, who is okay, but we're not really tight. My parents are real estate agents who keep really busy, so Daphne was in charge a lot. She thinks she's my mom and can't seem to transition into seeing me as a peer. My roommate and best friend, Kayla, and I have lived together since our freshman year of college. I graduated college a little over two years ago and now here I am."

"Hmm." She cracked some eggs into the mixing bowl. "What are your hobbies and interests?"

She may as well have been speaking a foreign language. "Hmm. I've heard rumors of those," I said playfully.

She chuckled. "You don't do anything in your spare time?"

"I haven't had any spare time for years. School and work have taken it all up."

"Not even quilting bees?"

I pulled a face. "I deserved that."

She patted my arm. "You'd better take advantage of your time here. You should go on hikes, learn to ride a horse, go into town and shop at our little stores. It would be good for you to become reacquainted with yourself and find out what you might enjoy doing." She paused and leaned close with a wink. "Enjoy having some handsome cowboys flirt with you too. We could all use a little more of that."

I bit my lips as they raised into a smile and nodded while stirring together all the ingredients I'd gathered into my bowl. "That's a good plan."

"Great." She took my bowl and began to gradually mix it in with her wet ingredients. "I usually bake most of these, but I freeze a few into cookie dough balls for when I need a little pick-me-up. You're welcome to sneak a few from the freezer yourself, if you'd like."

"I like." I was part of a cookie dough club and it was awesome!

"I thought you might." She turned off the mixer. "I've never had a guest as excited about mealtime as you."

"I never knew what I was missing out on." Now it was my turn to pat her on the arm. "You and I, we need each other."

She threw back her head and laughed heartily. "I think you might be right."

* * *

I took Willow's advice to explore and went on a walk through the meadow later that afternoon. The sheep were still in the higher pasture, so the fields near the house were open and dressed up for autumn, with the foliage turning golden and orange. I walked the same trail I'd ridden along with Daniel when we went to see the sheep earlier in the week, and was happy to see that it was lined with small wildflowers. I'd missed that detail from horseback. I picked a few as I walked along, mindlessly gathering a bouquet as I meandered toward the pines that stood as sentinels before the path began to climb into the foothills. I know I'd said it a million times, but I still found myself surprised by how different this place was from my normal life. At home my paths were surrounded by honking cars, the beeping of crosswalk lights, and the underlying hum of voices. Out here it was so quiet that I could actually hear myself think, which was a little foreign and unnerving. I didn't often have quiet like this, where I could let my thoughts flow. So, I thought I'd give it a shot.

Today's thought topic: What should I do for a hobby?

Willow had pricked at my mind with her question, and she was right that I needed something to do for no other reason than enjoyment. I'd worked really hard to get where I was, and I was working really hard to do a good job for Drake Enterprises. But now I could afford to take a little me time in the evenings and on weekends. I suppose step one was to do like Willow said and get reacquainted with myself, whatever that meant.

I trailed my hand along some tall grass and thought. I was still twenty-four and would be for another six months. I still had brown hair, blue eyes, and dark eyebrows that I swear I did not dye that color. I was still a little clumsy and distracted. Yeah, there was nothing new to read on the pages of Lucy Moore's life story. Reacquaintance complete. Check.

What did I like to do? Well, I liked reading, eating, sleeping, numbers and puzzles, and shopping the clearance racks. See, I did have hobbies. Why hadn't I thought of any of these when Willow had asked? These were all perfectly respectable hobbies. None of them were particularly active, though, so maybe I needed to get in touch with my sporty/outdoorsy/active side. I stepped off the meadow path and worked my way toward a stand of pines that created a circle in the middle. It looked cool. Once inside I stared up at the tunnel they made to the sky and dug deep to introduce myself to action-loving Lucy.

She's a shy one.

I scrunched my face, counted my heartbeats, and thought about PE class as a kid and how I'd shot the most baskets in my grade one semester, but lazy book-loving Lucy did not care. Book-loving

Lucy reminded me that no book had ever bounced off my head or slammed into my eye or given me a bruised shin. No book had ever jammed my finger, or caused a foul, or made my armpits sweaty. No book had ever blown a whistle at me, or made me lose a game. She had a point, there.

I gave up and opened my eyes. I was just going to accept myself and my no-contact habits as is. My mind was active and engaged, and my body was doing just fine. Plus, before I accused myself of true laziness, I reminded myself that I'd ridden a horse two times this week, I'd chased some sheep, and here I was outside in nature. What else was a woman expected to do?

Chapter Seven

I woke up Monday morning to a wall where nothing used to be. I blinked and rubbed my eyes, but no, it wasn't going away. Gone was my view of the kitchen and sitting area, and in its place was a black cloth wall within a wooden frame that I didn't remember seeing last night. Pamela's privacy screen had arrived. I looked at it while listening to her morning exercise routine. I had to admit, I wasn't hating it. Somehow it made me feel cocooned rather than cut off. Score one for the Pam-meister. Her neurosis had given me a small gift.

I hurried through my own morning routine, even though the screen had made me want to snuggle down in bed and hide away from the world, and skipped my way down to the main house for breakfast. Seeing what Willow had cooked up for us each morning always trumped more sleep. Thanks to daily yummy breakfasts with a side of eye-candy, I was much more of a morning person. (I'm talking about Alexander Drake, just in case all my ramblings about my shallow obsession with his looks hadn't made that clear.) Fine, I also enjoyed seeing what Steven and Jarrod would come up with as far as flirtations went. For all of last week I hadn't had to scoot out or push in my own chair, carry my breakfast dishes to the sink, or worry if my hair didn't look its best. Probably my favorite, though, was when Jarrod announced that he wished I was his mirror so that he could look at me every morning. That one had silenced the table. Mrs. Drake had laughed and told Jarrod to finish eating.

Today was a skirt day. Navy blue and flowy down to my knees, I'd paired it with my favorite white and yellow polka dot sweater. I was feeling adorable and looking forward to starting my second week of work. So far things had been going well. I'd moved on from the Harry Agaard thing and found satisfaction in going through the other client files and finding issues that no one else had noticed, or suggestions for improvements that Alexander himself hadn't thought of. I expected today he would give me more files to comb through, or, and this was a real finger-crosser, actually glance in my direction when we weren't talking about work.

Last night Kayla had gotten me rolling with laughter over ways to make Alexander notice me. I'd tried to tell her that between Steven and Jarrod I was flirting up a storm, but she'd pulled out the big guns by reminding me of a certain article I'd gone gaga over. Alexander had given an interview where he'd talked about his love of numbers and the many ways the use of them can improve our lives. It was pretty swoon-worthy material, and I caved to Kayla's wishes by dressing up and preparing for the day with breath mints and eye-catching red lipstick.

Daniel plopped down next to me at the table, interrupting my daydreams of Sudoku puzzles by candlelight. He smelled fresh from the shower and was wearing an easy smile. He hadn't entirely dried his hair, and there were dark spots on the shoulder of his blue t-shirt where it had dripped.

"Don't you freeze in the morning walking around with wet hair?" I asked.

He reached up to pat his hair as though he'd forgotten it was wet, then shook his head. "No. I live inside a house. So, I'm thinking we move away from Lucy all together and call you something like . . ."

I held up my hand. "The name is Lucy, and I'm happy with that. I don't need some funky nickname."

"Not even Peaches or Twinkie?"

I gave him a bored look. "Couldn't you have found something a little more condescending?"

"I'm feeling inspired by your shirt. How about Dottie?" I put my head in my hands and groaned. He patted my shoulder. "Don't give up. These things take time, but I'll figure something out we'll both like."

"I think we need to sit by different people from now on," I moaned.

"You'd miss me."

I didn't dignify it with a response, and he was probably right. Just then Steven and Jarrod came through the door and stuttered to a stop when they saw Daniel sitting next to me. That meant only one of them could sit near me. They tried to play it cool, but some elbows flew and Jarrod ended up sulking down the line to sit near Pamela while Steven took the seat on my other side. I wondered what Pamela would do if Jarrod tried to give her a few compliments this morning. That would be epic.

Even more important than seating arrangements were the four different frittatas in cast iron skillets that were being brought to the center of the table, causing my mouth to water in anticipation. Next came bowls of fruit and carafes of juices and milk. This was worth waking up for, indeed.

"Your love affair with mealtimes worries me," Daniel teased as he passed me a bowl of fruit.

"Your obsession with calling me anything but my actual name worries *me*."

"Fair enough." He grinned and popped a piece of orange in his mouth.

I scooped out some fruit and passed the bowl to Steven. He offered me a shy smile, and I was happy to see that his face no longer turned entirely red when he made eye contact.

"Polka dots look good on you," he said. I grinned and thanked him.

It took some work to steer Daniel away from nicknames like Tootsie and Foofoo, and I was happy when we found common ground discussing literature. I wasn't surprised at all to discover he was better read than I was. The man had an English degree, after all, and my reading ran more toward suspense or historical romance. But I did make the argument that there was such a thing as book snobbery and he'd probably enjoy some Mary Higgins Clark.

"What makes you think I've never read Higgins Clark?" he asked. "I'll have you know there's a shelf dedicated to her novels in the study."

"Really? I wonder if you have any I haven't read yet." I was excited enough by the prospect to stop eating and ponder the possibilities.

He laughed at the look on my face. "Check it out while you're in there today. If you find anything you like, you're welcome to borrow it."

I took a bite of frittata. "It's only fair to warn you that when it comes to books, I can't be trusted to return them. They have a way of becoming mine."

"I'll take the risk."

"Because you know where to find me?"

"Yeah. Plus, you're sort of borrowing them from your boss."

I pulled a face. "I thought they were your books?"

"Ours."

Oh, as in the Drake family's.

"Way to steal the joy out of thieving," I mumbled. Then I thought of something that might make the joy return. "So"—I tried to be super casual—"what did you guys end up doing for your family togetherness excursion on Saturday?" He chewed and pretended to be deaf, which is how I knew I really wanted to know the answer. "I baked with Willow and we had a nice talk about hobbies and stuff. She told me to flirt a little more. Then I did a little self-reflection in the meadow. It was a good day." He glanced over at me and raised his eyebrows. "This is called sharing. It's what friends do. Your turn. What did you do on Saturday?"

"She told you to flirt some more?" His eyebrows raised slowly.

I nodded and took a bite, chewing thoughtfully. "She seems to think I'm just what Steven and Jarrod need to brighten their days."

Something in his eyes shifted, but he looked back down to his food before I could try to read the expression. I did know that the flirting thing bothered him, and I hoped it was the same way I was bugged by his constant nickname stuff. This was fun.

I tapped his foot under the table with the side of mine. "Hey, don't worry. I can flirt with you now and then too, if you need the ego boost."

His tone was dry as dirt when he replied, "Gee, thanks" out the side of his mouth.

"So . . . back to Saturday. What's the deal?"

"Just family stuff." He took one last swallow of his juice and stood, scooting his chair back with a screech. "Busy morning, see you later."

My eyes narrowed on his back as he put his dishes in the sink and headed out the door. I smelled something fishy.

At the other end of the table, Alexander and Pamela were still eating, which meant Daniel had zipped off earlier than usual. They usually left the dining room a little before I did, but I liked to linger, visiting with the others until just before my work day started at eight. This morning, however, I decided to take advantage of Daniel's cowardice and get to the study before Alexander. That way I'd have a few minutes to select a book from the shelves to borrow, or steal depending on how things went.

I always loved entering the study in the mornings. It smelled like a library and yet had the more vibrant feeling of being a place where things were on the move. While I wouldn't consider Alexander and Pamela to be stimulating company, it was still kind of nice to work in the same room and have a little bit of camaraderie

I wondered how it would be back in Vegas when I'd have my own space and they wouldn't be as close. Whenever I thought about it I felt a little jittery about meeting all the new employees that I'd only had some brief email interactions with so far. I was the new kid and hoped I'd make friends and settle in comfortably.

I hadn't thought to ask Daniel which shelf the suspense novels would be on, so I veered in a direction that seemed to have more paperbacks and less old-fashioned looking embossed spines. There were more paperbacks than I'd have originally thought, but I focused in, running my finger along the spines as I glanced among the shelves. There seemed to be some order, but I didn't immediately hit on his shelving system.

"Looking for something?" Alexander asked when he entered the room.

I looked over my shoulder and gave him a winning smile. "Good morning. Daniel mentioned there was a shelf of Mary Higgins Clark novels in here."

"Hmm. He'd know better than I," was all he said before taking his seat behind his desk.

I looked back at the shelves to hide my expression. So much for him standing close to me and helping me search while a haze of romantic feeling enveloped us. Kayla's voice encouraged me to try again.

"Do you read?" I asked him.

"Doesn't everyone?" he replied.

Well, no, I thought. "What types of books do you enjoy?" I tried again, channeling Kayla, as I returned my attention to the shelves and the hunt, mentally crossing my fingers that he read decent books. It would be really hard to irrationally crush on my boss if he hated the written word.

"Mainly non-fiction, or occasionally World War II."

My balloon fantasy began to leak air. "That sounds pretty heavy," I tossed back lightly.

He glanced up and pursed his lips as he thought. "I suppose."

"Do you never read for fun?" I asked, hopeful.

"That's what the World War II reading is for."

He returned to his work, and I felt a curious mixture of deflated and hopeful. Deflated because sometimes talking to him was a painful exercise on my part. He just didn't seem capable of opening up at all. Yet, hopeful, because he'd engaged in some non-business there. At least I'd have something to report back to my best friend who was way too wrapped up in this potential love affair.

After another two minutes of looking for Mary Higgins Clark I gave up. I'd have to ask Daniel later where it was. Pamela had entered the room, signaling the official start to my workday. There were things to do, numbers to crunch, and financial empires to build.

"I'm a fan of the privacy screen," I told Pamela when we'd both settled into our desks.

"So am I."

Yeah, I'd figured that, seeing as she'd ordered it. "It came really quickly."

"Back in Vegas I can get things overnighted. Out here it took a full week." She clicked rapidly on her keyboard.

"I guess that's true. I wonder how Daniel, Willow, and the others get along without everything we're so used to." I clicked away at my own keyboard.

"The beauty of their surroundings makes up for the loss of some conveniences."

I'd never have pegged her as a nature lover. Now, while I don't typically enjoy banging my head against a wall, Pamela was being unusually chatty this morning, so I thought I'd shoot her a half smile and try to get some dirt. "Did Alexander tell you where they went for their family excursion on Saturday?"

She looked up at me with an irritated expression. "No. It's his private time and I don't ask." Okey-dokey, sunshine hour was drawing to a close.

"Curiosity killed the cat, huh?"

"Something like that."

Then a new thought. "I didn't see you Saturday. What were you up to?"

She was still looking at me the way you look at people who just can't take a hint. "I was in town."

Okay. Now I was done. I nodded and went back to my work.

Things were silent in our little study for over an hour before Alexander called my name. I'd been so focused on my computer screen that I had to blink a few times before I could focus on his face. When I did manage to look straight at him I went cross-eyed over his extreme yumminess. He beckoned me to join him at his desk and take a seat. I screwed my head back on and grabbed a note pad, having learned to always approach the desk prepared. He was looking back at his screen when I sat down, and the second my rear hit the leather he began rattling off a list of stocks. I wasn't sure why, but I immediately started writing them down, figuring he'd tell me when he was ready.

"I need you to do some research and analysis on these stocks. Are they ones we'd like to include in our portfolio of options? Have a report ready for me by Friday."

"Yes, sir," I replied.

"I'm also sending you our third quarter budgeting report. Something seems off and I'd like you to go over that."

I made a note on my paper and nodded. He released me back to my desk and I walked the ten steps over, wondering why we couldn't have had this conversation from our respective positions.

The thought made me smile to myself, as I entered the list into my computer. Seemed he was used to calling people into his office, even when we were sharing the same one.

At around 12:45 p.m. Alexander powered down his computer and left the study without saying a word. Not that I needed an explanation, just that he usually worked right up until one, if not after, so it hadn't occurred to me he'd change routine. He seemed to be a man of schedules. I kept my head down, busily researching the stocks he'd listed, fully intent on working until the lunch bell rang.

"Mary Higgins Clark will be in the fiction suspense section, third case from the door, about two shelves from the top," Pamela said quietly when he'd cleared the room.

I wasn't entirely sure I'd heard her correctly, so I popped my head to the side to look in her direction. Her gaze was without expression and unwavering as she gazed back. She wasn't going to repeat herself.

"Thanks."

She only offered the briefest nod in return and went back to her work. Huh. Looked like there was another reader in town.

Chapter Eight

It took me several days and a lot of persistence (begging) to get Daniel to tell me where his family had gone for their togetherness adventure on Saturday. Finally, when I'd pushed him to the brink, he grudgingly admitted they'd gone into Great Falls to take a ballroom dance class.

I could not have been more floored. "Did you have to partner with Alexander?" I asked in mock horror.

His lips pinched. "I knew I'd regret telling you."

I hurried to shake my head. "No, no regrets. I'm just curious about the whole thing." I tried to keep an innocent expression painted on, but inside I was auditioning to be a Dallas Cowboys cheerleader. My mind was painting a picture that brought me spoonfuls of joy. Not to mention the fact that I honestly could not picture Alexander willingly touching another person and wondered how *that* had gone.

"No. There are single women who also go to these classes."

I nodded seriously. "Any sparks fly? Can I expect to meet some lucky lady soon?"

He turned and walked into the barn. I'd followed him out after lunch, still wearing my cute black belted dress and purple cardigan. Now, following him into the barn, I was aware that my footwear wasn't really up to the muck. Still, I couldn't drop it now, not when I'd gotten him to open up, so I tiptoed around to keep the heels of my shoes from sinking in and did my best to keep up.

"No one special?" I asked.

He glanced over his shoulder. "No."

I skipped over some manure that needed scooping. "What was the age demographic, because I'm mostly picturing older people."

"Watch your step. There's another land mine here." He shot out a hand and pointed at another pile of manure.

"Um, shouldn't someone clean this up? It wasn't this messy last time I was in here." I side-stepped.

"Yes. It's my job today. I'm going to get the fork right now." He'd reached the back wall and retrieved something that did indeed look like a giant fork—sort of.

I stopped and looked around. "Well, that's good. Don't want poop on your boots next time you go dancing."

He chuckled. "Iris, these are not my dancing boots."

I wrinkled my nose as a chunk of manure went flying into a pile. "Iris?"

He pointed the fork at me, and I squeaked as I took a step back. "You're wearing purple today. Iris is a very popular purple flower and a possible nickname I'm trying out."

I filled my cheeks with air and blew it out slowly. "Lucy is a perfectly respectable name. What's your obsession with finding me a new one?"

"Same as your obsession with asking about my weekend. It's fun."

I wrapped my arms around myself, feeling a little chilled in the barn. "What dances did you learn?"

He bopped his head back and forth twice. "Just the usuals, I guess. I don't really know."

"The cha-cha, the foxtrot, the lindy hop . . ."

"Isn't foxtrot a military thing?" he asked.

"Uh, yep. Also a dance."

He stopped shoveling and leaned on the handle of the fork. "Says who?"

"Says everyone."

He went back to scooping. "I didn't learn a fox trot."

"Ooh, how about the pasodoble?" I offered. "Maybe the rumba? I hear it's the most romantic of the Latin dances."

He looked up again. "Where do you hear this stuff?"

I shrugged. "I watch TV."

"Maybe you need a new hobby," he muttered under his breath.

I decided he needed a minute before I pushed some more, so I looked around the barn while he went back to scooping, or shoveling, or whatever he was doing. It really was a nice barn. There were five stalls on each side with a really large open walkway down the center. You could probably park four cars side-by-side with no problems. Some of the stalls had horses in them, and they watched us with their heads over their gates. Other stalls were empty, and one was stacked full of bags that could have been horse food, or sheep food, or dirt. Who knew?

I looked back at Daniel, wearing an unbuttoned gray and black flannel shirt over his tee, his jeans worn and his black boots filthy. I wondered if he'd ever posed for a magazine cover like his brother. Imagining him dressed up like Alexander was as difficult as imagining Alexander out here scooping animal poop in worn down jeans. If it wasn't for their general coloring and similar eyes, you'd never guess they were related. It's funny how siblings can end up so opposite sometimes.

"Aha." I snapped my fingers. "The tango."

He threw one last chunk of manure onto his pile and walked back to the empty stall where I'd seen the pile of bags. When he returned he was pushing a wheelbarrow, the fork thing laid across the top of it.

"Nope."

I made a frustrated sound. "Well, what did you learn? Because you were gone all day and I don't know what other dances I haven't mentioned. Are you pranking me?"

He laughed. "No, I'm not pranking you. My mom really did drag us to a ballroom class where I really did dance with a perfectly nice elderly woman named Margaret whose head came up to my elbow. She was so tiny that my back ached from hunching down when the time was up."

"I'm guessing you made Margaret's day." I smiled big.

He continued as though I hadn't spoken. "I learned a few different dances and don't expect to ever do it again."

"What about when you get married?" I asked.

"Iris, if there's dancing when I get married it will be to country music and won't involve perfect posture." He mimicked the hold he'd been taught.

"But, will it involve Margaret?" I asked cheekily.

He paused in his shoveling and looked up in thought. "Possibly. From what she told me, she has a lucrative retirement account."

I burst out laughing, and he just grinned as he went back to shoveling the waste pile into the wheelbarrow.

"You know I'm not giving up until you tell me what dances you learned."

He nodded. "Yep."

The wheelbarrow was full, and he pushed it out the back door of the barn while I stood there wondering if I should follow or not. It was kind of cold inside the barn, and my wool tights weren't protecting me from breezes blowing up my dress. The cardigan was helping the upper half, though. Maybe if I buttoned it closed. I uncrossed my arms and began to button the soft material. Before I'd finished, he reentered the barn and hung up the fork. I watched as he returned the wheelbarrow to the holding stall and then took off his gloves.

"I can empty an entire manure pile into the compost heap and come back before you've gotten your sweater buttoned?" he said.

I pulled a face. "It took me a minute to decide if I should follow you or not."

He looked pointedly down at my heels. They were shiny and black. "You'd have been sunk."

I nodded. "Good thing I stayed put."

"So . . . I have things I need to get to, and . . . "

"And this is your friendly way of kicking me out." It wasn't a question, and it didn't hurt my feelings. "Fine, I'll leave you alone on one condition."

He groaned. "I don't accept. Your conditions scare me."

"You have known me, what, like ten days? You can't predict what I'll say. I just might surprise you."

"Ten days is plenty of time to know I won't like whatever you come up with."

"Wow. I didn't realize you kept chickens in the barn." I made a slow clucking sound and his eyes grew round.

"If I agree to your condition, will you stop making that sound? The horses are getting nervous."

I fell for it and looked around. The horses were watching me just as peacefully as they'd been watching before. "They seem fine."

"They're not. You'll have to trust someone with more horse experience."

I blinked and pursed my lips. "Fine. I'll stop clucking and leave you to your work if you'll show me one dance you learned."

"Pass."

I reached out and snagged his arm as he walked by. He stopped, thankfully, because his momentum had made me spin on my heels and now I was clinging to his arm for support, which wasn't really what I'd been going for. I righted myself.

"One tiny little dance and I'm out of your hair until at least dinner time."

He took a deep breath, but I could see he was amused. "I only learned couples dances and my preferred partner isn't here."

"Margaret?"

"Yes. I don't think I'll be able to do it right without her."

"I understand your concern, but in the words of Dante Aligheiri, 'The secret of getting things done is to act.'"

"Who?" he asked.

"Look him up. That's not what's important here. What dance are you going to show me?"

"How about if I call you Lucy and we never talk about this again?" he said.

I shook my head. "You can pretend all you want, but I know you're dying to dance one more time."

At this he laughed. "Okay, come here." He stepped close to me, put one hand on my waist, and took my other hand in his. "Do you know how to waltz?"

My smile widened. "I think so, but give me a refresher."

"Okay. Hold your body tight. Don't be all noodley." He stiffened his arms and I did the same, noticing how strong his arm and hand felt under mine. This was a man who worked hard every day, and it showed. I appreciated it, from a strictly educational point of view. "Now, I step forward with my left, so you go back with your right. Then my right steps sideways, your left, and we bring our feet back together. Then I'm back with my right, your left forward, and sideways, and . . . yes, good. Again."

He walked me through two more times, my forehead occasionally tapping against the brim of his hat until he took it off and tossed it onto a post. It was a nice shot. After the practice steps, he picked up the tempo until we found a rhythm and were turning in circles around the barn. When I felt confident in the steps, I started humming "Oh My Darling, Clementine," and then we were both singing the lyrics, dancing, and laughing in total freedom. I hadn't had this type of reckless, ridiculous fun in a long time. We sang and danced faster, his strength and balance making up for it when I tripped a bit over my heels, and I relaxed knowing he had me. It was the best. When we were both out of breath and couldn't take the repetitive words of the song anymore, we spun to a halt, holding onto each other's hands to keep us from falling to the floor.

"You're a great dancer," I breathed. "I'm guessing Margaret wishes she'd gotten your number."

He smiled and released my hands. "You surprised me after all. I didn't know you could dance . . . and who says she didn't?"

I straightened up with one last giggle, curtsied, and headed out of the barn back toward my cabin. "Those dance lessons were your mother's greatest idea," I said before popping out the door.

Maybe ballroom dancing could be my newest hobby, I thought, smiling the whole way back to my bed, where I flopped down with a sigh and let my shoes fall to the floor.

* * *

The next morning I couldn't get the song "Clementine" out of my head and kept smiling at the strangest moments. Pamela noticed—shocker—and finally asked if I was okay or needed the morning off. Alexander glanced at me, having heard. I shook my head stiffly and refocused, firmly shoving thoughts of spastic waltzing in the barn to the back of my mind along with a promise to call Kayla and tell her all about it. She'd be so bummed to have missed it but would love hearing about it anyhow. Besties are like that.

Thankfully I was in 'fake it 'til you make it' mode today, and eventually my fake work turned into real work. Alexander had sent me a list of stocks I'd never have expected him to take an interest in.

From what I could tell, they weren't good performers. I was unsure if he was considering taking them on as a risk, but I was having a great time shining my mental crystal ball and making predictions. Once I'd come up with some indisputable data, I'd started working on building a report for the items he'd asked me about on Monday. Today I was working on adding in some of my own 'gut predictions' and polishing it all off to hand over tomorrow. I hoped he'd like it. If so, week two of being a senior financial planner was going to be a good one.

When the lunch bell rang at one o' clock I wasn't quite ready to be finished.

"Willow won't hold leftovers," Pamela said as she stood.

I looked around to see that Alexander had already left. "That's okay. I have the fixings for peanut butter and jelly back in our cabin. I can eat there. I need to finish up this report for tomorrow."

She came around and looked over my shoulder, scanning what I'd prepared. "It looks adequate."

I resisted looking back at her to see if that was a compliment or not. While it was news to me that Pamela knew anything about analytic reports, I didn't doubt she could run the entire company herself. "It just needs a little polish and it'll be ready."

"You're missing out on a meal to polish up your already completed work?" If I didn't know better, I'd think I'd shocked her.

I turned in my chair. "Food isn't everything. It's important to me that I do a good job here."

She tilted her head. "That's good, because most women can't afford to be mediocre in the workplace."

My expression was serious when I replied. "I agree. Especially young women trying to prove themselves."

She stood up straight. "I'll see you later then."

She walked out and I got back to work, diving deep into the work to the point where I had total tunnel vision. This was my magic, and my happy place, working with numbers until they gave up their secrets and painted a picture for me. It was a full hour later when I looked up from my work and leaned back in my chair. It was done, and it was good if I did say so myself. No, it was great. I stretched my arms over my head and rotated my neck a few times. It wasn't until I leaned forward to grab the mouse and shut down my computer that I noticed a bowl of soup covered in plastic wrap with a roll sitting near it. Someone had brought me lunch.

I sat in the office eating that soup and falling in love with that roll, while I ran over the presentation once more in my mind. I credit that soup with giving me the brainpower that helped me push my presentation over the top and blow Alexander's socks off the next day. He'd been complimentary, and I thought maybe I'd seen a pleased expression enter his eyes. Week two's lesson was that a little hard work, along with an anonymous soup elf, can make all the difference in the world.

Chapter Nine

Apparently, traditions can be set pretty quickly, especially when there's nothing better to do. Here I was, back in Willow's kitchen on my second Saturday while the Drake family went on another family togetherness experience. After last week's dance class in Great Falls, I couldn't wait to ask Daniel what today's adventure had been. I figured it would be another doozy, and just thinking about the look on his face when I teased him about it made me feel happy inside. My tendency to tease and banter hadn't always gone over well with men, and I was loving the friendship that had formed between us.

Willow waved as I entered the kitchen area, and just like last week, she told me to snag an apron before she disappeared into the pantry only to reappear with an armload of flour. The kitchen was warm and cozy, with the permanent smells of lemon cleaner and fresh bread seeming to float in the air. I breathed deeply while I tied on my bumblebee printed apron over a red knit sweater that matched my lipstick perfectly.

"Today we're doing sweet breads," she said when I was ready. "Oh, and Alexander's birthday is next weekend, so I thought maybe you and I could brainstorm food ideas. Priscilla has the activity already planned, but I need to come up with a menu, and it needs to be something on-the-go because we'll be away from the homestead."

I blinked a few times in confusion. "I had no idea his birthday was coming up." Had none of my magazines ever mentioned his birthday?

"Yeah. It'll be a fun day to get out and play. You'll love it."

I stumbled over the words, "I'm invited?"

She chuckled, recognizing my brain freeze. "Yes, you are. Everyone on the homestead is."

The smile I gave her in return did not come out as casually as I'd hoped. There was so much to think about here. Did I get him a gift, and if I did get him one, would it be a boss gift or a friend gift? Would he actually talk to me if we were off site for the day? Maybe I could work some of the chill out of him in a more chummy setting. My mind was buzzing with the realization that this was a great opportunity. I needed a plan, I needed to crunch some numbers, I needed to . . .

"Lucy? You with me?"

I needed to pay attention.

Willow finished setting out the ingredients and we got to work, mixing and stirring. Somehow this week she had me pouring out all my woes about dating while mashing bananas. I was really unsure how it even came up, but she had mystical ways. I'd also like to add that mashing bananas is therapeutic.

"I must be a really odd duck," I complained, "because men seem to want nothing to do with me. I'm pretty enough to get asked out but not entertaining enough to keep dating."

She made a clicking noise with her teeth. "That's not true. Well, the part about you being pretty is true, but you are interesting and smart. Maybe you've been saying yes to the wrong kind of guys."

"I can't say yes to the right type of guys, because they never ask me out."

She pointed to a spatula and I handed it to her, watching her scrape down the sides of the mixing bowl as she creamed together eggs and sugar. She directed me to add some dry ingredients to a separate bowl and mix them together, which I did, all the while thinking there were too few men in the world who could keep up with my shifting thoughts and way of moving through life. It was a shame, because I'd be a good catch someday. I never eat other people's leftovers from the fridge, I always pay my part of the bills on time, I laugh at even the lamest of jokes, and I'm quite hygienic.

"This is the twenty-second century. You don't need to wait to be asked out," Willow stated. She wasn't wrong, but I'd never been good at chasing someone down, which is why my whole plan with Alexander was perfect. Crushing from afar and never making a move.

"Also, you can't say men don't like you. Steven and Jarrod practically trip over their tongues when you're around, and you've been spending time with Daniel. He's a good man." She reached for the dry mixture.

I instantly smiled. "He is. He's a lot of fun and we get along great. Which is my other problem. The same guys who never ask me out again are always happy to see me if we run into each other. I'm always everyone's pal, never the love interest."

Willow smiled. "I remember feeling the same way."

"Yeah, but one of them did ask you out and you were married," I said kindly, knowing full well it hadn't lasted.

"True," she agreed, flicking on the mixer once more, "but if I could do it again I'd shoot for friendship first. It would have helped our marriage, I think, if we'd built it on friendship rather than just attraction and proximity."

"Hey, attraction and proximity count a lot."

She handed me a bread tin and some shortening to grease it with. "True. Which is why you're lucky to live in Las Vegas and not here. You can't tell me there aren't plenty of bachelors in that city for you to choose from."

"In theory, yes."

"What does that mean?"

"It means, don't get your hopes up that you'll ever see them. I don't know where all those men are hanging out, but it's not any of the places I'm going."

She tsked. "You mean you're not finding them in grocery stores and libraries?" I rolled my eyes and she laughed. "Stop being a wilting flower and go meet some of them in a place you don't usually go."

"I'll think about it."

"Oh, and stop making eyes at Alexander. He is not what you want."

A blush crawled up my chest and over my face in a rush I hadn't felt since I was a teenager. "What are you talking about?" I pushed out awkwardly.

She stopped pouring batter into pans and raised an eyebrow at me. "Don't pretend with me. Alexander is probably the only person who hasn't noticed."

"I . . ." I had nothing to say to that. It was humiliating. The idea that everyone I'd been living with the for the past few weeks had noticed my puppy eyes. I couldn't believe that Daniel hadn't teased me about it. Oh, boy. "You don't really think everyone has noticed, do you?"

Her face softened. "Probably not. Really, though, Lucy, he won't make you happy."

I've found that embarrassment is a fantastic doorway to anger, which rose up in a wave. I clamped down on it hard, knowing she didn't deserve it and said, "I'm not sure you know me well enough to know what would make me happy." What I should have said was, "It's a silly little one-sided flirtation that will be out of my system soon," but pride and all that stopped me.

She plopped her hands onto her hips and scowled. "Listen, Alexander is an unusually attractive man, so I understand why he caught your eye. No woman under the age of sixty wouldn't feel their heartbeat creep up at meeting him, but you'd be bored by him and he'd be confused by you. Don't be that cliche. You're in a high position in a well-respected company. Don't give that up for him. He should be your boss and nothing more."

She went back to pouring batter, and I handed her another greased tin, trying so stinking hard to not be humiliated after her speech. "And you know all this about me after two weeks of watching me eat meals?"

She shook her head. "I see more than you know. Besides, the fact that you spend so much time with Daniel says a lot. He's discerning in who he opens up to."

Oh. So that swung pretty quickly to a compliment. "Thanks, I guess."

She carried the bread pans to the oven and slid them in to start baking. "Let's fill a few more and get them in the lower oven," she said, as though she hadn't just made my head all whirly with thoughts.

"Daniel is just a friend," I blurted out.

"I know."

"Okay."

Speaking of Daniel, he had warned me about Willow's ways and I'd been pretty arrogant in my reply. She'd definitely pulled me right into her sugar-coated trap. That didn't mean I was going to change anything, but she knew that I knew what she thought, and there was power in that.

* * *

I called Kayla the second I got back to the cabin after baking and felt myself relax the moment I heard her voice. It reminded me that I was only going to be here for two more weeks, which was a tiny, tiny blip of time in the span of my life. I gave her a rundown of my second week in more detail, since the majority of our communication had been via text. Then, I told her about Willow's pronouncement that Alexander was better left alone.

"No Christmas wedding?" Kayla said when I was finished. "Who is this Willow person really, anyhow? Does she get to decide what the life of Lucy Moore looks like? What does she know?"

"Well . . . She does know Alexander Drake better than I do," I admitted, still feeling a little flustered.

Kayla thought for a moment, and I could almost picture her face, eyes looking off to the side while she pondered something. Man, I was really missing her.

"Yes, she does know him better. However, and I say this in the kindest way possible, she only knows him as his chef when he's in residence, right? Or is there more of a long-standing relationship than we're aware of?"

"I have no idea."

"Even though assumptions can be the worst, I think it's probably safe to assume that they aren't super close. So, maybe it's okay for you to ignore what she said just a little bit."

Something niggled at the side of my mind, and I admitted it to her in the way one only does with a best friend. "We both know I'm not going to end up with Alexander Drake, though. Right? Because all my feelings for him are totally superficial, and so far we have nothing in common other than an appreciation of math. He doesn't even talk to me, and I try."

She sighed dramatically. "Yeah, but since when is a good old-fashioned, shallow crush a bad thing?" she pointed out. "You're off in the wilderness with your uber attractive boss. Of course you're going to indulge in a little daydreaming. When you get back to the real world you can settle your hormones down."

"So, I buy him a birthday gift?"

"Oh, yeah, you buy him a gift."

Kayla stayed on the phone with me, and together we looked up possible gift ideas online. Yes, it was a week early, but I was currently living miles from civilization and couldn't just pop out the day before to find something. What if I needed it shipped? (I for sure would.)

"Oh, oh," Kayla suddenly yelled and I nearly leapt off the bed at the screech in my ear. "I found the perfect list on this dating website. It's fifteen non-committal gifts for the person you just started dating. Now we're talking."

I laughed. "Um, that might be pushing the line a little considering we aren't dating, at all, and have only had one non-work related conversation that was short and disappointing." I still wasn't over him reading World War II books for fun.

"Well, I'm having a hard time finding a list of 'I'm a stalker crushing on you but it's nothing serious and will be over before you know it' gift ideas out there."

She had a point. I clicked on the link she'd messaged me and we scrolled through it together.

"Board game, cookbook, bluetooth speaker, scarf, hat . . . These are gifts for that co-worker whose name you drew for the office Secret Santa," Kayla said in annoyance, "not someone you're trying to make fall for you."

"Keep scrolling. Maybe there's something better the further we . . . Oh my. I found a little gem here." I covered my mouth with my hand and started laughing almost too hard to speak.

I knew the second Kayla came across it too. There was a huge gasp and then, "No way!"

"Matching underwear?" I squealed.

We died.

"How did we go from impersonal things like a nice cookbook to matching undies?" She snickered.

"I don't see that as an understated gift," I agreed. "These do not belong on a list of non-committal gifts. 'Here, new friend, put these on to cover your bum so you'll think of me all day long.'"

We were lost again to a round of roaring laughter.

Kayla was the first to be able to speak. "I don't even see myself wearing matching undies with the man I marry. What is that? Do people do this? Is this a thing out in the world?"

"I'd start searching that, but I'm afraid it would be a rabbit hole of couple's underwear that will leave me with a woozy and confused feeling," I said on a giggle. We both took a few minutes to bring ourselves back down, an occasional guffaw breaking through before I said, "Okay, but hypothetically speaking, if I bought matching underwear for me and my man, it would not be in that yellow smiley face print that's happening in this picture."

"You're saying a happy face print isn't appropriate for your most precious treasure to be sporting?" she cracked.

We were both gone again.

And so it went, with us finding one ridiculous thing after the other, none of them at all appropriate. It felt amazing to laugh with Kayla, but eventually I had to say goodbye and do a search on my own. Back to the task at hand. After a little more searching I remembered how I thought Alexander could use a little more fun. Why not take a risk here and help him expand his reading?

I searched unusual or unique books and stumbled across one titled *What If?: Scientific Answers to Absurd Hypothetical Questions*. It looked fun and different. With a few clicks I ordered it and paid the expedited shipping fee to have it delivered to the little book shop/ library in downtown Winterford. I crossed my fingers that he'd like it. Then I crossed my toes, because I didn't think he would without some cosmic intervention.

Chapter Ten

Monday morning flew by so quickly that I felt a little whiplashed when I stepped out onto the front stairs of my little cabin after lunch, having changed into what I referred to as my play clothes, and a Sudoku puzzle book tucked under my arm. I paused and took in the landscape. I had to say, autumn in Montana did not disappoint. Everything was golden and orange, with vibrant yellows and reds popping against the evergreen pine trees. I didn't have any definite plans for the afternoon, just thought I'd wander a little and see where things took me. The weather was cooling, and I was prepared with a white t-shirt under my black flannel shirt and a jacket over it. A bright red beanie matched my lipstick, and wool socks under my boots were all working together to keep me comfy.

The day was beautiful. I'd heard the winter light described as blue or gray and wondered what that meant, but up here I could feel a difference in the type of light that streamed down from the sky. I was sure there was some kind of science behind it, but I didn't care why it happened. I just liked it. I walked around to the front parking area and noticed some action happening near the barn. I had already been headed that way, considering hanging in the hayloft and doing a puzzle, so I wandered on over to see what was up. It turned out that something was definitely happening, and it involved chickens. I'm not a farm girl, so I had no idea if it was normal or not to have chickens squawking everywhere and three men hustling around with their arms spread wide, but I was assuming it was a problem. I paused to watch, and I have to say I had no clue what was happening. The men weren't really herding the chickens, nor were they trying to pick them up. I was at a total loss. And definitely curious.

I walked closer to enjoy the show, a half smile on my face because it was a little cartoonish. I'd almost reached the group when out of nowhere something loud and feathered came at me with claws out. Chickens have claws? Or was this another breed of animal I'd never heard of? It was making terrible noises and flapping its wings in my face while attempting to scratch out my eyes. I gave a little yelp and closed my eyes to protect them. Yes, I wear glasses and theoretically knew they'd protect my actual retinas, but my caveman survival brain doesn't think logically. I ducked my head, but the chicken just kept coming after me, at one point snagging a claw in my beanie and tearing it from my head.

I grabbed my Sudoku book and tried to slap the thing away when it launched at me again. "Stop it, stop it, stop it!" I yelled, terror turning to anger.

I made contact with the winged attacker, and it flopped back to the ground. I cracked an eye open, not believing for one second that it was going to just walk away and leave me alone. My first glance had been correct in that it looked like a chicken, and yeah, it wasn't done with me. Its white wings raised in the air, and it prepared to launch again. I readied my booted foot to connect with its head, raising my leg and staring at the creature with squinted eyes, Clint Eastwood style.

Before either of us could launch an attack, Daniel strode into view and grabbed that clucker right off the ground. Under it was my beanie. I glowered hard.

"What is that thing?" I cried, pointing at it.

Daniel took a second look, as if confirming that it wasn't some mythical beast. "A rooster." His tone was dry and, frankly, unappreciated.

"Someone could have warned me you had an assassin on the property."

He bit his lips together, not fooling me at all. He wasn't taking this seriously. "Sorry about that. We were a little distracted."

"He could have clawed my eyes out," I grumped, bending to retrieve my poor hat.

He nodded, dimpling. "I think that was his plan." I gave him a look. He finally cracked a smile, but at least it was apologetic. "Are you all right? Beau really didn't take kindly to you entering his brood."

"His name is Beau? I thought only domesticated animals got named. He's feral." I tugged my beanie back on and noticed I'd also dropped my Sudoku book. I picked it up and waved it at Daniel while pushing my glasses back into place. "Everyone makes fun of how much I love these puzzles, but this book may have saved my life."

"You two were definitely *at odds* with each other."

That didn't even deserve the air it would take to reply. So, I dusted myself off, took a deep breath, and moved along. "What's going on with the chickens?"

"There was a coyote attack last night that's got them all flustered. We usually let them roam free, but until we can find where the coyote got onto the property we're moving them into a coop and pen closer to the house. Things got a little nuts. Normally this is easier."

"I'll have to take your word for it."

He scanned me from head to toe, and I wondered if I'd put on my pants backwards or something. "What are you up to today?" he asked. "Besides puzzles and karate chopping helpless fowl?"

"Helpless fowl, my big toe." I shook my head. " I was innocently seeing where the day takes me."

He gestured for me to wait one second and walked across the yard to deposit good 'ole Beau back with his ladies. When he returned I finally had my breathing under control and was checking for rips in my jacket or pants, and scratches on the lenses of my glasses. Things seemed to be okay. I would never think of a rooster the same way again.

"How do you know if it's a rooster or a regular old chicken?" I asked him as I tugged off my glasses to rub them clean with the soft cotton of my t-shirt.

"Some people say the saddle feathers . . ." He trailed off and looked at me. "Do you really want to get into that level of detail? Because it's not as simple as you might think, and you don't seem like the type who wants to get into chicken anatomy."

I clicked my tongue and plopped my frames back onto my face. "You're probably right. I already know the important differences. If it's laying an egg, it's a hen. If it's flying at me with claws out, it's a rooster."

"Yeah. That'll do it."

"Do I want to ask if hens attack too?"

"Nope."

I eyed him, wondering if he meant to tease or if they really would attack me. In the end, I wasn't planning on gathering eggs anytime soon, so I'd just avoid them and we'd all be fine. Avoidance is bliss.

"Winter weather is supposed to be moving in," Daniel said when it became clear my Q&A session was over. "We're going to move the sheep down into the meadow close to the house today. Do you want to come along?"

"On what?" I asked.

"On horseback."

Considering the last time I'd been on horseback I'd also tried to flatten him like a pancake, I politely declined. "No thanks. The back seat isn't very comfortable, and I have no ability to dismount."

"Who said anything about a back seat? Look, you can't spend a month here and never ride your own horse. Today would be a great day for it."

My own horse? Um . . . "See, I disagree. Horses are big and I'm naturally a little wobbly, so it doesn't seem like herding day would also be a good day to learn to ride."

He laughed and reached out for my hand, giving it a tug. "Come on, Clementine. We have a smaller horse than Ford, and herding is actually a good day for it because the pace is slow and your horse will just follow the group. Nothing to it."

I glanced down to where his warm work glove was surrounding my hand, for once amused at his calling me a nickname. Clementine, in reference to our barn dancing, was one I could see the humor in.

"My gut says this is a bad idea," I argued.

"Nah. Trust me, you'll have a great time."

"Are you trying to pull the *wool* over my eyes?"

"Please stop," he said, and I laughed.

"The internet did say that for the most part horses are only aggressive when establishing dominance, which is something no horse needs to worry about from me."

He just shook his head and grinned, and I allowed myself to be tugged along until I fell into step beside him. He released his grip on me, and we entered the barn to find three horses tied with their saddles on. I recognized Ford and figured the other two belonged to Steven and Jarrod, who were still haggling with the chickens out in the yard while their mounts waited patiently in here.

"Ginger is still in her stall," Daniel said, referring to the horse I'd be riding. "I'll get her saddled up."

"Can I meet her first? I prefer not to jump on the back of something I've never met."

His chuckle made me blush, and I resisted swatting at his arm. "Probably a good policy."

"Shut up," I muttered.

Ginger, it turned out, was much smaller than Ford. Daniel told me she was technically considered a pony, but all it meant to me was that she looked a lot easier to get on and off of. She was a lovely golden color with a light mane and intelligent eyes. He opened her stall and I hesitantly entered, reaching out to rub her neck. She nickered and I jumped back at the sound. Daniel laughed, assuring me that was normal and not an angry sound. I spent a few minutes getting to know Ginger, which really meant talking myself into taking a ride. I wasn't afraid of new things. It was more that I'd liked to have tried riding around an arena first rather than being flung straight into herding. I'd seen *Man from Snowy River*.

Willow's voice sneaked into my head, telling me I should try some new things while I was in residence, and I caved. "Fine. Saddle her up. Be warned, though, that if I get hurt, embarrassed, or attacked by a coyote or a rabid sheep, I'm holding you responsible." I backed out of the stall and stood face to face with Daniel. "If she runs away with me on her back, kicks me in the stomach, or sneezes on my face, you and I will have big problems."

From here his eyes looked almost black in the shadows, but I could see them crinkling up at the corners and I felt a rush of heat that I attributed to nerves. He tugged on the brim of his cowboy hat. "Ma'am," he said with a totally straight face.

I moved to the side, and he led Ginger out of her stall and into the main area to stand by the other three horses. With her standing beside them I could see that she was definitely smaller, but I'd always thought of a pony as something you rode at the country fair while it walked sedately in circles. She was much larger than those horses had been.

"How do you keep the coyotes from killing your sheep?" I asked while Daniel grabbed supplies for Ginger.

"We have fencing that usually does the trick, but on occasion something breaks and one slips through. There must be a break somewhere near the homestead if it got a chicken. Gary and Colby are going to ride the line today and see if they can find it. We won't know if all the sheep are okay until we get up to the pasture."

"I've never seen any fencing," I replied.

"We opted to run fence around large chucks of acreage rather than several smaller sections. You haven't traveled far enough from the homestead to see it."

"You should send Beau the Angry Rooster to live with the sheep," I said with pinched lips. "Coyotes wouldn't stand a chance against him."

Daniel grinned. "I'm guessing that attack came as a surprise."

"I had no idea roosters did that."

He looked at me over the top of Ginger. "You brought out the best in him."

"I do have a way with men," I said in a playfully arrogant tone.

He cocked his head to the side, his face growing thoughtful. "I never thought to ask, but are you dating anyone back in Vegas?"

"Hardly," I snickered.

He stopped what he was doing, and I could practically feel his eyes running across my features. Warmth crept into my face under his scrutiny, and I looked away when it became awkward. He went back to work on the saddle, and I was relieved that the moment had passed.

"Why is that a dumb question for me to ask?"

Okay, moment still going.

I licked my lips and hemmed about. "You've spent some time in my company."

"And?"

"And . . . you know." I lifted my hands palm up.

Yeah, I didn't really know. I knew I wasn't a hideous monster with a terrible personality. I also knew, through experience, that men didn't seem very interested. As he was a man, I figured he'd inherently understand the mystery of why other men passed me over. So, it was supposed to be answer enough because I couldn't totally explain it. For Daniel, though, it wasn't.

"Okaaaay. Are you anti-dating? Too busy? Burned in a past relationship?" He tugged on a strap under Ginger's belly, and I was so glad he wasn't looking me in the eye for this.

"Uh." I took a deep breath. "I just don't date." It seemed better than saying, "I'm mysteriously repellent to men."

His hat bopped once. "Consider the subject dropped." He did a once over on Ginger's saddle and then patted her on the neck. "I think we're good here. I'm going to go see if Steven and Jarrod are done, and we can head out."

"Are you dating someone?" I blurted, suddenly very interested in his answer even though I couldn't put my finger on why.

He'd already taken a few steps away but turned back to face me. "No."

I nodded. "Anti-dating? Too busy? Burned in a past relationship?"

A big smile spread, his white teeth flashing. "Not enough inventory, probably too picky."

My lips tugged up too, imagining it couldn't be easy to find companionship in Winterford.

"Do you ever come to Vegas?" I asked.

"To find love?" He chuckled. "No."

"Probably smart. There's not much to be found there."

Chapter Eleven

I'm happy to report that horseback riding is not the worst thing ever, and I actually enjoyed my afternoon riding with Daniel, Steven, and Jarrod on the nimble and patient Ginger. Toward the end of the afternoon Steven and Jarrod made a game of each trying out their worst pick-up lines on me, as a joke, and I had roared with laughter more times than I could count.

Daniel hadn't joined in but had given them each a score between one and ten—ten being the most horrible. The winner had been Steven's line—"Do you have a name, or shall I call you mine?"—which had earned him an eleven. I'd nearly fallen off Ginger and had to tug her to a stop. All three men had worn big grins, and I'd come away feeling as light as the wispy clouds above us.

What I did not appreciate, however, was the mentality of sheep. They're either completely losing their minds, or following docilely in a little line, and there is no predicting it from one moment to the next. I'll leave it at that, considering this is not a story about sheep, and close with my suspicion that sheep are not actually easier to care for than cattle no matter what Daniel and the internet say.

I had enjoyed the afternoon enough that I allowed Daniel to talk me into joining him again the next afternoon to check fence lines. One hole had been discovered half a mile from the homestead, and a crew was working to repair that. Daniel felt it was worth walking more fence line, and I was happy to see more of their land.

We spent the day just the two of us, laughing and chatting in a way that I'd never experienced with anyone other than Kayla. To quote Anne Shirley, I'd found a 'kindred spirit' in Daniel, something I'd never have expected in the wide open country so far from home, and definitely not from a member of the illustrious Drake family.

I also felt a little cocky about my relationship with Ginger after our two days together. We'd formed a two-woman super team and no one could tear us apart. My inner thighs and rear end, though, were not in agreement, and I was a teensy bit grateful that the next day wouldn't involve a saddle

That evening I'd sat on the front porch and gone over the day with Kayla. I'd mentioned how much fun I was having with Daniel, and she'd teased me by asking if I was going to switch my relationship goals from one brother to the other. She'd laughed, and I'd tried to, but the idea that other people might wonder about my behavior felt like a thorn in my side. Daniel was my friend, and I didn't want to mess with that. Besides, I'd only be here for a little longer.

Today was the day I was heading into Winterford to pick up Alexander's birthday gift. I was pretty sure that he wouldn't like it, but I'm a glass-half-full type of girl and was surfing the optimism wave the entire drive. It wouldn't have been so worrisome if we hadn't had another brief encounter about books on Tuesday when I'd returned the ones I'd borrowed and selected two more new-to-me suspense novels to read by authors I hadn't heard of. Alexander had asked me what they were and then offered nothing but a "huh" when I'd answered him. Ugh.

The drive into Winterford was enjoyable in its silence. It had been a while since I'd really been alone, and while I'm a social person, I also value some quiet time each day. With a roomie who I both worked with and shared personal space with, and all the time I spent with various members of the household, it was kind of nice to sit and listen to nothing on the fifteen-minute drive. The little rental car made good time once I hit the pavement, and I was looking forward to visiting the library/bookstore in town. I had hours before dark would fall and the dinner bell rang, and I planned to peruse my heart out.

I parked in one of the angled spaces outside the Winterford World of Books. There were only two other cars in this section of Main Street, and I once again had the feeling of stepping back in time. The little shop had a bright blue canopy and two big bay windows where the library displayed books on one side and the book seller did the same on the other. Seeing as I didn't have a library card, I veered to the window with books for sale and looked over a few options. I found one that looked interesting, with a woman in a ball gown in front of a stone castle, and went inside.

The store itself was quiet, as I'd expected it to be at two o'clock on a Thursday afternoon, and I smiled to myself in anticipation of walking the rows and finding something that stuck out to me. But first, I needed to pick up Alexander's gift and ask about the book in the window. I made my way to the center of the big room where the cash register and customer service booth were shared with the library check out. An older couple were sitting in chairs, sipping from matching mugs, visiting quietly. It was the most adorable and cozy thing ever. I immediately imagined that they were spouses, one of them running the library and the other selling books. Maybe they'd fallen in love over a good novel, one of the classics. I nearly floated up to them.

The woman looked up with an open expression. "Can we help you?"

"Yes, hi. I'm Lucy Moore. I ordered a book to be delivered here."

She nodded and set down her mug before turning around to a stack of book-shaped packages wrapped in brown paper with labels affixed. She sorted through until she found mine and passed it to me. "Here you are. Anything else you need?"

"Yes. I was wondering about one of the books for sale in the window."

At this the man stood and came around to lead the way to the window. "Which one caught your eye?"

"I couldn't quite make out the title, but something about a duke."

"Ah, *Devastating the Duke*. I've sold several copies so far this month." His chuckle was as scratchy as his chin stubble looked. "A lot of people seem to want the life of a duke."

"Sometimes someone else's life seems a little less boring," I agreed, even though my life was nowhere near boring lately.

He grabbed a step stool and climbed it to pull down the little paperback. When he was back on firm ground he passed it to me, and I flipped it over to read the blurb on the back. He sauntered away, content to let me come to him when I'd made my decision, and I appreciated it. The story promised to be a lot of fun if the back cover was anything to go off. There were pirates and ships, the next-door neighbor's son, and of course the promises of forbidden kisses and an aristocratic title.

"If you turn that over and the lady is wearing a sagging dress while being held up by a muscled giant, it will really change my opinion of you," a low male voice said near my ear, warm breath skittering along my neck.

I squealed and spun, my pulse racing, and my free hand flying out in defense. My palm connected with a man's chest, and I looked up to discover Daniel standing there with an expression of satisfaction on his face. He was without his trademark hat and wearing clothing that was a little less country. He almost looked like someone I'd run into at the grocery store in Vegas, and it took me a minute to process.

"You look so normal," I said without thinking, my hand still pressed against him.

He glanced down at what he was wearing and back to me. "Thank you. I try to keep my own bulging muscles hidden when I come to town so the ladies can keep their ball gowns from falling off their shoulders."

"Oh my gosh," I sputtered, pulling my hand back and hugging the books against me to keep him from grabbing *Devastating the Duke* from out of my hands. "You're so weird."

"Weird, or really, really interesting?" His eyebrows shot up playfully.

"What brings you to town?" I asked as my surprise wore off. "It's the middle of your workday."

"Who says I'm not working?"

I purposefully glanced around the bookstore and back to him. "Unless you're buying books on the mental health needs of sheep?"

"That's not a bad idea, now that you mention it." He scratched his chin like he was thinking it over, before looking back at me with his head cocked to the side. "I came into town to get some parts to repair that broken fencing you and I found yesterday. I

96

was driving by and suddenly had a real hankering for a book about a Highland warrior and his lovely lass. I am an English major, if you'll remember."

I moved past him, grazing him with my shoulder as I headed down one of the rows of ceiling-high bookshelves. "Let's see if we can find you something. Maybe the hero of the novel would have a few pointers for you on how to find a lass of your own."

He gamely followed along, and I somehow knew his smile filled his face even though I refused to look back at him. His voice, deep and soft against my neck, had stirred up some unexpected feelings in me that had my head trying to float away. I recalled my conversation with Kayla last night and how important my friendship with Daniel was to me. I needed to stay in my lane, so redirecting seemed like my best move at this point. I walked through the rows, him following along, until I found one labeled Historical Romance.

"Here we are." I stopped and turned to face the shelf. "There are several sub-genres of Highland romance. What are you after?"

He wrinkled his eyes and pouted out his lips as though this were of the utmost importance. "What kind of sub-genres are we talking about here?

"Time travel, paranormal, historical, contemporary, immortal, witches . . ." I listed off without looking at him, knowing I'd crack a smile if I did.

"Wow. I had no idea." He stepped up closer to me, making me feel like he'd taken all the space in the row, and glanced closer at the shelves. "What do you recommend to a newbie? I'm kind of feeling witches, myself, but that might be too risky."

I made the mistake of looking up at the same moment he looked down. We were close, much too close. I wanted to back away, but before I could he froze me to the spot with a look of such pure—enjoyment?—that I was rooted to the floor. He looked at me like I'd made his day just by being there. Every other thing in the world faded, and it was just the two of us, hidden by dusty shelves, breathing slowly in time with each other. Then, as my throat began to feel tight, he reached up to where my glasses were slipping and nudged them back into place. His touch was feather light as the tip of one finger touched my nose.

I was in trouble here. Real trouble. Things I'd wanted to feel for Alexander were sort of leaking out toward Daniel, and confusion stole my voice.

"I think witches are too risky," I whispered.

He nodded. "Okay."

I watched in fascination as he blinked and leaned the tiniest bit closer, leaving his eyes closed for one second before opening them again, taking a step back and transforming into regular old Daniel.

"Why is your ranch called The Lucky Wolf?" I took my own step back, desperate to return to familiar footing.

"We named it after our Highland ancestor," he joked.

"That explains the interest in witches."

"Ha ha," he said, elongating the words. "Actually, when my parents came up to look at the property there was an old cabin where the house is. They got out of the car and went to see inside, but when they opened the door they were met by a growling mother wolf with her cubs. It was a stand off, her ready to attack and my parents fearing they'd be seriously injured. They backed away slowly and got back in their car without her springing at them. As they drove away mom said, 'That's one lucky wolf, living in a cabin in this beautiful valley.' So, when they decided to buy the place they named it The Lucky Wolf."

"I like that story." I smiled. "She *was* a lucky wolf."

"Yeah. We call her our lucky charm. Even though we tore down that cabin and built our spread, we've never had wolf attacks on our property."

"Cool."

"Yeah." He grew pensive again, his brown eyes darting over my face. "I'll see you at dinner?" he asked.

I cleared my throat and hugged both Alexander's book and mine against my chest. "Yep."

"Until then, Duchess."

Somehow he'd seen the title of my book, but he was gone before he could hear my reply.

* * *

I called Kayla the second she got off work that night. I figured she'd be in her car and we could chat while she drove home. Because I needed to chat and it had to be her. I was sitting in my little rental car, wrapped in a warm blanket I'd found in the bottom drawer of my dresser. I needed privacy, and this was the only place to get it, but I care about the ozone so I'm not going to sit in an idling car.

She picked up on the third ring. "Did you get the book today? How does it look?" she chirped, speaking about the book I was gifting Alexander.

"Yeah, I've got it. But, he's going to hate it."

"Why?"

"Every time I bring up books, or reading, he always goes back to non-fiction or World War II and doesn't seem interested in branching out. Then again, maybe I'm assuming things. He's really hard to talk to. This isn't working."

"Man, it's like he's your kryptonite, somehow breaking off your crush when he doesn't even know you have one. He's skilled," she said.

Amusement laced my tone when I replied, "No doubt. I wish I had the opposite skill and could make a guy fall in love with me when he's not paying attention."

"If you figure that one out, let me know."

"Nope. I'm selfishly keeping it. You have more dates every month than I've had in my life."

"You know what Alexander Drake needs?" Kayla said thoughtfully. "Someone to crawl up under his skin and make him pay attention."

I nodded. "Yeah. That's going to take one special lady, and all signs point to it not being me."

We chatted lightly about what we'd been up to while I tried to decide if I'd imagined those silent, heated moments in the bookstore with Daniel. Maybe it had all been in my head. But even now, I could still feel the path his finger had taken along the bridge of my nose. It had been completely out of the blue, and I wondered if he was feeling some of those same things I was starting to feel.

"I need you to tell me if I'm being crazy," I said as she was winding up to say goodbye.

"You're definitely being crazy, but I accept that about you."

"Wait, you don't even know what I'm talking about." I giggled.

She laughed too. "I assumed we'd circled back to Alexander Drake and his lusciousness."

"No. I know that whole situation is crazy."

"You can't help it that thousands of years of evolution makes your gene pool want to meet up with his," she stated.

"Yeah, but we both know it's just days away from fizzling," I replied.

"So there's something else you're being even nuttier about?"

There were a few beeps while Kayla locked her car door and I knew she'd arrived at our apartment. Thinking about that tiny little space, really no bigger than the cabin I was staying in, caused a pull in my stomach. I was a little big homesick right now and afraid that I was going to make a mistake somehow, that there was a pothole outside of my vision and I was going to fall into it.

"Yeah, well, you know me," I said.

I told her about running into Daniel at the bookstore and everything that had happened in the historical romance section. When I was done, she told me to walk her through it again. I did, and this time when I was finished she sighed.

"Daniel's single, right?" she asked.

"Yeah."

"If Alexander looks like he does, then I'm assuming Daniel's pretty good looking too. Unless it's one of those families where there's one hot sibling and the rest are totally unattractive."

I cracked up. "No. Daniel's good looking too."

"Is he make-your-eyes-cross good looking?"

I thought about it and didn't even realize I'd started smiling. "No. He's comfortably good looking."

"Dibs. You get Alexander, and you bring home Daniel for me."

I burst out laughing. "Not happening."

"Fine. I don't think you're crazy. You had a nice moment in a bookstore with a handsome guy. It's your evolutionary needs talking again."

"I might look into getting my needs some therapy," I replied and she laughed. "Okay. So I shouldn't overthink it?"

"Oh, yeah, for sure you're going to overthink this. That was straight out of a romance movie. Play that in your head for the next little while and you'll have some really great dreams." I could picture her grin, and it was my turn to laugh. "Then, you call and tell me about them."

"He's just a friend," I reminded her.

"Is there a law against friends being cute and you enjoying a look-see?"

"I don't want to make it awkward. I really like him. He's my best friend in this place."

Her tone grew serious. "Lucy, if he's your friend, then you don't need to worry or overthink. Just be cool and enjoy your time there."

"That's the other thing. I'm leaving soon."

"I'll say it again. Just be cool and have fun."

I could do normal, and cool, and super 'whatever.' Yep. As far as having sweet dreams was concerned, well, I could always use a few of those.

Chapter Twelve

Of course the day of Montana's first snowfall coincided with Alexander's birthday party on Saturday. Of course. I peeked through the kitchen window from my bed, my view occasionally blurred by the flying limbs of one Pamela Lin and her calisthenics routine. Big white flakes drifted down from the sky, and it seemed like all the sounds of life I had grown used to had disappeared. It wasn't like I'd never seen snow before. I'd traveled, and the mountain ranges around Las Vegas get snow every winter. It's just that snow doesn't really accumulate on the ground in measurable inches and cause life to pause while animals and people hunker down. This blanketed silence was new. Pamela huffing and puffing wasn't, but it didn't ruin the effect.

I got out of bed, hurried to wrap a throw blanket around my shoulders, and walked to the window for a closer look. After two weeks of living together, Pamela didn't even bother asking me to stay silently in bed, and I didn't even bother pretending I would. We'd reached a flow of working around each other, which meant I was free to move about the place while refraining from speaking or making unnecessary noises.

The view that met me was beautiful in its starkness. White covered everything in layers that seemed to drift with the landscape. Paths had already been shoveled from the four cabins to the main house and front drive. I couldn't see the parking area from here, or the barn, but I assumed it had been cleared with the same efficiency. This heavy feeling of hibernation explained why I'd slept like the dead last night in spite of my fluttery thoughts about the Drake brothers.

Added to those confused thoughts was the fact I was now 100 percent sure Alexander would hate my gift. He'd be polite, but he wasn't going to immediately open the book and start flipping through pages with a delighted look on his face. You know who would? Daniel. He was going to crack up so hard when he saw it, and when Alexander set it down with the other gifts and moved along, Daniel would snatch it out of the pile and start flipping through the pages. I'd bought a stinking birthday gift for the wrong brother, with zero time to do anything about it.

It was time to slip into blissful denial and pretend I really didn't care at all. It was a token gift, nothing big, and he'd appreciate the gesture. Hopefully.

"Dress warm," Pamela said when she'd finished the last of her exercises. "We're going out in side-by-sides today."

I spun to face her. "What are those and how do you know?"

"Those are off-road vehicles, kind of like a hugely modified golf cart crossed with a four-wheeler. Mr. Drake told me that a day off-roading through the hills around here and a picnic lunch is what he'd asked for. Snow isn't going to change anything." She sat down and placed her hands palms up on her knees. "Do you have appropriate clothing?" I mentally ran through my clothing items and came up with a nope. I shook my head. "I'm guessing Willow can get something for you. I'd be surprised if they don't have spares somewhere."

I blinked a few times. That was probably the nicest thing she'd ever said to me. She hadn't blamed me, she hadn't insulted my packing intelligence, she hadn't suggested I stay back. Wow. That was progress.

"Thanks," I said as I made my way to my side of our privacy screen. "Do you know what time we're meeting up?"

"After breakfast, which means you don't need to rush. You'll have some time to gather gear."

Two nice comments in one conversation. What was happening here?

I hurried to dress in jeans and a bright yellow sweater, shoving my feet in my everyday boots and zipping up a jacket. I ran fingers through my hair and pulled it back into a French braid before slapping a beanie over it. Glasses and lipstick completed my look, and my stomach growled just as I smacked my lips together. It was nice how my body was so in tune with the clock. Time to eat and see if I could get some spare snow gear.

The walk to the house was a bit frosty, and I arrived blowing warm air into my hands. That distance had been the equivalent of walking two doors down and my toes were ice-pops, so I was in trouble if I couldn't get warmer clothing. Thankfully I was early enough that Willow was alone in the kitchen.

"Good morning, merry sunshine. What makes you rise so soon?" she said when she glanced my way.

I assumed it was in reference to my bright yellow sweater, and I grinned, knowing the color was a lot. "I hear we're going out on side-by-sides today, and I have no snow gear. Are there spare things I could borrow?"

She nodded as she pulled a tray of hot muffins from the oven. "Yeah, in the mud room. Anything in the number six locker is extra and guests are welcome to it. Hopefully we have something that's small enough."

I almost thanked her for saying that last part. Hey, I'm good with my shape, but it's not like you're going to be angry with some-one suggesting clothing might be too large for you. I'll take my flattery where I can get it—even if I have to dig a little.

I made my way through the kitchen and into the mudroom that was attached to the laundry area. The mudroom was spacious with three lockers on one side and three on the other. These weren't normal sized lockers, but double wide and double deep. On the third wall of the room was a big cubby shelf full of footwear, hel-mets, and goggles. I'd reached the winter gear candy store, and that worried me a little bit because it must mean there was a big need for it here. I still had two more weeks to go. Exactly how frigid was it going to get?

I opened a locker that had a big number six stuck to it and found three pairs of snow pants and two coats. There was a pile of gloves on a top shelf too. After trying on all three pants I found one that worked, although it was too long and a little roomy around the waist. The smaller of the two coats hung off the end of my arms and down to my thighs, but it would keep me warm. The gloves were also too big, but again, I was grateful to have found some. I snagged a pair of goggles and boots, which were laughably large. Clothes you can make work, but stomping around in boots that are three sizes too big is another story. I figured I could layer on the wool socks and hope for the best.

I returned to the kitchen with an armful of clothing, my eyes barely peeking over the top, intent on depositing them in my cabin before eating. Other people were arriving and the scene was a little peppier than usual, everyone commenting on the snow and their excitement for a day off. A few birthday wishes were called to Alexander, and I was glad my face was hidden when I looked in his direction. He was wearing a slim-fit blue wool sweater, matching beanie, and sporting a lighter blue scarf tied around his neck. All that blue really pulled out the color of his eyes, and that slim fit was doing his body serious favors. Throw in black jeans and stocking feet and, well, hello—here was something to write home about.

I, unfortunately, kept walking while taking this all in and crashed into a wall. The wall said "oof" and turned out to be Daniel. Half of what I was carrying fell to the floor as he reached out to steady me. His hands were warm and solid around my upper arms, the remaining clothing pressed between us, when I glanced up to meet his laughing expression.

"Hey, Turbo, you're in a rush."

I started at the feel of one of his hands running down my arm to hold my elbow, and I felt oddly tempted to lean in a little more, remembering the way it had felt at the bookstore the other day. Not a great impulse, considering I'd just be ogling his miraculously beautiful sibling. Awkward and wrong and so confusing.

"I'm a busy woman," I replied with a smile, still leaning toward him in spite of the wrongness of it all.

He looked down at the load between us. "Snow gear? Will any of this actually fit you? I don't think we have any women's sizes."

My expression was playful when I replied, "Fortunately I'm a creative person."

He stepped back as though he were suddenly aware of how close we were standing and how many eyes were watching. The movement caused one last boot to tumble, and I chuckled as he bent to pick up the various items littering the floor around us.

"I'll help you carry this load," he said, his hands now full of boots, gloves, and goggles.

"My own personal donkey. How kind," I chirped as I stepped around him to lead the way.

"Flattery will get you places. You should give it a try sometime."

Our feet crunched in the snow as we hustled from the house to my cabin. Daniel wasn't wearing a coat, and my jacket wasn't making much of a difference, which meant that when we arrived inside my snug little room we were both puffing out cold air and stomping our feet. Pamela was nowhere to be seen. I took my armful and dumped it on my bed before coming back for his.

"I like the privacy screen. That's a good idea," he said as I turned to carry his load to my bed.

"Pamela."

"Ahh. Well, she does have some good ideas, and Alexander says she works really hard."

"Yes, she does. She's quite good at her job."

I came out from behind the screen to see Pamela standing in the open doorway of the cabin, looking at the two of us. There was no doubt she'd heard our conversation, and I immediately promised to remember this moment and be careful about gossiping, because that could have gone quite differently. Her expression was its usual blank, but there was something in her eyes that was new. Surprise and maybe a little gratitude.

"Willow gave me this scarf to wear today," she said. She hurried to place it on the kitchen counter and then spun back out the door before either of us could say anything.

Daniel turned from where he'd been looking at her and made a face of pure relief. "We seriously, *seriously* lucked out there. What if I'd been calling her a robot again?"

Our amusement bubbled over with the irony of that moment. When the laughter slowed down I noticed that while he wasn't dressed to the nines like his brother, he still looked really good in a gray sweater, dark jeans, and rough work boots—every bit as fit and masculine as Alexander. The two men were so different, and

I'd been so hyper focused on Alexander that I sometimes forgot Daniel was attractive too. Although standing here looking at the way his eyes danced when he watched me, and remembering how I'd wanted to lean into him, well . . . things seemed to be shifting. The thought killed the rest of my laughter, and I strode to the door to head back to the house. I was not going to let my romantic delusions transfer over to him and ruin our friendship that way.

"We don't want to keep the birthday boy waiting for his breakfast," I said in a rush of nervous confusion.

Daniel followed me out, his tone still sounding amused. "Trust me, Alex won't hold his birthday breakfast for anyone. We have nothing to worry about."

Oh, if only he knew that I had everything to worry about. I was a wreck, and I was heading out for a day riding in golf carts on steroids while wearing giant-sized snow clothes. Let's throw in the fact that I've never used the bathroom in the forest before and hadn't been known for my ability to hold it all day. Yet probably the worst was trying to stop thinking about how Daniel was so much more fun to be around, and how much I wanted to see if his hair was as soft as it looked.

* * *

Looking back at it, I'd have to say that the afternoon celebrating Alexander's birthday changed everything.

After a breakfast of muffins, fruits, and juices we dismissed to suit up. I dressed in layers of yoga pants under fuzzy pajama pants, a t-shirt under a sweater, and two pairs of wool socks, all covered by snow pants, a coat, and boots. I wore a beanie on my head and a scarf wrapped around my neck that I fully expected to pull up to cover my face. Goggles would complete the look once we got going. I could barely move my limbs by the time I was done. My only regret was that I hadn't thought to put on an adult diaper, because peeling these layers off for bathroom needs was going to be a true horror show.

Pamela had beat me out the door, so I was alone as I made my way haltingly down to the front drive, trying not to trip on my clown boots or have the gloves fall right off my hands. I wasn't sure what to expect, but Pamela's description of golf carts combined with four-wheelers hadn't made much sense to me, so I was anxious to see what I was dealing with. I rounded the corner to find four of the mystery machines parked out front. Hmm. Pamela's description hadn't been too bad, actually. Three of them had four seats, and one just had a front bench and an open back. Willow was sitting behind the wheel of that one, and in the back area were coolers and various items we'd need for food and who knew what else. My fingers were crossed it wasn't first aid.

Robert, Alexander, and Daniel were all standing near the driver's seat of a vehicle, which made knowing who was driving really easy. Outside of that, it seemed like seats were up for grabs. I watched as Priscilla came out the front door dressed in a top-notch snow suit, her hair still managing to look stylish as it peeked out from under a cute little cap. She made her way straight to Alexander and leaned up to give him a kiss. His face lost some of its usual reserve as he bent to receive it, and I thought maybe there was a human under all that sculpted marble.

Movement from the corner of my eye caught my attention, and I watched as Pamela inched toward the front passenger seat of Alexander's ride. I wasn't sure what to do. Daniel would be fun and make the day memorable. But there were some twirly thoughts regarding him that needed to be shoved back down, and that meant space was needed.

He looked my direction as though he knew I'd been thinking about him. He started to smile, but someone walked up next to him and he turned away. In that moment I made the decision to ride with Alexander and Pamela. I'd keep it simple and enjoy a fun day with my crush. The original crush. The *only* crush—come on, brain. I couldn't afford to think of Daniel in crush terms. I had a sinking feeling that if I let those emotions free it would only take the tiniest of pushes before I was truly falling for him. My time here was short, too short, and I liked him too much as a friend and . . .

I tried to walk normally and sedately, like I was taking in the scene and not really thinking about where I was going, while inconspicuously making my way over to the red death trap. Luck was on my side, and I leaned casually next to Pamela before anyone said anything to me.

"Oh, hey. You looking forward to the day?" I said to her. She looked sideways at me and shrugged. Too bad I needed it to look like we were palling around and I'd been invited to ride with her or something. "I've never been in one of these before. Do you think they're loud? How bumpy do you think the ride is?"

She shifted slightly and put a hand on the passenger seat door. "I'm riding shotgun."

I laughed like she'd really cracked me up and we were totally jiving, just in case Daniel was looking this way. "Yeah, obviously. I'll climb in back."

She could have the passenger seat. That was fine, but I was getting in this one or I was going to die trying. I mean, maybe Alexander was just as fun as Daniel. Maybe we'd never hung out before and I hadn't really given him a shot. Maybe being terrified and needing to use the bathroom all day would keep my mind off fuzzier matters.

I heard someone step up next to me and turned to see Jarrod all bundled up. "Hey, Lucy, you riding in this one?" he asked and I nodded. "Cool. Alexander is a hoot. Have fun."

"Yeah, totally." I had no idea what that meant, having never, ever thought of Alexander as a *hoot*, but gave Jarrod a wave as he headed over to the machine Daniel was driving.

I watched him walk away with a nostalgic pinch in my heart. Ever since our day herding sheep while he and Steven had tried to outdo themselves with pickup lines, the awkward flirting had ended. Now they were just really nice to me. It was a necessary adjustment but also a little bit of a bummer. Who doesn't like being the center of men's attention for a little while?

"Everyone's here. Load 'em up," Alexander called, startling me and almost making me trip over my too large boots.

I scrambled to pull open the door, but the glove fingers kept folding over and I wasn't getting any traction. Stupid big man gloves. Who really had hands this size? Did polar bears often visit and need to be suited up for extreme weather? Yeesh!

"Oh my . . . here." Pamela leaned over and tugged the door open for me.

"Thanks." I smiled like I was amused. I was not. I was embarrassed and feeling overly warm in my ensemble.

It took a few tries for me to get my massively padded body into the snug seating area behind Pamela's seat. My legs weren't bending as easily as they usually did, for one thing. I tried twice before I noticed a handle above my head that could be used for leverage. I reached up and as I was tugging myself into place I heard a rustle of laughter behind me. Strong hands grabbed my waist and hoisted me, the combined force almost launching me across the machine and into the chair behind Alexander.

When I could angle my body enough to look to the side I was met with Daniel's laughing brown eyes. "You have some serious padding there. I almost didn't know where your waist was."

"Cold is the worst," I stated, half happy to see him and half tortured. I knew I'd have more fun with him, but I couldn't bring myself to abandon . . . well, whatever it was I had cooked up in my head. I felt the train wreck coming and was holding it off as best I could.

"Good news is that you're not going to feel the bumps along the way." He squeezed my arm and I grinned in a way I hoped looked light-hearted.

"All a part of my master plan."

He pulled a face. "You have one of those?"

Alexander stepped gracefully into the driver's seat and leaned back to address his brother. "Dan, it's time to head out. Colby, Steven, and Jarrod are in your ride, ready to go."

Daniel nodded and I reached to close the door next to me.

"Thanks for the lift," I said, grateful he hadn't asked why I wasn't riding with him.

"See you at the top," he mumbled.

By a miracle that put physics to the test, I was able to get buckled in without having to suck in too hard or request a seat belt extender. A loud cheer rang out, and for a horrified minute I thought they were cheering me when they'd heard the click, but the engines revved and Robert made snow and mud fly as he led the way out of the parking area. In case you're wondering, yes, the machines are loud. The caravan took the road leading from the homestead back toward the main highway, and I was a bit surprised at how fast these machines could go.

I could hear Alexander and Pamela making conversation in the front seat, but they were yelling to be heard and I had no chance of naturally joining in. I thought about ways I could make myself noticeable and try to have some fun with them. I laughed loudly a few times when a really large bump in the road made us jump, but all I got was a glance in the review mirror and some side-eye from Pamela. When we passed under the arch, skidding from the grated dirt road onto pavement like a teenage driver on a freewheeling Friday, I let out a shriek. That one, at least, got some reaction as Alexander actually looked over his shoulder to see if I was okay. I gave him two thumbs up. I tried to ask where we were headed, but after Alexander saying "what?" three times I gave up. It was more important to stop being annoying than it was to ingratiate myself into the conversation.

Once I'd given up on being part of the dream team, I leaned back, pulled the scarf over my nose and mouth, dropped the goggles over my poor teary eyes—from wind, I'm not that weak—and hunkered down. This area of the country really was breathtakingly beautiful. Light flakes of snow continued to fall gently, almost like it wasn't falling at all. The trees and fields surrounding us were covered in a picture postcard way. I thought about taking some photos, but my phone was not in an easily accessible place. I'd have to make sure to take some when we had a break.

After a few miles we pulled off the highway back onto dirt roads. It was a little hard to settle in, as we were bounced all over, and I wondered why the speed seemed to be the same on the rough terrain. Shouldn't they slow down? However, Alexander had a huge grin on his face that kind of made everything worth it. I'd never seen a smile so perfectly imperfect, with one side lifting just a tiny bit higher than the other, giving off boyish charm. These thoughts were the dumbest but also seemed impossible to escape now that I'd made a habit of them.

I have no idea how long we drove along that dirt road, but by the time we stopped I was as comfy cozy in the back of the ride as I could possibly be. The layers had been a fantastic idea, and the bumps had lulled me into a trance. I'd been running through conversations in my head, things that had happened over the past two weeks, and the new people I'd met. I realized how lucky I was to be here. Some of it was because of skills I'd worked hard to develop, yes, but they could have just as easily landed me somewhere else.

The drivers parked in a line at the top of a ridge and shut off the engines. The quiet was almost painful after the constant hum of the engine and squeaking of the shocks.

"Beautiful," I said to no one.

Alexander turned and flashed me a smile. "It really is."

Now was the time to kick off the easy banter between us. I opened my mouth but had nothing to say. Absolutely nothing.

He unknowingly saved it. "Come on and check out the view."

That invitation got my brain moving again, and I was happy that getting out of the side-by-side was about a thousand times easier than getting in had been. Walking, however, continued to prove challenging, as I had to lift my feet high so I wouldn't catch the toes of my too-big boots and fall. I managed to join the group standing in front of the machines and looking down into the meadow. It was incredible, nature channel type stuff. The mountains were rugged around the meadow where a large moose was walking through, trailed by her calf who was young but not a newborn. Some taller grasses peeked through the snow, and the scene was so perfect that I decided it would be worth it to dig out my phone. It took some finagling, but I retrieved it and snapped a few shots.

"It makes for a nice picture," Alexander said as he stood next to me.

Okay, this was good. More non-work related conversation initiated by him. Maybe it was just going to take some time. Kayla's voice echoed in my head. *Be charming, Lucy. Make him laugh*, she nearly screamed.

"Moose aren't something I've seen much of in Vegas," I joked. Okay, yep, I could do better.

"Moose meat is some of my favorite."

Oh. Well, that wasn't very romantic, or at all expected. Even Kayla would need to regroup after that statement. So, new tactic. "Thanks for letting us all come share your birthday with you."

"No one else was free, and it's not as fun to celebrate alone."

I'm totally sure he didn't mean it the way it sounded, but I couldn't hold in a laugh that burst out of me in surprise. "Well, thank goodness for the B team then," I teased, in probably the most natural way I'd ever spoken to him.

His expression looked frozen when he turned to face me full on. "I didn't mean it that way."

I let him off the hook, him being the birthday boy boss and all. "I figured."

"I pride myself on honesty but not on being hurtful. I'm happy you could all join me."

I didn't reply, because I wasn't really sure what to say. Conversation did not flow with this guy, and I was not great at forcing chit chat. Forced conversation, with me, grew steadily more awkward the harder I tried.

I'm sorry, Kayla, I thought. *But this is getting exhausting.*

Thankfully someone was calling out for everyone to gather for a group photo. I was happy to oblige. I tucked my phone back into its carrying spot and joined in as everyone scooted closer together, bundled up in a variety of winter gear, cheeks rosy, while Willow stood in front of us directing things. She clicked a few pictures and then Robert called for everyone to load up again—we were heading to the lunch area. From the way he worded it, it sounded like we were headed toward a particular destination that the family liked. Cool.

Bodies jostled and I can't really say what happened, but my feet slipped in my gargantuan boots and the next thing I knew I was tumbling backwards off the edge of the ridge we'd been standing on. I yelped in surprise, and then I yelped in pain as my head hit something hard, followed by my arms, legs, and back getting pounded as I rolled and bounced. Fear coursed through me. The snow was deceiving, and I had no idea if this was a slight downward slope or if I'd be dropped off the sharp edge of something at any moment. I couldn't breathe as I panicked and tried to get some traction to stop myself. In the end, I slammed into a tree and had the breath knocked out of me before I discovered if there was a ledge or not.

I fought for air, tears stinging my eyes, my head pounding. I focused upward, disoriented and thinking odd thoughts about how nice it would be to die with the light snowflakes on my cheeks. Eventually my body did its job, and I gulped in a huge lungful of air. When that happened, sound returned. Someone was yelling my name and I could hear an engine start. I blinked a few times and looked around to try to figure out where I was. My left side was up against a tree, and I was flat on my back with my right leg out to the side. Not broken, I didn't think, just flung out like a rag doll. I rolled my head to my right and could see where I'd fallen from. I'd left a trail in the snow that three men were running down, hopping over bushes and rocks that had pummeled my body just seconds ago, skidding and sliding when it got slippery. Others were doing something with the machines, but I couldn't figure out what. My eyes felt glazed and I closed them.

Someone knelt down next to me, and I cracked my eyes open. It was Alexander. I'd always imagined that being rescued by my crush would be incredibly swoon-worthy, but instead all I felt was an unexpected disappointment that it was him.

"Are you hurt?" he asked.

My emotional reaction to that perfectly sane question was all-consuming. *What a stupid, stupid question*, I thought. He'd just watched me tumble down a hill making contact with everything possible. Of course I was hurting. I bit my lips together and nodded, then moaned and lifted a hand to my head.

Daniel arrived on scene, followed closely by Steven, who stood back and was calling directions to the people at the top of the ridge while the brothers knelt over me.

"Lucy," he said, his voice anxious. "Where are you hurt?" His tone softened, like he knew my head was pounding.

I closed my eyes. "My head's the worst, but basically everywhere." A tear felt warm as it ran down my frozen cheek. I hadn't realized I was crying.

"What happened?" Alexander asked.

"I slipped," I replied.

"You slipped? We're in the snow, here. You have to be careful."

I opened my eyes and blinked up at him, and in that split second all the fairy tale brightness I'd outlined him with in my mind, that

114

stained glass cocoon where he lived shattered. All that was left before me was a guy who happened to be attractive as heck but wasn't doing a thing for me in real life. Too serious, too deliberate, too caught up in work and his quest for perfection. Yeah, my infatuation hadn't even lasted a month. Willow had warned me and I'd admitted to Kayla that I doubted we'd ever be a thing despite her constant prodding, but what was unexpected was the sense of relief I felt, like I'd let go of the rock I'd never be able to push up the mountain.

How hard had I hit my head?

Daniel replied before I could, his voice tight with some emotion that sounded like anger. I hoped it wasn't at me. "You've got to be kidding me, Alex. I'm guessing she got the message delivered from the rocks and trees she just bounced off." I started to chuckle, comforted by his irritation toward Alexander and not me, but the movement hurt. I put a hand over my rib cage and tried to roll up into a ball. He pressed a warm hand over mine. "Don't move, Luce." He tried to smile when he saw me looking at him, but his brown eyes were anxious in a way I wouldn't have expected. "Tell me where you hurt and if you think anything is broken."

Every part of my body that I mentioned specific pain in was given a light inspection by either Alexander or Daniel. They chatted among themselves, with a few additions by Steven, about how they couldn't really tell with all my winter gear padding things, but it was too cold to risk taking it off. I was confident that nothing felt broken, and in the end they had no choice but to leave me protected from the weather and move me onto a sled that was being winched down. I almost asked about internal bleeding, but then they'd probably feel obligated to remove my warm clothes so I opted not to mention it. Besides, that examination would be done by a doctor, not laying in the snow with my boss as the examiner.

Alexander stood and reached down for me as though he was going to gather me into his arms. "Come on, the sled is ready. I'll carry you to it."

Without even thinking about it or really meaning to, I shrank away from him and reached for his younger brother. "I want Daniel."

And I did. He was the only person I wanted touching me or lifting me, or even speaking to me if it could be helped. Just him.

Steven and Alexander seemed to freeze in place at what was most definitely an insult, but Daniel instantly leaned over me, gently putting his arms around my back to help me sit up. It hurt, but he made up for my weakness with a strength that was solid and so dependable. Once he had me sitting up, he pulled my torso against his chest and told me to wrap my arms around his neck. Then, he scooted his other arm under my knees and stood without so much as a grunt. I was impressed and thought about complimenting him on it, but my ribs and back spasmed in protest, and stars filled my vision at the change in position.

"I see stars," I muttered.

I closed my eyes and turned my head. The action resulted in my nose pressing up against the warmth of Daniel's neck, just below his chin. Boy, did I like it there. It was like a cozy little nose garage, and I hoped to never leave.

"The sled is only twenty feet away," he replied, not seeming to mind my cold nose against his warm skin.

"I'm going to barf," I whispered against his collar bone.

Surprisingly, I felt a puff of air against my cheek, and he sounded amused when he said, "Please save it for the sled."

"Shouldn't you be worried about a concussion?"

At this he turned his head slightly so his mouth was pressed close to my ear. "Trust me, I'm about as worried as a person can be right now."

"Okay. That's good." My arms started to sag a little, feeling heavy, my hold around his neck loosening.

"Hang on."

"All these clothes are weighing me down," I whined.

For some reason that made him grin as he sat me down in the sled and tugged my hat back into place. "All those clothes probably saved you from a worse beating."

Chapter Thirteen

I have to say that bouncing back up the hill on a sled was only marginally better than being tossed down it had been. I'd managed to stay conscious despite the hammering in my skull but wasn't able to keeping from a little whimpering and groaning when my head was knocked or my midsection jolted. By the time I'd been lifted onto the bench seat of Willow's vehicle, my head was pounding harder than it ever had before. Daniel had slid into the driver's seat, and together he and Willow carefully pulled me toward him until my head was in his lap. Willow had rolled up a towel in a horseshoe shape and wrapped it around my neck to keep my head from moving much. I was covered in blankets and snow clothing but had started to feel a little chilled.

"Funny how warm I was earlier. Wonder why I'm cold now." My teeth chattered. Daniel's face looked tight and bunched, and I could feel the tension in his thigh as he guided the vehicle over the uneven terrain. "Did I ruin Alexander's birthday?" I asked groggily, yawning.

He looked down. "No. Try to stay awake." I tried to sit up, but his hand pushed me back down. "I insisted they go ahead with their plans."

I was a somewhat insulted. "You mean they're going to continue on to lunch while we go back? That's cold."

"I . . . maybe. I'm sorry if it is. I didn't think there was a reason for everyone to come back when just one of us can be in the hospital room with you. They'd be better off having their picnic than pacing around a tiny waiting room after driving for two hours to get there. And it wouldn't do any good for them to sit back at the homestead either, waiting for news."

He had a point, but it didn't mean my feelings weren't a little hurt. "Still."

He pulled a face I couldn't read from this angle and sighed. "Be glad you missed the fight. It wasn't pretty, and I can't say they'll actually have any fun. My mom was totally against sending you off with only me, but I reminded her that she's actually more of a stranger to you than I am."

"Oh." Well, that was good to hear. "It's probably for the best. I got Alexander a gift he'll really hate."

He glanced down at me. "Oh, yeah?"

"Yeah."

"What is it?"

"A book."

"Alex likes books."

"This book is called *What If? Scientific Answers to Absurd Hypothetical Questions*," I said, feeling a little silly that I'd ever thought Alexander would like it.

In fact, I was feeling waves of silliness over the fact I'd ever day-dreamed about him at all. I was going to chalk the whole thing up to an out-of-body experience and life would move on with no one the wiser.

"You should have gotten him a book called *How Not to be a Jerk: Lessons on Damsels in Distress*."

I laughed and then groaned and pulled my legs up toward my chest. My ribs were not happy with me. "Wait, did you say something about going to the hospital? Do I need to go to one? Can't I just go to bed and rest?" One of his hands left the steering wheel to brush against my forehead where some stray hairs had gathered across my eyes. It was then I realized that I wasn't wearing glasses. "Where are my glasses?"

"Lost. I'm sorry. We looked but they were nowhere to be seen."

"Insult to injury. Anything further than your face and I'm blind as a bat without them."

"We'll get you a new pair."

I closed my eyes. "Don't worry about it. I have a spare at the cabin. They're disappointingly plain."

Another stroke across my forehead and I felt my worry settle. I thought of our moment in the bookstore this week. I liked the way it felt when he touched me, even if his hand was covered by a glove right now.

"You need a hospital," he stated.

"How about we agree on some rest in my bed and observation? I really think most of this is just bumps and bruises."

"You might have a concussion, and head injuries can be serious."

He was right, but I really didn't want to go to the hospital and deal with all of that when they'd most likely send me back with a prescription for rest. I fell silent, not arguing, but not agreeing to go either. I wanted more time to evaluate myself first. My head was definitely hurting, and even though Daniel was being careful and moving slow, I could feel bruises forming under the padding of my winter gear—especially in my rib cage where I'd slammed into the tree.

"I'm okay. I'll be okay," I said after maybe five minutes, comforted by the fact that I didn't feel blood gushing around in my stomach like water sometimes does if you chug too quickly. I could move all my limbs, even if they protested a bit, and I wasn't feeling too dizzy. Laying down with a towel head support could have been part of the reason I wasn't seeing pinpricks of light, but I liked to think positively.

"Of course, you will," he comforted. "I'm not sure I will," he said under his breath. I heard him, though, and felt something bright in the center of my chest.

After an agonizing ride we made it back to the highway and were met by an ambulance from Winterford. I didn't realize one had been called.

"I don't want to go to the hospital," I said when Daniel turned off the machine.

"Lucy, you need to be looked over to make sure you're okay."

I looked up at him with my best attempt at puppy dog eyes. "Isn't there a clinic in town? What do you do here for emergency medical needs, or like a sinus infection or something?"

The EMTs had climbed out of the van and were heading our way. That van, by the way, wasn't instilling a lot of confidence in me. It looked like it was straight from the 1980s and someone had painted it red and white, slapped on some reflective stickers, and called it a day.

119

He sighed. "There's a town about thirty minutes the opposite way of Winterford. It's bigger and has a clinic."

"Let's go there."

Daniel got off the side-by-side and shook hands with the EMTs while I tried to listen in. He described what had happened and requested we be taken to the clinic first; then decisions would be made about the hospital. His tone said he didn't like the plan, and I really appreciated him not overriding me. The emergency responders walked around to the side where my feet were, and the bigger of the two men reached for my hands to help me sit up and get sliding across the seat.

The motion made me gasp for air, and something must have crossed my face because Daniel jumped in from the driver's side and supported my back and head while I was raised into position. I bit my lips to keep from admitting how much the movement had hurt, and closed my eyes to keep from seeing stars. I leaned back against Daniel, grateful for the support and once again wanting only him. It was a confusing emotion, the way I felt comforted by his presence. I turned my head back to rest against his shoulder and asked for one second to gather my bearings.

"Are they going to take me in that hating-it excuse for an ambulance thing?" I asked.

"Oh, yeah. The best Winterford has to offer."

"Are you ready, ma'am?"the EMT holding my hands asked.

I nodded and the three men moved me slowly until my feet were touching the ground. Each EMT put an arm around me, and we gimped over to the van, where I was grateful to find a bed waiting for me. The first order of business was to remove my extra gear and let the medics do a quick exam so that they knew what they were dealing with. Layer by layer of clothing was removed as considerately as possible until I was down to my yoga pants and t-shirt. They let me keep on one of the pair of socks, thankfully. Daniel stood outside of the van watching the process, occasionally telling them to take it easy if I flinched or bit my lips. The men took my heart rate, blood pressure, and oxygen levels, along with an exam involving a flashlight in my eyes and following their fingers. The light in my eyes hadn't felt great, and I'd closed my eyes and told them no more.

When they were satisfied that my life wasn't in immediate danger, I was covered with a soft, warm blanket and left alone. Daniel joined me in the back of the van and I reached for him, wanting that comfort. He didn't hesitate to reach back, taking my hand in between both of his. I dozed for most of the drive to a town I never did find out the name of.

When we arrived at the clinic there was a whirlwind of activity that ended with me settled in an exam room, in a gown, with machines beeping near my ear. My throat was dry and my head still had a painful beat behind my eyes, even though the sharpness was being dulled by whatever was running through those IV lines the clinic nurse had jammed into my arm. Daniel's winter gear, and mine, were draped over a chair, and he sat in the other, wearing jeans and a t-shirt, his hair messy.

A different nurse bustled into the room and offered me a comforting smile. "Hi there. I'm Kathleen, your nurse. How are you feeling?"

"Pretty good?" Rats. I hadn't meant for that to be a question.

"Dr. Baxter will be in soon to run a few tests. Would you like Mr. Drake to stay with you?"

Daniel and I locked eyes, and I knew he'd do whatever I was comfortable with. It was unnerving how much I wanted him in the room with me, but I also understood that this was probably awkward for him, and I didn't know if there would be flashing of skin that would make us both uncomfortable. I briefly wondered if anyone was letting my family know that I was in a clinic somewhere. Where was I? What would my family do from a thousand miles away? My eyes squeezed against another poker-like pain in the back of my head. No more thinking for me.

"I . . ."

"Hey, Ace," Daniel said and I opened my eyes. "I'll stay if you want, or I can go. No biggie."

"Ace?"

"Yeah, because you took a fall and kept on fighting." He gave me a thumbs up.

I gave him a thumbs down. "I feel like one of those aggressive sheep of yours kicked me square in the head, and then your horse

121

sat on me," I replied as he grinned, although it didn't make it to his eyes. "I don't think I'm cut out for life off the beaten path."

"Darwin would have considered you a weak link, I'm afraid. No survival sense at all."

That drew a laugh out of me, and I flinched against the ache in my ribs and back. "You know, we're barely past being strangers and it's really weird for us to be in an examination room together with one of us in a backless gown."

His smile grew. "Come on, now, we've known each other for three full weeks. I took you on a hayloft picnic and let you use me as a landing cushion. You introduced me to Highland romance novels. I'd say we're not strangers at all."

Another rush of dizziness had me closing my eyes again and breathing through my nose. "I probably know you better than I know my next-door neighbor of three years."

"Rest for now, Miss Moore," the nurse interrupted our exchange. "I'll tell the doctor you're ready and that Mr. Drake will be staying."

I took another breath through my nose and things began to settle. I was just happy I hadn't puked. I kept my eyes closed as we waited for this Dr. Baxter to arrive. At one point Daniel stood and came to the side of my bed, taking my hand in his and weaving our fingers together, which I found incredibly soothing.

"I'd be happy to call your family and let them know what's going on," he said softly.

"Let's wait until we see what the doctor says. No need to worry them yet," I replied in a way I hoped was casual.

In reality, I wasn't sure it would be worth it. They'd offer comforting words and maybe send some flowers, but they'd leave the Drake family to care for me. He squeezed my hand to let me know he understood.

When Dr. Baxter did arrive, Daniel retreated back to his chair while the doctor did a series of tests on my vision, hearing, strength, balance, and coordination, along with memory, ability to recall, and concentration. All the efforts made my headache spike again. Any part of my body that could have possibly come in contact with part of the forest floor was given a good once over. My poor, sad body. I blushed a few times too, sneaking a glance Daniel's way when I was worried he'd seen something, but at some point he'd stood and was facing out the window with his hands in his pockets.

When he was finished, Dr. Baxter patted my arm. "You're lucky, Miss Moore, that you were wearing so much padding. All those layers protected you from what may have been a much worse out-come." I'd never been more grateful for my over-preparedness. "As things stand, you definitely have a concussion and deep bruising on the ribs, although I don't believe any are broken. There are, of course, some bruises on other body parts, but they'll heal quickly and give you much less trouble than those ribs will. If you'd like, we can keep you overnight, but it's not necessary as long as someone agrees to sit with you for twenty-four hours. That said, if any symp-toms worsen over the next forty-eight hours, then you will need to go to the hospital in Great Falls for further testing such as a CT or MRI scan."

"I understand," I said.

"Dizziness, fatigue, and a headache are normal after an expe-rience like yours. You may feel nauseated as well. Those symptoms should begin to fade within the next couple of days. Treatment will be the same here as it would be at home. Rest, rest, rest. You need to be feet up, no reading or television for the next twenty-four hours, but those things should be fine by Monday morning unless they cause the return of symptoms."

He went on to fill my tired head with more information, which only served to bring on those issues he'd been discussing. The irony was not lost on me. I zoned out, floating in a bit of a daze, knowing the nurse would go over all of this again before I was allowed to leave and that Daniel was listening as well. My real takeaway was that I could go back to the Drake homestead, and not the hospital, which was what I'd really wanted anyhow.

* * *

The greeting I received a few hours later definitely made up for them not joining me at the hospital, almost to the point of embar-rassment. Steven and Jarrod had driven a truck to the clinic for us to come home in, and when Daniel pulled into the circular gravel parking area we were greeted by cheery yellow balloons tied to the front porch railings. How they'd pulled that off when it looked like they'd just gotten back themselves was a mystery. The front door opened and a large floral bouquet was followed by several people, some still in snow pants and boots.

"Hold up," Daniel said, leaning closer to me to see out the passenger window. "I'll come help you out."

I shook my head. "I'm good." I opened the door and he griped under his breath.

When my door opened, the greeting committee stepped off the porch and walked toward the truck. Daniel was in front of me blocking the view of smiling faces before I'd so much as put one foot on the ground.

"Put your arm around my shoulders and I'll help you balance."

"I'm good. I walked out of the clinic on my own," I said through clenched teeth while maintaining a smile.

"Actually . . ."

"Not a word." I held up a hand. I didn't need him to remind me that Kathleen had wheeled me to the parking lot and my walk had been all of four steps.

I slid easily off the seat and planted both feet on the ground. With one hand on the truck door I steadied myself before standing fully straight. The second I was upright, Daniel slid an arm around my back, his hand gripping my waist. My eyes shot to him, but he was looking up and smiling at everyone. Only from this close could the steel in his eyes be seen. There was no way he was going to let me walk without his arm around me.

Priscilla was the first to greet me, saying over and over how sorry she was to have a guest of hers get injured and how guilty she'd felt sending me off with only Daniel for help. I refrained from saying that her son had been more help than my own mother would have been.

She handed me the flowers, a gorgeous bouquet of dahlias in various shapes and shades of purples and pinks. It was incredible and I smiled as I sniffed at it. When I leaned down to sniff, my head felt a little woozy, and somehow Daniel felt the shift in my stance. His grip around my waist steadied me, and his other hand reached out to grab my elbow. It was only a moment, and I doubted anyone else noticed, before I was back upright and smiling. My smile, however, was a little tight with frustration. Frustration at my injury and frustration that most of my remaining time here was going to be wasted recovering, and a tinge of embarrassment because it was Alexander's birthday but I was getting balloons and flowers.

"I think Alexander found a lady with real grit when he hired you," Robert boomed from his place beside Priscilla. It was a strangely worded compliment, but I offered him a smile.

"Lucy really needs to rest. She's supposed to be feet up for another twenty-four hours." Daniel sounded like he was trying to be casual, but it didn't come off that way. Everyone in that group understood that he'd commanded them to let me be on my way.

"Thank you so much for this." I gestured to the balloons and held up the flowers. "I'm going to be just fine after a few days of rest. Don't worry, I plan to be back to work as soon as possible." I nodded in Alexander's direction.

Alexander, taller than the others, had been standing behind them with a polite smile. At my statement he replied, "Don't worry for even a moment."

"I hope I didn't ruin your birthday," I said. "I really didn't mean to take the focus away from you."

"Not at all."

The thing was, I totally believed him. My presence at his birthday celebration wasn't necessary, and probably the moment I went to the cabin they'd all return to whatever they were doing. I almost laughed at how little it hurt. I didn't care one bit. Even better, his book was still sitting wrapped on my bed, which meant the possible embarrassment could be totally avoided. He didn't expect a gift from me anyhow.

"Okay, well, thanks again." I gave everyone another smile while Daniel pointed out all the snow gear in the back of the truck to Willow, who would gather it up to take inside.

"Pamela and I brought you some more pillows and blankets," Willow said as she walked toward the bed of the truck. "There's also some food in the kitchenette to tide you over between meal deliveries."

I felt my face warm, unused to being the focus of service this way. "That was really nice, thank you."

Everyone else filed back into the house, and I turned to make my way around to the cabin path.

"Nope." Daniel was there, swooping me up and into his arms before I could take more than a few steps.

I didn't bother arguing. His shoulders were tense, his jaw clamped shut as he carried me toward my cabin. He was tired of arguing with me, and I was tired of arguing with him. It felt like all we'd done for the past hour was attempt to negotiate with neither of us bending. I wasn't an invalid. I had a concussion and bruised ribs. I also had enough giant Tylenol to keep me from feeling too much of it. Actually, let's be honest here, all the Tylenol did was keep me from caring that I was hurt. I could still feel the aches and pain.

"This is ridiculous," I pouted as he walked with easy strides. "I'm not a baby. I could have just steadied myself on your arm."

"Not up for negotiation," he said.

"I think you've said that at least fifty times today," I grumped, my arms wrapping more snuggly around his neck.

He nodded. "I'll probably have to say it at least twenty more. Man, you're stubborn."

"I'm stubborn?" I squeaked as he started up the cabin steps. I leaned out and turned the doorknob to let us in. "You're the king of Stubbornville."

He used a foot to kick the door open and turned sideways to get us in. "If I'm the king, then that must make you the jester."

I pushed against him in an effort to be set down. "Don't be rude," I huffed.

He relented but set me so gently on my feet that nothing could have possibly jostled me. "I'm trying not to be."

I made a sound of annoyance. "Oh my gosh, Daniel, I'm okay. All I need is rest on a bed or a couch, both of which I have right here." I pointed sharply at each item as I listed it. "What I don't need is someone schlepping me around everywhere." I set the flowers on the kitchenette counter with a thump they didn't deserve.

"Dr. Baxter said you should have someone with you for at least another twenty-four hours. You're still having moments of dizziness and a constant headache. What if you pass out?" he argued.

"You're worse than my mother." I stomped toward the couch.

He followed. "Oh, you mean the mother who offered a 'let me know how you get along' when you called her? I'm worse than that? For caring?"

I leaned against the back of the couch and slumped a little. He was right, and I said so. "I'm not used to being sick or having anyone take such an interest in my welfare. I feel smothered by it," I admitted in low tones. I sighed out a shallow breath, aware of my aching ribs. "I think the most disappointing part is that I'll be spending most of my last week here laying on the couch like a total bum. I'm embarrassed and upset, and that's just a lot of emotion right now."

The fight drained from him as well, and he turned so he too was leaning against the couch. "It is a lot. I'm sorry. For the record, I like it a lot better when we're being friends."

A smile tugged up one side of my mouth. "Me too. Can you go back to friend mode, please? Whatever you're doing now is a little much."

He sighed and ran a hand through his hair, his cowboy hat having been left in the truck. After the past several hours we were both a little worn out. I felt sympathy for my part in his exhaustion and reached out to move a lock of his hair that had remained standing straight up.

"I'm sorry," I mumbled. "I'm a terrible patient. I'll be nicer."

He reached for my hand and took it from his hair, lightly toying with my fingers. "I was feeling overprotective and might have slipped into caveman mode a few times there."

"You're forgiven," I teased, lightly squeezing his fingers.

His eyes met mine and he surprised me by growing serious. "I'm sorry, Lucy."

I smiled. "You used my actual name."

"I'm trying to be serious."

"You're doing a great job."

He made a sound of amusement. "Good. Now, can we please get you settled with your feet up? Do you want to be on the bed or the couch?"

"Let's start on the couch."

I walked around the couch while he snagged some pillows and a blanket that had been left nearby. When I was settled with my head and feet propped and a blanket to keep me warm, he sat on the floor next to me, his back leaning against the couch.

"We've sure been putting this new friendship to the test," I joked.

"I'm almost afraid to see what tomorrow holds." He grinned.

"Tomorrow holds you getting back to work. Sheep wait for no one. In fact, you really don't need to sit here and stare at me. I think I'm going to sleep for a while."

"You need observation through tomorrow," he argued.

"Pamela will observe the heck out of me, given the chance. It's her favorite thing to do."

He struggled for a moment, opening and closing his mouth a few times before a determined look settled on his face. "I don't trust anyone else to do it right. I'm the one who heard what the doctor and nurse said."

That caught me off guard, and it took me a minute to respond. "You can trust *me* with me," I said at last, eliciting a small smile from him. "Now go. Remind some animals who's boss, and I'll see you in a little while."

He stood in one fluid movement. "Fine. I'll bring dinner, and you'd better not have moved a muscle."

I reached out a hand to shake his in agreement, and he shook mine firmly before laying it softly on the couch and walking away.

Chapter Fourteen

I awoke to silence the following morning. No, that's not quite true. I could hear puffs of air—not quite snoring—coming from the other side of my screen. I felt a little disoriented, but I suppose conking your head on every rock in Montana will do that to you. I closed my eyes, analyzing how I felt. I ran my hands lightly down my ribs, willing the ache away or wishing I could fall back asleep. It hadn't been an easy night when every turn made my head and side cry out in complaint.

I hadn't been alone, though. Twice I'd gotten up for a drink of water and another pain pill and Daniel had been there, his dark eyes watching me from the couch. He'd jumped up before I could get halfway across the room and grabbed my cup from my hands, refilling it with the cool pumped-in well water and getting the pill bottle before walking me back to bed with his warm, large hand on my back. He'd wordlessly watched me drink and take the medicine, and then tucked me back in, fluffing up my pillows and making sure I was in a comfortable position.

My mind groggily realized it was the sounds of him sleeping that I could hear. Pamela was a silent sleeper, to no one's surprise. I doubted she ever rolled over or so much as sniffled. Plus, when she'd found out Daniel intended to spend the night on our couch she'd stomped to her bed and closed the privacy screen as tight as it would go. I hadn't heard a peep from her since.

Faded light was starting to come in through the blinds, and my bladder reminded me that I'd had two full glasses of water during the night. I pushed up to sitting, one arm around my ribs to support them, and swung my feet over the edge of the bed. When I touched down I immediately wished I'd thought to grab my slippers. The floor was cold, the stove having gone out in the night. I squatted down to see if my slippers were under my bed, but the action caused a shooting pain in my forehead and I put my hand over the spot while bracing my other hand on my bed. I don't know how long I sat there with my forehead near my mattress, trying to think straight, but Daniel's bare feet appeared in my vision a second before I felt his hand come to rest on my shoulder.

"What do you need?" he asked in a froggy morning voice.

"Slippers. The floor is cold." I swallowed, trying to clear the sleep out of my own throat.

He carefully pulled me back up straight and then sat me down on the side of my bed before hunkering down and reaching around to see where the fuzzy footwear had gone. After a few seconds he found them and pulled them out. Oh, yeah, they're koalas wearing pink bows, so that's fancy. He raised his eyebrows, definitely impressed with my choice of slipper, and I shook my head with a shrug. He put them on the floor and I slid my feet in, once again standing. I made my way to the bathroom with him walking alongside me.

"Do I need to ask you to wait out here?" I teased, and his lips lifted as he shook his head.

"I'll relight the fire."

I was slow to close the door, watching as he turned to go back into the sitting area. I was trying real hard not to notice how he looked in a white t-shirt with flannel pajama bottoms and bare feet, his dark hair rumbled and his eyes sleepy. I closed the door, blaming my thoughts on my head injury, and took care of my business. When I came out, Pamela's screen was open and she was gone.

"Did she come out fully dressed and ready for the day?" I asked Daniel as I made my way to the couch.

He turned from his crouching position in front of the potbelly stove. "Yeah, and I didn't even know she was awake."

I pulled a funny face. "I have a theory that she really is a robot and she just stands on a charging station all night long." He chuckled and went back to filling the stove with kindling. "Were you warm enough last night?" I asked as I sat down on the opposite side of where his blankets were piled. "It can get cold."

"I was plenty warm. How are you feeling? I know you were up a few times, and I thought I heard you tossing and turning here and there, but when I checked you seemed to be sleeping."

I blinked a few times, warmth tugging at my stomach at the thought of him keeping vigil. "You checked on me?"

He nodded, still facing the stove and now stacking on some larger pieces of wood. "That's why I'm here."

Well, that's true enough. "I'm a little sore, and my head still hurts quite a bit, but I think that's normal."

He struck a match and lit some paper before putting it in and making sure the kindling caught. When a few small flames were going he shut the door of the stove and latched it. He went to the sink to wash his hands and then came back to the couch, moving his blankets before sitting down. He tossed one my way, and I wrapped up in it, grateful that it was still warm from his body heat.

"Did you sleep at all?" I asked on an embarrassed sigh. "I feel terrible keeping you up."

He waved a hand. "Nah, you may have noticed that I'm a perfectly healthy man. We need little sleep."

My voice was amused when I replied, "Thanks for clearing that up for me." He nodded, watching the fire. "What are your plans for the day?"

He scratched at the beard coming in. "You're looking at it. Tending."

I arched a brow. "Tending?"

"Yeah. This fire isn't going to tend itself."

I rolled my eyes. "Go to work, Daniel. The sheep need you."

He pointed at my slippers. "I can't leave those koalas to fend for themselves in this northern country. They're not used to these temperatures."

I tucked my slippers further under me. "Are you seriously going to sit here all day?" What I didn't say, but my tone did, is I wasn't all that excited about the idea. I liked Daniel, but I would be miserable worrying about him giving up his work to watch me.

"Doctor's orders."

I sighed. "I'm going to say this in the nicest way possible. You have work, and I can babysit myself. I'll call you if I start to feel dizzy or something."

"Hard to dial a phone when you're having a seizure," he replied.

I groaned. "Send Pamela back when you find her, and go work. You can't be away from the homestead all day, and you'll go crazy sitting in this little cabin with me."

His gaze caught mine for a moment. The look in his eyes seemed to say that he'd love nothing more than to spend the day with me, but it was gone in a flash and I sure wasn't going to say a word about what I thought I'd seen. He stood and walked to the kitchenette, filling my glass once more and getting some of the pain pills the doctor had prescribed. When he returned to the sitting area he stood in front of me without a word, and I took the pills and water, drinking them down with a thanks.

"I'm going to shower and check on sheep, and say hi to my family. Then I'm going to come back here to spend a lovely afternoon with Floppy Moore, famous tumbling pro."

A laugh huffed out. "Floppy the tumbling pro?"

He nodded. "Don't try to shower or bathe until someone's here, okay?"

"I won't."

He took my empty glass and strode back to the sink. "I'll send Pamela back to sit with you. Be nice to her."

I tucked his blanket more firmly around my shoulders and looked out the window. "No promises."

"What if I promise to bring some food back with me?"

I looked back at him with a delighted expression. "Now you're speaking my language."

***

Patient's Log, Day Two of Cabin Lockdown
Monday, October something or other:

Patient is stir-crazy. Roommate says she's moving out until Nurse Daniel vacates the property. Nurse Daniel says he doesn't negotiate with terrorists. Unsure if he's speaking of patient or roomie with attitude issues. Today is Monday, and television has been given the go-ahead. Nurse Daniel provided subpar viewing options. Fight ensued. Patient led Nurse to believe he had won the argument, but she ended up with a bowl of ice cream and the fuzzier blanket.

"This cannot have been your favorite childhood movie," I said for the hundredth time. "What kid watches this?"

Daniel gestured to himself once again, as he had every time I'd made that comment. "This kid. This kid and his older brother, who are two successful men, I might add."

"What year was this movie made?" I scooped up another bite of mint chocolate chip ice cream.

"Why does that matter? It's a classic."

"They'd obviously just come out with color television at the time, or something. The picture is weird."

He sighed. "It's not weird. You're close-minded."

I gawked at him and spoke around a minty melting mouthful. "I'm close-minded? For never having watched a movie made before my parents were born?"

"Whatever. How old are your parents?"

"Fifty two and fifty four."

"So they were born in . . ."

"1966 and '68," I supplied. "What year was this movie made?"

"1956," he mumbled so low I could barely hear him.

I grinned. "I'll tell you what. I'm willing to forgive you because Charlton Heston is serious eye-candy." Another bite of ice cream filled my mouth.

His eyes grew large. "What? He's got to be like, I don't know, fifty in this movie."

I wiggled my eyebrows. "With those forearms? Please. He's not a day over scrumptious."

He blinked a few times. "You're kidding me, right?" I shook my head and licked my lips. "This guy's your idea of . . ."

"Of what?" I asked, making my eyes big and innocent.

He clamped down on the thought. "Never mind. You're making me regret watching this."

"Is it because coveting thy film star's body is against the Ten Commandments?" I said with a straight face.

At this he finally cracked, covering his eyes with one of his hands. "You're hopeless."

"So is this movie," I said out the side of my mouth.

"It's a classic."

"You said that already. What you still haven't answered is how a kid was hooked on an almost four-hour movie about the story of Moses."

"It's not four hours," he stated.

I held up my phone, showing him the screenshot I'd taken of the movie's details. "Read it and weep. Three hours and forty minutes." I set my phone down and formed my mouth into an O shape. "Did your mommy need a break from you, so she sat you and little Alexander down to watch your favorite show . . . for an entire half a day?"

He picked up the remote and turned the movie off. "You've officially ruined it. I was wrong to think I could share something so precious from my childhood with you."

I started to feel a little guilty, until I saw him glance my way, his eyes dancing with laughter, those gold flecks vibrant.

"We could choose one of my favorite childhood movies to tear apart," I offered.

"No, I think we've ruined enough memories for one day." He leaned back into the corner of the couch and looked my way. "Although, I am curious what your favorite movie was."

I grinned, knowing he'd get a kick out of my answer. "The *High School Musical* movies, all the way, baby."

"Please no." He shook his head.

I nodded. "Oh, yes. Troy and Gabriella forever. I could still sing you every single song from all three movies."

He closed his eyes. "I'll pass on that."

I sat my ice cream bowl on the end table and leaned forward, scooting into the middle seat of the couch and looking into his eyes, fluttering my lashes like I was blinded by love.

"Nah, nah, nah, nah, yeah . . . You are the music in me," I sang softly. Then, as the song did in the movie, I began to sing louder.

"When you dream there's a chance you'll find a little laughter, or happy ever after." He couldn't seem to stop a smile that started to take over his face, and I pressed on knowing full well my voice was terrible, but not caring. "When I hear my favorite song, I know that we belong . . . " I pulled back from where I'd been leaning toward him and stood, taking a moment to gain my balance through the tug on my sore ribs, while still humming. When I was steady I started bopping lightly. "Yeah, it's living in all of us, and it brought us here because, you are the music in me."

I reached down for his hands and tugged him up. He came willingly, that smile growing another inch, until I could practically feel his enjoyment all around me. I danced us around in small circles, slow and easy, trying to keep my aches at bay. It was nothing at all like the waltzing we'd done in the barn, but fun just the same. I kept singing the words to the song I'd sung thousands of times as a little girl, until it took its toll and I felt my head start to ache again.

I stopped, still holding Daniel's larger hands in mine, and stepped forward to lean my head against his chest. "Ooh, got a little dizzy there." I laughed.

He let go of my hands and reached around my back, running soothing paths up and down either side of my spine while closing the distance between us until we were pressed close together. I wasn't sure he even realized what he was doing, but I snuggled up against his strength willingly, resting my hands on his hips. It felt so good to be close to him. Too good.

"I can see why you think *The Ten Commandments* is a frumpy movie, when you've been exposed to such classical films as *High School Musical*," he said, his breath warm against my scalp.

I turned so that my cheek was pressed against his shoulder. "I'm only sorry you've been deprived."

His hands stopped moving, almost like he'd suddenly realized how close we were, and I felt something weighty fill the air. I hesitantly moved my hands from his hips around to rest flat against his lower back, a signal I wasn't sure I should be giving. His breathing stilled for a second but resumed as his own arms wrapped more firmly around me, fully cocooning me against him. It was the best I'd felt since . . . well, I don't know. Every part of me relaxed against him, and I adjusted until my head rested just under his chin. Comfort, pure and simple, flowed through me. He felt so big and capable, and fit so nicely in my arms that I had no thought of ever leaving this place. My heartbeat slowed, and my amusement faded until I could count each breath that we shared . . . until I understood that I might, once again, be in over my head.

Chapter Fifteen

I'm just going to skip over the next few days because after that, well, there wasn't much to report. Suffice it to say that I enjoyed (read: tolerated) visits from all the women every day, knowing full well Daniel had assigned each of them an hour to sit with me. At first I'd been a little like, "Wow, sexist much?" when I realized no men were coming to visit outside of Daniel. But then I'd quickly shifted to "Thank the heavens" because if the women were hard to be around, then the men would have been torture.

Willow's hour was okay because we were already friendly and she usually brought me a treat. Pamela just brought her laptop and worked at the kitchenette table, hardly saying a word and at one point admitted that Alexander had told her she was absolutely not allowed to talk work with me. She did, however, attempt a little chit-chat once or twice, which was actually nice of her. Priscilla's visits were kind of the worst. Oh, it isn't that she wasn't a nice person, because she was. She was kind and chatted comfortably for her hour every day. I learned that Priscilla was really into gardening, and her home in Vegas was a show piece. She also voraciously read romance novels and was a part of two book clubs. There was never a shortage of things I could have talked with her about, which meant I was the problem—awkwardness propped on pillows. What do you say to the mom of both your boss *and* the guy who's becoming one of your best friends? The mom of that best bud who both of you know sits with you every night and tucks you into bed before making his way into all of your dreams? The mom you never would have normally met this way? It didn't help the headaches, I'll tell you that much, but I was able to make some great strides on becoming a stellar listener.

Finally, on Thursday morning, five full days after my tumble down the hill and only two days before I was scheduled to leave this place, I was able to exit the cabin and venture out. The dizziness and headaches had finally said goodbye on Tuesday, and by Wednesday I'd felt pretty much normal other than the bruised ribs that would take a little longer to fully heal. At last this morning Warden Drake, second son, had given me the green light to leave my prison. Of course, I'd also spoken with Dr. Baxter, who'd cleared me as well, so, really, Daniel hadn't had anything to do with it. I'd just needed his cooperation.

It felt amazing to be outside again. No more snow had fallen, and temperatures had risen slightly, so the walkways were clear and I could hear trickles of water as the snow melted and ran down tiny pathways in the landscape. The air was fresh, the sky blue, and I simply stood on the top step outside the cabin door taking it all in.

"The lipstick is back, huh?" Willow called out to me as she walked out the side door of the house. "Get it, girl."

I pouted my lips out and cocked a hip, then shifted into another pose with my hand up behind my head. "Watch out, world." I stepped down to the gravel path and met her.

"What are you going to do today with all your freedom?" she asked. I shrugged. "Daniel hasn't given you your orders yet, huh?"

We both laughed, because truth can be funny that way. "So far I've given him the slip. Bonus to his daylight hours being so busy."

She pulled a face. "You and I both know that he's going to be keeping a close eye on you today, so watch your step."

I grinned, grateful that his watchfulness no longer bothered me but instead felt reassuring. "I missed breakfast. Any chance there are leftovers?"

"Didn't someone bring you a plate?" I shook my head and she rolled her eyes. "I think we have some pastries and fruit left over."

She turned to head back to the house and I stopped her. "No, please, go ahead with what you were doing. I can find my way around the kitchen."

"Okay. I'll see you at lunch." She continued on the path up to her little cabin, which was the last of the row.

I let myself into the house through the regular side door and felt a little sad as I walked through the kitchen and opened the fridge. I only had today and tomorrow left to enjoy my last meals cooked by Willow before getting in that little rental car and driving to Great Falls to fly back home. I'd miss it so much.

"Are you having a special reunion moment with your best friend, the fridge?" Daniel's voice came from behind.

I didn't bother to pull my head out and look at him. "I'd appreciate some privacy while I apologize for staying away so long."

He chuckled, but so did someone else. The new voice made me spin, and I was a little disconcerted to see Alexander standing there with a slight smile on his face. Oh.

"I'm sure Willow appreciates how much you like her cooking," Alexander said in an eerily relaxed and normal moment.

Daniel gestured to me. "Chompy here is Willow's biggest fan."

I dropped my head forward, closing my eyes until my chin was touching my chest. "Please, do not call me oddball nicknames in front of my boss," I said.

"Your boss is my brother, a situation I can't help, and brother trumps." Daniel sounded pleased with himself.

I opened my eyes and tried really hard not to glare at my boss's brother. "Lucy is a great name, one I'm a fan of. Please call me that."

"Are you ready to return home Saturday?" Alexander inserted, talking to me.

I shifted my eyes to him. "Sort of."

"I hope that means you've enjoyed your time at our ranch."

I nodded. "Very much. I'll be happy to get back to Kayla and my bed, but this is a beautiful place."

"Kayla's the roommate," Daniel supplied an answer to a question his brother hadn't asked. "She sounds like a firecracker."

I gave him a look letting him know that no one had asked him for his opinion on my best friend.

"This is a beautiful place, that's true," Alexander said to me. "I've got some work to finish up. I'll see you two later."

"Oh, I'm free to return to work," I said hurriedly, taking a step toward Alexander. "Do you need me to . . ."

He held up a hand. "Finish today how you'd like. Tomorrow morning we'll meet at eight for a quick planning meeting. The real work starts first thing Monday."

A week ago I wouldn't have known quite how to take that statement, but I now understood that Alexander always meant exactly what he said, which left no room for second guessing. I did expect I'd be working my hiney off when we weren't on Alexander's sabbatical anymore. A man who couldn't take a proper sabbatical wasn't going to be a slacker in the office.

When Alexander was gone I went back to the fridge. There was a bowl of fruit that looked promising, along with a pitcher of something. I grabbed both and turned to place them on the island. Daniel was leaning against that very island, watching me.

"What do you want to do today?" he asked.

"Eat," I stated, turning back to walk into the pantry.

"I meant after that," he called.

I found the Tupperware of pastries that Willow had mentioned and returned to the island with it in my arms. "I'm not sure. What are you up to today?"

He leaned over and popped open the lid of the pastry container while I got a glass, plate, and fork. "The usual. Sheep, fences, mucking out the barn, small engine repair."

I stabbed some apple slices and put them on my plate. "Small engine repair?"

"Yeah, one of the tillers stopped working at the end of the summer. This is the time of year I fix those things."

I popped a melon ball in my mouth and nodded. "So you're puttering?"

"No. I'm too young to putter. I'm working." He lifted a ball of melon out of the bowl and tossed it into the air, catching it in his mouth. "What you see here is a man in his prime."

I chewed "Oh, right. I remember something about women's shoulders suddenly becoming exposed when you walk by."

"Exactly."

"Probably best that you're out here far away from all the women in the big city." I poured from the pitcher, mildly annoyed to find it was cranberry juice. Yuck.

"What's the face about?" he asked.

"Cranberry juice. It's disgusting. Only old people drink it." My eyes brightened and I lifted the glass toward him. "Here you go. Keep your urinary tract healthy."

He made a huffing sound. "Uh, no. My tract is healthy, thank you, because I don't complain like a baby. I just drink the juice."

My eyes narrowed and I sniffed at the juice, regretting pouring a full class before I knew what it was. I looked back to him with that same narrowed gaze and chugged. So, I didn't chug as much as take a big gulp and then have to fight to get my throat to willingly swallow it. But, I held his gaze the entire time, his becoming suspiciously amused the longer I stood there holding a mouthful of cranberry juice without swallowing or spitting it back out. Through sheer willpower, I swallowed.

"I wasn't sure you were going to make it." He grinned.

I smacked my lips loudly. "Didn't whine at all."

"Your eyes were whining, trust me."

"My eyes were staring you down with the strength of a woman in her prime."

He laughed. "No, they were tearing up."

Whatever. I took the rest of my glass and poured it down the sink. I didn't have anything to prove to him.

"There's chocolate milk in the fridge if you need something to wash out the cranberry taste," he said.

"I'm just fine, thanks." I filled the glass with water and took a few sips before starting on my pastry. "I'm going to be mad if my pastry doesn't taste right because of that cranberry."

"I think Willow baked cranberries into the pastry, so you should be just fine." I looked up at him in horror and he totally cracked up. "I'm kidding. Your face."

I took a giant bite of the pastry, happy to find it was apple cinnamon, and chewed while Daniel got control of his hysterical self. "How about horseback riding? Could I take Ginger on one last ride?" I asked.

He sobered a little. "Would that jostle your head or ribs too much?"

I shrugged. "I'm not going to a rodeo. Could we ride out to the highway and back? It's a grated road."

He cocked his head to the side. "We can make that happen. Do you promise you'll tell me if it starts to hurt?" he asked.

"Yeah." Then I remembered he had a job here, unlike me. "If you don't have time I'll understand. This is kind of a vacation for me, but this is your real life."

"I can spare an hour or two."

I smiled genuinely. "I'd really like that."

"I'll meet you out at the barn in fifteen minutes. Dress warm, Frosty. I don't want you catching a chill right when I finally got you back to health."

I pulled a face and he left with a smile.

I finished my breakfast, cleaned up after myself, and made my way back to my cabin, where I layered up as requested. I was really excited about going on a horseback ride this morning. Ginger had proven up to the task of handling me on her back, and the two days I'd spent riding before I got hurt had helped me gain confidence. It seemed like the perfect thing to do before I had to leave Saturday. In fact, as I laced up my boots and tugged my beanie on, I reflected on just how bummed I really was to be wrapping up my time here. It had been a good experience for me.

I was studiously avoiding the thought of not seeing Daniel every day, knowing it was going to make leaving even harder. Better to focus on nature and hope to find more opportunities to spend time outside of the city in the future.

I shared that thought with Daniel once we were mounted up—thank you, feed crate, for the boost—and on our way down the road. It took me a minute or two to get settled back into the rhythm of Ginger's gait, but before too long I was looking around me and soaking in the view.

"I'm not sure where to go to find something like this, but I do think I need to be outdoors a little more, especially out of the city."

Daniel was thoughtful. "I didn't spend a ton of time in nature when I was living in Vegas, but there is Mount Charleston."

"Oh, yeah. I've heard of that. I think it's only like a for-ty-minute drive. That could work." I mentally ran through the things I remembered and made a note to check it out when I had a free weekend. "Lake Mead is another one people talk about, but I feel like that might be a boating lake in the middle of a city. I don't really know."

"How long have you lived in Vegas?" His question was genuine, which made my answer even more embarrassing.

"My whole life."

He nodded. "So, not from an outdoorsy family, then."

"No. My parents are real estate agents, which means a lot of their work happens on nights and weekends. My sister works at the Bellagio as a strategic planner."

"That sounds like an interesting job."

"Yeah. She owns a ton of pantsuits and is really good at bossing people around."

"Like you, minus the suits?"

I gave him an impish look. "She makes me look like a kitten."

"So no one in your family is spending a lot of time in nature. That explains your fascination with sheep when you first got here."

I laughed. "I'm still fascinated, but from a distance. Some things might be better learned from a book."

"Have you talked to your parents since letting them know you'd been hurt?"

"Uh . . . " I hesitated because people who come from families like his don't always understand families like mine. They think that because we don't dote on each other, or hang out much, that we must be missing out, or feeling unloved and incomplete. The truth is, I long ago accepted my family dynamic and have no real emotion about it, the same way I have no emotion about the change of sea-sons. It is what it is. We're independent.

"You're sure doing a lot of thinking and no answering," he prodded.

"Oh, yeah. I've texted my mom and Daphne. They both know I'm recovered and heading home on Saturday. They sent their well wishes."

"Tell me more about your roommate, Kayla," he said after we'd ridden without conversation for several minutes.

While Kayla was a favorite topic, I wasn't sure I wanted to break the mood of the moment with more conversation. In fact, the more we rode along listening to birds and the breeze in the leaves, the more morose I'd begun to feel. This wasn't my home, but I sort of wished I knew I'd be coming back sometime. It seemed such a shame to experience it once and never again. Maybe this could be an annual thing. I could accompany Alexander on his sabbatical each year. I'd get to see Daniel and Ginger and Willow. Okay, this thought process was not helping. I couldn't imagine seeing Daniel only once a year. The thought made me feel nauseated.

"You okay?" he asked, his voice laced with concern.

"Yeah. I'm fine." I cleared my throat and came back to the present. "Kayla and I met freshman year of high school. We hit it off, big time, and went to UNLV together, living in the dorms through our sophomore year of college. Then we moved into off-campus housing, which was a total mistake because the cafeteria disappeared from our lives, and we've had to fend for ourselves in a shoebox apartment ever since. We both graduated two years ago and have been working entry-level jobs as adults out in the real world. Our life goals are to get our student loans paid off as quickly as possible, afford food that doesn't come out of a box, and eventually upgrade our living situation."

"What's Kayla like?"

"She's funny. She has a great sense of humor. She's strong and confident."

"Makes sense. I don't see you being best friends with a lump on a log."

I glanced his way to see if he was teasing, but he wasn't, so I continued. "Yeah. She's really up for any adventure, always challenging me to do more or try something else. She's kind of like the pep squad leader." I laughed. "She dates a ton, so I might be living solo before too long."

"Are you okay living alone?"

"I wasn't sure, but Pamela has helped me realize that I could do it," I joked.

He laughed appreciatively. "Look at all the things you've learned during your retreat at The Lucky Wolf."

Yeah, I had learned a lot, actually. I leaned forward to pat Ginger on the neck and caught Daniel looking my way. I offered him a half smile, which he returned, and then I sank back into the sounds of the forest, wrapping myself up and holding on tight so that I could take this feeling home with me.

Chapter Sixteen

I made my way down the hall toward the study Friday afternoon, borrowed books in my hand, wishing I could sneak a few to take back to Vegas. I could imagine Daniel laughing when he figured it out and sending me some sort of funny text about it. It almost made me want to steal one after all, just for the excuse to stay in touch. I was really going to miss him.

The house was quiet, and I assumed the family was out together for their last afternoon before everyone said goodbye. Voices interrupted my meandering as I neared the study door. My head popped up and I paused. Men's voices. I recognized Alexander's first and slipped back against a wall to stay out of sight. I wasn't planning to eavesdrop, but as I turned to leave I swore I heard my name. So, yeah, there's no way I was walking away now. Forget good manners.

"Just say what you're trying to say." Daniel's voice entered the conversation, and now I was like a million times more committed to listening in. Just for a second. A tiny minute.

"I'm saying that it's obvious."

"What is?"

"Your feelings."

His feelings? About what? Maybe I hadn't heard my name after all. Maybe they'd said *laundry*, and Daniel really needed to wash his. I started to push away from the wall, but then . . .

"You're at least half in love with her," Alexander continued, not unkindly.

Silence. I froze. I think maybe Daniel did too. And, truthfully, Alexander was a pretty stoic sort, so there was no sound coming from that room at all. In the hallway my heartbeat cranked up a notch, and I held my breath. Daniel was at least half in love? With who?

When Daniel didn't say anything, Alexander pushed along. "Are you going to tell her?"

Who? Who was he going to tell?

"I . . ." Daniel let out such a loud huff of breath that I could feel his upheaval over this topic. "Well, honestly I'm a little shocked you noticed. You're not usually that observant about people."

Alex made a sound I couldn't quite decipher. "I notice the people I care about."

"Fair enough. As far as saying something to her, I'm not sure I should."

"Why not?" Alexander asked, and I silently thanked him for that.

Now there was movement. Footfalls on the carpet. Was someone pacing? I prayed they'd stay far away from the doorway I was lurking next to.

Daniel spoke again. "Are you honestly telling me I should? You, the guy who never takes a risk and overanalyzes everything?" He sounded irritated—no, more like he was stuck between two poor choices.

"You're right, I do overthink things, but you don't. Which is why I'm wondering what your hesitation is."

"I just met her. There's nothing about this situation that makes sense."

I mentally ran through what I knew about Daniel's schedule over the past couple of weeks. I'd assumed he was mostly here on the ranch, but I supposed I had no idea where he went or what he did when we weren't hanging out. Although, I felt like we spent quite a bit of time together, so when had he had the time? Agony, unexpected and sickening, filled my stomach. Daniel was in love with someone he'd just met?

Visions of him sitting next to me on the couch each night this week, reading me excerpts from books, discussing Mary Higgins Clark with me, or watching junk television filled my mind. Singing him the *High School Musical* song, and him holding me in the stillness afterward. After that we'd started sitting close on the couch, me leaning up against him, a blanket on my lap, while we killed the hours. I pictured the way his hair fell across his eyes when he'd walk me to bed at night before saying goodbye in a hushed tone that had made me sad the night was over.

As those scenes played across my mind, I wished more than anything that it could be me. The signs were there, right? I wasn't very experienced, but I knew my heart was warming to his. Yet, wouldn't he have told me if he was starting to feel something? We weren't exactly the type of friends who held things back from each other. I put a hand over my mouth to keep from hurrying in there and demanding to know who they were talking about. Me, or some girl who was about to get her car tires slashed.

"I'm leaving tomorrow," Alexander said. I swallowed hard, willing my head to stop spinning so I could focus on their words.

"I know."

What did Alexander's leaving have to do with Daniel telling this girl how he felt about her?

"Don't miss your chance," Alexander stated.

"I'm afraid she'll think I'm crazy," Daniel admitted in a vulnerable tone I'd never heard him use. "I don't do this kind of thing, but she doesn't know that. She won't know that I have never, ever had someone hit me straight in the chest like she has. She'll think that because of our family money I'm some sort of playboy who's had relationships all over the world, when the fact is that it's Dad's money and I'm living a really normal life here."

At this Alexander chuckled, and I realized through my haze that this was the most 'normal' I'd ever heard him act. "No, she won't," he was saying. "You'll have to trust me that you do not give off a player vibe. She'll believe you're sincere." More pacing, probably from Daniel. I wanted to join him and pace down the hall, but I was rooted, needing to hear how this played out. "When did you know you'd fallen for her?" Alexander asked in a tone laced with sympathy for his brother's struggle.

Daniel stopped, and when he spoke I could hear the smile in his voice. "I'd have to say seeing her fall off the ridge on your birthday was a big revelation. We've shared a few, um, other moments, I guess. Really, though, that first day when I rode up to her standing on the roof of her rental car yelling at her fairy godmother, something told me to watch out for this one; she was different."

Daniel chuckled at the memory, and no joke, I almost passed out. I managed to stay awake but did slide my back down the wall and sat on the carpet. Me? It was me! Who else had fallen off a ridge and stood on her car rooftop?

"Lucy's a good choice for you," Alexander agreed.

What now? Was I hearing correctly that my boss—who gave off the world's coldest shoulder—thought I was A-okay? Well, he'd had me fooled.

"I'm not sure what to do," Daniel admitted. "For me the feeling has kept growing the more time we spend together, but it feels too early to say anything, especially when I have no idea if she feels the same way about me. Honestly, for a while I thought she was into you."

I almost gasped out loud in horror over that. What an idiot I'd been. Alexander, thankfully, seemed equally shocked.

"Me? Hardly. Lucy has been nothing but courteous to me. There are no feelings other than professional regard from either of us."

I wanted to sink into the floor and was grateful when Daniel said lightly, "Yeah. You're right." He chuckled in a self-deprecating way that made me want to go in there and sooth that worry. He continued, "If time was on my side, I'd let it naturally take its course. But I don't want her to fly back to Vegas without me saying a word." Now he sighed. "Our lives are so different, and we'd be living almost a thousand miles apart, and . . . I guess the real question is, could she ever feel strongly enough about me to try to make that work?"

"These are questions you need to ask her."

Daniel sighed again, and I waited with my stomach in my toes to see what he'd say. "You really think I should?"

"The first step is admitting how you feel," Alexander teased.

"Did you read that in a book somewhere?" Daniel teased back. Then, after a short pause he said almost too quietly for me to hear, "I'm falling for Lucy." He sounded like he'd just been told some good news.

"Good. Now what are you going to do about it?"

I heard him clear his throat. "I have no idea."

I heard a slapping sound that made me think Alexander had given Daniel one of those back slaps guys like to do.

"This," Alex chuckled, "from the guy who took every dare and showed no fear of anything? The guy whose adventures I heard about from my friends and even business associates? Come on, you're not this guy, Dan. You know what you need to do."

I stood and raced down the hall, books clutched against me, darting through the kitchen and up the path to my cabin. Once there I barreled inside, locked the door behind me, and jumped right behind the screen onto my bed. Then, I stared at the wall in complete haziness. Once my heartbeat slowed I ran the conversation over and over in my head. Yes, Daniel had admitted that he was falling in love with me. Yes, he knew it had only been four weeks and that seemed a little . . . bonkers. Yes, I'd read so many romance novels where they fell in love at a weeklong house party and lived happily ever after. That was what we call fiction, though. Alexander and Daniel were talking about real life, *my* life.

What was I going to do? Was he going to actually tell me, or would he let it go and see how things went after I returned to Vegas? Should I try to act normal, or was that impossible with the knowledge I now had?

New thought edging in: Was I falling in love too?

This was a doozy and required pacing. I jumped off my bed and paced in circles around the living area. Some part of me understood that this was the price you pay for eavesdropping. Yet, a bigger chunk of me was high-fiving the heck out of myself because I could have been totally blindsided. At least this way I could react in private and be ready to face it head-on when the time came. If the time came.

Okay, time to list some facts. Facts I can work with.

1. Daniel has romantic feelings for me.
2. Daniel is hard-working, dependable, down to earth, courteous, funny, educated, intelligent, kind. So, he's a real catch.
3. He's easy on the eyes and deliciously warm and strong.
4. He's the first person I want to share my thoughts with, or tell a joke to, or tease, or sit by at meals, or . . .
5. Oh boy.

I paused in front of the potbelly stove and looked out the kitchenette window toward the barn. I'd been so distracted by Alexander's good looks, learning my new job, and exploring this new part of the country that Daniel had sneaked right in and latched himself onto my heart. I'd had an inkling that my own feelings had shifted over the past week, especially during a few real intense moments, but I hadn't imagined that he felt the same. It wasn't the path that my life usually took.

I'd never had an actual boyfriend. I knew what flirting felt like and was familiar with guys acting attracted to me, but it had never materialized in any way. And so I'd begun to discredit myself when I thought maybe a guy was into me. I'd learned to ignore it, squash my hopes down, and assume I'd still be single me at the end of whatever the situation was.

A guy like Daniel, actually falling for me? Never in a million years did I see that coming.

I plopped on the couch and let my head sag back. So, like Alexander said, the first step is admitting something. I'll go ahead and admit that I was super duper interested in Daniel Drake. I could also finally admit that I'd been doing my best to squelch those feelings, as I knew I'd be returning to Vegas and didn't see anything coming of them. But yeah, he floats my boat and I like that feeling a lot.

Was I in love? Maybe. It's never happened to me before, so it's hard to be sure. Do I feel like I'd rather lose my leg than never see him again after this week? Yeah. Because when I think about how life will be back in Vegas, with no teasing brown eyes and him challenging me at every turn, well, it doesn't feel like much of a life at all.

A life decision this big needed some big space to think in, so I changed into more weather appropriate clothing and headed out for a walk. I wouldn't go far and I'd keep it sedate, but I was going to follow the road back toward the highway and see if I could make sense of all I'd learned, and maybe even make a plan for how to move forward.

I walked for a long time, definitely missing the lunch hour, but I didn't mind. I felt rejuvenated and more lucid than I'd been in a long time. I had the chance here to grab for something, a chance that shouldn't be missed. Of course, there was always the possibility that it would end in heartbreak, but I had a gut feeling it would be worth it either way.

Daniel came upon me on my way back, when I'd almost passed out of the tree line into the open area where the homestead sat. He was on foot, and it wasn't easy to see his expression between the shade cast by his cowboy hat and the shadows created by trees. He was wearing a coat, hands in his jeans pockets, walking purposefully but not striding like he was worried or angry. Anticipation rose in my chest at the sight of him, and I smiled when he looked up. He returned the smile as he picked up his pace, not waiting for me to close the distance. I still couldn't see his eyes when we came to a stop a few feet apart.

"You missed lunch," he said. "You okay?"

I nodded. "Just needed to stretch my legs. I've been doing a lot of sitting the past week. What are you doing out here?"

"Practicing my tracking, looking for our missing guest."

I took a step closer to him. "Guest, huh? I thought I'd at least have been upgraded to warmly regarded acquaintance."

He shook his head. "I think you've been downgraded, actually. Impertinence."

"That's a fancy word. I didn't know I was capable of such behavior." Another step forward.

I was now close enough to see his eyes. They were wary, unsure of what I was doing. Considering I was attempting to be flirty, his confused look might not be a good thing. Then again, if it kept him off-center that was cool. I liked to keep him on his toes.

All at once a big cloud of snow fell on our heads from a branch that had been weighted to its tipping point. Chunks fell down under my collar, and I shrieked as icy cold ran down my backbone. He laughed and pulled off his hat, slapping it against his leg before looking to see how I was faring. Not well, I'll tell you. I wasn't wearing a nice cowboy hat with a wide brim like he was. My beanie hadn't protected my face at all. I reached up mittened hands and pulled off my glasses with one while I wiped at the snow with the other.

"What's wrong with you, Montana?" I grumbled.

This was a two-hand job, so I tucked my glasses into the pocket of my jacket and moved to rub at my face again.

"Here." He stepped forward, and I cracked open an eye to see he was holding a bandana. An honest to goodness kerchief of the old west.

I was so caught off guard by it that I remained frozen, so he took it upon himself to wipe at the wetness clinging to me. His touch sent a riot of sparks through every inch of my body. At this range I could see him clearly without my glasses and was rewarded with those golden flecks in his eyes. His skin was smooth and tan except for where his beard was starting to come through. I tugged off one of my mittens, the urge to run my fingertips across that roughness too strong to resist. He'd been so focused on wiping my face that he hadn't seen me coming. My fingers were light as silk as I ran them from his ear to his jaw. I wanted more, so I continued on, lightly running my fingertips over his lips.

Now it was his turn to freeze. His hand stayed where it was, the bandana pressed against my own jaw, as his eyes moved to meet mine. They were full of questions, and I happened to have a few of the answers. I slid my hand around to the back of his neck and gave the tiniest of tugs until his head lowered and I was able to press my lips to his. It was like coming home. Like the greatest puzzle piece had slipped into place. The forest grew silent, and the bandana fell away from my face as his hand tensed in what I hoped was surprise and not unwillingness. My other hand reached for his upper arm, wrapping around it and pulling him closer. I wanted this, I wanted him, and I didn't want to wait until he got around to saying something. His mouth was warm, if a little tense under mine, and I wanted to laugh at the feeling of it all.

Knowing that he secretly had feelings for me made the entire experience that much better. As I pulled him closer he thawed and came back to life, his own arms wrapping around me, pulling me as close as we could get with layers of flannels and coats. He deepened the kiss and something inside of me broke free from the place it had hidden for so long. Sparks, tingles, fireworks—whatever you want to call them—ran up the back of my knees and through my spine at the same time that my heartbeat stepped it up a notch.

I was soaring safely in his arms and loving every moment of it. I had never, ever been kissed by someone who loved me, and I was finding out here in this snowy forest that being loved made all the difference in the world.

I raised up onto my toes, wanting to be closer, and his hands left my back to move under my coat and press against my shirt, eliminating some distance in a way that made my breathing hitch. I dared to move my mitten-free hand into his hair while my other wrapped more snuggly around his neck. Yeah, I had no idea where his hat had gotten off to and truly did not care—I was too busy fulfilling a secret yearning I'd had to run my hands through his dark locks like I'd watched him do. It was heavy and soft between my fingers and tickled against my palms. I couldn't imagine anything feeling better.

After a few moments he pulled away and pressed his forehead to mine. "Lucy?" His breath tickled my lips.

I shook my head quickly. "No. Don't say anything, don't ask anything."

He nodded and I heard him swallow as he pulled me into a hug. I could feel the energy humming through him and how he wanted to talk about what had just happened, but I just wanted him close to me. Plus, maybe I wanted a second kiss. Then, that idea became so appealing that I lifted my head and kissed him right where that pulse in his neck liked to stick out when he was working hard or feeling aggravated. He sucked in a breath and looked down at me.

"Are you looking for trouble?" he asked, with a new glimmer in his eye.

"Trouble is my middle name." I leaned forward and closed my eyes and didn't have to wait very long to see just what was going to happen.

Chapter Seventeen

I finally had the delightful opportunity to ride front-seat on Daniel's horse Ford when he took me out after dinner that night. My last night. He said we needed to ride together because it was dark and chilly, and it had only been a week since my injury, and he needed to make sure I wasn't going to relapse on horseback. (Guess he'd forgotten that I rode all by myself the day before, but who was I to argue with his reasoning if it meant being close to him?)

This time we rode bareback, which I'd never tried and was somewhat hesitant about. How would I stay up without a saddle? However, all my fears flitted away when Daniel swung up behind me and held me firmly against him. Riding along under the stars with him pressed along my back, his arms around my middle, was not the worst way I'd spent an evening. I had the feeling he'd never have gone the bareback route if I hadn't kissed him earlier, and then I'd have missed out on this royally swoony moonlit ride. Full disclosure: kissing him had been one of the best choices I'd ever made.

Ford walked along slowly, feeling the lack of urgency from us, and I relaxed into the motion that had been totally foreign such a short time ago. One of my hands wrapped around his mane, and the other held the reins loosely.

"Can we talk about this afternoon?" Daniel asked when we'd gotten settled and were away from the house.

"Nothing really stands out to me," I replied lazily.

He retaliated by brushing a feather-light kiss on the side of my neck, and really, all that did was encourage me to keep being a pain.

"It's not every day that I'm kiss attacked in the forest," he pressed.

"Well, good," I teased, leaning more fully back against him. "I'd hate to be one in a long list of women . . ."

"You're not." He cut me off. "Not at all."

His tone was so serious, so sincere that I couldn't tease him. I remembered what I'd heard him tell Alexander, about how worried he was that I'd think of him as a playboy.

"I know that," I soothed.

Poor Daniel. I hadn't let him have "the talk" earlier. Instead, after spending another heat-inducing, skin-flushing ten minutes kissing in the forest, I'd taken his hand and walked back with him in silence. I'd known that the talk would involve the long-distance thing and other difficult topics, and I'd just wanted to enjoy the total magic of discovering something without it being tainted by the real world.

"Lucy, you're leaving in the morning, and I know we haven't known each other long," he said, his arms tightening around me like he was afraid I'd jump off the horse and run away screaming, "but I don't want to just say goodbye and have that be it."

"I feel the same."

His arms relaxed and I put my free hand over one of his. "I've been thinking a lot and, well, maybe first I should say that . . . uh . . . I'm not sure where to start."

I squeezed his hand, wanting to ease this moment for him. "I maybe know some stuff already."

"Like what?"

I wanted to face him, but balancing on top of a roundish shaped object was making that hard. "You chose the top of a horse to have this conversation?" I joked. "Where I can't see your face?"

"It was the most private place I could think of," he replied.

"Point taken." There were some downsides of living so communally. "Okay. Well, let's hypothetically say that earlier today I was on my way to the study to put back the novels I'd borrowed, and in theory there were two men in there talking, and I possibly heard my name, so instead of walking away I maybe listened in for a minute."

He reached around me to grab the reins and tug Ford to a stop. I turned as best I could to see him blink a few times and then surprise me by grinning. "You heard Alexander tell me to fess up to my feelings," he stated. I nodded, biting my lips. "That makes this talk a little easier."

He leaned forward and gave me the best, softest kiss ever. My stomach swooped and I darn near fell off that horse, reaching out to grab a handful of mane while my heart slammed against my still-healing ribs. I grabbed his knee for balance as he continued the kiss, light and sweet, but still stealing my breath. Too soon he pulled back.

"We're supposed to be talking," he said with a smirk. His hat had been bumped back on his head, and he tugged it forward with a warm look in his eye before he got Ford moving again.

I faced forward and settled back in against his support. "We don't have to talk. I'm good living in this magic bubble forever."

"Agreed. I wish you could stay for another month or two so we could take it slow, but we don't have that luxury," he stated. I nodded. "I've been obsessively thinking about it, and it really comes down to the fact that our lives are so far apart. How do we cross that hurdle, or do you even want to try? You said the other day that this place is like a vacation to you. Will you go back to Vegas where there aren't memories of me everywhere and see this as a fun fling?"

I felt mildly offended. "Of course not."

"You know, I feel embarrassed to admit this, but if you told me I got this short time with you and then it was over, I think I'd still be grateful for what I got."

Touched, I bit down on a smile. "This isn't a fling. I think we should try to . . . " My voice faded away.

"To what?" he said when I didn't continue.

I shook my head and felt a little melancholy. My shoulders sagged. "We really do live worlds apart."

He gathered me more fully against him, until his cheek pressed against my ear. "No, don't go there. Not yet. Not in the first talk we have. We're in the hopeful zone, right?"

I nodded, but my heart pinched. "How long can we really go with just phone calls and never seeing each other, though?" I asked, a lump forming in my throat. "I don't know."

He pulled Ford to a stop again and slid off. "Come here." He reached up for me, and I put my hands on his shoulders. As soon as my feet touched the ground he wrapped me in his arms. "It sounds like you're getting a little overwhelmed, and that's not going to work. I don't want this . . . relationship . . . to be a source of unhappiness for you."

I sank into him, nuzzling up under his chin and swallowing down my worries. "You make me happy. Being apart makes me mopey."

His voice was filled with self-reproach and a little humor when he said, "That doesn't bode well, seeing as we live apart."

I squared my shoulders and pulled back, a soldier ready to face down the land mines. "All right. What's our plan?"

He smiled and took my hands in his as he stepped back. "First, do you want to see where this goes?"

"Yes."

"Good. Me too. Second, the biggest issue is distance. How do we go about navigating that?"

"We'll obviously talk every night."

"Agreed," he said. "On camera so we can see each other."

I nodded and mentally crunched some numbers. "The flight from Vegas to Great Falls is only about two hours. Plus another hour and a half drive—give or take—to here. So, three or four hours of travel one way." I paused and thought some more. "We could probably see each other on the occasional long weekend, right?" I tried not to feel overly worried about the cost of round trip flights, or how few and far between those weekends might be.

He nodded. "Yes. We'll alternate who goes where?"

"Yeah."

"And if we have a chance for more, we take it."

I nodded while fighting back a lump in my throat. I reached for him, needing the reassurance. "If we have the chance, we take it."

He offered me all the reassurance I could possibly ask for, saying all the right words and holding me tightly, but leaving me still wondering how a couple that was always apart could ever hope to really be together.

* * *

I don't care who you are, goodbyes are blah. If you're in love, they're heartbreaking. If you're best friends, they're a bummer. Saturday morning, though, I stumbled on a new level of awkward goodbye-ing known as "we're barely friends but we shared some stuff and I might never see you again" . . . and it's unpleasant. Plus, I hadn't attempted to say goodbye to Daniel yet, a situation that was guaranteed to peel my heart out of my chest.

I ate an incredibly delicious final breakfast and then stood to return to my cabin to gather my things and head out. Robert and Priscilla shot me a wave from the end of the breakfast table, wishing me well and assuring me they'd see me around Drake Enterprises every now again. Gary and Colby—the workers who had witnessed some of my shenanigans but never spent much time with me—called out well wishes. Willow hurried to my side from where she'd been sitting and gave me a giant hug, then snagged a gallon baggie of cookies from the pantry for me to take home, which made all of us laugh. Pamela offered me a nod and double checked that I'd packed all my things and none of hers, while staying seated. Alexander, though, stood and came around to where I was. He seemed to have relaxed a little with me, and I wondered if it was because his brother and I were sort of in a relationship and the lines had been blurred, making us no longer simply boss and employee. He gave me a handshake, thanked me for my first weeks of work, and said he'd see me at the office first thing Monday morning. He and Pamela were flying out early the next day after one last Drake family experience.

No one had been surprised when Daniel rose to walk me to the doorway of the house, saying he'd see me off. It was well established that we were friends, at the least, although based on Willow's expression she knew what was really happening, and she was fully supportive. However, I was totally caught of guard by Steven and Jarrod standing too and walking with us to just outside the homestead door.

Steven handed me a book he'd bought from the Winterford World of Books called *Vying for the Viscount*, and I darn near teared up. He blushed when I laughed and took the book to read the back blurb. Then, I spontaneously gave him a hug and he patted my back rather roughly.

"Are your parents bakers? Because you're a cutie pie," he said against my head, and I squeezed harder in reaction to another cheesy pickup line. He really was such a sweetheart.

Jarrod was up next, handing me two tubes of my exact shade of lipstick. I giggled as I opened one of the tubes, applied it to my lips, and pulled his head down to plant a big kiss on his forehead where everyone could see. "Thanks for flirting with me," I said.

"Anytime." He smiled somewhat shyly, his eyes dancing.

Daniel reached for my hand, signaling that it was time to go, and I offered a slightly watery smile to both of the men who had added something special to my time here. Daniel and I walked hand-in-hand along the path to my cabin. For two people who had never found conversation difficult, we were strangely silent as we entered and gathered my two suitcases. Daniel picked them up before I could, and I stood with my purse in my hands, looking in a slow circle around the space. It really was the cutest place, and I wished this wasn't such an open-ended goodbye. I bit back on emotion, feeling slightly ridiculous. I was making a mountain out of nothing. It was time to go home, not ship off to Mars to start a new colony. I'd talk to him tonight, and if all went well I would see the cabin again.

I nodded to Daniel and held the door for him to pass by with the luggage. When we were both to the bottom of the steps I tried to take a suitcase, but he only shook his head and started walking. I trailed behind him, mostly because I wasn't in a hurry to go. I watched him with new eyes, seeing his confidence, his athleticism, and smooth way of moving. I'd noticed it all before but hadn't allowed myself to enjoy the view. He joked and teased, pushed and prodded, but he was dependable and solid. He'd been my friend from day one, which only sweetened the new things developing between us. My life didn't overflow with friendships, and tears pricked at my eyes when I thought about how much I appreciated having his. He was every bit as swoon-worthy as his brother, and I couldn't wait for Kayla to meet him. She'd go bonkers for him. The thought helped soften the edges of some unnamable feeling bubbling up while watching him carry my bags away.

We circled around to the side of the parking area where my rental sat, and I pulled out the keys, clicking the button to pop the hatchback. Daniel loaded my bags and shut the door, and then it was time to say goodbye. But all I could do was stand there staring at him while trying to choke down a lump that had formed in my throat. Tears built up behind my eyes, and I did my best to blink them away while I scolded myself, telling my heart that this was not forever.

My voice was thick when I started to speak, so I swallowed and tried again. "I guess this is the part where we say goodbye and thanks." He nodded, still looking down at me wordlessly. "Thanks for, uh, not running away when you saw this weirdo standing on top of her car yelling at her fairy godmother." I managed a soft laugh at the image. "And, um, thanks for really just showing me why I'm glad I don't have an older brother."

At this his expression softened. He reached for me, his fingertips pressing into my waist, and I grabbed onto his forearms. "Thanks for the comic relief," he said, pulling me close.

I went willingly, running my hands up his arms and around his neck as his arms closed around my back. I hugged myself to him, scared to say goodbye. With him I'd found a new place to belong, and I wondered where my luck was now. Why couldn't he and I be in the same location? I sniffled a little, and his hold tightened, his head dipping to press against mine.

"I'm being a total pansy," I said in a wobbly voice. "Do you promise to keep me up to date with the latest in sheep drama or chicken attacks?"

I felt his chest vibrate against mine. "We could start a book club of two, and our first read would be something about an untamed Highland witch warrior goddess."

I grinned and sniffled. "The sad thing is, you could probably look it up on the internet and find that exact book."

"I'm counting on it."

There didn't seem to be anything else to say, neither of us wanting to say goodbye out loud. It didn't matter in that moment that we'd promised to fight for this new spark, because all I could see was the thousand miles between us. Added to that, the thousand miles between our lifestyles, and, well part of me was terrified that all of this would fade until he was a happy memory from a place out of time, the one that got away.

"Will you call me when you land in Vegas?" he asked. He straightened a bit and pressed a kiss to my hair.

"Yeah."

"And then again before bed?"

"I'll prop my phone on the sink while I brush." I nodded and pulled back enough to lean up and press a kiss not on his cheek but next to his mouth. "Take care of Ginger," I said as I planted another kiss on the other side of his mouth. "She's too young to understand why I have to leave."

I fell back on humor to get me through, but his expression was serious when he leaned down and pressed his lips against mine. I tightened my grip on his neck, pulling up onto my toes to show him how I felt. All my feelings rushed out, coursing through me and begging him to never let go. His arms contracted, holding me so tight I could hardly breathe. There was urgency, and some heartache in that kiss, both of us knowing there were no real promises between us. We were going on hope and genuine affection for each other, but would it be enough?

After a few moments I lightened my hold and sank back down onto my flat feet before softening the kiss and then ending it all together. He let go of me, and I turned away to get in the car. He followed closely behind, bending to pull my car door open before I had the chance, our fingers fumbling together for one unexpected moment. I didn't look up at him. I kept my head down. I was afraid of what I'd see written on his face. I was afraid of what he'd see written on mine.

* * *

Kayla was waiting for me at the passenger pick-up point outside the airport when I arrived back in Las Vegas. She leaned up against her car, arms folded across her chest and hip cocked out in her usual pose. Dressed in leggings and a t-shirt with white sneakers, she was so herself that it made me smile, until I got a little closer and saw something that was definitely new.

"You put pink in your hair?" I said when I was close enough.

"I missed you too." She laughed, bypassing my luggage and giving me one of her exuberant hugs.

I let go of my luggage handles and hugged her back. "Now, let go and let me see your hair."

She stepped back and swished her head around, making the strands of pink she'd used around her face disappear in the dark brown waves and then reappear. It looked pretty cool. A little hint of edginess in a way that she could totally get away with in the business world.

"It looks amazing," I said. "What does Graham think of it?" I asked, referring to her uppity boss.

"He's handling it," she replied with pinched lips, which meant he didn't like it but she wasn't taking it out. "I know, you're bummed out that I didn't wait for you. It'll have to be touched up next month, so you can come flirt-i-fy yours too."

"When did you do it?" I asked as she opened her trunk and reached for one of my bags.

"Last week."

I made a face and grabbed the other bag. "What happened to telling each other everything?"

She made the same face back. "I'm wondering the same thing. Last week you were falling down a mountain. Now you're home, and I'm sure there are a lot of blank spaces in between. You have a lot of gut spilling to do tonight."

She had no idea, really. I hadn't had a chance yet to tell her about the developments with Daniel and how my stomach was tied in knots already, missing him hard. She shut the trunk and we got in the car, starting the engine and pulling away from the curb.

"Can you turn on the air? I'm hot," I said.

She looked over at me and waved her fingers in my direction. "You may want to drop a layer."

I glanced down, having completely forgotten that I was wearing a flannel shirt over my tee. I unbuttoned it and pulled my arms out, catching a whiff of Daniel's scent before I threw it into the already littered backseat of Kayla's beat down car. I shook my head, willing visions of his sad eyes to fade.

"Remember what a shock the fifty-degree weather was when I arrived in Montana?" I forced a laugh. "Now the shock is going the other direction, especially because Montana had dropped down to a balmy forty degrees when I left." I glanced at a billboard we were passing, and it said it was currently seventy degrees outside. It felt great. "Actually, can we roll down the windows? I've forgotten what it feels like to have warm air on my skin." I pushed the window down button without waiting for her reply.

"You act like you were up there for two years." She laughed but gamely opened her own window.

It was definitely cooler than it had been when I'd left a month ago, but it felt warm and dry and smelled like Vegas—exhaust and garbage and the occasional whiff of a buffet. Kayla maneuvered out of the airport and onto Paradise Road, toward the UNLV area, where our apartment was located. We drove past all the stores and restaurants that I hadn't seen in a month, and I felt some part of me begin to settle back in. It may have been the Dunkin' Donuts sign that told me things would be okay.

For a split second my heart went out to Daniel. Here in my home I had no memories of him, but on his homestead there would be memories of us together all around. He'd gotten the short end of that stick. I pulled out my phone and shot him a text.

> **Me:** Landed. Cruising around with the windows down and no extra layers.

My phone dinged almost instantly.

> **Daniel:** Lucky. I'm wearing three.

> **Me:** I'll call you later?

> **Daniel:** Ok.

"Who's that?" Kayla asked.

"I promised to let everyone at the ranch know when I landed safely," I said. Why didn't I admit it was Daniel? This was my best friend. What was I hiding? "I was sad to leave, but it feels good to be home."

164

"I doubt it was the Drake ranch you were sad to leave." I glanced her way, but her eyes were on the road, dark hair blowing behind her. "You can admit it's Daniel you're missing and him you're texting."

"Yeah," I sighed. "We had a little development in that area, actually."

Her eyes grew large, and her smile followed. "Ooh, do spill."

I told her all about my eavesdropping—cause friends don't judge and would probably actually join in—and the revelations that came afterward. "You once asked me if he's as attractive as Alexander, and yeah, he totally is. He's not just a pretty face, either. He's funny and kind and hard working." I was warming to the subject now, speaking quicker than normal. "At first I didn't think he'd be my type. He's really outgoing, and kind of silly, and quick to join in my banter. I tend to go for tall, dark, and brooding, thinking that's so dreamy, but it turns out that his sense of humor is really what makes him . . ." I struggled to find the right word.

Kayla reached a hand to my arm and stopped me in my tracks. "A good fit."

I looked back out my window. "Yeah." I made a frustrated noise. "I've wasted so much time thinking guys who are serious and mysterious were what I'd like, and because of that it took me weeks to realize how perfect he is. He just fits, you know? If I hadn't overheard him admitting he liked me, I don't know what would have happened."

"Do you think he would have said something if you hadn't?"

"I hope so. If not, I'd have come home a little grumpy."

"You'd have come home acting like Oscar the Grouch, and I'd have poked and prodded at you until you realized that you were missing him."

"And then I'd have completely gone bonkers trying to figure out a really nonchalant way to get in touch with him while playing it cool because I'd lived with him all that time and not realized what my true feelings were. Talk about beating yourself up."

"So, how was kissing him?" She grinned.

I gave her a mysterious grin of my own. "Amazing."

"When do I get to meet him?"

I shrugged. "We're going to try to visit each other and talk on the phone a lot, so hopefully soon."

We fell back into silence for a moment while the ache in my chest grew. I was used to seeing him every day, and now I had no idea when it would happen again.

"There's no food in the apartment," Kayla said, bringing me back. "Do you want to grocery shop or stop at Whitecastle for a burger?"

You all know by now that given the choice I won't cook for myself. "Whitecastle. Do they still have those brownies on a stick?"

Kayla laughed. "You were gone for a month, Luce. The brownies didn't go anywhere."

I'd only been gone for a month. So why did it feel like I'd stepped away for half a lifetime?

It didn't take us long to grab burgers and head back to our apartment. I lugged my large suitcase, and Kayla did the same with my carry-on and the bag of food. Two flights of stairs and a little grunting later, and we were right back where we'd left off. We dumped my luggage next to the front door and headed straight for the couch, me on the right, her on the left. We were a little rigid in our seating preferences, and on the extremely rare occasion when someone else was over we had to pretend to be okay with sitting somewhere different.

"Do you realize it's been an entire month since I had a burger?" I said as I unwrapped mine.

Kayla was already on her first bite but didn't bother to wait to answer. "No way. Did you eat out at all?"

I shook my head. "All home-cooked meals. There may have been a diner in town, I didn't really look. The meals at the ranch were so good, I didn't miss restaurant food."

She chewed thoughtfully. "Do you feel healthier?"

"Maybe. I was definitely more active too."

"I hear activity and eating at home are good for you."

I grinned. "If rumor is to be believed."

While we ate, we caught each other up on the little things we hadn't talked about while I'd been gone. Her job was going well—or at least as well as it had ever gone. She'd gone on a few dates that hadn't seemed newsworthy at the time but had me rolling now. I told her about Pamela actually talking to me, and getting attacked by Beau the killer rooster. I told her more details about Daniel and some of our funny conversations and things that had happened. She oohed and aahed appropriately over the romantic moments we'd shared, which was the best. We finished eating before we finished talking, so Kayla followed me into our tiny bedroom and sat on her bed while I unpacked.

"So, I did some thinking on the flight home," I said while hanging up shirts. "We should look for a new apartment next month. Away from campus."

A smile lit up her face. "I was thinking the same thing. No offense, but there was a lot more space here this past month with you gone." I made a noise and threw a pillow at her. "I said 'no offense.'" She squealed. "Do you think we could afford two bedrooms?"

We both got quiet, imagining such a luxury. "Maybe," I said after a moment. "Let's get our next paychecks and see how it goes, but dreaming got us this far, right?"

She tossed my pillow back to my bed. "Could you imagine a kitchen where we could actually pass each other?"

I laughed. "It might almost be enough to get us cooking. Almost."

Chapter Eighteen

Monday morning the alarm rang on my first actual day in the corporate offices of Drake Enterprises. Yes, I'd been doing real work while in Montana, but it was part-time from the family study. Today I would be in a tall glass building, entering my first real office, and meeting new faces.

I'd thought way too much about my outfit last night, as though I was reliving high school, and had firmly decided that I'd avoid polka-dots—at least for the first few days while I got the lay of the land. Red lipstick, however, was non-negotiable. I'd ordered new glasses, missing my animal print frames, but they were another week out, so I was going to have to make do with my boring black frames.

I hit snooze on the alarm and kicked my covers off while staring at the ceiling and wishing I woke up as easily as Kayla did. She was finishing in the shower, though, so maybe it was good that I was slower to wake. The differences in our wake-up ability had kept shower sharing from being an issue. The light in Vegas was different from the light in Montana, I reflected. Here it was tinted more yellow, and if light could be lazy, then Vegas light in November was lazy.

My phone dinged and I reached for it on my nightstand.

Daniel: Willow isn't okay.

Attached was a picture of Willow holding a quiche and frowning. I chuckled to myself as a second text dinged.

Daniel: No one is patting her on the back like you did.

Me: That looks amazing. My mouth is watering from here. Does she ship?

Daniel: No to the shipping, but you put a smile on her face by asking.

Me: She put drool in my mouth, so now it's me who's frowning.

Daniel: :) I'll eat some in your honor. Good luck today. Your office is on the 10th floor.

Me: I've always wanted an office.

Daniel: Good news: you have one. Bad news: it's next to the bathroom. The walls are thin.

I laughed out loud just as Kayla stepped out of the bathroom with her hair wrapped in a towel. "What's so funny this early?" she asked.

"Daniel." I didn't look away from the screen but hurried to text him back.

Me: So it wouldn't be a good idea to put nails in the wall?

He took a second to reply, and I hoped it meant I'd made him laugh too. Man, I missed sitting together talking.

Daniel: Go ahead and hang the pictures, but invest in buckets.

Me: Good tip. Hope the sheep are kind today.

Daniel: Hope Alex is too.

I dropped my phone into my lap and leaned back against my headboard.

"You've got it bad for this guy." Kayla smirked.

"I know. I wish I knew when I'd get to see him again." I swung my legs over the side of the bed and went to my closet to gather clean underclothes before heading to the bathroom, still feeling a little glow.

"First day at work, huh? Are you ready for the corporate world?" she asked.

169

"I figure I survived a month on the Drake family ranch, so I'll be okay."

She grinned. "Yeah, I can see how all those home cooked meals and kisses on horseback were a real trial."

I pulled a face and closed the bathroom door behind me. By the time I was done, Kayla had left for her job, as her commute was longer than mine. I snagged a Costco protein shake from the fridge and shook it while I locked the door and took the stairs down to the parking lot. There were no covered spots in this cheep complex, which meant that I was always grateful for the cooler months when I didn't have to air out my car before I could get inside.

I got in and popped down the visor, giving myself a once over. Brown hair in an updo with the front side-swept, make-up looking passable, giant front bow on my silk maroon shirt tied, and black pencil skirt was free of fuzzies. I was ready to go.

* * *

Pamela's was the first face I saw when I exited the elevator on the tenth floor of the Harris Office Tower in downtown Las Vegas. She was standing next to the reception desk, and it was apparent she'd been waiting for me. She was without her usual handful of files but still armed with her typical "you're wasting my time" expression. She was also wearing a black pencil skirt, but it seemed pointier than mine. I purposely darted my eyes to the receptionist and put on an award-winning smile.

"Hi, I'm Lucy Moore, the new senior financial planner." I stuck out my hand.

The guy manning the desk was young, probably around my age, and he stood with a smile of his own. "Welcome. So nice to meet you. I'm Corey." He was cute with curly brown hair and white teeth. Maybe Kayla needed to meet him.

"Miss Moore, Mr. Drake is waiting for you in his office," Pamela said as soon as Corey and I had finished shaking hands.

"See you later, Corey," I called over my shoulder.

Once we were out of earshot Pamela said, "I hear you and Daniel are dating."

"Maybe," I teased.

She pinched her lips. "He's a good guy. Nice."

I nodded, dropping the tone. "He is. I have no idea how I got lucky enough to attract his attention." I stumbled to a halt when I saw Pamela's mouth shift into a half smile. "I don't think I've ever seen you smile," I said.

She'd walked on a few steps without me but then stopped. The smile was still there. "I find things funny, even if I don't show it. Like how you caught a guy by falling off a mountain wearing thirty-two layers of snow gear. I have to give you points for creativity."

I blinked and then grinned. "I'm assuming you can snare a guy on your own, but if you ever need pointers . . ."

She held up a hand, shaking her head. "My dignity couldn't handle your tactics."

I started walking again, falling in alongside her. "I'll have you know I never once used any of your labeled beauty products while we were in Montana."

She nodded. "That's why we're still on speaking terms." Aaaand—she was back, although somehow she didn't scare me quite as much anymore.

We took a path through a large open area containing about twenty cubes, the same path I'd taken when coming to interview. The big difference was that this time I'd be entering Alexander's office rather than the conference room a few doors down. I saw one or two faces that looked familiar to me as heads popped up to watch the new lady parade along. Pamela led the way with confidence and never once glanced to the side or greeted anyone. I wondered if she preferred it, or if she felt lonely. Maybe she was the social center of an entire community outside of work that I knew nothing about, and this was her anti-social down time. Who knew?

Alexander's door was open, and he was seated behind his desk. I was caught by the view behind him. Two full walls of glass showed off the city as it spread its way through the long, flat valley. From here I could see a few of the large casinos on the Strip. It was pretty epic. Pamela knocked lightly on the door frame and he glanced up.

"Welcome." He stood and crossed toward me as I entered, hand out to shake.

"Hi, Alexander. This is a killer view," I said, taking his hand in mine and hardly noticing how handsome he was anymore. Really, the shine was gone, and now he was just a regular guy in my eyes. "Oh," I realized when our hands released. "I'm sorry, it's Mr. Drake now that we're back in town."

A barely perceptible shake of his head and tug of his mouth said not to worry about it. Pamela murmured something and left the room. I watched as she took her seat at a desk situated just outside of Alexander's—Mr. Drake's!—door. She settled in, flashed me one last look letting me know she'd be watching, and focused in on her screen.

"Please, come with me." Mr. Drake gestured for me to walk ahead of him back out the door. I did and then stood aside to let him lead me wherever it was we were going.

"Daniel says she's a robot," I said quietly after we'd passed Pamela. "If she is, I'd look into mass producing her, because the woman has skills."

His face softened at the mention of his brother. "I've never regretted hiring Miss Lin."

It wasn't meant unkindly, but it was a good reminder that we were no longer chumming around the family homestead. The familiarity we'd sort of accrued at the end of the month now needed to be put back in its box. I cleared my throat and my mind, reorganizing my energy and settling into my new role as Miss Moore.

We walked a few doors down to an office next to the conference room. He pointed out the names of the people in the two offices we passed, but neither of them were there. "Heather Allen is the senior marketing manager. Travis Johnson is over HR. And, here you are."

"I seem to remember meeting Heather and Travis when I interviewed," I said.

"Yes. I'm sure you'll recognize them."

I entered my first ever office with excitement. My nameplate was next to the door, and while I didn't have an entire two walls of windows, I did have one wall, which was the coolest thing. "This looks good," I said sedately, while inside I had butterflies of celebration. I couldn't wait to text Kayla and Daniel. Maybe I'd send them a shot of my nameplate too.

"You, Ms. Allen, and Mr. Johnson share an administrative assistant. Her name is Angie Peters, and her desk is there." He pointed to a cubical situated right in front of Travis Johnson's office, which put it between the three of us. I nodded. "I'll let you get to it. You already know how to get logged in. It's all the same as it was in Montana. If you need anything, Ms. Peters and Miss Lin can help you."

"Thanks so much. I'm happy to be here." It had been nice of him to personally show me my new office.

He nodded and left. I closed the door behind me softly and then walked to my big window wall and looked over the city I'd called home for my entire life. The view from the tenth floor of a downtown office building was very different than anything I'd had before. After a few minutes of grinning like the Cheshire cat, I got out my phone and started snapping pictures before I shot off a text to Daniel.

> **Me:** This office is the size of my entire stinking apartment.

Which was followed by five pictures from different angles and two selfies of me hamming it up in front of the window.

> **Me:** Please put Ginger on the next plane. She can live under my desk and save me on gas money.

Next I sent a text and pictures to Kayla.

> **Me:** Forget apartment hunting, I think I can hide a bed and portable shower in this office!

Kayla surprised me by texting right back, which must have meant her boss was nowhere near.

Kayla: There's room for at least two of us there. What's the employee lounge like? Vending machines?

Me: Ooh, hold please.

I tucked my phone into my skirt and opened the door, then wandered down the hall to where I assumed it would be. Sadly, I only saw two cafe-style tables for four, a coffee station, a sink, a mini fridge, and a microwave.

Me: No vending machines.

Kayla: We can make do with a mini fridge if there is one.

Me: You're in luck. We're moving on up.

Kayla: Celebration time!

Kayla sent some winky faces, and I made my way back to my office with a cup of water. Couldn't look like I was just an oddball wanderer.

As I was sitting down at my desk, Daniel chimed in.

Daniel: That view is amazing, but I'm sorry to tell you that Ginger doesn't know how to use a toilet.

Me: Can sheep be potty trained?

Daniel: Doubtful.

Me: I maybe told your brother that you think Pamela is a robot, just so you don't get blindsided by that.

Daniel: You broke code?

Me: Yes. But it won't happen again. Consider my wrists slapped.

Daniel: Forget the toilet, I'm sending Ginger. You
need someone to guide you through life.

I laughed and put my phone back in my purse, then put the
purse into a large drawer. Playtime was over. It was time to earn
my keep.

* * *

My cell phone buzzed in my purse as I was pulling into my
apartment complex that night. I fumbled to answer as I parked in
the first empty stall I could find. No numbered and labeled stalls
here. We just fought it out like gladiators.

"Hello?"

"Hello, dear." It was my mom.

I turned off my car, dropped the keys into my purse, and leaned
back in my seat. "Hi. How are you?"

"I'm good. I thought I'd check in and see how you're getting
settled in back home and how your first day of work went."

Honestly, it was nice of her to remember, although technically it
wasn't my first day. Still, I no longer worried over those details with my
family and just accepted what they could offer. I told her about my office
and the work I was doing. I mentioned that Kayla and I had talked about
looking for a new apartment, and it was like pushing a big red buzzer that
powered up Realtor Mom. I could practically see her face light up.

"That's great, honey. Your dad and I have never liked that little
apartment where you live. Can we help you find something?"

"I need to work out the ifs and whens with Kayla first, but
when we're ready I'll give you a call." My parents were pros, and
they'd care where I ended up, so why not? "Our budget won't be
big, though, Mom."

She made a scoffing noise. "I know you're just starting out in
your careers, Lucy. I work with all sorts of budgets."

"Great."

"We were hoping to have you and Daphne for dinner on
Wednesday night. Would you be free to come?"

Dinner invitations were never something I turned down, because cooking. "Sure."

"We're doing some showings until six p.m., so dinner will be at seven."

"Thanks for the invite."

"Of course. We're all looking forward to hearing about your adventures in Montana."

We said our goodbyes and I went inside, happy my mom had reached out but wishing I was still having adventures in Montana.

Chapter Nineteen

My parents' names are Jim and Judy Moore. They run the Moore Real Estate firm, and their slogan is "No one will move you Moore." It's horrid but successful. People laughing at your slogan are still people who have seen it and will remember it. They stay busy and credit it to their catchy phrase. I credit it to their bus stop benches and my mom's giant blonde bouffant hair sticking up off the top of taxi cabs around town. Regardless, they've always been gone when I was home and home when I was gone. That's the biz.

Daphne, four years older and starting to trend toward a blonde bouffant herself, took on parenting me in their absence. It's made a sisterly relationship hard to achieve, which is probably why Kayla had become my sister in all the ways that matter. Anyhow, Daphne works hard and serial dates all the high-rollers that come into the Bellagio. She has a strict code of ethics, though, which can be summed up with the phrase "dinner and done." That's it. She goes out to dinner with whomever invites her, is a charming and fun companion, and then when the check has been paid she heads her own way. She's also kind of grumpy, and I think I would be too if I went out to dinner almost every week with an old guy looking to make me into his next piece of arm candy.

"Hey, Daph," I said when I entered my parents' house in Henderson, a quiet suburb of Vegas.

"Luce." She was sitting on a couch, flipping through *People* magazine and didn't lift her eyes.

"How's work?" I sat down on the recliner next to the couch and flipped the leg up loudly, like I knew she hated.

177

She glanced my way, knowing I did it on purpose. "It's good. Busy."

"Mom and Dad not back from their showing yet?" I asked, looking at the giant clock that hung in the family room.

"Nope. I think dinner's in the slow cooker, though." She crossed her legs, and I noticed what she was wearing for the first time.

"Daph, are you wearing leggings?" I blurted out, not used to seeing her in anything but something crisp and professional.

She stuck out the leg she'd crossed and wiggled her toes. "They're so comfortable. I hate myself for wearing them, but I can't seem to stop. The second I get home from work I'm in these and a t-shirt." She was grinning in an abashed way, and I loved it.

"Well, your legs look amazing. Have you been working out, or just hiding them?"

Her smile grew, but she looked back down to her magazine and put her leg down. "Just nature, little sis."

"Dang, nature. I need some of that."

She chuckled. "You doing okay after your concussion?"

I thought about it. "Yeah. My ribs still ache a little if I sneeze or move just right, but overall I'm doing great."

"Good."

The scent of food was heavy in the air. We fell into silence while we waited for our parents to arrive. After another five minutes I flipped on the TV, stopping on *Jeopardy*.

"You know," I said to my sister, "I'm realizing that you don't have to be a genius to know these answers. You just need to live for a while and life teaches you stuff. I'm thinking I could go on the year I turn forty and give them a run for their money."

Daphne closed the magazine and put it on the coffee table. "Five bucks says you can't get ten of them right."

I put the legs of the recliner down and turned up the volume. "You're on."

By the time our parents finally showed at 7:25 we were both standing up, yelling at the TV. I was winning, Daphne hated it, and the bet had spiraled into something so silly we'd gotten the giggles over it. It was a mixture of laughter and fighting that fell to an abrupt stop when Dad picked up the forgotten remote and turned it off.

"What?" Daphne and I both yelled, spinning around.

"We just need five more minutes," she pleaded.

"Please, Daddy." I put my hands in prayer position and pouted out my bottom lip.

Dad glanced to Mom, who shrugged her shoulders. Dad turned it back on.

"Final Jeopardy," I cheered. "If I get this one right you owe me two cases of butterbeer from the Universal Hogwarts experience and three pantsuits of my choice from your closet."

"You'll never get it. No one ever gets these right."

"Stop it. The contestants get this right all the time."

Daphne harrumphed. "Yeah, the contestants. Not twenty-some-things at home trying to hustle their siblings."

"The category is Asian Geography," I read aloud. The room got quiet and my parents paused in setting the table to watch, caught up in the drama. "It's the only country that borders both the Caspian Sea and the Persian Gulf."

I scrunched up my nose and looked around at my family. Daphne shrugged and my parents both shook their heads. Okay. I could do this. What did I know about the Caspian Sea and Persian Gulf? I'll tell you what I didn't know . . . I had no idea they were considered part of the Asian continent, or whatever. My knowledge of the globe outside of North America was pretty slim. I needed to travel some more.

The countdown song came to an end and Daphne squealed. "You have to tell us your answer now!"

"I . . . I . . . " I sank down into the recliner. "I have no idea."

Daphne jumped up and down, pumping her fists in the air, blonde hair flying. "You owe me two jars of creamy peanut butter, two weekends of washing my car, and a gift card to the movies."

I clicked off the TV and pulled a face. "Man. I was so close to pulling it off."

"How would Daphne have gotten you butterbeer from Hogwarts?" Dad asked. "I thought that was a fake castle from a wizard book."

Daphne and I looked at each other and started laughing. "Don't worry about it," we said.

Mom called us in and we all took our assigned seats at the table, Mom and Dad at the heads and me and Daphne facing each other in the middle. Dad said grace and I smiled the whole time, thinking it had actually been pretty nice so far, reconnecting with my sister.

"Daphne, dear, when did you start wearing leggings?" Mom asked as she took her first bite of food.

Daphne's face shuttered a little. "Oh, they're mainly for exercise. I came straight from the gym." She eyed me and I wasn't about to give her away.

Dad nodded. "That's good. Exercise is good. As long as you're not wearing them to work. They're not very put together looking, you know." Daphne nodded again, shoveling more food in. "Hey, girls, what room are zombies afraid of?" Dad continued.

I groaned. "No, Dad, please."

He winked. "The *living* room. Get it? Because zombies hate the living?" He chuckled.

"Jim, you don't explain the joke after you tell it," Mom said. "That takes the fun out of it."

Daphne and I met eyes over the table and exchanged amused glances.

"Okay," Dad said. "Here's another. Want to know exactly where your property line is?" We all looked up. "Just watch your neighbor cut the grass."

I smiled, as did my sister, but Mom giggled. "Oh, Jim, that's too true. A neighbor will never cut even one blade over what he has to." Mom turned to me. "Lucy, tell us about Montana. How do you like your new boss? What was his property like? Do you think it'll ever come onto the market?"

For the rest of our meal my parents shot questions back and forth between Daph and me. It had always been that way. When we did manage to get together as a family, they sought all the information they could get out of us in the moment. Maybe it helped them feel like they knew what was happening in our lives if they could get a huge chunk of info every so often.

"Sounds like the Drake family is lovely," Mom said at last, standing to clear her place. "And Daniel, was it? The one who helped care for you after your injury?" I nodded. "He sounds just nice. Is he seeing someone?"

Dad stood too, taking mine and Daphne's plates to the kitchen. When their backs were turned I locked eyes with Daph and mouthed, "I'm dating him," while pointing at myself.

Her eyes grew large, and she leaned forward and whispered, "Are you going to tell them?"

"Should I?" I asked under my breath.

"Is he rich?"

At this I almost broke our silent exchange by laughing, but I kept it together. "Sort of? Maybe? I'm not sure, exactly. His family is, though."

"Don't tell them yet."

"What are you girls whispering about over there?" Mom came back to the table to get more dishes.

I looked up and gave her an innocent smile. "Just what brand of peanut butter Daph likes best."

Mom waved her hands. "Oh, you girls and your bets."

We jumped up and helped with the dishes. When the dishes were done I gave my parents a hug, thanked them for the food, and waved at Daphne as I headed out the door. Overall it hadn't been bad.

I called Daniel on the drive home, putting my phone on video call and snapping it into the dashboard holder I'd bought. I was hoping to someday have a car new enough so I could connect my phone to the car speakers, but for now this was working out, especially for doing a face-to-face call.

He picked up quickly, and the sight of his smiling handsomeness almost had me pulling over, unable to drive. It had been four days and I was lonely for him. I remembered how it felt to be held close against him, and it sounded as good as a bubble bath on a cold night.

"Hey, Red," he said.

"Red?" I laughed.

"Yeah. The lipstick."

"What is with you and nicknames? I'm the only person you do that with." I flipped on the blinker and turned out of my parents' neighborhood. When I realized he hadn't answered, I darted a look back at my screen to see if I'd dropped him. "Daniel? You still there?"

He was, and he was making a face. "Not sure if I'm ready to answer that yet."

"Well, now I'm intrigued and you have no choice but to spill it."

"Not to be too literal here, but I do have a choice. You're a thousand miles away and can't do a thing about it." He'd meant it as a joke, but it let a little air of my happy balloon. "I didn't mean to make you sad." His face came closer to the screen, and I wished I could use my finger to smooth the worry lines that had risen between his eyes.

"Of course you didn't. I just miss you tonight."

"Same," he replied. "What are you up to?"

I came to a stop sign and paused to make eye contact. "I just had dinner with my family where I lost a *Jeopardy* game to my sister, so I owe her peanut butter, car washes, and movie tickets."

He whistled. "Your family doesn't mess around with betting."

"Yeah." I giggled as I pushed the gas to get moving again. "If I'd have won she'd have had to fly to Hogwarts Universal experience and bring me home butterbeer, plus give me some of her pantsuits."

"You like butterbeer that much?"

I nonchalantly shrugged. "No idea. I've never had it."

I was rewarded with his hearty laugh, which made my heart reset and start to beat properly again. I still found myself a little confused about how I could feel so lonely for him when we hadn't admitted our feelings for each other until just a few days ago, but it was more than simply attraction and affection. He'd become my friend, and I missed him in all the ways I could miss a person.

"How is Alex treating you at work?" he asked.

I held up a finger and took a minute to merge onto the freeway to head back across town to my apartment. "Sorry. Had to drive for a minute."

"You realize a video conference while driving is a terrible idea, right?"

I nodded. "Yep." He grumbled something, but I hurried to keep talking over the top of what I was sure would be a lecture. He didn't care enough to make me hang up, after all. "Mr. Drake is polite as always. Pamela actually smiled at me the other day, so that's cool. Angie, the group admin assistant, is really friendly."

"You're back to calling him Mr. Drake?"

"Uh, yeah. He calls everyone Miss or Mister, never by their first names. So, I'm just fitting in."

"He's so pompous sometimes." He laughed, but it had no sting. "Dad didn't run his business that way."

I shrugged. "It's no biggie. I think it's probably good that he keeps me at arm's length. Otherwise I'd be pestering him about you all the time."

"That's not a bad idea. Maybe I need to get your sister's number. Or Kayla's?"

"No way. Right now you still think I have redeeming qualities. If you talk to them you'll find out the truth."

He was still for a second before replying. "I already know the truth, and I'm happy with who you are. Want me to share a truth with you?" Intrigued, I nodded for him to go on. "You want to know why I call you all those nicknames? Two reasons. First, to get your attention. And second, because you weren't ready to hear what I really wanted to be calling you."

My breath felt thick as the feeling in the car changed. "Well, you succeeded in getting my attention. What is it you really wanted to be calling me?"

"I'm still not sure you're ready."

"What's your measuring post, here? Because I feel really ready," I joked, trying to get feeling back in my fingertips.

Out of the corner of my eye I saw him look off to the side, but I couldn't see what had distracted him or hear what was being said.

"I'm so sorry, I have to run. We'll talk tomorrow?" he said in a businesslike tone, making it clear he wasn't alone.

I sent a smile as best I could while still driving. "No worries. Have a good night."

He leaned closer to the screen, so all I could see was his mouth, and said in a whisper, "Goodnight, sweetheart." I heard a click and my screen went black.

All I thought about the rest of the drive home was how much better it would have been if he'd called me sweetheart in person for the first time and then kissed me goodnight. Black screens and silent drives weren't doing a thing for me. I was left to feel the butterflies all on my own.

Chapter Twenty

It was mid-morning on Saturday. Kayla and I were a couple of miles into a trail that worked its way around Lake Mead, and she wasn't having it. I'd spent a week at home, and nature was impatiently calling to me. Kayla said Montana had ruined her perfectly good city-loving best friend, but I'd promised her that time out of the city would be good for the soul. Apparently, it wasn't good for the feet.

"My blisters are having babies," she half yelled as she sat down on a boulder and glared up at me, the pink streaks around her face seeming to glow in the sunlight.

"I told you to wear comfortable shoes, not new ones," I replied as I stepped off the side of the trail to stand near her.

"Well, your shoes are horrible."

I looked down at my tennis shoes. They were hating it, but they were soft on the inside, and that made all the difference. "They're nice to my feet." I put my hands on my hips, having said this at least a hundred times this morning.

She untied one of her sparkly athletic shoes and slipped her foot out, rubbing at her heel. "I thought there would be more cute guys here."

"Aside from the fact that guys don't keep an eye out for glittering shoes, we didn't come to flirt. We came to refresh our souls."

She grimaced. "My soul is super fresh already, and I did come to flirt. Everywhere I go, I go because I might be able to flirt. Work, flirt. Grocery store, flirt. Clothes shopping, flirt."

I laughed. "You must be exhausted from trying to make magic happen in the produce section."

She pulled off her sock to examine her toes. "You have a boy-friend, so you don't notice guys anymore. I still do."

I scoffed and scratched at my hair. It still felt strange to hear I had a boyfriend, when it was so new and he wasn't around. "My eyes didn't fall out. I can still tell if a guy is good looking or not."

She gestured to my shoes. "Your shoes tell a different story."

I looked down. "I'll have you know I wore these shoes in Montana and came away with a man. Your theory needs revamping."

I sat next to Kayla and stayed quiet, enjoying the view of the water in the distance while she grumbled about blisters and going septic from infection. The sun was shining and people were out making the most out of the early November temperatures. This was a time of year when tourists came, and the trail was no exception. Families were walking and cycling, people were jogging, and others were walking their dogs. It was a friendly feeling I didn't get much when I was surrounded by pavement.

While it was nowhere near as peaceful as The Lucky Wolf had been, it still gave off the same sense of settling down my heartbeat and realigning something inside of me. I missed the dense trees and tall wild grasses of Montana, but the bright blue water and almost purple colored hills around Lake Mead were pretty too.

"Have you ever waltzed?" I asked Kayla, a smile coming to my lips.

"Uh, no. But based on the way you just disappeared into your head, you have."

I nodded dreamily. "Yeah, in a barn with Daniel before I knew I was crazy about him. In fact, that might have been when I started falling."

Kayla interrupted my dreamy soul healing. "How come you never realized you hated the city until you went to the country?"

I looked at her. "I don't hate the city. I just learned that I enjoy nature too. I'm trying to figure out how to live in both places."

Her lips pinched. "I keep telling myself it's a phase and that you'll snap out of it."

I frowned. "This is the first time I've really spent outside since I got home. It's not like I looked for a lease on a cabin in the mountains and replaced all my toothbrushes with pine cones."

She faked an alarmed look. "You've brushed your teeth with pine cones?" I bumped her with my shoulder and she chuckled. "You know we could always just go to the Bellagio gardens if you need plants in your life."

I nodded thoughtfully. "They are incredible."

Kayla wiggled her foot. "But it's not the same?"

"It's inside."

"Okay." She put her sock and shoe back on and stood with a determined expression. "Let's get this over with, because this afternoon it's my turn to pick the activity and it's going to be city all the way."

I stood too. "This section of trail isn't a loop, so we can head back whenever you want."

"Now." She spun on her uninjured heel and began walking back toward the parking area, making me laugh with her exaggerated limping.

We walked for a while in the comfortable silence of two lifelong friends, setting a slower 'Kayla's feet are in terrible agony' pace. Eventually, though, conversation picked back up and we chatted about all the non-important things of life that add up to feeling connected to someone. New songs we'd discovered, a TV show everyone was talking about, if I could successfully raise a cactus—the consensus was no—and other odds and ends.

"So, I got paid yesterday," Kayla said as we neared the parking area where we'd left her car. "I did some number crunching, and it's looking good. Do you still want to apartment hunt?"

"Honestly, I keep expecting to be handed my check and then have someone jump out from behind an office plant and yell 'fooled you' in my face. It's not just the paycheck, but the whole job. Luck was definitely on my side, because even I know how completely unrealistic it is for me to be in a senior position."

"Are you needing more time to make sure you're not being pranked?"

I chuckled. "I'm still in. The Jim and Judy Moore Agency said they're happy to help with the search if we're interested."

Kayla's eyes lit up. "They always find the best places. How grown up would we be, taking a real estate agent around in search of properties?"

"I'm game if you are. I just need to tell Mom the budget and she'll line some things up."

We reached the car and Kayla clicked to unlock the doors, moaning in relief as she sat down on her seat and took off her shoes. "Yes, I'm driving without shoes and if we get pulled over I'll show the cop my blisters. He'll give me a giant award for bravery and probably a police escort home."

I held up my hands and shook my head. "I wasn't going to say a word."

My phone rang as we were pulling out of the parking area, and my stomach flipped when I saw Daniel's name on my screen requesting a video chat. I quickly answered and was rewarded with tingly toes when his smiling face appeared. His hair was wet, and I wanted to reach out and touch one of the dark water spots on his t-shirt. He looked relaxed and happy, and I wished we were in a hayloft sharing a box lunch. This time, that romantic setting wouldn't have gone to waste.

"Hey, how's my favorite city slicker?" he said, and I laughed.

"Sweaty. Me and Kayla just got done walking a trail around Lake Mead." I was suddenly flung forward when Kayla slammed on the brakes. Daniel asked what had happened at the same time I glared at my roomie. "What the heck, Kayla?"

She held up her hand for my phone. "I've missed every single one of your conversations, and other than some internet stalking I've never seen this guy. I need to look Daniel in the eye."

I looked back at my screen to see Daniel's eyes crinkle up. "I'm game," he said and I handed my phone to Kayla.

"Scoot back a little," she bossed him. "I need a better overview. Do you have something you can prop your phone on so I can see your whole body?"

I gasped. "Kayla, knock it off."

She sighed. "Fine. Let me get a look at your face at least."

Daniel sat quietly, but I could see the corners of his mouth tugging while Kayla completed her examination, asking him to turn his head back and forth a few times, then to hold the phone over his head so she could see how much of his hair he still had left. It was like watching a horror show. I couldn't keep my eyes off what she was doing.

"Hold on, Dan," she said once she was finished. She put her hand over the camera to block his view and mouthed to me, "He's seriously delicious, and this is on the phone where no one looks good. Comfortably attractive? You lied." Then she moved her hand and smiled at him. "You've passed the attractiveness test, which is very shallow and judgmental. Now we move on to the character questions. Here, Lucy, hold your phone while I drive."

She handed me my phone, but I continued gawking at her for a second while she got the car moving again.

"You don't have to do this," I said to Daniel. To Kayla I said, "He doesn't go by Dan."

Kayla smirked. "He does if he wants my blessing on this relationship."

Daniel laughed and I rolled my eyes. "Before you ask," I said to him, "yes, she's a little bossy."

"No wonder you handled living with Pamela so well," he joked.

"That's going to be a point off your score," Kayla inserted as she entered the flow of traffic. "I know about Pamela, and I'm nothing like her."

I made a face for Daniel to see, but Kayla caught me, and we all busted up laughing.

"My tyrant of a roomie needs a second to get us merged with traffic, so tell me about your day," I said while Kayla negotiated the heavier traffic making its way back toward Vegas.

He told me about the meals Willow had cooked, which was the way I always asked him to start our conversations. I made the appropriate 'poor me' and 'lucky you' sounds while he told me about stuffed French toast with real cream and strawberries. Even Kayla joined in with me, feeling sorry that all we had waiting for us at the apartment was a pre-made hoagie sandwich from the deli at our local grocery store. It wasn't going to be very good.

He also told me that breeding season was kicking off for his sheep in order to have lambing season in March or early April, and

I loved hearing him talk about something he so clearly enjoyed. He was a meticulous planner but also understood that nature had a way of doing what it was going to do regardless of anything he desired. I mentioned the possibility of being on-site for lambing, and he seemed excited about that idea. I nearly broke my face smiling because that meant he still expected us to be together four or five months from now.

Kayla took the conversation back over once we were flowing along on the freeway.

"Okay, Daniel," she said, with special emphasis on saying his entire name, "here's my first question. What song could you listen to every day for the rest of your life?"

I laughed as Daniel's face screwed up in thought. He hadn't expected that to be on her list, I was sure.

"'Don't Stop Believing' by Journey," he eventually said.

"Okay. What was the song you really thought but didn't say?" she asked.

His expression went a little slack and he glanced at me. I raised my eyebrows, and his voice was hesitant as he answered. "'What's Up?' by 4 Non Blondes."

Kayla nodded. "Interesting, but weird. Next question."

I laughed. "It's not weird."

Daniel and Kayla both said at the same time, "Yes, it is."

"So . . ." Kayla got the attention back on her. "What reality show would you want to be on?"

"Easy. One of the adventure racing ones that goes around the world and completes challenges."

I grinned. "That would be cool. Only I'd just come along to cheer for you and try different foods."

He nodded. "You're a woman of priorities."

"The good news is he didn't say *The Bachelor*, am I right?" Kayla said loudly out the side of her mouth to me, which cracked me up. "Next question. Who was your first crush?"

"Melissa Larkin, eighth grade. I had it bad. She had really long black hair, and sometimes it would fall over my desk so I couldn't write or anything, and I didn't care one bit." He put his hand over his heart. "Sadly, she was madly in love with Craig Parker and I didn't have a shot."

"So you know what heartbreak is like, then?" Kayla giggled. He nodded. "So far, you're doing well. What do you do when you can't sleep?"

He chuckled. "Would it be too much if I said I count sheep?"

Kayla and I joined in his amusement, and she agreed to let the question drop. She held up a finger to signal a pause in her interrogation as we exited the freeway back to surface streets. Once we were flowing again she resumed her questioning. "If you could only splurge on one thing, would it be house, car, clothes, or vacation?"

It was a good question, and I pondered it for myself while he did the same. Overall, I think I'd have to say house because that's where I spent most of my time, and my relationships and memories centered around home. I wondered what he would choose.

"Vacation," he replied after a few seconds. "Cars get beat up in my line of work, and so do clothes. I don't need a large, expensive home, but I'd love to travel the world and have some adventures along the way."

"Lucy would have said house, for the record," Kayla replied as she came to a stop at a red light.

His eyes shifted to me, and his smile was intimate somehow. "Oh, yeah?"

I bit my lip and nodded. "Yeah. I'd want a really great place so that my family would all want to get together."

He nodded. "Good to know."

"Lucy wants to one day have the family she doesn't have right now. They're nice, but they're distant. She's looking for cozy and committed."

I slapped at Kayla's arm. "Shut up," I said. I didn't need her sharing things for me.

"What? He's your boyfriend, right?"

My face warmed as I smiled. "Well, yeah," I said, and he pumped a fist in the air, which made something inside of me relax. Guess I wasn't the only one who'd been wondering what we were calling this. Thank you, Kayla, for shoving us into the conversation face first.

"Okay, last question because we're almost home and you guys want to talk without me around." Kayla turned into our apartment complex and found an open spot. "If you could be any animal for a day, what would you be?"

"Hmm, as an animal lover that's a tough one." He scratched at his chin, and I could hear the scruff of his beard. My fingertips tingled, remembering how that had felt under my hand. His eyes lit up and he looked right at me. "I'd be a wolf. A lucky wolf."

My heart rate sped up. "Living in a little cabin in the forest?"

"Exactly."

My smile grew and I wanted more than anything to touch him, kiss him, lean my head on his shoulder. This long distance thing was the worst. I finally had my first boyfriend, and this wasn't how I'd ever thought it would be.

Kayla turned off her car and opened her door. "Will you lock the doors when you're done?" I nodded. She leaned close to get back into the screen. "Bye. I guess I'll call you Daniel, then, because you passed. It was nice to meet you. Hopefully I'll see your actual face someday." Daniel nodded politely. "It goes without saying that if you hurt Lucy you'll answer to me?" He chuckled and nodded again, and she was gone.

"I'm sorry about that," I said, feeling oddly relieved that Kayla was gone, but also a little unsure of how he'd felt about her.

"She's fun," he said. "The pink in her hair is a nice touch." And just like that any worry was gone.

I launched into telling him all the details of the past few days, including that Kayla and I were going to be apartment hunting. That brought up the fact that I'd never taken him on a video tour of where I lived, so I made my way inside, showing him all the really impressive—sarcasm—gardens and lawns in the complex along the way. The tour of the apartment was brief, and he agreed that it hadn't been much of a sacrifice for me to live in the cabin on his property.

I sat down on my bed as we finished chatting, and when it was time for him to go take care of his land and animals I felt that familiar tightening in my throat. I didn't want to say goodbye, and I didn't want to show him videos of my life. I wanted us to be in the same place, wherever that happened to be. I kept hoping this would get easier, but instead it was like every day apart kept getting harder.

We hung up at the same time that Kayla walked into the room. I put the phone down and met her eyes, then burst into tears. Kayla immediately came to me and wrapped me in a hug, not needing me to explain what it was obvious I felt. Daniel was amazing, but being apart was not.

Chapter Twenty-One

The next two weeks were an absolute blur. On the Monday after our Lake Mead walk I'd called my mom and given her the go-ahead to search for apartments. By Wednesday we were searching, by Friday we'd found one we liked, and by the following Friday we were packing boxes to move in on Saturday. Yes, normally moving doesn't happen that fast, but my mom had found us a great price in a good location, and the stipulation was we sign the year-long lease agreement and be moved in by November twentieth or they'd give it to the next person on the list. Basically, my mom had pulled some strings to get us priority and we'd jumped. Whew!

It was a little bittersweet packing up our run-down mini apartment. On the bright side, it wasn't going to be a huge pain to move because we weren't moving the furniture. Still, it's amazing how many little things crawl out of the woodwork when you're packing. Things you haven't seen in ages suddenly reappear, or you find a random cupboard you'd forgotten about. With our busy day jobs we packed as much as we could in the evenings, but the reality is that you can't pack too early, because you still need the stuff to live.

"Toss this in the miscellaneous box," Kayla called from the kitchen, and I looked up from the living area in time to see a hot pad flying my way.

I snatched it mid-air and tossed it into a large box in the corner of the room that we'd started filling with random things. "Where was that?" I asked.

She laughed. "Under the microwave, along with seven tooth-picks and a packet of ramen seasoning."

I went back to my job of packing up the TV and blu-ray player and getting all the electronic cords wrapped up and labeled. "What are you most excited about with our new place?"

"Besides the obvious awesomeness of having our own bedrooms? I'm pretty pumped about a bathroom with a door between the vanity and the shower and toilet. We can both get ready at the same time."

I nodded. "Covered parking spots will be huge in the summer."

"A kitchen where we can pass by each other without standing sideways."

"Those separate bedrooms come with separate closets." I cheered.

"A dishwasher."

I stopped what I was doing and looked her way. "Oh my gosh, yes. A dishwasher."

She paused too, holding our toaster in her hand. "Laundry in the apartment. No more lugging baskets to the scary basement and then standing guard against thieves."

I grinned as she did a little jig and put the toaster in a box on the kitchen floor. It was going to be amazing to have so many amenities after years of living with the bare minimum. My parents had often said that sacrifice brings rewards, and I was suddenly so filled with excitement about nabbing some of those juicy rewards we'd worked so hard for.

Kayla turned on some music and we sang along, occasionally doing some dance moves as we stacked the filled boxes next to the front door. While we worked my mind wandered to where it always did these days—straight to Daniel. It had been an interesting two weeks for our relationship. At this point we'd been apart for longer than we'd officially been together. The nice thing about long distance is that when we talked on the phone we really talked, you know. We weren't distracted by other things, just entirely focused on each other. We'd shared a lot of things, told childhood stories, explored our families and their differences, and slowly something had shifted to where I was calling him before Kayla, telling him stories before Kayla, and confiding in him more than her. Kayla hadn't said anything, but I was sure she'd noticed. One of the best things about her was her independence. Kayla wasn't needy or clingy. Yet,

I was sure it stung a little to watch herself slowly being replaced as the number one in my world.

I'm going to be honest and say that after the initial high of admitting we were falling for each other in Montana, I'd come home and wondered if those feelings would fade. It would be so easy for me and Daniel to slip back into our normal lives and begin to grow apart. I'd sort of braced myself for it, a corner of my heart holding itself closed off in preparation for the logical end of this romance. Instead, I felt closer to him now as a deeper friendship had emerged. Which made life a little like a seesaw ride. High when we were talking, low when my life didn't include him.

As a rule, most of mine and Kayla's Friday nights involved pizza and a movie, but tonight when the clock struck midnight we stacked our last box of belongings next to the door and stood facing the pile, our hair and clothes a mess, and our energy sagging. Even Kayla, who seemed to have limitless resources of go-go juice, was beat.

"That's a much bigger stack than I'd expected." She grimaced. She reached up to tug her hair out of its ponytail and started massaging her scalp.

I tossed the packing tape dispenser onto the couch and sighed. "How many loads are we going to have to take in our little cars?" I mumbled.

"A lot. We shouldn't have turned down your parents' offer for help."

I nodded. We'd thought we could do it ourselves because we weren't taking anything other than boxes, a TV, and our microwave. It had seemed pointless to take up my parents' Saturday—their busiest workday—with something we could handle. I was regretting it a little bit just now.

"It's going to be a long day carrying it all down two flights, loading up our cars, driving across town, carrying it all up two flights, driving back . . ." I was doing a terrible job of pep-talking us.

"Do Jim and Judy have a truck we could at least borrow?"

I shook my head. "They drive sedans."

"Are their trunks bigger than ours?"

"Maybe, but they aren't going to take clients around in my little Civic or your two-door coupe."

She sighed and then rotated her shoulders and stood straight. "We're just tired right now. We've got this. After some good rest we'll be fine."

We went to our bedroom, where we'd left out some pillows and blankets to use on our bare mattresses. After our nightly routine of brushing teeth and washing faces—one at a time—we laid down and stared at our ceiling. Last night in Memoryville.

"Remember when you were taking a shower and the showerhead fell out of the wall when you tried to adjust it?" Kayla suddenly giggled.

I smiled. "Or when the water heater went out and the manager couldn't get to it for a few days, because he's a mean troll, so we boiled water for dishes and to take a warm bath. That took so many stupid pots of water."

"Or when you forgot to put water in your microwavable macaroni and cheese and burned it so bad that our apartment stunk for a week?"

I laughed. "And when I opened the microwave door all that yellow smoke billowed out. Bright yellow. I haven't eaten that stuff since, because the yellow smoke made me wonder what was in that macaroni."

"Oh my gosh, when I went to open the fridge and the door fell off?" She squealed with laughter and I joined in. It had been hysterical, the look on her face. She sighed as the laughter died. "We've had such a good run."

"Yeah. I think it should be a law that everyone needs to live in a dump at one time."

"School of life," she stated.

"Yeah."

We were silent for a minute, but I felt the shift in her and waited to see what she wanted to talk about.

"Are you worried about our new lease being for a year?" she asked.

I'd seen her cautious expression when we'd signed, and knew she was worried about what the future might hold for me. I turned my head to look at her. "Not at all."

"Things seem to be going really well with Daniel, and who knows what a year will bring."

I nodded. "Yeah, but things are going really well with my job too, and he lives in Montana. I can't really plan around what-ifs. What if he moves here, or I move there, or we lose our jobs, or there's a volcano that wipes out Vegas? I'm moving forward in ways that make me happy, and I'll figure out the speed bumps as they come."

"Are you calling Daniel a speed bump?" she teased.

"Yes." I pulled a face. "The dangerous kind."

*   *   *

We woke early the next morning, dressed in old jeans and raggedy too-big t-shirts, slapped our hair up into messy buns, and after a champion's breakfast of protein shakes we were once again standing in front of our pile of boxes. While it didn't look quite as daunting as it had at midnight, it still looked pretty big. It was going to be a long day.

"How do you want to do this?" I asked Kayla, knowing she'd probably already figured out a plan. That's how her mind worked.

I was right. She did have a plan. "Let's load your car first, because with four doors you have a little more room, and then see what's left." I nodded and she made a resigned face. "I'm not trying to be a whiner here, but I wish we had a truck and some muscle-bound workers. It's going to be a long day."

I filled my cheeks with air and let it out slowly. "Yep."

"I need to use the bathroom. My bladder is throwing a nervous fit."

Kayla walked into the bathroom just as my phone rang and I reached into my back pocket to snag it. Daniel's name popped up and my heart immediately lightened. He wasn't video calling, which was kind of unusual, but I was always happy to hear from him in any form.

I answered. "Hi, you."

"Hey, Luce. How's moving day looking?"

I flopped down onto our couch and laid my head back. "Honestly, long. We may have underestimated how much we have, and overestimated our muscles."

197

He sounded sympathetic when he replied, "I'm sorry. What can I do to help?"

I smiled to myself. "Nothing. Unless you can magically appear at my front door with a truck and some burly muscles."

"Done."

I laughed. "Right. I wish."

"No, really. Listen."

Three sharp raps sounded on our front door, and I frowned in confusion. "What . . ."

He laughed. "Don't believe me? Okay, once more."

Three more knocks had me sitting up straight and staring at the door. "Don't tease me. I can't take it today."

His voice dropped, warm and quiet. "Sweetheart, come answer the door."

I jumped up like lightning had struck, tossed my phone onto the couch, and tore the door open. There he was. My heart soared, my fingers felt shaky, and a blush of happiness rose on my face. He was here, real, in person and looking so amazing I thought I'd die on the spot. I didn't wait until he'd stepped in but rushed to him with my arms open and reached up to wrap them around his neck. His arms were immediately around me, pulling me against his strength and making my stomach flip. He lifted me up enough to get my feet off the ground and walked us through the door, closing it behind me and lowering me back down while I blubbered nonsense and tried to stop the tears of complete happiness that were trying to fall.

He nuzzled into the side of my neck. "It was too long. I couldn't wait anymore, and I thought maybe my girl could use some help moving."

"You were right on all counts," I replied as I wrapped my finger around a lock of his hair.

He pulled back enough to look into my eyes, and my stomach felt another swoop at the look on his face. I closed my eyes and leaned toward him. He came to me, and the last few weeks apart melted away as our mouths pressed together. I was no longer in my ratty Vegas apartment but in paradise. He felt so large and steady, and I just wanted to sink in and let him carry me for a while. He held me close, his palms pressing against my back while his mouth told me he'd missed me as much as I'd missed him. I moved one of my hands down to his chest where I could feel his heart beating along with mine. The kiss was like air to me, and I pushed up to get closer.

"Well, this is a surprise," Kayla's amused voice broke into our little reunion. "I hope you're Daniel, but I can't tell for sure because your face is all mashed up against Lucy's."

The kiss ended, but I couldn't bear to let go of him, and he didn't seem to be in a hurry to release me either. I leaned my head against the front of his shoulder and slid my arms down around his waist.

"Don't you have somewhere to be?" I grumped back to her.

She and Daniel laughed. He raised his head, and I knew he was smiling as he spoke. "Hi, Kayla. Nice to finally meet you in person."

"You're taller than I'd pictured," Kayla replied.

"Oh yeah?"

His hold on me relaxed, but his palms still rested lightly along my sides. I sighed, pressed one last kiss against his throat, and stood straight, stepping out of his embrace.

"You sure now how to kill a reunion," I smirked at my roomie.

She came forward with her hand out and Daniel shook it. "I sure hope you have a truck," she said.

"It's your lucky day," he replied, reaching into his pockets to pull out a set of keys. He held them in the air and wiggled them around. "Boy Scout motto, always be prepared."

"Were you a Boy Scout?" I asked.

"You're looking at an Eagle Scout." He bowed at the waist and Kayla and I chuckled.

"Well, Eagle Scout, we're glad you brought a truck. We also need muscles. Any ideas where we can find some?" Kayla joked.

Daniel surprised us both by pushing back the sleeves of his t-shirt and flexing his biceps. Oh, okay. I'd felt them under his shirt, but they were, you know, acceptable in a really swoony kind of way. Like if I were the wise man, I'd build my house upon that rock.

Kayla painted on a thoughtful look. "We'll need to see your abs too, before we make our final decision."

Daniel raised his eyebrows and started to lift up his shirt, prepared to take on the challenge, but I snagged the hem and tugged it back down. "Some things aren't for your viewing plea-sure, Kayla."

He glanced down at me and ran his thumb over my cheek. Making his voice unusually low he said, "These abs are all for you, baby."

I cracked up, which was his intent, and patted his stomach. "Please, cage the beast."

He nodded with a gleam in his eye and leaned down to press a butterfly light kiss on my smiling lips. "Fair warning," he whispered against them, "you may not be able to get rid of me."

I pressed a kiss back. "Good."

"All right." Kayla clapped her hands together. "Let's get this show on the road."

Chapter Twenty-Two

Sunlight, bright and white-ish, woke me the next morning. I reached up a hand to cover my face as I rolled to my side away from the light. It was strange, I thought, to be woken by sunlight. Did Kayla forget to close the blinds last night? I slitted open one eye, and it was then I remembered that I was in my new apartment, in my own room, sleeping on a blow-up air mattress on the floor. It was me who'd forgotten to close the blinds. I rolled onto my back and worked to open my other eye. It was so quiet. I was used to the sounds of Kayla dozing next to me and traffic outside of our window. This new apartment was in a more residential area, away from university living, and all I could really make out were the sounds of birds. It was a nice change.

Now that I was awake, that meant my bladder was too, because nature is cruel to women sometimes. I rolled off the slightly deflated mattress onto my hands and knees, pushed to standing, and shuffled out into the hallway bathroom. When I was finished, I pulled my hair up into a ponytail, brushed my teeth, splashed cold water on my face, and made my way to the kitchen for a drink. Normally, water on an empty stomach makes me feel like I've just gotten off a roller-coaster, which isn't exactly a nice feeling, but my throat was parched. I noticed a few aches in my back and neck as I walked, reminders of how much lifting and shoving we'd done the day before. Moving wasn't for pansies.

I stumbled to a stop when I reached the living space, noticing Daniel still asleep on the floor. In my early morning brain fog, I'd forgotten he had spent the night. We'd taken almost the entire day to lug things from one apartment to the next and get basically all moved in. Daniel was a workhorse, that was for sure, doing twice as much lifting and moving as Kayla and I had done. He'd stayed cheerful the entire time too, and it was one more thing I'd come to appreciate about him.

I'd had the forethought to borrow two blow-up air mattresses from my parents for Kayla and me to sleep on, but we didn't have any other furniture yet. That was today's goal. I'd offered to share a bed with Kayla and let Daniel have the other mattress, but he'd insisted we each celebrate our new living situation by sleeping in our own rooms. In the end, we'd made a pile of blankets and done our best to make the floor a little more comfortable, but I was guessing his back wouldn't feel great today.

I padded over and knelt next to him, just wanting to look. My eyes had strayed to him constantly yesterday, and his had done the same. It was like finding an oasis after a long journey through the desert. Every chance he'd gotten he'd touched me on the shoulder or back, pressed a quick kiss to my hair, held my hand, or lightly caressed my arm, until I was so filled with his energy and light that I felt recharged somehow.

His dark hair was messy and his t-shirt twisted. He still wore jeans, but his feet were bare. He was lying on his back with his arms over his head, and while I didn't want to disturb his sleep I did think maybe I needed to be close to him for a few more minutes. I lay down on my side and got as close as I could without actually touching him. He smelled like he always did, of fresh laundry and something almost citrusy. I imagined how it would be to see each other every day, and then clamped down on the same melancholy that thought always brought.

Daniel stretched, taking in a deep breath, and turned his head toward me, his eyes peeking open. "I could get used to waking up to this view," he said, his lips tugging up.

I spontaneously leaned forward and kissed him. Nothing major, but still enough to make me sigh. "I could get used to you carrying all the heavy stuff. Gallons of milk, laundry detergent, canned goods . . ."

He reached an arm around me and tugged me up against him. My head came to rest on his shoulder, and he wrapped his arm around my waist, his other hand reaching for mine and playing with my fingers as they rested against his chest. "You paint a romantic picture," he replied, his voice still raspy from sleep.

"On a scale of one to ten, how bad is your back going to hurt today after sleeping on my floor?"

He thought about it. "Hard to tell, but I'm guesstimating a three."

"That's all? Lucky."

"I've been attacked by sheep and bucked off horses. Your floor doesn't even make the list."

"I'll have you know that my air mattress was one of the orneriest beasts I've ever come across. I almost needed a cane to walk in here."

His chest rose on a laugh, and he squeezed my hand. "Did your air mattress deflate?"

"Don't they all?"

He nodded. "Yes. It's a marketing ploy to keep people buying new ones."

"Diabolical."

"Speaking of mattresses, I still have use of that rental truck today. Are you hoping to go do some furniture shopping?"

I nodded against his shoulder. "There's a few second hand stores we wanted to check out. We also need to find a used washer and dryer, but Kayla's been watching the community ads for those."

"Sounds good. I just need to swing by the house to get cleaned up, and I can come back for you in a little while."

"What house?"

He leaned his cheek against my head. "My parents' house. My luggage is there."

I blinked a few times and then lifted my head to meet his eyes. "You slept on my floor for no reason?"

He shook his head. "I slept on your floor for one very important reason. It's where you are."

I leaned down to kiss him again and felt his arm contract around me. My hand that had been against his chest now moved up to his shoulder as I leaned further, but before I could deepen it as much as I wanted to, he ended it and tucked my head back down. When I made a noise of complaint he ran a hand down my back.

"Love, I haven't brushed my teeth since yesterday morning, and I'm not looking to introduce you to my dragon breath at this point in our relationship."

I made a sound of amusement, relaxing against him again. "Maybe we're still in that smitten phase where we don't notice things like breath and body odor."

Now it was his turn to be amused. "Not a risk I'm taking."

"Fine."

"I'm proud of how maturely you handled that."

"I'm the most mature person I know."

We laid there, snuggled up in the stillness of the morning, chatting about this and that, until my hip complained about the lack of softness on the floor and his bladder came knocking. He stood first, reaching down a hand to help me up before making his way down the hall. Kayla came out of her room at the same time he disappeared into the bathroom, and she gave me a look as she came near.

"Don't we have a clause in our lease about men stealing our bathroom time?"

I grinned. "Good morning, roomie. How was your very own bedroom?"

"My mattress deflated."

I moved into the kitchen. "They always do."

* * *

Daniel had waved goodbye after one more hug and having to settle for a kiss on the cheek, and disappeared to wherever his parents' house was for an hour. When he'd come back to pick up me and Kayla, he'd been dressed casually in faded jeans and a gray t-shirt that looked like it had been washed a million times and wanted my nose to be pressed against it. We'd loaded into the truck and headed for the first second-hand store that had popped up on our search.

Furniture shopping with Daniel was not the party I expected it to be. It had been a bust. The couches looked like they'd been rescued from a seventies sitcom, there were no TV stands or dressers, and Daniel refused to even discuss the mattresses. In fact, he'd high-handedly stated that he was against second-hand mattresses at all and would just buy us both a bed. I'd pursed my lips and ignored the comment, fully intending to do what I'd already planned on doing, which was buy my own stuff.

The next store was more successful, even though Daniel had asked me to drive so that he could spend the entire fifteen minutes looking up reasons used mattresses shouldn't be purchased.

"I think it's pretty obvious that bodily fluids are the number-one reason not to buy used. Bedbugs are another huge worry. Mattresses are breeding grounds for them, and then they can move from there to couches, chairs, clothing. It's disgusting, really." He'd paused while scanning some more.

"Every time you sleep in a hotel, you're sleeping on somebody's used mattress," I'd argued. "When I stayed at your homestead I was sleeping on a used mattress."

He'd glanced at me and scrunched up his face. "You're right."

"I know."

It hadn't stopped him from going on. "A mattress can't be washed and sanitized. For all you know, that used mattress was sitting out back and got rained on and slept on by a stray dog before they brought it into the store. They cleaned it up, but the inside's rotten. Also, an old mattress will be shaped to whoever slept on it before you, so you'll be stuck in someone else's body print. Doesn't that bother you?"

I'd pulled into the parking lot of the second store and put the truck in park. "Daniel, all you've done is make my stomach queasy. It doesn't change the fact that I can't afford all new things. So thanks for planting those thoughts in my head that will just make sleeping harder . . . on my used mattress."

I'd tossed him the keys and stomped inside. I'd heard Kayla say something to him, but I wasn't sure what it was. Hopefully it was a gentle reminder that he wasn't in charge here.

Now here we were, looking at couches. Daniel hadn't said anything after my outburst and I was glad. I didn't like it when our differences in money came up. My gosh, here I was moving into my first real adult space, buying my first furniture, and feeling excited about standing on my own two feet. I didn't need him sucking the joy out.

"Do you think that pea green color will blend with the oak of our kitchen cabinets?" Kayla said, half seriously, pointing to a couch with a gray and green print.

"It'll remind us to eat our veggies," I replied. Daniel wandered off, some dressers seeming to catch his eye. "Good riddance," I muttered.

Kayla grinned. "I love it when you get all feisty."

"Well, am I wrong? He's being a little much about mattresses."

She nodded. "He just wants you to be safe from fluids, bed bugs, and feral animal fur."

"Yeah. He's not buying us beds, though. Can you imagine? I'm not a freeloader."

Kayla wandered over to another couch and I followed. "No, I agree with you there. He's not buying us anything. Unless it's dinner tonight. I can accept that charity all year long."

I was amused enough to smile. We stopped in front of a light blue, almost gray, couch. It was simple and looked clean. In silent agreement, we turned and both sat down. It wasn't too bad. We wiggled around, bounced in the seats, and leaned back. I gestured for Kayla to move, and I lay down to test its napping comfort level.

"I think we have a winner." I sat up.

Kayla looked at the tag. "Only three hundred dollars." She gave me a thumbs up. "I'll go get a sales person and have them mark it 'sold.' Then let's go check out lounge chairs."

"We're getting some chairs too?"

"Oh, yeah. It's the big time."

She wandered off, and I stayed seated so that no one else would get any ideas. It was easily the best couch in the place. Daniel was still investigating dressers and possibly TV tables when Kayla came back with the salesperson. He stuck a giant 'sold' sign on the couch and took down our info. We moved along to chairs, testing a bunch out and trying to match something to the blue-gray couch we were buying. Daniel continued to give us space. It was starting to feel a little like the cold shoulder treatment, which was not my favorite.

I jumped up from the seat I was testing. "I'll be back," I said.

Kayla's eyes looked toward him and then back to me. "Going to battle?"

I nodded, lips pursed, and walked to where he was opening and closing the drawers on an end table. He stood up straight when he heard me approach, his eyes wary.

"Are you giving me the silent treatment?" I asked.

"No. I'm giving you space, which is what I assumed you wanted." It was a reasonable response.

"Well, it felt like the silent treatment."

He tucked his hands in his pockets. "I obviously ticked you off over the mattress thing, so . . ."

"You're still the King of Stubbornville," I said.

His gaze softened as one side of his mouth tugged up, and I felt a wash of affection rush over me. He ruined it a little bit by saying, "I'll gladly wear the crown if it means saving you from a gross bed."

I shook my head and held up a hand. "Last night you slept on my floor. That was probably gross. Besides, I'm paying for the stuff, so you just have to let me make my choices."

"Luce . . ." He took his hands out of his pockets and reached for me, but I stepped back.

"No using your handsome, eye-candy, charm factory on me. I'm serious."

"So I'm just a truck and some muscle?" His eyes had taken on a glint, and I found it both intriguing and annoying.

"No. You're more than that. Those are just like the side dishes to the main course of who you are." His eyebrows dropped. Maybe he wasn't following my thought process there. "I mean to say, I'm glad you're here in a supportive role."

"Ah. Supportive. As in keep your opinions to yourself." His hands went back into his pockets.

"I'd want you here even if you didn't have a truck, okay?" I crossed my arms. "Are you feeling offended right now?" I asked and he nodded once. "Kind of like *I* was feeling offended when you wouldn't stop spouting off about how terrible used mattresses are, the whole time knowing I can't afford all new stuff?"

His expression shifted again, and now he was looking at me thoughtfully. "There are a few dressers over there that look good," he said.

I tilted my head to look him in the eye. "We're getting that couch." I pointed to the one with the giant sticker.

"It looks good."

"Yeah, it does." I uncrossed my arms and took the final step toward peace. "I saw you messing with a night stand over there. Did you at least get her name first?"

He grinned and reached for my hand, peace offering accepted. "Come on, I'll introduce you."

An hour later we were back in Daniel's truck, this time with him driving and no internet searches happening, headed back to our apartment. We'd been able to fit two lounge chairs and two dressers into the bed of the truck but would need to go back for another load, including the couch and two small night stands. Delivery wasn't part of the deal at second-hand stores. We still needed beds, a kitchen table and chairs, and a washer and dryer, but we'd made a great start to filling up the place.

Emptying the first load and getting it up to our second-floor apartment hadn't been too bad. With Daniel on one end and Kayla and I on the other, we'd navigated the stairs and turns and done it relatively quickly. The couch, however, wasn't going well. Plus, it was now past lunch time and I was probably fifteen minutes away from flipping over to hangry (hungry + angry = hangry).

We were jammed in the staircase landing and needed the couch to go up and over the railing. Daniel, bless his heart, was trying to call out instructions, but the arm of the couch kept smashing into his face and muffling his words. Then Kayla yelled out "pivot!" from the famous episode of *Friends*, and the two of us got the giggles. It's a scientific fact that you can't lift heavy objects while having a laughing fit or you'll pee your pants.

"Stop laughing and lift," Daniel called when his mouth was free again. Maybe he was getting hangry too.

"Okay, okay," Kayla and I agreed, shoving down on our laughter and reengaging our muscles.

"Turn left, yes, now lift right, yes . . ." Daniel was calling, but we weren't sure if he meant his left or ours and kept accidentally lifting the wrong side. "Your other left, your other right."

"There's a lot of grunting and inappropriate words coming from that end of the couch," Kayla whispered to me, which got me giggling again and I had to hold my legs together.

"Stop," I whispered. "I refuse to wet myself in front of Daniel." Seriously. If he couldn't kiss me with dragon breath, then urinary accidents were out of the question.

"What kind of guy doesn't love a girl who's willing to be vulnerable and honest about who she is?" Kayla cracked.

"One last lift, now," Daniel called over our chatter.

We heave-hoed and the couch made the turn so suddenly that I caught my foot and fell backwards on the stairs, my side of the couch landing in my lap. Kayla, luckily, still had hers in the air, but she was a step above me now.

"Ouch," I said. I pushed to stand and got my part of the couch lifted back up.

Nothing more was said as we navigated through the door of the apartment and set it down in our living space.

"Dibs on the bathroom," Kayla called, launching herself down the hallway.

Daniel was wiggling his arms and shoulders as he came to where I was standing rubbing my elbow. Guess it had gotten banged when I'd fallen. He reached for my arm, running warm fingers over the space that ached.

"Did you hurt yourself?" he asked. I nodded. "Do you need me to kiss it better?" It was meant as a joke, and I smiled.

"Yes. But it's hurts the most right here." I pointed to my lips, and his eyes shifted into something less playful.

He gathered me close. "What kind of monster doesn't know her left from right?" he asked, kissing me between words.

I wrapped my arms around him, running my fingers up his nape and into his soft waves of dark hair. "What kind of monster doesn't laugh when someone yells the word *pivot*?" I replied, pressing my mouth against his.

He pulled back with a smirk. "I was laughing, but I had a mouth full of couch so you couldn't hear it."

"Poor baby," I pouted. "Let me kiss that better."

And I did. Thoroughly.

Chapter Twenty-Three

Want to hear the best news? Daniel was going to be in town for a full week. This coming Thursday was Thanksgiving, and so he'd decided to make a long trip out of it. I'd assumed that we'd be saying goodbye again on Sunday afternoon when he came to have dinner and hang out, but when he'd kissed me goodnight—finally sleeping at his parents' house rather than on our floor—he'd told me the good news. I'd hardly been able to sleep last night, so thrilled to know I'd actually see Daniel in person for the next several nights. Don't even get me started on how we had Thursday through Saturday off work. He was flying home Sunday morning, and my head was already full of things we'd do together.

Drake Enterprises was running full steam ahead when I arrived Monday morning. I'd basically floated on over, barely remembering the drive as I painted romantic fantasies in my head. I greeted Corey at reception with a bright smile and Angie at her desk with the same winning look. They'd both offered me a 'good morning' in return. I entered my office and walked directly to the huge window wall. I was going to kick some butt this week. I felt alive, pumped, and totally ready to take on the world, knowing my man was out there in the same city I was currently gazing upon.

"Your skirt's on backwards." I turned around to see Pamela standing in the doorway. Her words finally registered, and I looked down at myself.

"Crud." She was right. I set my purse on my desk. "Do you mind closing my door for a second?" I asked.

She stepped into the room, and as soon as the door was closed I unzipped the back of my skirt enough to make it spin. The skirt was knee-length, dove gray, and cut slim with a cute, big bow that sat on one hip. Which meant the bow had been sitting on my rear end, and I have no idea how I hadn't noticed that I'd zipped it up the front instead of the back. At least my white blouse was tucked in and on the right way.

"Thanks," I said once I'd straightened myself out. "Guess my head was somewhere else this morning."

She nodded, and her expression wasn't unkind when she said, "Could have something to do with Daniel being in town."

I couldn't stop the beaming smile that filled my face. "Yes, and he'll be here through this coming weekend. We get an entire week together."

She offered a small smile in return. "That will be nice."

I shook my head and redirected my thoughts to the business world. "What can I help you with this morning?"

She set five blue file folders on my desk. Blue, in Alexander's world, was for stocks or portfolios that were middle performers; green, for the high performers; and red, for ones he wanted to cut, the low performers or money losers. Early in my employment I'd asked Pamela why Alexander still dealt with printed out sheets and file folders rather than sending it all electronically. She said he'd preferred to see my thoughts at a glance, rather than have to scroll through or click on comments. So, I was given a folder and a red marker where I circled, underlined, and wrote feedback. Everything at a glance. It was fine. His company, his game.

"These are giving Mr. Drake some problems. He initially thought they would do better and wants your thoughts on why they aren't, and if they need to be adjusted somehow," she said. I nodded. "He's also emailed you some classified information on a prospective client, someone who has requested our services but Mr. Drake isn't familiar with. He'd like you to look over the man's financials and see if he's someone we're interested in working with."

"Sounds great. I'll get right on those items."

She turned to leave, and I sat at my desk, intent on diving into work, but the day moved at a snail's pace. Knowing Daniel was actually out there within reach and that I had to wait until that pesky clock struck five before I could see him made the hours drag.

I tried to bury myself in numbers and predictions, but by three o'clock I was hitting a wall. The truth is, it was starting to make me mad. I wasn't the girl who lost her head. I was a hard worker, practical, dedicated. I was twenty-four years old, for heaven's sake. I wasn't sixteen sneaking peeks at my first crush in biology class. I stood and took a walk around the building, and then firmly took my brain in hand. Alexander deserved at least two productive hours out of me today.

When the clock ticked to 5:00 on the dot I was up and out, moving quickly through the office, down the elevator, and through the parking garage, not a minute to be wasted. I sped home, fingers crossed that today would be the day all the cops weren't paying close attention. I was going to meet Daniel at my place, and then we were going to dinner at my favorite Chinese restaurant. We were going on a real date, just the two of us, without friends or family around. I couldn't wait.

He'd taken the rental truck back on Sunday morning, but I recognized his parents' spare sedan that he'd been driving when I pulled into my parking lot. Anticipation thrummed through me as I hurried from my covered space and up the stairs to my apartment. This was better than Christmas.

Daniel stood from the couch when he heard me come in, and I ran my eyes over him. He looked so *city* down here, his clean jeans and cotton button-up shirt a far cry from the cowboy boots, flannel shirts, and cowboy hats of Montana. In all honesty, I may be a city girl, but I'd always choose the rugged cowboy who'd stolen my heart.

"You look amazing," he said as I came forward to give him a kiss. "That little bow on your hip is a nice touch."

I shimmied my hips and grinned. "Thanks."

His hands skimmed up and down my arms from shoulder to elbow and back. "Have I ever told you how gorgeous I think you are?" I tried to choke on a swallow, and shook my head. I understood he found me attractive, because kissing and stuff, but he'd never actually said the words. "Well, I should have. You're beautiful."

I looped my arms around his shoulders. "The feeling is mutual." He gave me a hug in return, but it was brief because I wanted to get to dating. "I'm going to change, and then we can do our couple thing tonight. Are you so excited for a real date?" I said as I pulled away and readjusted my glasses.

He planted a kiss on my hand, making me grin. "I am."

I kicked off my heels and picked them up, letting them dangle from my hand while I walked down the hall. I'd planned out my outfit already, during those long hours when I couldn't focus on work. I was going to change into black skinny jeans and a . . .

I froze just inside my bedroom, confused. There was a bed in there. As in bed frame, box spring, mattress, headboard, and sheets. No quilt or comforter, but still, a full on bed. I stepped back out and looked into Kayla's room. Same thing. So that made two beds, just missing comforters. I went back into my room and sat down on the bed. It was new. I could tell after having tried out no less than fifteen used mattresses over the weekend. The air mattress I'd been sleeping on was folded nicely next to the bed.

I wasn't sure how to feel. On the one hand, it was a relief to have a bed. On the other hand, it meant someone had been sneaky behind my back, and I wasn't a fan of that either. I took a minute to think it over, not wanting to go with an instant reaction but to approach it rationally.

"I don't hear any yelling, and nothing's been launched at my head. Does that mean you're not mad, or so mad that you're frozen in place?" Daniel entered the room, leaning against the door jamb.

I glanced at him. "I'm trying to decide how to feel."

"Please choose grateful, relieved, and looking forward to good sleep."

"What if my first reaction was that my boyfriend shouldn't be buying beds for me and my roommate?" I replied, but there was no anger in my voice.

He stepped closer. "You sound less thrilled than I'd hoped you would."

"Did you really expect ecstatic?" I ran a hand over the mattress.

"Not really."

I sighed. "I'm not sure what to say. I understand you have money, but I don't feel comfortable with you using it this way." He opened his mouth and took another step toward me, but I stopped him with a look. "On the other hand, it's so kind of you. It's really expensive to furnish a place, and this is really generous."

I heard the front door close seconds before Kayla's head popped into the bedroom. Whatever she'd been about to say died on her lips when she noticed the bed. "Wait." She disappeared and then came back with a huge smile on her face. "Beds!" she screamed, then disappeared again. I could hear her bouncing on hers. "This is amazing. Thank you, Daniel," she called down the hallway.

Daniel smiled at me and I laughed. "This is more the reaction I was hoping for."

"Well, I haven't been able to jump on mine yet, like she is."

He leaned forward and picked me up, making me squeal, before tossing me onto the mattress. I laughed out loud as I landed, cushioned by the best mattress I'd ever claimed as my own. I rolled around a few times and did a worm-like movement until I was satisfied. Then I sat up and gave him two thumbs up.

He reached out and grabbed my hands, tugging me toward him until my feet were dangling near his legs. "So, yes to the bed?" he asked, combing my hair away from my face and adjusting my glasses.

"Yes to the bed." I wrinkled up my nose.

"You know why I bought them, right?" he leaned forward until our noses were practically touching.

"Brownie points with Kayla?" I quipped.

"Wrong." He cupped his hands on either side of my neck, his thumbs landing lightly on my jaw, and pressed his lips to mine, whispering against them. "I love you, I love you, I love you."

I melted . . . I melted . . . I melted.

* * *

"What I need to know is, who taught you how to fold a t-shirt?" I said, pressing my lips to keep from laughing as I watched Daniel on the other side of a large folding table.

"My mom," he defended, laying the unidentifiable garment on top of the other mangled attempts.

"Mm-hmm. I'm guessing if your mom were here she'd be on my side."

Daniel held up another shirt and wagged it at me. "Please, dear professional folder, teach me."

I grinned and shook my head. "You're too set in your ways at the age of twenty-eight. There's nothing I can do to help you." I grabbed the shirt from his hand. "I think you'd better stick with matching up the socks."

We were in the laundry room of his parents' house, and let me just tell you that the place was unreal. When pressed, Daniel had admitted that it was over thirteen thousand square feet. It was done in clean, modern lines with natural tones and lots of windows, and I instantly loved the place. Sadly, we hadn't been able to find a washer and dryer for our apartment yet, and clothes needed washing. Kayla had been going to visit her family anyhow, so she schlepped along her dirty clothes. I'd been debating what to do myself when Daniel had offered his parents' house. That was a no-brainer for me. I was itching to see it.

"Sock duty? You wound my pride," he said, but he reached for a pair of socks.

"Did your parents buy this house when they moved to Las Vegas?" I asked, refolding a few items.

"Nope. We lived in another house a few miles away. They built this house about five years ago, the same time Dad retired and Alexander took over and I moved up to Montana." He sounded a little, I'm not sure, but like there were some *feelings* about all of it.

"You sound a little sad about it," I said, my eyes on my clothes, playing it super chill. "Did you want to get the company?"

"Not at all." The firmness in his tone confirmed that he had no interest in running Drake Enterprises. "Alex is well suited to it, and I'm happy with what I'm doing."

He took a deep breath. "To answer your question, it was hard enough when we left our simple life to move to Las Vegas, but I adjusted and had a good high school and college experience here. I even felt like my family was pretty normal in spite of my parents' money. Then, five years ago it felt like everything about our old life was dropped and a new life was created, so I think I just feel a little nostalgic. The houses I had grown up in were nothing like this one. This is kind of over the top. But it's a catch-22 because all that money also brought me the homestead, and I'm happy there."

It wasn't like I didn't know that, but somehow hearing it opened up a vulnerable place inside of me. Where did I fit? What did he think our future held? Was he expecting me to chase him to Montana? I didn't know, and I wasn't sure this was the time to ask. I didn't want to mess up our week together.

"So are you planning on the homestead being your forever place?" I asked. Again, trying to play it cool but realizing we were wandering into territory we hadn't really discussed yet.

"I don't know if I'll live in Montana forever."

Obviously this led me down the path of wondering where he'd go if he wasn't in Montana. What would he do? Did he see me in whatever future he was planning? Did he even have a plan?

I turned and gave him what I hoped was a winning smile. "I guess you never really know. Life is full of surprises."

"Like you." He grinned, bending to kiss my hair. "You were a big surprise."

Chapter Twenty-Four

P lease believe me when I tell you that I do not make a habit of eavesdropping, because my track record doesn't look good. Once again, on Wednesday afternoon, I found myself lurking around a corner and straining to hear what was being said. This time I was standing outside of Alexander's office and had apparently happened upon a Drake family meeting—about me.

"What, exactly, are your plans for Miss Moore, Daniel?" Mr. Robert Drake asked in a booming voice.

I mean, *come on*. The man talks like he's projecting off a theater stage. What was I supposed to do? I'd been walking down the hall with my stack of blue folders, all prepared to give Alexander my thoughts, but I froze a few feet away when I heard that sentence. Can you blame me? No one in the world wouldn't have done the same.

"As of now my only *plan* is to have her over for Thanksgiving dinner tomorrow," Daniel replied in a reserved tone.

I'd started to turn away, really. No, I'm lying. I had no intention of walking away from this conversation. But I did turn to make sure they couldn't see me, and when I did it was to lock eyes with Pamela, who was standing directly behind me. Her eyes looked as big as mine.

"They're talking about me," I whispered.

She nodded. "I heard."

"Eavesdropping is never a good idea. You almost never hear good things," I said.

She bit her lip and leaned up against the wall. "Do you want me to listen in and report the basics back to you?"

I smiled, both shocked and pleased at her offer, and shook my head. "I'd just pester you for details. It's best I hear it myself."

We fell silent again, listening in, while I hugged the folders to my chest like I had done with the paperback mystery books outside the study a month ago.

"Of course, she's welcome to dinner," Mrs. Drake's voice entered the discussion. "She's a lovely girl."

"Thanks, Mom," Daniel said while I gave her a silent cheer.

"We aren't discussing if she's a lovely girl or not." Mr. Drake was back. "We're discussing the fact that she's one of Alexander's employees and that Daniel has no right to mess with her."

"The last thing I'm doing is messing with her." Daniel's voice was sharp.

Alexander interceded. "Dad, Miss Moore is an independent person. She doesn't belong to me, or to you, or to Daniel. I'm not sure why this needs to be a conversation."

He sounded firm and I appreciated it. The next time I saw Alexander I was going to give him the highest five of his life, possibly even a high-ten.

Robert replied in an equally firm tone. "She's an employee of Drake Enterprises, which means this situation is filled with possible lawsuits: harassment, coercion, fraternization, to name a few."

"I'm not her boss, or her supervisor, or in any way involved with the company," Daniel argued.

"What if it goes south? What if she takes you to court claiming she was only dating you because she felt pressured into it while on a family retreat? You're the boss's brother and she feared for her job if she said no," Robert pressed.

The room fell silent, and both Pamela and I sucked in a breath. "I would never," I hissed between my teeth. I felt Pamela's hand on my shoulder—another shock, but a welcome one.

"It isn't like that," Daniel stated.

"Robert, you only have to see the two of them together to see they care about each other," Mrs. Drake said, her voice filled with reprimand.

"You should know that I encouraged Dan to pursue her," Alexander said into the quiet. "I could see he had genuine feelings for her, and I believe Miss Moore feels the same about him." His tone lightened when he said, "For the past two days she's floated around this office with her head in the clouds simply because he's in town."

Alexander was getting a double-high ten. High-twenty.

"Oh, Daniel, you've waited so long to find someone you care about," his mom said happily.

"I believe this takes us back to my original question," Mr. Drake plowed forward. "What are your plans for Miss Moore? Are you giving up Montana for her, walking away from everything we've set up there? You've already been away for five days, and ranchers—even sheep ranchers—don't get to take that amount of time off to chase a woman around the country."

"Robert, he's your son, not your employee. Have a little sympathy," Mrs. Drake said in a quiet undertone I almost didn't catch.

Ah. The confusion cleared and I heard the real question beneath it. The fact was that the Drake family counted on Daniel being the keeper of the homestead, and I threatened that. I was about to break eavesdropper code and waltz in there to inform them that I'd never ask that of Daniel, and that I took serious issue with Mr. Drake saying Daniel was chasing me around the country, but before I could move Daniel spoke.

"No, Dad. I'm not walking away from anything."

What did that mean? No, he wasn't giving up Montana? He wasn't sacrificing anything . . . for me? I . . . what else could it mean?

I turned and handed Pamela the blue folders I'd been holding, while my blood drained from my body and pooled around my feet. "Could you please see that Alexander gets these?"

"Lucy," she mumbled, "I don't think it's what it sounds like."

I shook my head, swallowed, and mustered a smile. "It doesn't matter what he meant. I shouldn't be listening in. I'll just chat with Daniel later."

She didn't offer me any more empty condolences, although, really, she'd been amazingly human there—and I didn't ask for any as I held my head high and walked back to my office.

Thirty minutes later I was snuggled up on my bed, the one Daniel had bought me, wearing leggings and a long sweater. After folding laundry we'd gone to pick out the new comforter that was currently wrapped clear up around my head so that only my face was showing as I laid on my side, looking out my window. I could see some palm leaves blowing lightly, which was the only thought that registered. My door was closed and I wasn't making any sound, so it wasn't surprising when Kayla came in and went about her business without disturbing me. Roomie code says to leave closed doors alone.

My phone chimed a little while later and I ignored it. It did, however, wake me from my funk and get my brain going again. I hashed and rehashed the conversation between Daniel and his family. What had Daniel said or done in front of them to make them worry that I'd tear him away from his ranching? I knew he loved Montana, and I wouldn't ask him to give that up. If things ever got serious between us we'd talk and compromise. Maybe I could work remotely from Montana. Maybe we could winter in Vegas while the sheep were resting in the colder months. Then we'd go back for lambing season and spend the summer months there. There were a million solutions, but it was too early to talk through them all now. Yet, it felt like Mr. Drake had not only addressed the elephant in the room, but he'd also pushed the elephant off the cliff, not giving us time to react.

I'd been fine with Robert Drake when we'd been in Montana. I hadn't tried to strike up a friendship or anything, but we'd been pleasant to each other. Now I was just mad. He was meddling and I didn't like it. Stereotypical rich man, pushing in to make sure his world stayed how he liked it. I thought all sorts of other mean thoughts about him, trying to pump myself up and out of the blues that had settled into my chest when Daniel had said he wasn't walking away from anything.

I hunkered deeper into my cocoon, imagining all the mean things I could do to get revenge. Admittedly, I'm not much of a revenge person, so the best I was coming up with were things like putting a red sock in with his white laundry or putting a 'please honk' note on the back of his car. Yes, they were hopeless ideas, but it didn't mean I wasn't enjoying imagining it all. A knock on the door pulled me out of my daydreams of delivering a pie with shaving cream rather than whipping cream on top. I didn't answer, waiting for footsteps to walk away. They didn't. Another knock, this one a little louder.

"Lucy, sweetheart, I know you're in there," Daniel called, and darn it if my heart rate didn't kick right up.

I ducked my head into my comforter. "No, I'm not."

"I saw your car outside."

"Other people drive Civics."

"Pamela pulled me into the women's restroom and I'm scarred for life," he said through the door.

I wanted to smile, but I also didn't want to smile. "Did your life flash before your eyes?"

"Yes. She told me something about an ancient art of war she's familiar with, and that she can immobilize a man with a single flick of her wrist. One word from you and I'd be chasing sheep in a wheelchair. It was terrifying."

I smiled under my covers. "Good."

"Can I come in, please?"

Might as well get this awkward conversation over with. "Yeah."

But I wasn't coming out of my cocoon. It was warm in here, and I didn't want to see his face in case he said things I didn't like. I didn't want him to know I was so in love with him that my heart would crack if he tried to pull the plug on our romance. I heard the click of my door opening and then closing again, and then shock ran up and down my entire body when he climbed into the bed beside me and cuddled up against my back. An arm draped over my side and he pulled me in close.

"Lucy Clementine Moore, what are you doing in here?"

"Hibernating," I replied, enjoying the feeling of being held.

"Not running away?"

"No. Plotting evil things."

He made a humming noise, and I felt it against my back and down through my toes. "Tell me what your evil plans are. I might want in."

I pulled the comforter down to my shoulders and was rewarded with a light kiss on the back of my head.

"The usual things. Toothpaste Oreos, cling wrap on the toilet."

"Classics."

"Yeah."

"When Pamela finished threatening my life she told me what you heard." He chuckled softly. "I kind of wish she'd lead with the part about you overhearing, because it took me a while to figure out why my legs would be coming out of my shoulder blades."

The thought of her calling him out lifted my spirits. "She was very un-robot-like for a minute there."

"Eavesdropping usually doesn't end well."

"Yeah. I tried to turn away, but your family has really interesting conversations about me. It would help if you could stop."

"Luce, you know I'd never walk away from you," he said softly and in a serious tone he rarely used. I shrugged, but it was a decoy shrug because I wanted him to go on. Sue me, I liked hearing it. "I'm serious. I'm in love with you. My dad doesn't get a choice in who I love, or what I decide to do."

"He's sort of your boss in a lot of different areas. One, your dad. Two, your actual boss. Three, he pays you money because he's your boss."

He squeezed my side and I stopped. "That's true, but he's not my boss-boss. I can quit anytime I want."

I nuzzled my head deeper into my pillow. "You can't quit being his son, and I don't think you want to quit being the guy who herds sheep. You love the ranch."

"What I said was, 'I'm not walking away from anything', and I'm not. Not you, not the homestead, not my own hopes and dreams. I'm keeping it all because I'm selfish that way."

At that I wiggled until I could roll over and face him. He scooted back a bit, putting some space between us, his arm falling to his own side of the bed. His expression was worried, in spite of the light tone he'd just used. I sat up and leaned against my headboard, and he did the same.

"Why the face?" I asked.

"I'm worried I might be committing patricide later tonight."

Man, I loved dating an English major. He came up with the best words. I nodded. "I can see that causing some stress."

He reached a hand over and pulled my glasses off, cleaning them on his t-shirt. "Please tell me that we're okay. I can't stand the idea that you were hurt by the things my dad said." He handed me my clean glasses and I put them back on.

"How do you propose to keep it all?" I asked, instead of answering.

"I don't know. So far things are going well, and I wasn't really ready to have this conversation yet." I tensed a little and he reached for my hand. "It's not because I don't want to. It's because I don't want to push you. I think I'd scare you off if you knew my real thoughts. You're only twenty-four, and you just scored your dream job and got into your first real apartment. Me, I've had years to make my choices and settle into life. I know what I want, but I'd never ask you to choose between me and your job, or between Montana and Vegas. What if next month you meet a total hottie down here and decide old sheepherders aren't to your liking?"

I bit my lip to keep from smiling. "Do you think that's likely to happen?"

"I don't know. You seem to fall pretty easily. You did fall for me, and I'm not much of a prize."

"You're *the* prize," I said.

That now familiar rush of love for him started at the top of my head and trickled through my entire body until I had to flex my toes. Daniel. How had I gotten so lucky? I pushed my comforter down to my waist and reached my arms out for him. He was there in a heartbeat, pulling me up against him and meeting my mouth with his. Only now that we were close could I feel the tension in his arms and shoulders. He'd truly been worried that I would turn away from him after what I'd overheard. I deepened the kiss, trying to express that he had nothing to fear from me. Heat swirled between us, making the comforter on my legs feel heavy. I put my hand on his cheek, softening the exchange before releasing him.

"I love you," I whispered, finally saying it out loud. I propped my forehead against his and closed my eyes, letting the things he'd said fill me with peace. After a few more heartbeats I sat up, scooted out from under the covers, and stood. "Do you want to come with me to buy some toothpaste and Oreos?" I asked.

He grinned, his eyes going back to their familiar playful look. "Make it double-stuffed and I'm in."

I walked around the bed to leave my room, but he met me at the door and placed his hands on my shoulders. "We're okay?"

I nodded and rose to my toes to give him one last sweet kiss. "Always."

Chapter Twenty-Five

Kayla and I went shopping on Black Friday—without Daniel, lesson learned—and found a washer and dryer on a killer deal. We'd searched for used ones and come up empty handed, which we were secretly okay with because it was kind of exciting to buy something new. We each paid for one of the appliances, with the agreement that we could buy each other out if the time came. Delivery wasn't available until the following Friday, but when Daniel heard, he decided this was an area he could help with. He rented a truck, again, and met us at the appliance store . . . with Alexander in tow.

Kayla was a wreck the second Alexander stepped out of the truck and the two men started walking toward us. I'm talking such a sweating mass of pre-teen style angst that I thought she'd actually faint. It was incredibly out of character for the girl who flirted her way through life.

"Get a grip," I hissed out of the side of my mouth.

"In person . . . better . . . so handsome . . . Pictures don't do him justice," she mumbled almost incoherently.

"He will not be interested in someone who can't pick her jaw up off the floor," I stated with a pointed look.

She took a deep breath and pulled herself together, mouth closed, face passive. Thank goodness. Not that I didn't get it. I'd been a fool over Alexander too. Boy, I hoped I hadn't looked like that. I probably had, though. He was impressive. Still, it was a little strange for Kayla to be all gaga over someone. She was confident and flirtatious with men from all walks of life, and it was usually the guy who acted flustered and incoherent. I tucked a smile back in, thinking that this might be fun to watch.

I walked over to meet them. Kayla did her best to glide along beside me, but she totally looked like she'd recently broken her toe and couldn't walk normally.

"Hey, guys." I met Daniel with a light kiss and gave Alexander a smile. "You've been recruited for muscle, I see," I teased.

Allow me to insert here that things had blown over, mostly, with the Drake family. I'd had Thanksgiving dinner with them the day before. Just the five of us. Thankfully everyone had treated me kindly, the food had been amazing, and I'd decided not to feed anyone my special toothpaste Oreos. I didn't want to risk coal in my stocking for Christmas, after all.

They didn't know that I knew that they'd talked to Daniel, so I played it cool and made sure Daniel had nothing to worry about from me. I'd chatted lightly with Priscilla in the kitchen, helped Daniel set the table, and even managed to thaw one more layer of frost off of Alexander, thanks to holding up under Mr. Drake's scrutiny.

Over pie I'd had an answer for all of Robert's financial wizardry questions, and before too long he'd relaxed back into his chair and watched me with a pensive gaze. Now he probably wanted me to marry Daniel and bring my amazing head for numbers into their hot as heck gene pool. Together we could create a race of super babies with looks and smarts.

Anyhow, now we were at the appliance store, and my best gal pal was trying to surreptitiously wipe sweat from her forehead. I didn't even want to know what was happening under her arms, but she was flapping them lightly like a bird testing out the wind pre-flight. I nudged her with my elbow and her arms fell. Thank heavens.

" I believe I have," Alexander replied to my comment about his muscles. He wasn't smiling, but his expression was relaxed.

"Yeah, we really needed extra brawn. Last time Daniel was left with a mouth full of couch and a bad attitude," I replied. "So thanks for coming."

At this Alexander's lips twitched. "I heard. He wasn't interested in a repeat performance." Then his eyes scrunched. "Oh, and I'm forbidden from using the word *pivot*?"

Kayla finally snapped out of her trance and we laughed. "I think it triggers him," she said.

Alexander spared her a glance, but I couldn't read what he thought of her. Probably nothing. His head was too full of business.

"Where are the machines?" Daniel asked.

"They're bringing them out," I replied, wanting to tease him about calling them machines rather than appliances.

"Check the boxes before we load them up," Alexander said. "I bought a set once, but they accidentally sent me home with two washers and the store was closed by the time I noticed."

"You mean you didn't have a delivery service handle it?" I dared to tease.

Alexander shook his head. "I'm not totally helpless."

"Agree to disagree." Daniel slapped his brother on the back.

Two store employees came out of the front doors with hand trucks and large boxes. They looked relieved when they saw Daniel and Alexander standing with us, which was insulting. Kayla and I weren't exactly wimps. We could heft things, too, even if we were secretly relieved to let the guys handle it. As it was, we stood to the side and let the four men put the boxes into the back of the truck—wouldn't want to get in the way. Just because I could, I watched Daniel appreciatively. It was a compliment, really, the way I freely ogled him working those muscles.

When they were done, they thanked the store employees and Alexander got in the passenger side of the truck. Daniel, however, turned my way with a teasing look on his face.

"Were you checking me out?" he asked.

I nodded with a sly smile. "I was and I liked it. I'm planning to do it again when you carry the 'machines' up the stairs at my complex." I did finger air quotes when I said the word *machines*.

He laughed and swooped in, picking me up off my feet and planting a warm, deep, delicious, and terribly short kiss on my lips. He set me down and spun me toward Kayla's car, where she was already waiting in the driver's seat. I walked on unsteady, but happy, legs and got into the passenger seat.

"You two are ridiculous," she said as she started the car, but there was a smile in her tone.

"So, Alexander Drake, huh?" I teased.

She got us going, following Daniel's rental truck to make sure nothing came loose, before replying. "I owe you and your ancestral gene pool an apology," she said. I chuckled, remembering how I'd told her my genes wanted to hook up with Alexander's genes. "Yeah, that's a pretty strong pull."

I patted her arm. "Don't worry, my genes have moved on to greener pastures. He's all yours. Feel free to sweat as much as you want."

"I was not sweating."

I scoffed. "Please. You looked like you'd just walked out of a waterfall."

We bantered back and forth for the entire drive back to our apartment, and in the end she admitted she'd maybe been a little bit caught off guard by him in real life.

The Drake brothers had the appliances up the stairs and through our apartment door with very little struggle. They seemed to inherently understand each other's directions, and I chalked it up to family stuff. They'd obviously had to work together in the past. The smooth progress didn't last, though. The dryer seemed determined to mortally wound Daniel as he lay on the floor next to it, trying to hook up the sharp, flexible venting. Alexander stood above him, his height allowing him to lean over the top of the dryer and give directions. From what I could tell, Daniel didn't want the directions but sort of needed them.

"This is like trying to fold a fitted sheet," Daniel snarled.

Having watched him fold laundry where even t-shirts had escaped his grasp, I couldn't imagine him attempting a fitted sheet. I spluttered out a laugh without meaning to.

"I heard that, Luce," he grumbled.

"Have you ever tried to fold a fitted sheet?" I asked.

"Once. It was hard."

Now Alexander smiled and Kalya laughed. Kayla was standing with me down the hallway, keeping much quieter than usual, and totally checking out Alexander every chance she had.

"Try bending the . . . yeah. Now clamp the . . . exactly. Tighten the . . . perfect," Alexander said.

"They speak a form of brother code that's even more epic than our roomie code," Kayla said. "It must have taken them years to perfect it. Is there hope for us?"

I shrugged. "I eak-spay ig-pay atin-lay," I said.

Kayla pinched her lips and rolled her eyes. "Yes, but they don't even have to complete their . . ."

"Sentences with each other. Hey . . ." I held up my hand for a high-five and she laughed. "We've got it, girl. Don't you . . ."

"Wonder?" she supplied.

"Yeeees . . ." I said very slowly, because *wonder* wasn't the word I'd been thinking. "I meant *worry,* but *wonder* can work too."

She put her palm to her forehead. "I've let down the team."

"Don't sweat it. After they leave we'll practice. Next time they won't have a . . ." I gestured at Kayla to finish the sentence.

"Chance."

I nodded. "Exactly." It was a lie. I'd wanted her to say 'clue.' They wouldn't have a clue what we were talking about. It didn't matter, though. The idea was the same.

"I don't have a *clue* what you're talking about right now," Daniel said as he let out a groan. There was a scraping noise and then, "Yes. I did it. Let me scoot out, Alex. Then you push it into place."

Daniel had used the word *clue*. He got me. It was cute.

Alexander pushed the dryer into place once Daniel was clear, and they went to work hooking up the water and gas lines. When both units were in place, Daniel suggested we give them a test run before we called it good. Kayla grabbed a few dirty towels and threw them in the washer. The four of us stood there shoulder to shoulder, listening for any signs of a problem. It looked good to me.

"You don't want to hang out for forty minutes and wait for towels to wash," I said to the guys—well, mostly Alexander, who never seemed comfortable in a social situation. "You're off the hook if you want."

Alexander looked to Daniel, who was about two inches from having his rear end planted on my couch.

"Oh." Daniel stood, once again picking up on Alexander's unsaid words. "Did you have somewhere else you needed to be?"

Alexander's smile was the same polite one he usually used. "I'm sorry, but I do."

I didn't know if it was a lie or not, and I didn't care. Either way, it had been kind of him to come help out.

I stuck out my hand and gave him a gratitude handshake. "Thanks for coming, Alexander. Daniel said way less bad words with you here."

"I said zero bad words last time," Daniel protested.

"The jury's out on that." Kayla giggled. "Some of your words were muffled and sounded a lot like things your mom wouldn't have liked."

Alexander headed toward the door. "I was happy to help. Sorry to drag Dan away."

I shook my head and walked them out. "It's okay. He'll be back. He's drawn to me like a moth to the flame, like metal to magnet, like . . ."

"A dog to its vomit," Kayla said under hear breath.

Alexander heard it, though, and his face opened up into a true smile. He laughed. He actually laughed. Kayla and I blinked in surprise, and not just because it was a blazingly incredible smile but because I'd never seen him like that. It didn't last long, just a few seconds, but I owed Kayla a fist bump when the guys were gone.

"All that aside," Daniel said, "we're having dinner with her family tonight. I'll pick you up at six?" he said to me.

I automatically leaned in when his fingertips brushed my waist, pulling me to him. "Yeah. Six is great." I kissed him. "Wear something nice so they'll like you."

Alexander headed down the stairs when Daniel leaned in for another quick kiss. "The theme of the night is eye candy?"

I smiled and nodded. "With a side of reformed rogue."

"Should I use a Highland accent?" He stepped back and out the door.

"For sure. It'll seal the deal."

"See you soon."

I waved and closed the door when he was halfway down the stairs. Eye candy, indeed.

* * *

As though the clock striking seven had sent my world into a parallel universe, my family was behaving very badly. It had started the moment we'd arrived. They hadn't meant to, and maybe some of it was my fault for not keeping them in my life loop, but dang they were coming across as a bunch of vultures with an IQ of ten, falling all over themselves to get in the good graces of the Drake family while simultaneously insulting them. It was bizarre, and I'd never thought to prepare Daniel for it because I'd never in a million years seen it coming. My parents were realtors, for the love, whose entire business model involved schmoozing people. My sister ran a department at the huge Bellagio casino, which dealt with wealthy people on the daily. They knew better. I'd thought, anyhow.

When we'd entered their house, it had smelled wonderful. My family tradition for the past several years had been to do Thanksgiving dinner on Black Friday. This was because Daphne had needed to work Thanksgiving Day quite a bit while climbing her way up the corporate ladder. It had worked for us, and tonight was no exception. Mom had gone all out, cooking all our favorites and a few extras. Once I'd told her I was dating Daniel Drake and had invited him to join us, she'd gone into a bit of a tailspin. I figured we could feed twenty people tonight. The thought of taking home leftovers made me very happy.

I'd made introductions, and everyone had gotten through that appropriately. Daniel was dressed to kill in dark slacks and a forest green sweater that made his eyes look like deep pools of 'I wanna jump in.' He made me drool as much as the food did. I'd remembered to bring Daphne her peanut butter and movie tickets, although I still needed to find a time to wash her car.

It began to unravel after the turkey was carved and we were passing our plates to Dad to serve us a piece.

"Does your family carve their own turkey?" Dad asked Daniel.

I scoffed. "Dad, come on."

"It's a fair question," Mom inserted. "I don't think the Drakes probably cook their own meals."

While I didn't know what happened in the daily life of Robert and Priscilla, I had eaten Thanksgiving with them and knew for a fact that Robert Drake had carved his own dang bird. I opened my mouth to reply, but Daniel's warm hand was on mine as he took over like a champ, with a self-deprecating smile.

"You're right, Mrs. Moore, my parents do have a cook. However, we didn't always have money, and there are some meals Mom still likes to cook herself. Thanksgiving is one of those times. My brother and I even pitch in. This year Mom loved having Lucy there to help out."

Mom shot Dad a satisfied look before smiling at Daniel. "Please call us Jim and Judy. Nothing formal around here."

"What do you do for the corporation?" Daphne asked him, dishing up some stuffing and passing it to me.

"I live and work in Montana on the family ranch."

Daphne looked up at him curiously. "I didn't realize you lived, like, permanently up there. I thought you were there for the family retreat, or whatever took Lucy up there."

He smiled again. "Nope. That's my brother, her boss, Alexander. He lives here in Vegas. I stay in Montana, running sheep and maintaining the acreage."

"I didn't realize the Drake family raised sheep," Daphne said while scooping out some green bean casserole.

My smile was tight as I yanked it out of her hands. "There are a lot of things you don't know about the Drake family."

"Mm. Apparently."

"How long have you been a shepherd?" Mom asked with a smile, like it was totally normal to have your baby girl bring home a rich sheep guy.

"Going on four years. Started with cattle, but decided that was a bigger operation than I was after. Sheep are more my speed." Daniel passed the green beans to Mom without taking any. In any other setting I'd have teased him about being allergic to green foods, but now wasn't the time.

Talk settled in and Daniel did a beautiful job of directing questions away from him and toward my family. It's always flattering to be asked about yourself, and they weren't the exception. My parents went on and on about their real estate business, sharing funny anecdotes that had us all laughing. Daphne threw in a few of her own, and she certainly saw her fair share of craziness in her line of work. However, it wasn't meant to last, as they circled around to Daniel again.

"Now, how long have you and Lucy been dating?" Dad asked, leaning back in his chair, his plate cleared of food.

I answered. "We met last month and have been an official couple for, what, a month now?"

Daniel nodded. "It seems like longer, but I guess that's all it's been."

"Well, don't go rushing into any big decisions." Dad smiled. "Lucy just got her new job, and it sounds like you're pretty busy with your sheep. There's plenty of time to see how things pan out. Long distance isn't easy on any relationship."

I smacked my lips, making a popping noise. "Thanks, Dad."

Mom patted my hand. "Don't get your insides in a knot. Daddy's got your best interest at heart." She leaned forward to see Daniel better around me. "Are you a provider, Daniel?"

I almost choked, waving my hands in between her and Daniel. "You do not get to ask him that," I nearly shouted in horror.

"Yeah, Mom." Daphne laughed. "You do know he's a Drake. Providing for her will not be a problem."

"Daphne," I cried, shifting my focus. "Stop. I can provide for myself."

"That's true, Lucy, but there are more ways to provide for someone than financially," Dad added calmly. "Emotional and mental support are every bit as important."

Daniel's expression was amused, and I prayed he wasn't faking that, because I was dying over here.

"I'm so sorry," I said to Daniel, taking his hand under the table. "They're usually house-trained."

Mom tsked. "What a thing to say, Lucy. We're your family. We just want to make sure you're not being taken advantage of."

Daniel squeezed my hand. "I'm afraid she is being taken advantage of. I take advantage of her kindness, intelligence, sense of humor, and loyalty every day. You've raised a lovely daughter. I consider myself very lucky."

And, my parents melted like ice cream on a sunny Vegas day. Daphne, however, twisted her mouth up in an effort not to laugh before shoveling in some mashed potatoes and chewing violently.

The rest of the meal went okay, but I wasn't able to eat another bite. I owed Daniel an apology for thinking his family was being nuts when they'd talked about me. It had been pretty darn mild in comparison, and none of it to my face. I owed him an even bigger apology for my idiotic and unbalanced family.

After dinner we played one round of charades—shoot me now—before we could make our escape. By the time we climbed in his car I was barely able to swallow down the huge lump of frustration in my throat. That frustration was quickly turned to misery as I replayed the conversation and his reactions to everything. He was a stinking saint, and I didn't deserve him. Okay, maybe *I* did, but my family didn't.

Tears were running down my face before I even noticed them. I wasn't sure why I was crying. It wasn't really like me to be an emotional wreck. But, it also wasn't like me to have a boyfriend and introduce him to the family. A lot had happened in the past weeks —getting a new job, going to Montana, meeting a man, moving— and maybe some of it was catching up to me through my tear ducts. I brushed at them, willing Daniel not to see, but of course he did

"Hey now, blue eyes, none of that." He reached over his free hand and wove his fingers through mine.

His voice and touch opened the flood gates. "They were horrible," I sobbed. "I feel humiliated. They're never like that."

"It's fine. They were just nervous around me."

I sniffled and took his hand in both of mine. "I judged your family so harshly, but now they come off looking like prize winners compared to the nut house we just left."

"Lucy, sweetheart, I wasn't upset. You kind of sprang me on them, and they were confused about how to act." I took in a shaky breath and nodded. "Don't waste your tears worrying about me, please."

"Do you want to just run away with me?" I sniffled.

"Yes. In a heartbeat."

I nodded and bit my lip to keep it from quivering again. "Where should we go?"

He squeezed my hand. "I have just the place."

Chapter Twenty-Six

Sunday night found me as bummed as I'd ever been. Kayla and I sat on our couch watching reruns of a popular comedy show, and I couldn't even laugh at some of the jokes that made this show what it was. The problem? Daniel was on a plane headed back to Montana, and he'd taken my heart with him. We'd had the best week ever experiencing things as an official couple—some fun, some awful, but all of them together.

I think my favorite night had been Friday night after my parents' dinner disaster. He'd driven me silently through the dark streets of Vegas, holding my hand and letting me control the radio, until we'd ended up at his parents' house.

"They're gone to Palm Springs for the next two weeks. We may as well make use of their paradise," he'd said.

The pool house had extra swimsuits for spontaneous guests, and we'd both found one that would fit. Then, we'd floated in the heated pool for hours. Most of the time we hadn't even talked. We'd just held hands from our floaties and watched the stars. It had felt good, and peaceful, and I'd allowed my frustrations with my family to wash away. Eventually, when I felt up to it, I'd told him a few more stories from my life and shared a few bucket list items that made him laugh. He'd done the same, and through that we'd found a new level of connection that had made today's goodbye ten times harder than the goodbye in Montana had been.

I ached.

Even worse, this entire apartment was now filled with memories of him. Sleeping on our floor that first night, moving in furniture, surprising us with beds, hooking up our washer and dryer. When

I'd tearfully mentioned the fact that the whole place reminded me of him, Daniel had laughed and pulled me close.

"Now you know how I've felt the past month. The homestead isn't the same without you there." He'd kissed me so softly, nothing like the heated exchanges we'd shared over the past few days. It had made more tears fall and he'd grinned, handing me one of his bandanas. Guess you couldn't quite leave the cowboy in Montana.

I still held that blue bandana in my hand, wrinkled from my tears last night. Today it was my comfort object, helping me feel like he wasn't quite so far away.

Kayla laughed beside me and I tuned back in to watch, finding a little humor in the show, but not enough to laugh.

"Okay, Luce, I'm giving you today to mope, but tomorrow you're going to have to dust yourself off and pull it together. You didn't break up. He's just gone back home. He'll call you tonight, and things will go back to normal."

Easy for her to say. "We ruined our normal by having this week together," I whined. "Now I really, really know what I'm missing out on."

"That might be true, but I know you wouldn't take it back." She reached out and patted my knee. "What do you need to eat to feel better?"

"Reese's peanut butter cups."

She nodded. "On it."

I heard her rummaging around in the cupboards, and she returned with my requested pity party food. I thanked her and munched a little, the peanut butter and chocolate reviving me enough to smile a few times, which was good progress.

"You know I'm not going to make it another month without seeing him, right?" I said while a new episode queued up.

"Yeah. I know. I'm figuring one of you is going to be on a plane within the week." Then she chuckled. "I did predict an engagement by Christmas, if you'll remember. I just got the wrong Drake brother."

I handed her a peanut butter cup and grinned, not even registering what she'd said about the engagement. I was stuck back on the idea of an airplane. There was no reason I couldn't go see him. I'd just need to talk to Alexander the next day about working remotely for a couple of days and make sure he was okay with that. A spark of hope fluttered inside. I held on to that spark and fanned it until it reminded my heart how to beat.

*   *   *

I looked at myself in the mirror the next morning and felt as Monday-ish as I'd ever felt. I was a little pale, but my leopard print glasses had arrived on Saturday night, and I'd done my hair in a professional-looking updo. I painted on my signature cherry red lipstick and tried out a few smiles. I'd put on a pink sleeveless, knee-length dress with a skinny black belt and some strappy heels. With a black jacket over it I looked good, which was my way of trying to feel good. Fake it 'til you make it.

Things were humming along like normal when I arrived at work. Corey and Angie were cheerful in their greetings, Pamela had given me an almost-smile rather than side-eye, and there were new blue folders on my desk for review. I settled in, willing myself to focus. This job was really important to me, I liked it, and I reminded myself once again that I wasn't going to lose my head over love.

Love is supposed to make you better, not a blubbering mass of weakness, I said to myself as I opened the first blue folder. Thankfully, work sucked me in and became a great escape from my loneliness, until around four o'clock when the phone on my desk beeped. Alexander's name popped up on the caller ID. I picked up quickly—he'd never called me directly.

"Mr. Drake, how can I help you?"

"Hey, Lucy, can you come down to my office, please?"

"Sure thing."

I kept my tone light, but I was immediately worried. He'd called rather than having Pamela do it. Then he'd called me Lucy instead of Miss Moore. Something was up, and I knew it was going to be related to Daniel because he wasn't being Mr. Business. I stood and walked nonchalantly down the hall to his office. No need to get any tongues wagging over my hustle.

I knocked on the door jamb, and he invited me in, asking me to close the door. I did as he asked while he stood from behind his desk and moved to a small sitting area near one of the large window walls.

"I'm guessing your mind is going a thousand miles a second wondering why I called you down," he said as I approached.

I nodded and clasped my hands together as I came to a stop in front of one of the matching leather chairs. "Yeah."

"First, take a seat, please." We sat and he didn't lean back like he usually did. "I don't want you to worry. Daniel is just fine." He reached out like he was thinking about patting my shoulder, but then his hand fell back in his lap. Still, that was progress, the fact he'd thought about possibly trying to comfort me. "He did have a small accident, though."

I was instantly tied in knots. "What happened? I just talked to him last night, and he was home and fine." I sat up straighter in my chair.

"He was out working on some farm equipment this morning in the barn, which he does in the winter, and well, to be honest I'm not totally sure of the particulars. My understanding is he was working on the riding lawn mower and one of the blades was loose, but he didn't realize that. When he tipped it up to access underneath, the blade fell off and his foot was cut pretty badly."

I gasped. "He cut off part of his foot?"

Alexander looked the most unsure I'd ever seen him. "I don't think so. No one said anything about missing toes."

"Missing toes?" I gasped.

He was quick to shake his head. "No, no. I'm saying he still has his toes."

This conversation was not going well. "Is he in the hospital?"

He shook his head. "They took him to the same clinic you went to. I'm told he's on his way home now. Steven is taking care of him."

"Steven?" I nearly shrieked, and had to take a deep breath. "Sorry. They didn't think a major wound required a hospital visit?"

"This is ranching country. The clinic sees farm accidents regularly."

"Well, maybe *they* do, but Daniel doesn't. He should have received the best possible care." I was suddenly angry, an unfortunate side effect of fear. "So they're just taking him home to rest up in the middle of nowhere?"

"Willow and Steven will keep a close eye on him to watch for infection. They'll keep him off his feet until the recovery is complete."

I nodded sarcastically. "Right. Because Daniel is the most cooperative person I know." I took a breath and looked away from Alexander and out the window while I grumbled under my breath. "Of all the asinine, ridiculous . . . what were they thinking—a clinic?" I cleared my throat and looked back to him. "Can he talk or is he loopy from pain medicine?"

"I have no doubt that as soon as he can talk, you'll be the first person he calls."

That did little to soothe my worries. How much pain was he in? Who really cared enough about him to make sure he was getting the rest he needed? Did he, or did he not have toes?

Willow and Steven already had busy jobs. They didn't have time to add nurse to the list. I crossed my legs and jiggled a foot while I thought about what to do and which homestead staff member I was going to murder first for not taking him straight to the hospital in that van ambulance thing.

"Lucy," Alexander called my attention back to him. "I'm assuming you'd like to go be with him?"

As soon as the words left his mouth, I realized he'd said out loud what I hadn't dared to. I had to bite my lips to keep tears from forming. I nodded. "Yeah."

"Then go. I've already had Pamela look into arranging a flight for tonight. Take the company laptop. You can work there remotely, and we'll play it by ear on your return."

I stood, and he did the same. "Really?"

"Yes."

"Thanks." I spun to head out the door. Guess that answered the working remotely question.

"Oh, and Lucy?" he called. I stopped and looked at him. "Pack warm. Montana isn't known for its palm trees and sunshine this time of year."

My first real smile of the day broke across my face, and I spontaneously walked to him and threw my arms around his waist. I could feel his shock in the way he tensed up, but after only a second he relaxed and patted me on the back. *How funny*, I thought. *I'm actually hugging Alexander.* Hugging Daniel felt about a trillion times better, for the record.

"Thank you," I said as I squeezed him and let go. "I owe you one."

He stepped back, doubling the distance between us, but his expression was mildly warmer than usual. "Just make sure my brother is okay."

I flew out of his office and stopped at Pamela's desk, where she handed me a one-way ticket on a flight that left in two hours. I thanked her as I jogged down to my office, not even trying to pretend I wasn't flustered and in a hurry. Angie asked if I was okay, and I gestured for her to follow me into my office. I gave her a brief explanation of what was going on while powering down my laptop and packing my things. When I finished she was silent, so I glanced up quickly.

"You're dating Mr. Drake's brother?" she said in awe.

"Oh, I thought it was common knowledge." I smiled.

"No. The hot one who was in here last week and works in Montana at their ranch?"

I nodded, possibly a little smugly—I'm only human. "Yeah. The hot one."

She gave me a sassy grin. "Nice."

She was right; it was nice. It was even nicer that I would see him before my head hit the pillow tonight.

* * *

I'd called Willow when I was waiting for my flight to take off, and she'd promised to have someone meet me in Great Falls to take me out to The Lucky Wolf. I didn't want to eat the cost of a rental when I wasn't sure how long I'd be there —yes, I will be cheap until the day I die. I'd typically feel a little bad about asking someone to drive three hours round trip this late at night, with no warning, but I was desperate to see Daniel and wouldn't sleep until I had.

Kayla had been amazing, leaving work early to help me pack and drop me off at the airport. I had no doubt that her boss, Graham, was going to be a total twit about it, which made me all the more grateful to her. When she'd walked in the door, I'd allowed myself to finally cry as I told her what was going on. I was worried, angry that I hadn't been there, terrified he wasn't getting good enough care. I finally understood why he'd been so overprotective when I'd gotten hurt. I got what he meant when he'd said he didn't trust anyone else to take care of me. That was exactly the feeling coursing through my entire body while I threw in all the warm weather clothing I'd originally packed two months ago.

Kayla had hugged me tightly when she'd dropped me off at the airport, telling me things would be okay and making me promise to keep her updated. I'd hugged her back, wiping at more tears that had leaked out and thinking how lucky I was to have someone who'd not once reminded me that this wasn't a fatal injury and that he really would be okay. She'd just let me have a total freak out and packed my toiletries.

The flight had felt like hours, my body tense the whole time. By the time we landed at 7:30 p.m. I was a ball of nerves. Willow herself picked me up in one of the farm trucks, apologizing that I'd had to wait for half an hour for her to get there. The roads were snowy and slow going, turning the usual ninety-minute drive into a full two hours. I was relieved to see her and gave her a warm hug, which she happily returned.

On the drive to the homestead she filled me in on the details. Daniel had been in the barn alone when it had happened. He'd torn off his coat to press to the wound and called her before calling 911. Willow had brought towels and called Steven in from the pasture where he'd been putting out extra feed for the sheep. Together they'd cut off his boot and elevated his foot while keeping pressure on it. Willow said that the cut was actually further in than just where the toes connect to the foot, so there would most likely be long-lasting nerve damage. She said he didn't say much, just laid there with his eyes closed, breathing hard through clenched teeth, and it had been devastating for her to watch. For a sliver of a moment I was grateful I hadn't had to witness that pain. I wasn't sure I could have handled seeing him like that.

When I questioned her about the choice to take him to the clinic, she reminded me of how long it had taken her to get to Great

Falls, and how long it was taking us to return. The clinic staff was well-versed in these types of situations, and time was a factor in cuts this deep, especially because of infection risks. After that, I settled in and accepted that they'd done the best they could. I thanked her for that, meaning it from the depths of my heart.

By the time we arrived at the homestead it was a little after ten p.m. Willow had helped me carry in my luggage and put it in the room inside the main house that Alexander used when he was in town. It was next door to Daniel's and would make it easier to hear him if he needed anything in the night. I thanked her and took a minute to freshen up in the en suite bathroom, washing my face and brushing my teeth. Finally I kicked off my shoes and crept down the hall in stocking feet to peek in on him. I was guessing he was drugged up and totally exhausted from the event, so I didn't expect him to be awake, but I needed to see for myself that he was breathing and alive.

The room was dark with a sliver of moonlight coming from a partially opened drape. He was laying on his back with his injured foot raised up on three pillows to keep it elevated. A light blanket covered him from his knees to his chest, and his strong arms were resting at his sides. I stepped closer, not wanting to disturb him, but to watch his chest rise and fall with his breathing. A breath I hadn't realized I'd been holding escaped when I saw him up close. His coloring looked okay. His face wasn't twisted up in pain. My shoulders relaxed, my stomach unclenched, and I nearly fell asleep standing right there.

I turned to go to my room but changed my mind when I noticed a recliner in the corner next to a bookcase and end table. Decision made, I pulled the throw blanket off the back of the chair and settled in to spend the night right there, which was exactly where I wanted to be.

Chapter Twenty-Seven

Luce?" A raspy, low voice pulled me out of the deep sleep I'd managed to fall into around three in the morning. I fought to open my eyes but then cringed when I felt the kink in my neck from sleeping partially sitting up. When I did manage to open them I was rewarded with Daniel laying in the early morning light, looking at me like I was an angel. How drugged up was this poor guy? His hair was wild, and his overnight beard growth made his jawline look shadowy. I thought he looked amazing.

I reached for the handle on the recliner and sat up, stretching as I did, the throw blanket falling to the floor. Mental note: jeans aren't comfy overnight clothing.

"Hey, cowboy," I said with a smile as I stood, feeling amused at calling him one of those nicknames he liked to throw around.

He blinked a few times, like he was pulling out of a dream and had thought I was a figment of his imagination. "You're really here?"

I walked to the side of the bed he was laying on and brushed my hand along his forehead, happy to notice it didn't feel feverish or clammy. "Yeah. I'm here."

He seemed to deflate a little as he closed his eyes. At first I was a little offended, because it seemed like that meant he was disappointed, but then his lips tugged up and he said, "Best medicine ever."

I liked that he thought of me as medicine, and I leaned down to press a kiss to his forehead. "How are you feeling?"

"Groggy, hungry, tired." He reached a hand out and wrapped it around my forearm. "Glad you're here."

"Good. I wasn't sure if you'd be mad that I was told or not."

At this he popped those brown, chocolate eyes open at me. "Why wouldn't I want you to know? I'd kill someone if you were hurt and I wasn't told."

I definitely liked that we were on the same page as far as that went. "Can I get you anything?"

"Some water, and it might be time for my pain medicine again." I could see the lines around his eyes pull tight and realized he must really be feeling it.

"I'll go check in with Steven and Willow. We'll get you sorted."

I hustled to the kitchen, where I figured Willow would have all the doctor's information that I needed. I was right. It was lined up next to the sink, and thankfully Willow was already in the kitchen to explain everything Steven had told her. The instructions were a little overwhelming. Daniel needed to be off his feet for three days, his foot elevated and iced every couple of hours. Antibiotics for infection twice a day. Pain meds every four hours for the first day and then backing off until he was weaned off after those three days. Daily bandage changes at home, which Willow said she'd help with. He could move to crutches after the three days, but still no weight on the foot. Sutures out on day ten back at the clinic. Meanwhile, the foot needed to stay dry and elevated periodically throughout the day. Willow said the clinic doctor told Steven that Daniel would be in a walking boot for at least a month, with limited activity for two.

I sighed and rolled my eyes. "Yeah, because Daniel's going to obey all those rules."

Willow agreed, handing me his medicine and a cup of water. "I think we can get him to stay off it for the three days. That was one heck of a wound and he knows it. However, once he's on crutches, well, watch out. He's going to be trying to ride and herd and all the other things he can't seem to live without."

I tried not to flinch too hard at the whole 'things he can't live without' part. It was a reminder that we still didn't know what we were doing long term in this relationship, and the possibility that we'd eventually stumble upon an impasse. What if he always wanted to live here and I never wanted to leave Vegas? It just felt like someone was going to have to give up something, and . . . it was more than I wanted to think about today. For now, it was good enough that I was here and that Alexander had been generous with allowing me to work remotely for a little while.

I got Daniel his drink and medicine, and promised him that some breakfast was coming soon. Then, I settled onto the recliner and asked him to tell me what had happened. I soon asked him to stop because it was too gory and I thought I had a pretty good grasp.

The meds started to kick in before breakfast had come, but in this case I thought sleep was what he needed most. I stood and covered him with the blanket, and closed the door behind me. I wasn't sure how long he'd sleep, but I planned to eat breakfast and shower, let Alexander know things were under control, and then check back in on Daniel. I hope it's not considered selfish to treat myself to one of Willow's delicious breakfasts while my boyfriend sleeps after an injury. Nah, I stand by the choice.

I went to the kitchen first, and Willow told me it would be another ten minutes. That was plenty of time to wash my body and put on fresh clothes. I only washed my hair every couple of days anyhow, and up here they wouldn't care if I ran around in a messy bun or ponytail.

I found my luggage where we'd left it last night, and got my first glimpse of Alexander's room. Like I'd mentioned before, the homestead was laid out in an H formation. On one side of the H were the mud room, laundry, kitchen, family room, and study. The other side of the H had four bedroom suites. The two sides were connected by an all-glass walkway, which also had the front door in the center of it with a large covered porch.

Alexander's room, while the same size and shape of Daniel's, was stark in comparison. All done in grays and blacks, it felt upscale and not lived in, which was fine by me, as I expected to not be doing much more than sleeping on that giant king-sized bed. My eyes grew large. The comforter was definitely real down, and it puffed so high I could believe it was filled with actual clouds. Yeah, sleeping here was not going to be a hardship.

The bathroom attached to Alexander's room had a big tub and an even bigger shower, which I gratefully stepped into, washing away the travel and the worry. I felt about a hundred times better when I finished and dressed in clean clothes, leaving my hair in the bun I'd used to keep it dry and skipping the make-up. With my glasses in place I checked the clock, happy to see it was just after 7:30 local time, which meant it was only 6:30 in Vegas and I had some time to eat before checking in with Alexander. I made my way back to the kitchen, where I could hear subdued voices.

Willow and the four permanent guys were seated and digging in to a giant stack of waffles. A variety of toppings were being passed around. It should have been a scene of Willy Wonka style joy, but the smiles were missing. It was understandable. They were worried about Daniel, and I wouldn't be surprised to find out that there was a little guilt over none of them having been there when it happened. Honestly, what could they have done anyhow?

"Hey, Lucy. How's Daniel?" Willow called as I entered the room fully and took a seat next to Jarrod.

Jarrod offered me a smile and I returned it.

"He's resting. I'll take him some breakfast when he wakes up. How are you all doing?" I asked, looking around and making eye contact with all of them. They all offered me a kind nod, but no one really spoke. "That good, huh?" That rustled up a few grins. "Listen, I feel like I walked into Eeyore's support group. None of you need to blame yourselves or think 'if only.' It's not helpful, and no one is to the blame. It's called an accident for a reason. If Daniel were here, he'd say the same thing." I looked at each of them again and felt a little buoyed by the color returning to their faces. "Now, pass me the whipped cream and tell me how I can help out around here while the boss is recovering."

* * *

Hindsight being what it is, I sort of wished I hadn't offered to take on a few of Daniel's easier chores while he was incapacitated. Not that I'm not a team player. I'm just allergic to chickens on a cellular level, and one of my jobs was to feed them. I smiled and nodded when Steven asked me to do it, asking him if it was okay for me to do a little bit of my real job first and then head outside at lunch time. Steven agreed.

After breakfast I spent my morning working in Daniel's room and seeing to his needs. He was changed into clean clothes—courtesy of Steven, let's not get ahead of ourselves—fed, drugged up, and resting peacefully. Willow brought me a sandwich mid-day, and I ate in his room while watching Daniel sleep, which was less creepy than it sounds.

I also spoke with both Alexander and Priscilla. My conversation with Alexander was short and informational only, with a stint about financial planning after we'd covered the topic of his brother's injury. My conversation with Priscilla, however, was all emotions and a lot of me promising that she didn't need to jump on a plane, that I could take care of him, and that I'd have him call her every day. Boy, she was an involved mother—and I tamped down on the jealousy. I may not have had a mom who would jump on a plane, but I was going to be the kind of mom who would. Daniel was lucky. And I felt lucky that she trusted me to take care of him.

Finally it was time for me to approach the chicken coop. I'd acted all chill when Jarrod had shown me where the feed was and what to do. He swore it was easy. All I had to do was take the bucket of feed, enter the coop, spread it around on the ground, and leave again. Sure. Easy. You know what else had been easy? Beau the rooster sneak attacking me. This time, however, I was prepared for him. I'd taken one of those metal garbage can lids from the barn and was holding it like a shield with the feed in the other hand. No, I did not think about how I'd sprinkle the feed one-handed, thank you very much. I was thinking only of fighting off any attacks.

I entered the pen stealthily, watching for any sign of Beau. The hens heard the clanking of the bucket and headed toward me. Jarrod had told me there were only two dozen chickens out there, but to my nervous eyes it looked like there were at least seventy of them.

I set the bucket on the ground, intending to gather handfuls and just chuck them in the general direction of the hen house, but as soon as the bucket was down all one million and five of the hens went after it. I kept reaching down to pick it back up, but my hands would get pecked by those greedy little things and I'd have to pull it back out. Oops. How bad was it for hens to eat too much feed? I decided to try to get my booted foot in there and scoot the bucket behind me while holding out the trash can lid shield until I could pick the bucket back up. It worked, and I gave myself a mini cheer as I picked up the bucket.

I looked around. Still no sign of Beau. I bravely set the lid on the ground and then launched a few large handfuls of feed away from me. The hens took the bait, clucking their way to the new piles of food. I grabbed the shield and made a smooth exit out of the pen. Then, I checked my hand for puncture wounds where I'd repeatedly been pecked. There were a couple of scratches, but I seemed to be okay.

Jarrod was in the barn when I went to put everything away. Thankfully, he didn't ask about the trash can lid, but he did ask if I was up to coming with him to feed the sheep out in the pasture. I glanced back at the house, not wanting to be away from Daniel too long, and not wanting to abuse Alexander's kindness. Still, I knew the animals' needs were high priority so I agreed. Turns out, it was my lucky day. All the hay was loaded into the back of a farm truck already. He just needed me to drive it and he'd toss the feed along the route.

I followed him, which is how I found myself driving through the snow for the first time in my life. There were good tracks, and the truck was in four-wheel drive, but it was still a different experience, as it would occasionally slip, or it would slide to a stop in a way I wasn't used to. It didn't take long before I was parking the truck back near the barn door. I hopped out and Jarrod met me as I came to a stop near the back.

He smiled at me, and I remembered how he used to blush and make a fool of himself. "Hold on. I have something for you." He opened the back door of the truck and leaned in, rummaging around for a second while I wondered what treat he had in store. He popped back out, carrying a dirty brown cowboy hat, which ended up sitting on top of my head. "You're becoming quite the ranch girl." He grinned. "Thought I'd better make it official by gifting you your first hat."

My first hat smelled like the backside of a mule and was too big, but my heart rose in happiness. "Thanks. Can it be washed?"

Jarrod laughed. "Yeah. Willow will give you some pointers."

I pushed my hat back from my forehead and made my way into the house, brushing hay and dust off of myself and leaving my boots in the mudroom before making my way into the kitchen.

"I have a hat," I announced to Willow.

She turned and took it all in. "The butterfly leaves her cocoon," she said with a chuckle.

"It needs a bath." I wrinkled my nose and pulled it off my head.

Willow gestured for me to follow her into the laundry room, where she taught me how to wash the hat. When it was sitting out to dry I headed to Daniel's room to check on him, nearly floating in happiness over the gift of a really trashed cowboy hat.

Maybe I could find happiness here in Montana. Maybe Daniel and I would be able to find middle ground and keep the things we couldn't live without.

When I arrived back in Daniel's room he was sitting up watching TV with a sandwich in his lap. Rats, I hadn't been there when he woke up. He turned to see me enter the room and gave me a once over.

"I like the way you've dressed up your hair with hay." He smiled.

I walked over to the mirror above his dresser and laughed at the three pieces of hay sticking out of my ponytail. "Just giving it a little zhuzh." I grinned at his reflection. "Did you get your medicine?"

"Yeah. Willow brought it with my sandwich. What have you been up to?"

I walked to the side of the bed he wasn't on and climbed up, facing him with my legs crossed. "I fed chickens and sheep." I nodded and pointed at myself. "Yes, I maybe took a shield with me, and yes, I've never driven in a snow-covered field before, but I did it."

He smiled, his eyes warm on my face. "I'm not surprised at all. The shield was a good idea."

"I'm full of them. So full of them that Jarrod gave me my own hat. Which is why my hair smells a little mildewy."

"Congrats. Was it the old one in the back of the white truck?" he asked with a glint in his eye. I nodded and he laughed. "Yeah, that would definitely make your hair smell."

I shrugged. "Willow helped me wash it, so it'll be as good as new."

He nodded, unconvinced, and changed the subject. "I wasn't really tuned in earlier when we talked, so tell me again what your plan is."

"For what?"

"How long are you staying, are you taking vacation time or working, what are you missing out on?"

I explained that Alexander had said I could work remotely and that I'd offered to pitch in around the homestead too, that my return was open-ended depending on what Daniel needed. I expected him to be happy, but instead his brow wrinkled up, and by the time I was finished he seemed upset.

"What's wrong?" I asked.

"I don't like you giving up your life for my injury."

I laughed, thinking he was being silly. "You'd do the same for me. In fact, you did when I fell down a mountain."

He pulled a face. "Yeah, and remember how you shoved me out the door to make sure the animals were okay every day?" I nodded. "Well, I don't want Alexander to be disappointed in your work because you're here. I have plenty of people to help me out."

My smile faded. "I also remember you saying that you didn't trust anyone else to care for me. The feeling is mutual."

"Yes, but you did let other people come during the hours I was working, and I was only allowed in at night when you thought my work was done."

Now it was my turn to make a face. "I'll bet you hated that. Now that the shoe is on the other foot, I have to say that was very mean of me."

"Lucy, you're not listening."

"Fine, what are you trying to say?"

His lips pinched. "I'm saying, maybe now that you can see I'll be okay, you should get back to your life."

I stood and put my hands on my hips, hurt beyond belief that he didn't realize *he* was my life and that there was nowhere else I could have possibly been right now. "You're being a hypocrite and very ungrateful, but I'll forgive you because you're also hurt and on medication. You're not going to get rid of me. I love you like the barnacle loves the boat, so good luck." I walked over and snatched my laptop off his desk and headed to his door. "You need a nap and I need to scrub hat goo out of my hair and do some work. We can talk again when you're ready to be reasonable."

"You should go home," he said firmly.

"Fat chance."

I slammed the door behind me and walked to the room I was using, slamming that door for good measure. He'd have to be the dimmest bulb on the Christmas tree to not realize he'd ticked me off, which was fine by me. I wasn't here at his whims. I was here on my own. My heart pounded as I gathered clean clothing and made my way to the luxurious bathroom. I scrubbed my body and hair a little more viciously than usual, which kind of helped with the mood. I dried and dressed, braided my wet hair, and sat at the desk in Alexander's room to get some work going. I worked furiously for a couple of hours until a timer on my phone beeped, signaling it was time for more pain meds for Daniel. I stood and stretched, feeling a little less mad and now just plain irritated.

Willow was in the kitchen prepping dinner, and I sniffed the air in a way that made her laugh. "I've missed you. My food has missed you," she stated.

I stood at soldierly attention. "You are the empress of food, and I salute you."

I filled a cup of water and got some pills together, and promised Willow I'd come back for a plate of food for Daniel. "In fact," I said halfway out the door, "I'll plan on eating in his room with him tonight."

"I'll miss watching your face while you eat," she teased.

"I'll have Daniel take a video for you."

I made my way down the hall, shoulders squared and preparing for a skirmish. Daniel wasn't going to win this one. I was here to stay until I was good and ready to leave, and no one could tell me otherwise. Not even Alexander. It was my choice.

I knocked on Daniel's door and pushed it open when he called. He was lying down again, his pinched face a sure sign he was ready for the pain relief I brought with me. My heart softened and my resolve to punch him in the throat faded. He needed my sympathy, not my salty words.

"Hey," I said as I crossed to the side of the bed. He pushed himself up to sitting, tugging down his t-shirt as it tried to ride up, and I hurried to put some pillows behind his back to support him. "I have your medicine. Looks like you're ready." I handed him the glass and the pills, and he took them down in one quick swallow.

"Thanks."

I took the glass from him after he'd emptied it. "Do you need any help with the bathroom or anything before I get your dinner?"

He shook his head, his eyes like lasers on me, their brown color even darker in the low light. "Lucy Moore, what am I going to do with you?"

I put the glass down and stood next to him. "The first step is to stop trying to boss me around. It never goes well."

"Agreed."

I reached for his hand, lacing my fingers through his. "Does that mean you're not telling me to go home after all?"

He grimaced and shook his head, giving my fingers a squeeze. "I was trying to be all noble or something, because I don't want you to give up things for me, but the truth is that I want you here. If I hadn't hurt my foot I'd have been flying back to you by the end of the week, guaranteed."

"Oh thank goodness, because I was all prepared to have one heck of a battle tonight." I smiled.

He used our joined hands to tug me toward him until our lips nearly touched. "How about we skip straight to the making up part then?"

I happily complied.

Chapter Twenty-Eight

Daniel graduated to crutches on Friday morning, and by lunch I'd already had to shoo him out of the laundry room and even caught him shuffling his way down to the barn. I wasn't very pleasant in my efforts to get him back to the house and onto a couch where he could rest with his foot up.

"You're a worse patient than I am." I scowled as I put a few pillows under his feet. "Seriously, you make Beau the rooster seem like a walk in the park."

His eyes danced, proving he found my efforts amusing. "What kind of saying is that, anyway? Strolling in the park is the epitome of relaxation? Shouldn't it be floating on a cloud, or licking an ice cream cone, or . . ."

I fluffed the pillow and walked away with a growl. "I have work to do."

He twisted around to look at me as I left the room. "What are you working on?"

"That one job that pays me." I blew him a kiss.

Saturday morning when I looked out my bedroom window, I saw him attempting to enter the chicken coop, using only one crutch and carrying the feed bucket. How was this possible? My alarm hadn't even gone off yet, and there he was dressed and trying to go about his day. I tugged on a jacket, slipped my feet into boots, and trudged out to get him. Of course, this meant feeding the chickens myself while he stood outside the coop and watched, but they no longer scared me and I hadn't seen the feathered monster all week.

"You're killing me here," I said as we headed back to the house. I was shivering, and tired still, and worried about the fact that he wouldn't slow down.

"I'm not a man who does well with sitting," he half apologized. "Do you want to play a card game?"

I held the front door open for him to negotiate through. "Babe. No. It's six-thirty in the morning."

"Does your brain only do games after a certain hour?" he asked.

Honestly? "Yes. My brain only does *everything* after a certain hour in the morning."

"Noted."

Sunday he was driving the truck with the hay bales for the sheep . . . and it was his right foot that had been injured. I didn't ask how he'd managed it, just told him to knock it off.

Monday he was tinkering with the small engines again in the barn when I took a break from work.

Tuesday he was trying to run a flat tire into the repair shop in town and fill up the extra gas cans. Was he using his left foot to work the gas pedal and brake? I wasn't sure I wanted to know.

Wednesday afternoon I watched out the window of my bedroom as he hobbled on his crutches toward the chicken coop again. I sighed and dropped my head on the desk where I was working, not even trying to stop him.

Thursday was suture removal day, at last. Then he could be in a boot and I could stop worrying so much about him banging his foot on something while he wandered the homestead. He had an appointment at the clinic at three, so at two o'clock I began the search for him. He wasn't in the house, or the chicken coop, and all the trucks were parked in their stalls. That left the barn. I entered, listening for sounds of him. I heard his voice talking and caught him in Ford's stall, brushing the big guy down while he chomped something in a bucket.

"What are you doing?" I asked.

"I just finished grooming Ginger, and now it's Ford's turn. He's been feeling neglected with me out of commission."

Just then Ford lifted his head to look at me and shifted sideways a bit. Daniel moved out of the way of those big hooves, and it occurred to me that one of those stupid horses could have stepped on his injured foot. I flipped. No, I exploded. I could barely breathe for all the anger flowing through me in that moment. The days and days of worry and begging him to be careful. The extra work I'd tried to share on the homestead while still managing my job. The flight I'd caught, the terror I'd felt, the dressing changes, the pain medicine and antibiotics, all so he could stand in that stall and brush his horse?

"Of all the idiotic things you've done this week, this is the worst," I said, my voice low and hard, my fists bunched at my side. "I can't believe you'd let me worry over you, and drop everything to be here for you, and then put yourself at risk this way. I'm done. I'm so done."

His face had gone slack. "Lucy, I'm just grooming Ford like I have hundreds of times."

"Yeah, and you've fixed lawn mowers hundreds of times too, but now you're healing from a major wound. All that big animal has to do is shift just right and he's standing on your foot. Your injured foot. The one you don't seem to remember you have." I turned and stormed off. "Your appointment is in forty-five minutes. I'll be in the truck."

I didn't wait even one second for him, but marched straight to his truck and climbed in the driver's side, tossing my purse onto the bench. I fumed, absolutely livid, and didn't bother trying to cool myself down. The second we got back from the doctor's appointment I was buying a plane ticket home. It was clear that my feelings and wishes were obsolete. I was out of here.

He came out a few minutes later, hobbling along on the crutches and climbed in the passenger seat. He looked at me, but I ignored him, cranking on the engine and pulling away from the barn to head out to the highway. I didn't say a word as we bounced along, but that didn't mean my thoughts were silent too. Oh, no. They were going in circles over how angry I was. We'd all been so happy that there'd been no signs of infection and that during the daily bandage changes everything appeared to be healing well. It was a miracle, because he couldn't be credited with helping in his own recovery.

"Lucy," he said when we finally reached the pavement and made the right turn away from Winterford and toward Juniper, the bigger town where the clinic was.

"No. Don't. I'm too mad at you right now." I slammed on the gas as we made the turn, and the truck bed slid around before getting traction.

He held onto the door but didn't say anything about my speed demon moment. "Look, I'm sorry, I . . ."

"I know," I interrupted rudely. "You're not a guy who can be tied down. You're bored."

"I didn't realize you felt this strongly about me taking it easy."

At this I finally did look his way. "Oh, sure. I can see how you'd be getting mixed messages from the way I chased you all over the stinking homestead and dragged you back into the house to prop up your foot." Sarcasm oozed out of every word. "You're in luck. After this you'll be in a boot, and I can stop playing bad cop all day long. I didn't sign up for that thankless position."

"I don't remember you being a model patient with your concussion," he grumped, clearly not enjoying being on the receiving end of my displeasure.

My teeth slammed together, and I spoke with a tense jaw. "Don't you dare compare the two. I may have whined and complained, but I didn't set foot out of that cabin until the doctor cleared me. This is not the same."

He looked out his window and I glared straight ahead, happy to not talk at all for the rest of the drive. When we arrived at the clinic I jumped out and went straight to the door, not bothering to help him with his crutches or, well, anything really. He was an independent man who couldn't be tied down. I did, however, hold the clinic door for him to pass through. If I'm being totally honest, it was because the clinic staff could see and I didn't want them to know I was on the verge of murdering my pig-headed boyfriend. I had appearances to keep up.

I sat on a seat and let Daniel check himself in. I was done playing nursemaid. I pulled out my phone and started looking up flights right then, and when he came to sit beside me I turned my phone screen away so he couldn't see what I was up to. I wasn't having *that* discussion right now. That could be saved for our fight on the drive back.

A nurse came out to call him back before too long, and I told him I'd be in the waiting room when he was done. It was the ulti-mate snub, and I knew it. His expression said he knew it too. I regretted it the moment he disappeared behind the door with the nurse. I might have been mad at him, but I shouldn't have left him on his own for the suture removal and all that went along with it. A stone settled in my stomach, and I walked up to the reception desk.

"I'm so sorry," I said to the smiling woman. "My boyfriend, Daniel, just got called back, but I wasn't able to make it at that moment. Can I please go back now?"

Thankfully she nodded and pushed a button to unlock the door and let me through. "He's in room three," she said, and I thanked her profusely.

When I found room three I knocked lightly on the door before letting myself in. He was laying on the exam table with his foot propped up and a nurse removing the bandages while asking him questions about fevers or discomfort. I met his eyes quickly, his look surprised and maybe a little grateful, before taking a chair and focusing entirely on the nurse. Being in here didn't mean I wasn't still furious, because I was. I was committed to not saying anything unless asked directly, and I held to it. If the nurse found the silence uncomfortable, or strange, she didn't let on, but went about her job cheerfully. Daniel's responses to her questions were short and he too remained stoic.

When she left, he looked over at me. "Thanks for being here," he said.

I nodded, still avoiding his eyes. Silence descended again, this one heavier than the last, until the doctor came into the room. It was Dr. Baxter, the same man who had helped me when I'd been hurt. He remembered me and asked how I was doing. I was polite and chatted with him for a minute before he turned his focus to Daniel. My vow of silence was back on, but I lis-tened closely to his instructions. Daniel would be getting his boot today, but he was still on restricted activity through Christ-mas. Daniel should come back the first week of January, and the doctor would look it over and make a decision about returning to full activity at that time.

Daniel thanked him, and I shook his hand as he left the room. The nurse came back in quickly to re-bandage his foot in some lighter cloth and get him settled in with the boot on his foot. She gave him instructions the whole time, showing him how to wrap his foot and get the boot on and off. I watched too, although part of me wondered why I was paying such close attention when I wasn't going to be around to make sure everything was done correctly. Daniel had proved he wasn't someone who needed looking after.

Just so we're clear here: I like strength and independence. I wouldn't be nearly as attracted to a needy man. However, I also appreciate using your brain and following doctor's orders, and not making your caregiver's life a royal pain.

When the nurse finished—and I was honestly surprised it hadn't involved her slipping him her number—we made our way out to the truck. Technically, the doctor said Daniel shouldn't be driving with the boot on, but I still paused next to the truck to see if he was going to let me drive. He walked to the passenger side, so I got in and drove us back.

"How long are you going to give me the silent treatment?" he asked once we were cruising along the highway.

"I'm not giving you the silent treatment. I'm protecting you from the yelling treatment," I replied.

"I think I'd rather have the yelling."

I glanced his way. His face was serious. "Fine. I'm ticked. You don't care at all how I feel about any of this, and that's like a kick in the face by a mule." He nodded, and I went on. "I've been banging my head against a wall for days and I'm tired, and angry, and my feelings are really hurt."

"Why are your feelings hurt?"

"Because when you can't be bothered to do what I'm asking you to do, which is nothing more than following the doctor's orders, it makes if feel like you don't care what I have to say. Like I'm pointless."

"You're not pointless."

I sighed, the anger beginning to fade into hurt. "I'm going home, Daniel. You don't need me here."

His head swung in my direction. "What?"

My voiced dropped as a feeling of dejection settled in. "I looked up flights while we were waiting at the clinic. There's one that leaves tomorrow morning. I'll have someone drive me to Great Falls."

"Sweetheart . . ."

I held up a hand. "It's okay. Willow explained to me how you can't live without your animals, and being outside, and taking care of the land. I get that, and I love that you've found your happy place. You're healed up enough to get back to most of it. So, I'll head home and get out of your way."

I swallowed hard, not wanting any of those queued up tears to fall. It was heartbreaking, feeling like I could barely function in Vegas, wishing so hard that he was there, but he didn't need me here at all.

"Are you serious?" His voice was stricken. "How can you think you're in my way?"

I didn't answer, just smiled sadly at him. I could tell his mind was churning, but he kept all his thoughts to himself, and I . . . well, I just kept on driving.

Chapter Twenty-Nine

I sat on the front steps of the cabin I'd shard with Pamela after dinner that night, wrapped in a blanket, just watching the moon. A light snow was falling, and the flakes seemed to be as large as silver dollars, each floating lightly down, but none of them touched me under the cover of the cabin roof. It was beautiful, and I was once again struck by how everything grew still under the blanket of snow.

Willow had announced at dinner that it was high time she decorated for Christmas, and invited me to join her the next night after work. I'd told her I was flying home in the morning and could feel the mood of the room plummet. Steven patted my back, while Jarrod offered me a sad smile. Willow had become strangely focused on her food, and Daniel had remained silent. The other two staff members, Colby and Gary, just kept eating, but I wasn't surprised—I'd never really interacted with them anyhow. I'd tried to keep up some light conversation, but people weren't dumb. They knew something had gone wrong.

I pondered all of it, sitting there in the silence. Where *had* it gone wrong, and what did this mean for mine and Daniel's relationship? This wasn't break-up material, was it? I mean, it was obvious that we were in the middle of our first real fight, but I kind of assumed I'd fly home and it would blow over. By this time next week we'd be laughing over the entire thing . . . right?

What if I was wrong? I'd never been in a serious relationship. Was flying home in the middle of a fight the kind of thing that shoved cracks in the foundation? Should I be seeking him out to make sure we were in a good place before I left? Did he realize how much I wanted to stay? Should I tell him that?

As if my fairy godmother was once again at work, Daniel's shape materialized around the side of the house. He was carrying another blanket and what looked like a thermos. Ooh, I hoped it was hot cocoa, because I was starting to get a little chilly. He limped along, adjusting to his boot, and came to where I was sitting. He looked at me with a question in his eyes. I scooted and he sat down.

"Willow thought you might like some cocoa." He handed me the thermos and I smiled.

"She thought right." I unscrewed the lid and took a sniff. "I'm sad to be leaving her cooking behind again."

He took a deep breath. "You know, the entire flight home from Vegas last week I alternated between kicking myself for leaving and trying to make myself believe that it was fine because we could have a solid long-distance relationship." He rubbed at his face. "The thing is, what is a *solid* long-distance relationship, and why is that something to shoot for?"

My stomach sank a little. "Meaning?"

"What I mean is, shouldn't we want more for our relationship than occasional visits and nightly phone calls?"

I thought about it and nodded, the dread disappearing. I could see what he meant. What was so great about being so far away from the one you loved? Eventually something would have to change, because staying long distance was never the end goal. It wasn't even my short-term goal, if I was being honest.

"I've had a lot of time to think this afternoon, and I've come to a few conclusions," he said, turning to face me more fully. "First, I'm sorry about everything. You're right. You dropped your life and jumped on a plane when I was hurt, and I shoved it back in your face by making it impossible to care for me. I hope you can forgive me."

The words cracked the last sheet of ice I'd packed around my heart. "I hope you can forgive me for losing my mind today."

I leaned forward to press a kiss to his mouth. Oh, my goodness it felt good to kiss him. I slid closer and pressed my lips more firmly against his. He was so delicious, and I felt electric currents running over my limbs.

He kissed me twice more, forgiveness granted on both sides, before continuing with what he'd come out here to say. "Second, you're dead wrong that I don't need you here. It's not really working for me to be apart from you. Before I'd even gotten into bed after my flight home last week I'd already looked at options to fly back to Vegas. I wouldn't have lasted one week away from you." He shook his head, seeming almost embarrassed to admit it. "I love you too much . . . and even more, I really like you. Being around you makes me happy."

I grinned as warmth flowed from my head down. "I was looking at flights too. In fact, we may have crossed paths in the air because I was heading here to see you the first chance I got."

He reached for me, pulling me into his arms and pressing his cheek to the top of my head. "You realize you're going to have to marry me, right?" he whispered against my hair.

A bazillion fireworks went off in my heart, and I clung to him. "Oh, yeah? How do you figure?"

"Lucy Moore, there's no way I can let you leave this place without me, and I'll never be able to leave Vegas without you again."

I was having a hard time sitting there and not jumping up and down. "You sound pretty serious."

"You should know before you make a decision that I'm looking for babies, and roots, and forever kind of stuff."

"Hmm." I pretended to think about it, but in reality my heart was pounding out *yes, yes, yes!*

He squeezed me tighter and kissed my hair. "What do you say? Think we can make a go of it?"

"It turns out I'm looking for those same things, and I think you're just the guy to make my dreams come true. So, yes, Daniel Drake. I will marry you."

"Guess you owe that fairy godmother of yours an apology," he said. "She knew what she was doing when she locked you outside of your car and set off the alarm."

I leaned slightly out of his hold on me and pressed my mouth against his before saying, "Every species has their specific mating call."

"Heaven help me," he said.

We hugged each other close as we laughed, the sound echoing through the night . . . a sound I hoped to hear every day for the rest of my life.

* * *

I never booked that flight home, and two nights later we stood looking at the Christmas tree we'd helped Willow set up the night before. It had been a night of celebration. Willow, Steven, Jarrod, Colby, and Gary had all been thrilled by the news of our engagement. We'd listened to Christmas music played too loud, and Willow had whipped up some peppermint cupcakes for a treat. Today we'd called our families to tell them the news, which had resulted in more jubilation and a lot of squealing from Priscilla. Robert had seemed oddly happy, and I figured it was because he could stop worrying about a lawsuit . . . or maybe because he really was hoping for those genius babies after all. The next generation of Drakes.

Now it was just the two of us in the house. Alone. Everyone else had gone to bed in their cabins. Daniel stood behind me, his arms wrapped around my shoulders as I leaned lightly against him, well aware that his balance was still a little off with the boot and recovering foot.

"Do you think Jim and Judy Moore will come down from the high of finding out their baby is marrying into *the* Drake family?" he teased, his breath warm against my ear.

I shook my head. "Don't be surprised if their ads go from taxi cabs to billboards with a photo of you." I laughed. "And if we don't have the wedding at the Bellagio, then I think Daphne will disown me."

"I can think of worse places to get married."

"How do you think our two moms are going to get along?" I asked curiously.

He leaned down and pressed a kiss along my neck, making my fingertips tingle. I leaned my head back against his shoulder to give him better access. He could keep doing that and my holidays would definitely be merry and bright. "I think we can distract them by talking about all the babies we're going to have."

"Mm. How many do you want?" I asked, goose bumps racing over my arms.

He moved his mouth to just under my ear. "A dozen should do it."

"That's a no from me. How about two?"

"Two dozen?" he said in mock horror, pulling his lips away from my neck.

"Stop it. I meant two total and you know it."

"Didn't you ever wish there were more of you? Another sibling for the days you hated Daphne?" he teased. "Because let me tell you, there were a few years there where Alex was not my favorite."

"Okay. Three."

He made a sound of disagreement. "But then someone always has to ride alone at Disneyland." I stepped out of his arms and turned to face him. He made a sad face. "Come back."

"Now that I know you want twelve children, I'm rethinking this engagement," I said.

"It was a jumping-off point in negotiations." He tucked his hands into his pockets.

"Who starts at twelve when talking about kids?" I laughed. "You'll notice I started at two."

"I like to shoot for the stars."

I stepped up to wrap my arms around his shoulders. "That explains why you went after me. I'm about as good as it gets."

His own arms wove around my hips and tugged me close. "Absolutely."

I kissed him, loving the feel of his lips against mine and wanting to pinch myself over the fact that I got to kiss him every day for the rest of forever. His fingertips pressed into my lower back, telling me he felt lucky too. When we pulled apart I took his hand and led him to the couch, where he sat and I took a seat on his lap, snuggling in against his strength.

"Now, for the hard stuff. Where are we going to live?" I asked. I'd been thinking about this a lot and still didn't have a perfect solution. "Everyone is going to start asking us, and I don't want to have to hem and haw and talk crazy because we don't have an answer."

"That's easy," he replied, wrapping an arm around my knees. "Together."

"Be serious. I need to talk with Alexander."

"I am serious. We're going to live together. No more long distance anything."

"I appreciate the sentiment, and totally agree, but my boss doesn't want to hear 'I'll be living wherever your brother lives' as my official statement."

He grew quiet, absentmindedly swirling a strand of my hair around one finger while I soaked in the setting of Christmas lights and the scent of pine. It really was so cozy here. Of course, a lot of that had to do with his lap and the fact I wanted to sit there all night.

"Okay. I want you to hear me out before arguing," he said in a firm tone that actually made me smile.

"You just automatically assume I'm going to argue? I'm the picture of flexibility." I fake pouted. He lightly pinched my side, which made me squeak. "Fine, fine. I'm listening with an open mind."

"I've waited a long time for this. Actually, I wasn't sure I'd ever find someone. Winterford is a small place, and ranch life doesn't make dating easy. Now that you're in my life I'm never going to risk losing you. We'll live wherever you'll be the happiest. If that's Vegas, then I'll sell the sheep and this place can return to more of a vacation home. If you want to live here, we'll try to convince Alexander to let you work remotely. If you want a mixture of the two, we can hope to figure out a rotation of some sort, although that's not my first choice. I don't see how we can realistically maintain a full life in both places."

My initial reaction was a mixture of pure love and irritation. "Why do you get to be the martyr? I don't want all that pressure of deciding your future. Maybe you should decide where we live."

He grinned and moved his hand to the back of my head, where his fingers weaved through my dark hair until they were up against my scalp. "No arguing, remember?" he said as his fingers lightly played in a soothing way.

I wrinkled my nose. "Not arguing. I just don't want you to make all the sacrifices. You love it here. What would you do if you sold it all and moved to Vegas?"

"I'd live with my gorgeous wife and put my English degree to use somehow. Probably teaching. There are always teaching jobs available."

I bit my lip and turned to look at the twinkling Christmas lights while I thought. He squeezed my knees, and I settled down further, resting my head on his shoulder. Behind the giant pine I could see the moon reflecting off the snow and the mountaintops in the distance. I could hear crickets, and picture the soft clucking of the hens and the shuffling of the horses in their stalls. In a lot of ways it felt like my real life, my real heart, had started the moment I'd climbed off the top of my rental car and onto the back of Daniel's horse and ridden into new territory. This place had gotten under my skin in a major way. Yes, even though the temperatures were a little frigid for several months of the year.

I felt the rise and fall of Daniel's breathing against my side and soaked in the peace that he always carried with him. For the first time, I understood that a lot of that peace came from living in a peaceful place. I couldn't take that from him, in spite of his willingness to leave it all behind. Of the two of us, my job was the only one that could be done remotely. There was no such thing as a video meeting for lambing season. Marriage and having a strong relationship would require sacrifice, but I'd never be happy knowing I'd plucked him from this place and stuck him in the hustle of Vegas.

"I want to live here," I whispered, almost afraid to say it out loud. Yet, as soon as the words left my mouth a warmth crawled into my chest that confirmed my thoughts.

"Are you sure?" he asked. I felt the way his body seemed to stop breathing and tense up, like he was scared to believe that I meant it. Which was even more confirmation that it was the right choice. Nothing tied me to Vegas the way he felt tied to the ranch. Besides, Kayla and our families were there, and—fingers crossed—my job, so I knew we'd visit regularly enough to fill up my city girl cup.

I sat up. "Yes. I'm sure. I don't know how Alexander will feel about it. He might fire me."

"I doubt it. He has nothing but compliments about your work."

"If he doesn't fire me, he might want me to travel to Vegas regularly."

He squeezed my knees. "I'll come with you."

I laughed at the rightness of it all, fully relaxing into the brightness of my future. "We're going to have the best life," I said.

He leaned forward to kiss me, and I could feel his relief and excitement, confirming once again that this was the right path for both of us. "You and I, against the world."

I kissed him back, my heart soaring higher than the tops of the pine tree whose glittering lights were a reflection of exactly how brilliant my life had become.

Epilogue

KAYLA

The first time I saw Alexander Drake was on the cover of a *Financial Life* magazine that my roommate, Lucy, brought home. I'd have to have been blind not to notice he was a tasty morsel, but I wasn't one to swoon at someone in a picture. Pictures couldn't be trusted. Who knew what had been edited out? Maybe he had a third nostril in real life.

Then, in a stroke of unbelievable luck, Lucy had been hired by his company to work directly with him. We'd immediately gotten online and looked up more pictures. It was possible, after looking at no fewer than twenty pictures, that he didn't have a third nostril. I immediately predicted that Lucy would fall in love with him by Christmas. It wasn't the first time I was wrong about something. Well, not entirely wrong. Lucy did fall in love by Christmas, but it was with Alexander's brother, Daniel.

The first time I saw Alexander Drake in person he was walking with that brother toward me and Lucy at an appliance store. I swooned. Hard. He was even more impressive in person than in his pictures. The pictures couldn't capture how vital and intelligent he was. I possibly had a small brain aneurysm while introductions were being made. To make the whole thing even crazier, he'd come to our apartment and helped Daniel install a washer and dryer. There he was, in the flesh, hooking up wires and hoses. While I'm normally chatty, confident, and social, I didn't manage more than a couple of lines the whole time he was around.

That was four months ago. Now, I'm looking at Alexander Drake again from my seat in a dimly lit Las Vegas restaurant where Lucy and Daniel asked if he'd be the best man and I'd be the maid of honor at their upcoming wedding.

"Tell me what you want done and I'll make it happen," Alexander replied, pulling out his phone and starting to take notes.

There was no excitement in his expression or tone. He looked like a guy trying to close a business deal, and he'd not looked at me even once. It was obvious I had no effect on him, even though he made my palms sweat just by being in the same space. I was unbelievably disappointed in myself for wishing his bright blue eyes would look my way, and suddenly I wanted nothing more than to ruffle his feathers and see if his face was capable of anything other than that politely aloof expression he always wore . . . to see what could happen if I became a force in his little life bubble.

"I'm in," I said to Lucy, but I was looking at Alexander the entire time.

Oh, yeah. I was all in, but the four of us were definitely not talking about the same thing. I was going to shake up his world.

See what happens between Kayla and Alexander in the second book of the Drake Duology, coming in 2022.

Acknowledgments

As always, my gratitude goes out to my husband, Steve. He lets me think I'm hysterical, takes me on road trips, and continues to spoil me by putting me first in everything. I can't imagine what I did to deserve you, but I'm so lucky. (I haven't ruled out my own fairy godmother!)

My four kids. I think of you every night before I fall asleep, and my heart fills with happiness. You came good, kind, and funny. I'm thankful for your friendship, your patience, and the way you stretch me into a better version of myself.

My extended family. Oh boy, do I like this group. We're a disaster, but we laugh a ton, and I wouldn't want it any other way.

I've always been blessed to have amazing friends. People who celebrate, commiserate, and kindly motivate me to be better through their examples. I "friended" up.

The lovely people at Cedar Fort Publishing, for continuing to help me along this publishing path. Thanks for acting excited when I turn up in person! It makes me feel pretty good.

To my readers—WOW! Thank you for your kind reviews, and for your messages, and for loving my characters as much as I do. You're keeping the dream alive.

To my beta readers. As always, your input is invaluable! Seriously. Believe it.

Lastly, a special acknowledgment to Charlie Rockwood, who will never see this in a million years! Charlie's farm was two doors down from my childhood home. He had something like twelve horses, and it came to my brother Ben's attention as a boy of ten that Charlie could use some help exercising those horses. So, Ben approached Charlie and a deal was struck. A deal that, looking back as an adult, is pretty amazing. Ben was "gifted" a horse or two that needed some extra time, and he recruited me (age twelve) to help him. We had full and unlimited access to them, and we spent countless hours riding around Charlie's arena. When we were comfortable, and had built a relationship with the horses, we were set free. We rode all over the mountains near our home, spending our summer days exploring on horseback. Their names were Magic and Fire, and on their backs I learned confidence and how to dust myself off and get back in the saddle. Invaluable lessons. Charlie, you blessed my life. I know you loved Ben like we all did and that you miss him like we do. Thank you for making two children's dreams come true. Those memories are some of my ultimate best.

I'd be remiss if I didn't also mention Charlie's son, Bryan, who became like another brother. Bry, thanks for continuing the tradition by letting my kids come ride from time to time and giving them a little slice of "Uncle Ben" in his place.

About the Author

Aspen Hadley loves nothing more than a great story. She writes what she wants to read: clean, sassy, romantic comedy novels that give you a break from real life and leave you feeling happy.

Outside of writing, Aspen's number-one hobby is reading. Number two is sneaking chocolate into and out of her private stash without being caught. Other favorites: playing the piano, listening to classic rock, eating ice cream, traveling, a good case of the giggles, and riding on ATVs over the mountains and deserts of Utah.

Aspen shares her life with a patient husband, four hilarious children, and one grumpy dog in a quiet suburb in the foothills of her beloved mountains.

Scan to visit

www.aspenmariehadley.com